GENERATIONS OF LOVE

GENERATIONS OF LOVE

WENDY PULFORD

Matador
9 Priory Business Park,
Wistow Road, Kibworth Beauchamp,
Leicestershire. LE8 0RX
Tel: 0116 279 2299
Email: books@troubador.co.uk
Web: www.troubador.co.uk/matador
Twitter: @matadorbooks

ISBN 978 1788039 475

British Library Cataloguing in Publication Data.
A catalogue record for this book is available from the British Library.

Printed and bound in the UK by 4edge Limited
Typeset in 11pt Minion Pro by Troubador Publishing Ltd, Leicester, UK

Matador is an imprint of Troubador Publishing Ltd

ACKNOWLEDGEMENT

My grateful thanks to various authorities in Canada and Britain who have given their assistance, to Lorena and Mello and Catherine for their editorial advice, Hannah and team for their publishing expertise, family and friends for their unstinting support, but most importantly to Sergei Rachmaninov in whose music I found the inspiration for this story.

PREFACE

Harold Wilson's first term of government gave way in 1970 to that of Edward Heath. During Heath's term the United Kingdom was taken into the European Union, but with divided ranks. Committed to British industry, Heath bailed out Rolls-Royce and Upper Clyde Shipbuilders in an effort of support, but subsequent attempts at legislation against unofficial strikes led to the work to rule by the miners with consequent power cuts and damage to British industry, all amid continuing oil difficulties and Irish problems. In 1974, Heath went to the country on a 'who rules' platform, but lost to Harold Wilson, who in his second term of office again found trouble with the economy and, faced with obtaining a loan from the International Monetary Fund, suddenly resigned in 1976 amid alleged rumours of MI5 interest. James Callaghan took over as leader and imposed deep cuts in public spending, dislike for these leading to the 'winter of discontent' in 1978.

With this background of industrial unrest, racial tensions because of the Ugandan Asian influx and problems starting to build in some of Britain's high rise housing, the findings of a BBC poll showed the British public were worried.

PART ONE

CHAPTER 1

The fishing boat *Patsy* set down anchor just off the Ayrshire coast about a mile outside the Ardrossan harbour an hour before dusk on a cold February day. With the light almost gone, a dinghy with two men on board slipped unseen towards the jetty. One man came ashore and hurried up onto the main road and waited, a brisk wind tugging at his clothes. Within minutes a Ford Cortina slowed to a halt beside him. The driver wound down his window and took a package from the waiting figure. No words were exchanged. The car drove off and the man returned to the waiting dinghy. By first light the *Patsy* had weighed anchor and was back out at sea.

*

As a fine example of a Georgian interior, the private dining room of the Grosvenor Club near Regents Park was one of the best. Although it was now late in the evening, a fire was still burning in the large white marble fireplace, throwing flickering shadows around the high moulded ceiling. Rich gold damask curtains were drawn over the tall windows to keep out the chill of the night.

Out of the six dining chairs at the long table, three were still occupied, one of the four original diners having just left. The remaining men were enjoying another brandy, alone now, the waiters having cleared the table and withdrawn.

'We're on track then, Lionel?' The speaker's accent was typical public school but with a faint Scottish burr.

'It seems that way from what our friend has just implied, Gregory,' confirmed his companion on the left nearest to the fire. 'We now have a firm medical prognosis and definite retirement date. Our guest has had some good results of late and that will stand him in good stead as a candidate' he smiled 'with, of course, some lobbying of the right people.'

'There will be other choices.'

'Indeed, Gregory, and no doubt some good ones. We need to be subtle.'

The speaker reached for the brandy decanter, refilled his glass and offered it round to the other two. They both declined, and with a shrug, he returned it to the tray in front of him.

The third person present had contributed very little during the whole of the evening. A display of complete boredom was still evident on his dark, almost swarthy face, as he studied the remaining contents of his glass. As with the others, he too was in his middle fifties, and they all had about them the air of those who feel they have reached a certain elevated position in their chosen profession. He now raised his gaze and surveyed his companions.

'And if he isn't given the post, Lionel?'

'Then we're no worse off, Geoffrey.'

This sharp, censuring retort identified Lionel Franklin as the acknowledged leader of the three. Even so, the third diner once more tried to make his point.

'As I see it, if he did get the post he would have even more constraints than he does now. More eyes on him too. It's a fine idea, but it might not work as we hope.'

Franklin gave the other man a cold, hard stare.

'Look, Geoffrey, it was decided at the start that this was worth attempting and nothing has changed. It's come at the right time, with the current problems in the country. We must grasp the opportunity. With the position secure, as I've said before, consider

4

where this could lead; think of what other personnel could then be put in place.'

With another pointed look, he turned back to his brandy glass. He had dealt with Geoffrey Villiers for some years but never ceased to be exasperated by the other man's lack of drive. Villiers enjoyed the prosperity and lifestyle that had come with his thriving legal firm, and certain other business interests, but through the years it had been Franklin's own energies pushing the other man along.

Catching the eye of Sir Gregory Hamilton sitting across the table, Villiers gave a shrug of resignation and remained silent.

Hamilton stood and moved over to the fire.

'How is your other matter going, Lionel?'

This remark appeared to lighten Franklin's mood and, with a rare broad smile, cradling the refilled brandy glass in his hand, he went to join Hamilton.

'It's all going to plan, Gregory. No worries at all.'

Keeping his smile in place, he studied the other man. As a non-executive director at the Bank of England and numerous other companies, plus a family estate in Scotland, it might be thought that Gregory Hamilton had everything he could have wished for to enable him to live a long life to the full. However, his ample waistline and reddened cheeks spoke more of indoor excesses, rather than outdoor pursuits in the Scottish hills, which might well shorten those odds somewhat. Over the years Franklin had nurtured his association with this man, always making sure to conceal his distaste for the false aura of refinement he portrayed. That said, Hamilton's banking contacts had proved to be very useful and, Franklin hoped, would continue to do so.

Whilst the other two seemed to revel in their mutual amusement, Villiers still gazed into his almost empty glass.

'What about your niece, Lionel?' he commented. 'Time is moving on, you know, not long to go before she's twenty-five. That gives us a year or two, but we need to think about things before then.'

Both men by the fire turned to look at their companion with some irritation, but for different reasons. With a trace of annoyance, Franklin tossed back the contents of his glass.

'As you say, Geoffrey, things there haven't gone to plan. I shall have to revisit the problem.' He shot a glance at his fireside companion. 'What's the latest position, Gregory?'

'I've done all I can, Lionel. The laddie says he's beginning to lose interest.' In his annoyance, Hamilton's Scottish burr was more pronounced.

'A mistake, I think, from his point of view. He knows it would be worth his while in the long run. Perhaps a little more effort?' The remark was firm and decisive. 'Geoffrey here' he nodded towards the table 'has reminded us of our time limit in this respect and I might have to give serious consideration to other contenders.'

'I'll have another word, that's all I can do,' muttered Hamilton, throwing Villiers a vicious look.

'Good. I'll see if I can move things on at my end.' Franklin crossed to the table and replaced his glass on the tray. 'Well, I think we've covered everything we can tonight.' Then he turned back to the man by the fire. 'No, just one more thing. When is the next arrangement in Scotland, Gregory?'

Hamilton looked at his watch. 'With any luck there should have been one tonight, if the weather was favourable. It is February, after all! There's one scheduled in a month or two and then one more several months after that.' He reached inside his jacket and pulled out a small diary which he consulted for a moment, then tore out a blank page from the back of the book, wrote on it, and handed it to Franklin. 'These, as far as I am aware, are the dates. If, as I said, the weather is suitable.'

The other man consulted the paper and then placed it in his jacket pocket. After a moment's thought he stated, 'I'm going to suggest we close that particular avenue down. It's been useful, but our friends are being a bit difficult at the moment. Perhaps then they might come to realise how helpful our mutual association is, rather than playing the superior partner. Serve them right.' Hearing the obvious contempt in the choice of words, his companions glanced at each other, but said nothing. Franklin went on, 'If we need any movement the other way, we can try something else.'

6

He stared at the other two until they nodded their agreement.

'I'll speak to Aubrey about it,' he muttered. 'Pity he ever got himself involved with them in the first place. I told him they'd be trouble.'

*

The dark blue Porsche purred through the wet London streets. At this time on a Sunday morning, combined with the poor weather, the traffic was light. Despite this, and the fact that he knew he was late for his first shift of this new detail, Alex Hartman had no intention of breaking any speed limits and he suppressed the urge to feel the undoubted power of the car. With the problems posed by the fuel crisis it was a shame he did so little long-distance driving. Apart from the occasional longer run, he seldom found the chance to appreciate the car's true performance. However, he promised himself, when he had some leave, he'd take a trip over to Europe and let it loose on the autobahns and see what it could do. His grey eyes shone in anticipation. Yes, you needed something to look forward to in the downcast air of the country at the moment.

Although purchased secondhand, the Porsche 911 was his most prized possession, a present to himself for years of hard work; and he had worked hard, damned hard. An East End boy with a bad start, now a Detective Inspector in the Metropolitan Police, and just moved to the Special Branch. Not bad! During his time in the Army, uniformed police and then CID, he knew he'd been noticed not just for his natural ability but also for his single-minded application. He was well aware that there were people who disliked him for his ruthless approach to his career, but it didn't bother him. In fact, he smiled to himself, he was amused to notice how colleagues never minded being involved with his operations; they just hoped to be pulled along themselves by his own success, and it was his intention to climb even higher. His handsome face became dark and serious. They were all unaware that the experiences of his youth had given him this compulsion to excel, to make sure that no one ever again abandoned him, forcing him, without warning, to fall back on his own inner resources. No, he told himself, it would never happen again. He was in charge of his own life now.

As he made his way out to Richmond he sensed again the strange feeling that this particular detail was somehow important.

Several days ago, he had been finishing up a report on a previous assignment when he was passed urgent instructions on his next. This new job was to head up protection for a High Court Judge who had received a death threat letter. It was thought possible that the threat might be related to a case being heard by him at the moment, but despite this, the Judge had been adamant about continuing with his involvement. The CID were investigating the circumstances surrounding the origins of the letter. After his own perusal, however, this appeared to be of little use: standard plain typing paper with the words cut out of newspapers and magazines. He, himself, was detailed to be in charge of all security matters relating to the protection of the Judge at work and at his home in Richmond.

Then, a sealed note was delivered to him requesting his attendance at a meeting in Whitehall that evening. The note was unsigned, and no one appeared to know from where it had originated. At first he thought about ignoring it as someone's idea of a joke. However, the more he thought about it the more intrigued he became, and he decided to follow it up.

With growing curiosity, he had followed instructions and was surprised to find Sir John Fraser, the Metropolitan Police Commissioner, no less, waiting for him together with another man, more his own age, introduced as 'Mr Francis'. No further information about this person was forthcoming, but as the meeting progressed Alex suspected his possible identity.

The Commissioner had apologised for the clandestine manner in which he had been summoned and referred Alex to his new protection assignment.

'You in particular have been selected to be in charge,' he explained. 'You are to deal with the matter as routine, to all outward appearances, but we require you to keep your eyes and ears open during this duty, at the end of which you are to report back to either myself in person, or Mr Francis here. Any written reports are to be kept under your own confidential control.'

Uneasy about the lack of further explanation, Alex had decided he must make a comment. 'It would be useful to have more of an idea of what I'm supposed to be keeping a look out for.'

It appeared, however, that neither Sir John nor Francis would be drawn any further on the matter. The latter muttered vague terms like 'operational necessity' and 'something he need not know at the moment', and went on again to make the point, 'I must impress upon you that any extra enquiries made must be kept as low key as possible.'

Alex considered the whole matter strange to say the least and his lack of operational information and freedom to act would, he knew, cause considerable difficulties.

'I will require to bring in other people. I need at least two others, but how much can they know?'

Francis had deferred to Sir John on this.

'You can choose your team, but get the best. We need you, however, to be more hands on than otherwise might have been the case. However, as far as your colleagues are concerned, this is a straight-forward protection detail; but inform them that they must report all that happens during their own shifts to you, and discuss it with no one else.'

When Alex had left the meeting he'd felt frustrated with the lack of definite instructions and began to ponder just what the real reasons were behind all this super security.

CHAPTER 2

With the Porsche idling at a set of traffic lights on the outskirts of Richmond, Alex thought again about his first visit to the Judge's property yesterday. He had taken with him Detective Sergeant Douglas Johnson, the man he had chosen as his second in command. They had worked together on several occasions in the past. At thirty-eight, Dougie was a couple of years older than himself, not ambitious it appeared, but reliable enough and intelligent, and Alex considered that for this particular job they would work well together.

Both he and Dougie had made a tour of the house and gardens, checking on security, and had identified some weak areas. While he went to his first meeting with the Judge, Alex left Dougie speaking with the members of staff, Arthur and Grace Painter. The Judge owned an ageing Rolls-Royce and Painter acted as chauffeur, manservant, butler and handyman. He lived in the house with his wife, who performed the duties of housekeeper and cook. It would be useful, Alex thought, to see what Dougie could find out about the daily activities of the household.

On being shown into the Judge's study, Alex found that he was more interested in the man sitting behind the large desk than in noticing much of his surroundings. His first impression of Judge

Lionel Franklin was of a small, slim man. However, the pale blue eyes were the most arresting feature, now fixing him with an intent gaze, although lacking either expression or warmth.

From reading the background notes provided for him, Alex knew that Judge Franklin was a Senior Judge and had overseen some important cases. However, in private it wasn't considered by his peers that he would rise any higher in the judiciary. There was no explicit reason given for this assessment but several independent comments had confirmed the same thought, and also gave the unspoken impression that he was not liked. Alex had wondered if this might be a touch of class snobbery, as, although well educated and a Cambridge graduate, Franklin's original background was from a working-class family. According to the notes, his parents' endeavours over the years had created a successful engineering business, allowing a good education for their two sons, offering a chance of increasing their career opportunities in life.

The Judge did not stand to greet him, nor offer him a seat, and Alex masked his slight irritation at the lack of immediate courtesy.

'Good morning, Judge. I'm Inspector Alex Hartman, and as you know I'm heading up your protection detail. I'm in touch with CID and I've seen the letter involved. In my view I don't think it will tell them much. However, I've asked them to inform me of the results of the fingerprint report. I presume you handled it?'

'I did, Inspector. Once I saw what it was I took appropriate care with it. I do know about these things.'

Alex ignored what he felt was a sarcastic remark.

'Judge, I need to ask if you have any idea who might have sent it. The wording is in broad terms, appearing to threaten you if you dispense anything less than proper justice. Do you feel it relates to your current case? And if so, do you suspect the defendant himself, or someone unconnected? For instance, a person with a grudge against you for something in the past.'

The Judge gave a slight smile. 'Inspector, in my walk of life there will be a lot of people bearing grudges against me. Some people have not been slow to voice their opinion about the outcome of some of the cases in which I have been involved over the years. So far, I have remained free of this kind of joke, but to answer your question, it might be connected somehow. Then again, it might not. However, I intend to do my duty under the law, whatever the provocation. I have no doubt that everyone else will be doing the same and making all appropriate enquiries.' An eyebrow was raised in query.

Alex disliked the apparently disparaging remark and took a deep, calming breath. 'Yes indeed, Judge. As your current case involves the attempted illegal sale of weapons, any number of factions might have an interest, domestic and foreign. Let's hope that, as you say, it all turns out to be a joke. Meanwhile my Sergeant and I have reviewed your security and consider you should make some small changes.'

A look of irritation crossed Franklin's face. 'I can't imagine why you think that anything needs to be done.'

Alex knew he had to stand his ground. 'I would advise that you put extra security lighting around the house, and upgrade the alarm system. I also suggest that care needs to be taken with the other members of your household, for their own safety. I assume you have total trust in your staff? How long have the Painters worked for you?'

The Judge regarded him for a long moment and then shrugged. 'If you feel extra security lighting is required then I will have to organise it, I suppose. I'll deal with it for Monday as a priority. As to my staff, the Painters have worked for me for over seven years and have given me no reason to think they are not trustworthy.'

'I will require them to inform my colleagues of their movements at all times, please, Judge. I also understand that your niece lives with you. The same will apply to her, unless you are able to send her away somewhere for the time being.'

'Inspector, my niece will remain here. We don't want to create an unnecessary air of lurking danger, do we? However, having said that, I am sure we all feel comforted by your presence.'

Patronising bastard! Alex could feel the anger building in him, but he tried to remain civil. 'As you wish, Judge. It's my duty to make my views known to you. Is there anything else you wish to raise with me?'

'I would just stress that the less contact you and your colleagues have with members of my household, the better. No doubt there will be contact of a sort, but nothing too familiar. We all have our jobs to do, after all.'

'I quite understand, Judge.' Alex had already come to the conclusion he wouldn't want to pass even the time of day with this man if he could help it. 'Was that all?'

'I'm sure you've covered every angle, Inspector. You appear a very capable young man.' Franklin paused. 'I would suggest you have done very well for yourself.'

Alex could feel the other man's eyes running him up and down and was glad he had decided to wear one of his better suits.

'Tell me, Inspector,' Franklin settled back in his chair, 'what in your professional opinion do you think of today's law and order?'

Alex was off guard for a moment. He hadn't expected this form of personal questioning. 'As with anything else, Judge, it could be a lot better, but we achieve a fair amount I believe.'

'Mmm… any pet grievances on administration in any quarter? What about those in charge today, for instance?'

Alex could see no reason why his personal views were valid in this situation, and had no intention of becoming involved in any form of debate.

'I'm sure some things could be better whoever has the ultimate power. I just concentrate on doing my own job to the best of my ability. Now, if you will excuse me, Judge, I need to speak with my Sergeant before I leave. He will be with you until tomorrow morning. No doubt you will organise the security lighting changes as discussed. I will see you tomorrow, Judge. Good morning.'

As he left the study Alex was conscious of the tension in him. What was that all about? Odd that the Judge appeared to shrug off the possible threat, yet sound just as happy to accept protection. One thing Alex was sure about, however: he was relieved to be out of the man's presence.

He found Dougie in the kitchen with Grace Painter.

'I'm off now. Can I see you for a moment?'

He smiled and nodded to Mrs Painter and led the way outside.

'Did you find out anything worthwhile?'

'Nothing that useful. The Painters appear to be quite happy for any changes to their routines and have been on the whole helpful and pleasant. Reading between the lines, I estimate that they consider the Judge an adequate employer, but they don't enthuse about him.

'Arthur Painter told me that he always makes a habit of doing a security check on the Rolls every day but was happy for us to do so as well if we wished. It would seem there are few, if any, visitors to the property, which helps us quite a bit. There's a newspaper delivery every morning at about seven-thirty. The Painters deal with any grocery purchasing themselves.

'The Judge, I'm told, is part owner in the freehold of a gentleman's club, The Grosvenor, and goes there a lot, both during the day and at night. I'll organise a check around their premises, if that's OK?'

Alex gave him a nod in reply.

'Without any prompting, Grace Painter has told me quite a bit about Catherine Franklin. It seems she lives with her uncle as part secretary-researcher and hostess, although as I've said the Judge does very little entertaining at home. She's twenty-three years of age. Her parents were killed in a flying accident in Europe when she was fourteen. Although Lionel Franklin was eighteen months younger than his brother and a bachelor, he gave Catherine a home and has seen her through schooling and then on to a prestigious finishing school on the Continent. Since then she has lived with him, performing her duties as and when required, otherwise helping around the house and garden. It's obvious that the Painters have a soft spot for the girl.'

'OK, well thanks for that, Dougie. I don't suppose any of it helps us, though. I'd be interested in what you think of the Judge when you meet him. He's a strange character. Anyway, see you tomorrow morning.'

*

Lionel Franklin banged the desk with frustration.

'Why the hell didn't you tell me you'd be away. I've been trying to get in touch with you for two days now… Alright, alright Aubrey. I wanted to talk to you about the Scottish runs. I'm considering ending them, at least for our current clients… That's just it, Aubrey, they're becoming picky, trying to take over. I warned you about them. Why you couldn't deal with our Italian connections, or even further afield, I just don't know. It would have been far better… Yes, that's your trouble, you're just looking at it from the political point of view… No, I'll deal with it my way. I have an idea already… What? Oh yes, that. It's all swung into action… No, Aubrey, I want some of the interest deflected… Yes, they've put quite a team of bodyguards in place… I've just met the officer in charge. Seems pretty sharp and on the ball – might have to watch that a bit… No, there's nothing to worry about, Aubrey. Nothing at all.'

CHAPTER 3

His mind still running through the events of the last few days, Alex finally turned into the driveway of the detached Queen Anne property, his tyres crunching on the gravel. At least no vehicle could turn up unannounced, was his automatic thought. Sure enough, Dougie was at the side kitchen door to greet him.

'Sorry I'm late, Dougie. I took longer on my run this morning than I thought.'

Dougie grinned at him. 'I haven't the energy for all that sort of physical stuff on any morning.'

Alex smiled back. 'Everything OK?'

'Yes, fine, no problems. A quiet night.' He grimaced. 'The usual Sunday morning, seven o'clock and no one's up and about, except us. I've turned off the alarm, though, just in case. Oh, I gather none of them is intending to go anywhere today, Boss.' Dougie had slipped into this form of address despite Alex objecting on the point. 'Last night Arthur said he would wash and check over the Rolls today ready for tomorrow.'

'OK. I'll take over now until six p.m. You take over again from then, and I'll be around for the drive in tomorrow morning. I've asked Carl to be here from when I leave tomorrow, to oversee the security men doing their alterations. I would prefer to have someone checking on them. I've warned him about confirming their security details when they arrive, and told him what changes are being made. Any departure from that and he's to contact me. I should be back with the Judge when you come tomorrow night, but in any case Carl will stay on to hand over to you.'

'Right-oh. I'll be off, then. See you.'

Alex watched with some amusement as, with great care, Dougie manoeuvred his Ford Escort around the Porsche and drove out of the gates. He then went inside and through to the kitchen. Much to his surprise he encountered a young woman busy preparing a breakfast tray. This must be Catherine Franklin. His immediate impression was of someone younger than her twenty-three years. She was very attractive: slender, with dark brown hair curling below her shoulders – and the most remarkable green eyes he had ever seen! He wasn't prepared for his reaction, and found himself in the ridiculous situation of having problems with his breathing. Aware that he must have been staring, he cleared his throat.

'Good morning, Miss Franklin. We haven't yet been introduced. I'm Inspector Alex Hartman.' In an effort to put her at ease he added, 'I've already had my breakfast, thank you.'

Cool green eyes studied him. 'This tray is for my uncle, Inspector Hartman. I always prepare it on a Sunday to give Grace a lie in. Perhaps I should have added the information to my list of movements that you requested.'

Her hostile attitude puzzled him. He sensed in her tone a suggestion of aloofness, almost superiority. He grimaced to himself. No doubt young ladies of her station were not used to lads from the East End. He had no idea why that impression had formed in his mind, or why he found it rankled as it did. After all, she knew nothing whatsoever about him or his background for her to be able to form any opinion. He had long ago realised that his father's deliberate insistence in correcting his East End dialect was now an advantage to him, and understood why his father had been so strict about it.

He gave her a slight smile. 'Unless the food has been laced with

17

arsenic, Miss Franklin, I'm not sure that I'm all that worried.' He realised his own remark was a bit waspish, but God knows he didn't want to contend with opinionated little females first thing in the morning.

Her attitude annoyed and, for some strange reason, unsettled him. Then again, perhaps his initial judgement was unfair and this was her normal wary reaction to a stranger, also bearing in mind her uncle's comments about any contact. What did it matter, anyway? In a week or so he would be moving on to something else. He must confine himself to concentrating on the important things to do with this job.

Leaving the kitchen without waiting to see her reaction to his remark, he crossed over the wide oak panelled hallway and entered the Judge's study. He moved over to the French windows and stood for a moment looking out over the well-tended garden. He rattled at the lock, knowing full well that Dougie would already have checked them before he left.

Why on earth had the girl got under his skin like that? Should he try to find out the reason why her attitude was so hostile? Then again, what was the point? Damn these stuck-up society people with their airs and graces! He took a deep breath to calm himself, then turned and looked around the room.

From his earlier brief tour around the inside of the large house, this room, as all the rest, was well proportioned and quite spacious. There were dark oak bookcases along one wall, either side of a fireplace which looked as though it was used for the purpose. On the opposite wall hung a large watercolour, and although Alex was no connoisseur he was of the opinion that it, like other paintings he had observed around the property, might well be an original and also valuable. Likewise, the large bronze sculpture of a horseman standing on the mantelpiece was obvious in its quality, as were other ornaments he had seen dotted about the various rooms. Franklin, he considered, was a man who, although not wishing to appear ostentatious in his wealth, still enjoyed being surrounded by the finer things in life. All the more reason for proper security!

He returned his thoughts to the room in general. There were two metal filing cabinets on the short wall near the door, together with a small but robust looking Chubb metal safe. The desk was positioned with its back to the window, something Alex wondered about changing, but he considered that if you were sitting in the substantial high-backed chair at the desk there was no ideal field of view for anyone who might have made their way into the garden. There were other properties on all sides with their own large gardens, but each boundary had a six foot fence topped with three strands of wire, and the extensive mature shrubbery would make it awkward for someone to gain entry with any ease. The neighbours had been checked out some days before and all seemed satisfactory.

Again, the bizarre request to keep his eyes open came to him. He was still uneasy about the unusual aspects of what he had been asked to do, and at the moment could determine nothing out of the ordinary. What was he looking for? He cast a glance over the papers on the desk. Most of them appeared to be typed case references on which handwritten notations had been made, and a transcription of Friday's Court hearing. This particular case was relevant to the illegal trading of firearms by a member of an up-and-coming London gang who had been apprehended whilst attempting to negotiate a sale; unfortunately for him, to a covert team of Metropolitan Police. You could understand someone being sore, but enough to threaten the presiding Judge of a potential open-and-shut case? Alex wasn't sure that it would be worth the effort, but you never could guarantee anything, and his job was to be ready for the unexpected.

Except for the likes of Catherine Franklin! Damnation! Somehow she had come into his thoughts again. He wasn't busy enough, that was the trouble, and he had the whole of Sunday to get through yet.

He glanced along the bookshelves, wondering if the Judge would allow him to borrow a book to read. Most of them were law books of various kinds, all neat and regimented in their chronological order. Some, he noticed, were quite old. In one section however he found a more varied selection. One or two books were to do with psychology, useful in Court, no doubt; and several related to economics, both domestic and worldwide. There were also other titles relating to global political doctrines of one persuasion or another. He even found one book on firearms. It looked up to date. On a bottom shelf he caught sight of a book entitled *A Yachting Guide to the West Scottish Coastline*. He pulled it out. It was an old edition by several years, but no doubt the Scottish coastline wouldn't be changing all that much! Perhaps the Judge owned a boat of some sort. He replaced the book on the shelf.

He looked at his watch: nearly seven-thirty and the paperboy would be coming, if he was on time on a Sunday as well.

CHAPTER 4

Just as he left the study and went out into the hall, he heard the scrunch of footsteps on the gravel. Yes, the paperboy was on time. He opened the front door and was met by a cheery grin just about discernable through extensive layers of scarves and a wool hat.

Alex thanked the boy, who struggled off with his bulging bag. He turned back inside, shut the door and looked at what had been delivered. Well, that was interesting, at least. As well as the predictable *Sunday Times* and supplements, there were also others from across the whole political spectrum. The Judge must keep his ear very much to the ground.

Catherine Franklin was crossing the hall with her loaded tray. She stopped and looked at him. 'You can leave the papers there, Inspector Hartman, I will deal with them when I come down.'

'If you tell me where to put them I can do it for you, if you like?' One more attempt at politeness wouldn't hurt.

'You can leave them in the kitchen for now. Er, thank you.'

She turned up the stairs and for a moment Alex watched the small, slim figure, then counting himself lucky that he had received a civil reply, went into the kitchen, deposited the papers on the table, and decided on a walk around outside.

The rest of the day was boring. He saw nothing at all of the Judge, who was either in the dining room or in his study. Neither did he see any more of Catherine Franklin. He spent most of his time wandering around inside and out, although not intruding on closed doors, and talking to Grace and Arthur Painter. He declined Grace's offer of a cooked meal, but accepted a sandwich and coffee. He found himself relieved when Dougie arrived at six p.m. to begin his shift.

Alex was about to leave when Catherine Franklin came into the kitchen with a plate and mug which she left on the draining board. So, she had at some time been down into the kitchen when he hadn't been present, Alex thought.

'Good evening, Sergeant Johnson.' This greeting was accompanied by a brilliant smile as she turned to go. It filled her already attractive face with warmth and vitality, and Alex again found himself staring at her.

'Good evening, Miss Franklin. I hope you've had a pleasant day.'

Dougie at his most urbane, thought Alex.

'Oh, just the usual Sunday I'm afraid.'

Then the smile died on her face as she saw Alex watching her, and she turned and left the room.

'So what do you have that I don't all of a sudden?' he found himself remarking, glancing at Dougie.

'Well, I'm sure I don't know. She seems pleasant enough to me. I'd have thought that you of all people would have had no trouble with a pretty girl.' This remark was accompanied by a sly look.

Alex just shrugged. 'I must be losing my touch. See you tomorrow.'

He felt glad to be leaving the house, and this was just the first day! Perhaps he needed an evening out.

It was a spur-of-the-moment decision, but Alex already felt himself relaxing as he made his way to Sunbury. It would be good to see Luigi and Maria again. He had known the couple since he was a small boy. Although Luigi and his wife had both been born in London, they still retained a lot of the Italian way of life, with a love of family and good food. They had run a successful restaurant in the area where he had grown up. He was fond of them both. They

22

had provided him with unfailing support and guidance at a difficult and troubled time in his life, plus a meal and place to stay if ever he needed one. They had retired from the restaurant a year or two ago and opened a small bed and breakfast business near the Thames. He tried to see them as often as he could, but at times it was difficult.

He drew up in front of the three-storey whitewashed building and, lighter in spirit, bounded into the front entrance hall.

'Luigi?'

A short, rotund man in his middle fifties came through from a back room, his face wreathed in a broad smile. He thumped Alex on the shoulder. 'Good to have you here again, boy. It's been a while. I thought I heard that jet engine of yours!'

Alex grinned back at him. Luigi had always considered his choice of vehicle excessive.

'Come on through and let's surprise Mama. She's in the kitchen, as usual.'

Alex followed him down the hall and through a large door into an impressive kitchen. Putting his finger to his lips Alex motioned Luigi to remain silent. He tiptoed over to the range where a small, dark-haired woman was concentrating on stirring the contents of a pan. He slid his arms round her ample waist and kissed her on the cheek. She shrieked with surprise and dropped her spoon to the floor.

'Alessandro, you naughty boy! You always have to creep up on me. Now look at my floor!' The smile on her face belied the tone of her remark.

'I'll clean it up for you, I promise. How's my favourite girl?' Alex encircled her again with his arms.

'If I'm the best you have, you must be losing your touch.' She gave him a light smack on his arm and he released her.

'I've begun to think the same,' muttered Alex, thinking the words out loud, and he had a sudden vision of large green eyes. God damn it, couldn't he get away from her, even here? Annoyed with himself, he pulled out a chair from the kitchen table and slumped down, not noticing the glance that passed between the other two.

'What have you been doing with yourself all these weeks? We

were just saying you hadn't been down for a while. The last time was when you brought that very stylish blonde lady with you.' Luigi gave him an enquiring glance.

'It's the old story, I'm afraid. Irregular hours play havoc with your private life. I think we were both happy to leave it in the end.'

'Well, you'll have to find a girl who doesn't worry about all that, as long as she's able to see you enough. There can be other compensations.'

Luigi looked over at his wife and gave her a fond smile.

Of late this had begun to be their usual line of questioning and Alex was keen to change the subject. 'Yes, well, I've no doubt I'll find one some time. I'm not fretting about it. How's business, Luigi?'

'Quiet at the moment, but it's the beginning of the year. Are you staying the night? We have the space.'

'No 'fraid not, Luigi. I'm on shift work with a new case. I like the smell of whatever Maria has in that pot, though.' His mood now improved, he grinned at both of them.

'Well, if you leave me in peace I may have something for you a bit later. Luigi, go find a bottle of wine for us.'

'Yes, Mama.' With a grin, Luigi went to do her bidding.

Maria turned back to her cooking, but glanced over at Alex. 'You look tired. Are you alright? Are they working you too hard?'

'Don't worry, Maria, I'm fine. I know one thing for sure, though, when this current job's over I'm putting in for leave. I thought I might take the car over to the Continent. Maybe do some hiking.' He watched as Luigi returned and dealt with opening the bottle. 'If I get that far I might even pop in on Vincenzo. Are they all well?'

'Yes, it seems so, thank goodness. The little ones are growing up fast. I know Maria would like to see more of them, but it's difficult with the distance involved and our commitment here.'

Luigi moved over to his wife and gave her a quick kiss. He turned and picked up some wine glasses.

'I'll just have one glass thanks, Luigi. I'm driving, and I ought to keep a clear head for my latest job.'

'Something important? Or shouldn't I ask?' Luigi settled himself at the table.

Alex took a slow sip of his wine. 'It might turn out to be important. I'm not sure yet.'

A strange, almost anxious feeling came over him, but with an effort he shrugged it off.

CHAPTER 5

Alex had spent part of the day liaising with the Court's own security, but now, the Judge's session having risen earlier than normal, they were making good time back to Richmond. Alex was pleased about the slight change in schedule; it might keep someone guessing, and was one of the security measures he wanted to enforce. In the back of the Rolls the Judge was working on his papers, and Alex left Arthur to concentrate on his driving.

Carl had arrived at the house in his Mini before they had left in the morning. Detective Constable Freeman was young and bright, someone who had caught Alex's eye. True to form, on offering him the opportunity to join his team, Alex wasn't surprised to find it accepted. Another example of someone who considered it did their own career no harm at all to be involved with him. The lad appeared keen, although at times Alex wondered if his attention to his job was too easy to divert. As anyone's could be, he was honest enough to admit, remembering his own lapses of the last couple of days.

Before leaving that morning Alex had repeated his instructions, as to both general security and, in particular, the expected workmen.

As the Rolls pulled into the drive and the Judge started to collect his belongings, Alex was looking around, then said over his shoulder,

'Judge, please stay in the car.' He turned to Arthur. 'Move off, and don't come in the drive unless you are instructed to do so.'

Exiting the car, he walked round to the kitchen door. Any care he now took was a joke, he thought, because their arrival could not fail to have been heard.

But the fact that it had not became clear as he entered the kitchen. He could hear sounds of laughter coming from the hallway. He opened the door to the hall and gazed at the scene in front of him. Carl Freeman was standing on a chair in the middle of the hall, endeavouring to replace a light bulb. Catherine Franklin was steadying the chair, with Grace Painter hovering in the background with a fluffy duster. Everyone was laughing so much they had not heard Alex approach.

'What, in God's name is going on!' he thundered.

The three faces turned in his direction and Carl overbalanced on the chair and almost fell.

Now worried and embarrassed, he blurted out, 'Well, you see the workmen caught this light with their ladder and broke the bulb, so I was just…' His voice tailed off as he saw the look on his superior's face.

'You know very well you should be doing no such thing. I gave you orders and I expect them to be carried out, no matter what other diversions present themselves.'

Alex threw a look at the other two figures. He could see Catherine Franklin about to challenge that remark, but she must have recognised the anger in him, and in a wise move remained silent.

'Now go outside and bring in the Judge, and tell Arthur to park the Rolls. Then you and I will have a further few words together.'

As Carl climbed down from the chair and rushed off outside, Alex rounded on the two women. 'Next time you need any help with domestic arrangements please do not utilise my colleagues, who have more important things to do. I had left orders that any approaches to this property were to be observed at all times. We have arrived just now to find that not so. As far as I was aware, any sort of emergency could be about to present itself. I sent the car away again just to be safe.

27

Any attention diversion of my operatives, for whatever reason, might prove fatal to someone. Do I make myself clear? I am, as instructed, trying not to interfere with any of your daily routines, but my job is the Judge's safety and that is paramount. Light bulbs can wait!'

The front door opened and the Judge came in, briefcase in hand.

'A false alarm, I gather?' he said, with a sardonic look in his pale eyes, and, raising an eyebrow at Alex, he went into his study and closed the door.

With a muttered oath Alex marched off outside to confront the unfortunate Carl, passing Arthur on his way in.

'What's been going on? The young boy came out looking as though he'd been hit by a whirlwind.'

'More of a hurricane, I would have said,' replied his wife.

'It's unfair to blame us,' said Catherine, 'we didn't ask for his help. We've replaced that bulb by ourselves many times. That man is an arrogant bully.' Her tone didn't quite carry the conviction of her remark, however.

They put the chair away and Grace went into the kitchen to start the evening meal. Catherine wandered into the room.

'Do you want any help, Grace, or shouldn't I ask?'

Grace wondered at the relevance of that remark, but then saw Alex passing through the hall and, the kitchen door being open, realised he must have heard. However, he went into the Judge's study without any comment. Grace was about to question Catherine as to why she was being so unpleasant which, for her, was so out of character when Dougie Johnson arrived.

'Evening, ladies,' he said, 'a spot of bother I hear.'

'A lot of fuss over nothing, I think,' commented Catherine.

'You could be wrong there, my dear. Alex must have been on the alert to sense a possible danger. He did the right thing. The lad slipped up, but he's young and he'll learn.'

Catherine caught the polite censure in his tone. 'I suppose Carl Freeman will be in trouble now.'

'Not if I know Alex. The lad's had his dressing down, and that's as far as it will go for him. Alex is no doubt in with the Judge now, accepting the blame for the situation on the principle that the buck stops with him. Whether the Judge wants to do anything about it will soon become clear. Don't be so hard on Alex, my dear. He's good at his job.'

'Well, it seems as if it's my day for being told off.' With a rueful smile she turned to leave the room. 'I'd better go and change for dinner.'

As she reached the door she almost collided with Alex coming in from the hall. He put out a hand to steady her, which she avoided, but she did glance up at him and, with a small smile, and 'Goodnight Inspector Hartman', she disappeared upstairs.

Watching her go, Alex remarked, 'Well, I suppose something good has come out of today, but I'm off before anything else happens.'

*

The rest of the first week's run to and from the Court proved uneventful, and so too the first two days of the following week. The next day, Alex arrived back at the house to find Catherine Franklin had a visitor. Introduced to him as an old school friend, now a hospital Sister, Sarah Jennings was sitting in the kitchen with a pot of tea and a plate of biscuits on the table in front of her. Sarah was blonde, bubbly and seemed, from the start, warm and outgoing. When Grace offered Alex a drink and he accepted, she patted the chair next to her, and gave him an admiring glance.

'I've been hearing a lot about you, Inspector Hartman.'

Alex glanced over at Catherine Franklin who was studying the bottom of her tea cup.

'All of it good, I hope. I would hate to disappoint.'

'I can't imagine you ever doing that, Inspector.'

The tone of the banter was acknowledged by each of them for what it was, but in a sudden move Catherine Franklin stood up, and, with a pointed look at her friend said, 'Shall I see if Arthur can drive you home, Sarah?'

'Um, well… Oh, yes, if you're sure it would be alright.'

'I'll go and ask him.' With that, she left the room. Alex didn't miss the glance which passed between Sarah and Grace.

'How did you get here?' Alex asked.

'The Tube as usual, then a taxi from the station. Why?' enquired Sarah, looking at him bird-like with her head on one side.

Some perverse demon made Alex carry on. 'This is just a suggestion,' he said, 'but if you would care to wait until my relief gets here in about half an hour I would be glad to drive you into town. It would save Arthur another journey today.' He realised he had made the offer to goad Catherine Franklin without thinking about it, although on reflection it seemed a polite gesture. 'Where do you live?'

'South Kensington.' Sarah caught his surprised glance. 'My parents' property, you understand. Don't forget, I'm an impoverished nurse,' she laughed.

'I'm relieved to hear it. I was thinking of making a career change if your salary runs to that sort of area.'

'Would it be out of your way?'

'Not too much. I have to go to Kennington, just over the river.'

'Well, if you're sure, that would be very nice.'

Catherine came back into the room. 'Arthur says my Uncle might want to go to his Club tonight and—'

'Don't worry, petal,' interrupted Sarah, sorting out her coat and bag. 'Inspector Hartman here has been very kind and offered to take me home.'

'But—!'

'I've assured Sarah' Alex made sure that he emphasised her Christian name 'that it would be no trouble at all.'

Observing the horrified look that appeared on the other girl's face, Alex was amused that his ploy had worked. It was clear that she was put out, but then found himself annoyed at the actual amount of reaction she had shown.

Grace smiled at Alex. 'I'm sure Arthur would be most grateful.'

Alex heard tyres crunching on the gravel outside.

'I'll be ready in a few moments if that's OK, Sarah?' He got up and went outside.

As he left, Sarah looked at Catherine in puzzlement. 'What's wrong with taking up his offer? I can't think of any reason why you should disapprove. Anyone would suppose he was a criminal of some sort, rather than an officer of the law! A very attractive one, too. The original tall, dark and handsome.'

'What would Jerry think?'

'He would no doubt be quite glad I wasn't using public transport at this time of night,' Sarah replied, her tone firm. 'What's wrong with you? Don't be so Victorian. He seems very nice.'

'You seem to be getting on alright. I would imagine he must have a lot of practice in chat-up lines.'

'Catherine, dear,' Sarah got into her coat and picked up her bag, 'with his looks and charm I don't think he would have to do much chatting up, the line of willing females forming in front of him would be far too long.'

She turned to her friend in time to observe the wave of colour flooding her face.

'Oh Catherine, what am I going to do with you,' she chuckled.

She gave her friend's cheek a kiss, just as Alex and Dougie came into the kitchen. Introductions were made and then Alex looked at Sarah.

'All ready to go?'

'Yes, fine. Bye all.' She glanced once more at her friend and smiled. 'I'll ring you,' and she winked.

Alex said goodnight to the room as a whole, but looked in particular at Catherine Franklin, who had crossed over to the sink. He couldn't see her face but her back view was eloquent enough. He shrugged and opened the back door for his companion.

CHAPTER 6

As the sound of the car faded into the distance, Catherine dried her hands and then made to leave the room.

'I'm going to finish off some work before dinner, Grace. Call me if you need me.'

She closed the door of the office behind her, and sat at her desk. She had no intention of doing any work. She had needed a quiet moment to herself. Watching the interchange between Sarah and Alex Hartman she had begun to feel envious of their apparent ease with one another.

From her bedroom window the first day anyone had been aware of police at the house, she had watched the two men walking around the garden. Grace had told her that one was an Inspector, and observing the body language between the two she could tell which one was in charge. Some people had a natural aura of rank about them. As they both neared the house the man had glanced up at the windows and, moving back out of sight, she had noted that he was an attractive man. No doubt his air of casual arrogance came from the fact that he knew this and used it to his advantage. She had never felt comfortable with that sort of person, and made up her mind to keep herself detached and have as little to do with him as she could.

So why, since she had first met him face to face, had she begun to experience a strange mixture of anticipation and excitement whenever she thought of him or saw him in person? Something she was at a total loss to explain. And what made her behave in so unpleasant a manner to him? His attitude was always polite; at least, on the surface. She had the impression, however, that this wasn't what he was thinking. It was much nicer to have the easy friendliness that she found with the other two, but with Alex Hartman she felt unnerved and out of her depth. In any case, she remembered the warning Uncle Lionel had given her on the first night of their arrival. He was adamant that she was to have as little contact with any of them as possible, and in the event of any direct questioning she was to say nothing, in particular about his work. She was disappointed that he had found it necessary to remind her of this. He should have known she would do no such thing. She gave a small sigh. There was no point in letting it worry her. In a week or two this problem would all be over and the household would revert back to its usual quiet boredom. Why was that thought so unwelcome?

*

'Umm, this is luxury,' said Sarah with an appreciative look around the interior of the Porsche.

'My one weakness, I'm afraid,' Alex replied, 'a lucky tip off on the Stock Market gave me the money.'

'Just the one?'

Alex chuckled. 'You're the sort of tonic I need at the end of the day. I feel better already.'

'Oh, I soon found out in my initial training there's nothing like an hour or two in A&E or theatre to encourage some insane chatter.'

'Do you specialise?'

'Not at the moment, but I want to. I want to go into Rheumatology, in particular with children. Not the most sought-after career path, but it just interests me. Jerry, my intended,' she explained with a smile, 'wants to specialise in paediatrics, work with children, you know and it would be nice if we could work together.'

'Are your parents medical?'

'Yes, they're doctors with the World Health Organization. They're off crawling around a South American jungle at the moment. They're often away.'

'So that explains the boarding school.'

'Yes. The downside of having parents in certain professions. Although mine always used to make sure one or the other, or both, were always there for my holidays. For some it didn't work out as well.'

'I know the feeling,' said Alex, his voice quiet. 'I wasn't lucky with having family around and I've spent most of my leave since I was seventeen on various courses and the like. Mark you, I suppose it's stood me in good stead, but it can be a little on the solitary side.'

'I've said to Jerry, if we have children I'm going to make sure I'm around for them.'

'So it's not just a career then? You're looking for the ideal scenario: career, home and a family?'

'It sounds as if that's something you don't subscribe to. Is it not for you?'

Alex thought for a moment before replying. He'd never spent time considering the matter with any seriousness. If he was honest, he had for the most part always tried to avoid the whole subject.

'I'm still working on my career, I suppose. Time and circumstances will alter things, I imagine, and there's still plenty of both left.' In the end it was all he could think of as a reply, and endeavouring to change the subject, he glanced at his companion with a smile. 'Well, we do seem to have got on to a serious topic all of a sudden.'

She grinned back at him. 'There are some people you feel you can talk to, and others not.' She gave him a considering stare. 'I think I like you, Inspector Hartman.'

Alex laughed out loud. 'Well, thank you, Miss Jennings. It restores my confidence in myself. I was beginning to wonder.'

'What's between you and Catherine? She seems quite odd towards you. Not her normal self at all.'

Alex concentrated on his driving for a while.

'I couldn't say. I don't know what her "normal" is, do I?'

'I think she's just overwhelmed. She's not used to dealing with experienced powerhouses of men like you.' Alex shot a surprised glance at her for a moment before turning back to the road. 'The men she's ever had any dealings with have been these empty-headed wealthy old family types introduced by her uncle who talk about Daddy and polo and not much else. I've tried to get her to come to some of the hospital dances. I'm sure she would be a wow there, but she doesn't seem to be interested. It's a pity she ever agreed to work for her uncle. She should have found a proper job or gone to college. She's bright enough. I know she loves history.'

'Perhaps she feels she owes her uncle something for giving her a home.'

'He hasn't had to expend that much. Her parents' estate paid for her schooling, as I understand it. The rest of it is left to her in some sort of trust for when she's twenty-five. The strange thing is, Catherine's not bothered about the idea of money, hers or other people's. She's very generous, as I know all too well, and she enjoys being so, but she's quite happy curled up at home with a book rather than being out partying; and you can imagine what a hit she would be. It's a shame.'

'Sarah, you shouldn't be telling me all this.'

'Oh, I would imagine with all the things you must see and know, and have to remain quiet about in the course of your job, all this is quite tame to you.'

'Nevertheless, I'm sure she wouldn't like the idea of you talking to me about her.'

'That's the strange thing; as I've said, I find you very easy to talk to. I'm surprised that Catherine hasn't found the same. For some reason I feel that she's quite the opposite.'

'Well, it doesn't matter. In a few weeks all this will be over, and our paths won't cross again. Now, it's time for you to give me some directions.'

Alex followed her directions and tried to keep his mind off the fact that some small part of him felt that the acceptance of him by Catherine Franklin did matter.

He pulled up as instructed outside the terrace of white, bay-fronted villas.

Sarah turned to him. 'Well, here we are: Number Twenty-Nine. Now, don't get the wrong idea, but would you like to come in for a drink or something? Jerry should be along in a moment, and I'm sure he would like to meet you. Perhaps we could all have something to eat. Unless, of course, you have something more interesting arranged.'

She was back to her banter again, Alex realised. 'No, that's the best offer I'll have tonight, so yes, thank you very much.'

When they went inside the first floor flat he looked around with interest. 'Umm, very nice. Much better than mine, by quite a distance.'

'My father bought it many years ago as a sort of investment. They don't seem to spend much time here, though. It's handy for the Brompton Hospital. Sit down, Alex, make yourself at home. Would you like a drink?'

'Nothing alcoholic, thank you.'

After making him a coffee she busied herself in the kitchen, starting to prepare a meal. Jerry arrived a few minutes later. He also worked at the Brompton Hospital. He greeted their unexpected guest with a warm smile and, as Sarah had anticipated, was grateful to Alex for his generosity.

'It was kind of you to put yourself out. I don't like the idea of her doing a journey of that distance on her own at this time of night when it's dark.'

Over the meal Alex found himself, under gentle questioning, which he recognised but somehow didn't mind, explaining about his own career choice.

'It started when my father put me in the Army to straighten me out, as he put it at the time. I must admit I didn't appreciate the imposed discipline at first, but once the rough edges had been knocked off, sometimes in a literal sense, I came to enjoy it. I might have stayed in, but I was still young and thought there were other things to do. It was strange that I went straight into the police force.' He smiled at them. 'It was a good move, though. I was lucky, and I've now reached Inspector and want to go higher.'

'I would imagine your father is proud of you.'

Although Sarah's comment had been expected, he didn't quite know how to reply. After a moment he spoke the truth. 'When my father put me in the Army he went off to Canada and I haven't seen or heard of him since.'

The other two were silent for a moment and then Sarah commented, 'Well, families, as we said earlier, are not always ideal. Good friends can be a real help, though. Now we've come to know you, perhaps we can keep in touch.' She looked over at Jerry, who nodded.

Alex felt quite moved. In a gallant action, he grasped her hand and brought it up to his mouth and planted a kiss on it.

'You wouldn't have done that if you'd known what I was doing this morning!'

As the laughter died away, it was inevitable the talk between the two men came round to cars. Jerry appreciated the Porsche and began to tell Alex how Sarah's father had left him in charge of a 1930s Aston Martin held in a lock-up mews garage a few streets away.

'He co-owns it with two friends who are also abroad quite a lot. She's a beauty, four cylinders that make the most marvellous noise, soft top, spoke wheels and chrome to die for. I take her out for a spin when I have the time and the weather is OK. Next time, suppose I contact you?'

Sarah went into the kitchen to do the washing up, listening to them chatting away. It was nice to see that although Alex was a little older, they were getting on so well. She had noticed his slight hesitation in answering her questions during the car journey, and what appeared to be his unease at the topic of family. Now, learning about what must have been quite a traumatic time in his early life, she was beginning to form the impression that on the inside he was not as cool and in command as he liked to portray. Well, she thought with a shrug, being the handsome, eligible bachelor he was, he ought not to have too much of a problem when he did want to find someone special.

Rather like Catherine, she realised. Her friend was just the same. She thought about earlier on today, of the almost electric atmosphere in the kitchen between Alex and Catherine, and Catherine's strange attitude to him. How interesting!

*

Alex arrived home to find that a message had been put through his door. It was short and to the point: 'Whitehall. 10 p.m. tonight.'

After the enjoyable evening he had just experienced, the message brought him back to reality. He looked at his watch. He would just make it.

CHAPTER 7

Johnny Clarke looked out of the window and watched the traffic, lighter now at this time of night. He downed the rest of his gin in one swallow. Would that old rogue Franklin pull it off again, he wondered? Villiers had promised him he would. What the hell did Atkinson think he was playing at, getting caught in that way! Dabbling in weapons for the first time, you had to be sure of your contacts. Too greedy, that was his trouble. The sniff of a profit and he was there like a rat up a drainpipe. He should have spotted the police a mile away, instead of getting sucked into their little game. Now he'd been forced to work hard, calling in favours to get the stupid bugger out of a hole. A lighter sentence was all he could hope for. Serve him right if he had to do a full stretch.

The trouble was, Clarke thought to himself, things like this were making him too reliant on people such as Franklin, and the favours being asked in return were getting expensive.

He didn't trust the Judge. Villiers was more his sort of man. One of those snooty, successful lawyers, who wasn't afraid to do deals for his own benefit in some less orthodox ways. They had done each other several lucrative favours over these last few years. The problem was, Clarke thought, he was losing some of his bargaining power.

Although only in his late twenties, he had been making a name for himself in the pecking order of the London underworld, much to his satisfaction, and had become known as someone prepared to do anything for anybody as long as there was money in it. The trouble was, it didn't make him look too clever at the moment, considering it was one of his own associates in the dock. He'd have to throw some weight around to regain lost ground. Old Jack Ellison must be having a good laugh at his expense. He knew he regarded him with contempt as a young contender to his throne, with little chance of taking it. Perhaps he might have to think up something very interesting that wouldn't look too good on Ellison, just to try to even the score.

He turned and looked at the young woman sprawled on the bed, still fast asleep. He'd wake her up in a minute. If she didn't perform better this time, he'd teach her a lesson. She was beginning to bore him anyway; time for a change. She'd also been asking too many questions for his liking. Just because she'd been his regular for some time, she was beginning to get airs and graces. Yes, little Miss Lucille Prentice, you'd better watch your step, or Johnny Clarke will show you who's still boss.

He put down his glass and moved towards the bed.

*

Alex was able to park using his pass. Wondering if he was going to hear more intrigue, or at last find some answers, he went up to the same office as before. The security guard in the lobby must have rung ahead, as Francis opened the door when he approached.

'Good evening. I wondered if my message would catch you tonight.'

Taking a seat, and seeing they were on their own, Alex felt a little uncomfortable that his superior was not present.

'Sir John doesn't like to undertake duties at this time of the day.' Francis was correct in interpreting Alex's thoughts. 'Are you aware that he has some, er... health problems?'

'Yes. I gather he's about to retire.'

'Indeed, and who will succeed him, I wonder? Any thoughts yourself?'

'Assistant Commissioner Rankin seems to be proactive with various initiatives, with some success of late, but I haven't had much association with him so I'm not that aware of him as a person. The powers that be have never seemed keen on a straight, moving-up appointment; more of a new broom opportunity.'

'Quite. It's a powerful job. The right man could control quite a lot… or even the wrong man.' Francis gave Alex a keen look. 'If the wrong man were in that position, there could be all sorts of quiet irregularities possible.'

'But that's what these watchdog committees are for.'

'Even they can be suborned.'

'That sounds to me like something in the realm of fantasy,' Alex retorted with a frown. 'No one could trust anyone else if you follow your logic through.'

'It would be unsettling, I grant you, but just humour me for a moment and think about it. Imagine if, over a wide spectrum, certain people holding certain positions were not all working for the greater good, if you want to put it that way. Not all of those need to be in high-profile jobs, just the ordinary working man or woman, causing disruption in one form or another. A lot of damage could be done. Small damage, but drop by drop it could make a difference. Countries have fallen in the past because of one small action.'

Alex stared at him, astounded. 'Are you trying to tell me you think something of the kind is happening?'

No answer, just an impassive stare.

Alex stood and walked around. 'That's crazy! It would have to have some sort of control. It couldn't just happen. Someone would have to pick out the person, position, timing… and that could take years to achieve.' He sat down again.

'But you're right. It could do enormous damage.' The more he thought about it, the more alarming the idea became.

He looked over at the still silent Francis. 'Are you suggesting to me that the Commissioner's post is… suspect?'

'It would be a good opportunity, don't you think? Get your own man in there and… well, you can use your imagination.'

'Have you any evidence for all these suspicions of yours?'

'Nothing so far that would look too good in a court of law, but I have some interesting facts and figures. Sir John knows of my ideas. He, too, is concerned, and he agrees that someone should be utilised in any capacity that would assist in this investigation, but on a confidential basis. He considers you have the aptitude to be of assistance as a representative of the police force.'

'You consider me that trustworthy?'

'You've been checked out. After a rather shaky start in life you have proved yourself capable and you appear to have integrity. Your father was also a good policeman, until he went astray, albeit under a certain amount of duress.'

Alex was rather startled to hear reference to his father. They must have been doing some digging!

'Is my current detail something to do with this matter?'

'As we said, for the moment we would like to know a bit more about what goes on in the Judge's household. We've been given a unique and unexpected opportunity to get on the inside. That's all I'm prepared to say at present.' He studied Alex for a while longer. 'Are you willing to assist us in investigating the wider issues?'

Alex didn't hesitate. 'Yes, I think I am. Am I under your control or Sir John's?'

'You will be operating under your ordinary police procedures, as we mentioned before. Finish your current duties at Richmond, and then set something up. I want you to do your own thinking and probing. Sir John is arranging for you to be seconded to the Anti-Terrorist Branch with a special assignment; say, organised crime links with terrorism. You will from time to time also be given orthodox jobs, as cover. The transfer will give you a chance to poke around a bit. If you need any special permissions, contact me. You can have someone to assist you but they must not know the whole story, and I cannot impress upon you enough the need for secrecy. By its own nature we cannot be sure who is on the inner circle. One false move or remark, and tracks will be covered.'

'Yes, I understand that. I wonder if my present Sergeant would be interested. Can I speak to him?'

'Yes, but under the proviso I have already mentioned.'

Francis wrote on a piece of paper and handed it to Alex. 'This is a secure number on which you can reach me at most times. If not, it's always manned, so you can leave a message if you have to. Memorise it and destroy the paper.' His smile was thin. 'You don't have to eat it!'

In a complete change of tack he asked, 'What sort of make is the Judge's safe? It's in his study, I take it?'

Alex had to think for a moment to remember but then it came to him. 'It's an old Chubb, and yes, it's in his study.'

'Yes. Mmm… of course.' Francis made a note and then rose.

'Well, I think we've done enough at this time of night. I will leave it to you to speak to your Sergeant and then you can get to work. Give it some thought meanwhile.'

Alex drove back to Kennington, thinking hard.

*

After relieving Carl the next morning, Alex did a tour of the house and grounds. Not so much checking on the security arrangements, but trying to see the property through new eyes. It was his last day roster and after a day off he would return for nights.

There was just one way in and out of the property at the front, and with the new extra security lights at the front and back, any approaches in or out should be well observed. The thick tangle of shrubbery all around the back garden would, in his eyes, still pose a problem for an easy entry or exit. This left a check on the inside of the property.

Returning to the house, he walked through an archway in a hedgerow into the vegetable area. His approach had been on grass and therefore silent, which is how he came upon Catherine Franklin before she knew he was there. She was standing on the gravel path dressed in a heavy coat and Wellingtons, her dark brown hair caught back in a ponytail. However, it was her face which held his attention: a picture of beautiful serenity. She appeared to be gazing up towards a nearby tree. He himself became aware of a bird trilling its heart out, and realised she was listening too.

The bird stopped and he said, 'They make an amazing sound unequal to their size.'

Startled, she jumped and spun round. For once there was no aloofness in her expression. She was still caught up in the wonder of her experience, and Alex felt a sense of pleasure from just looking at her, wishing that she was always like this in his presence. He could see a smudge of dirt on her cheek and had an insane desire to reach out and rub it off. He gave himself a mental shake.

With an embarrassed smile, he heard her murmur, 'Excuse me', and she went to move past him.

Nettled that she appeared to be so keen to get away from him, and against his better judgment, he commented, 'Oh, by the way, Sarah arrived home safe and sound last night. We spent a very entertaining evening together.'

He regretted the remark the instant he made it as he saw the unhappy expression cross her face. She made no reply, but turned on her heel and trudged off out of sight.

Hell's teeth, he fumed to himself, why on earth did he want to do that? She wasn't in the same league of banter as Sarah Jennings by a mile, and appeared to think the worst of him anyway. Even so, she ought to know her friend better than to think she had also taken advantage of the supposed opportunity. He'd formed the impression, after his talk with Sarah, that they were more like sisters. He sighed. She was a mystery to him, but he regretted any worsening of the situation between them. He would have to find a way of making things up with her. Then again, perhaps he ought to just keep out of her way. He had a job to do. With a shake of his dark head he carried on back to the house.

*

Catherine dumped her gardening things in the scullery and went through to the kitchen. Grace was washing the breakfast dishes and looked up as she entered.

44

'Ah, there you are, your uncle has been asking for you. He also wanted to know where Inspector Hartman was. Have you seen him?'

'Oh yes, I've seen him alright, and I hope I don't have to again.'

She disappeared through into the hall, ignoring Grace's enquiring call, and went into the study. Her uncle was on the phone but gestured for her to wait. When he finished his call, he glared at her.

'There you are. What have you been doing? We've been looking everywhere for you. I need to take those notes with me today that you were typing.'

'I was just in the garden. I'll get them.' She turned to leave.

'Oh, have you seen Hartman?'

'Yes, he's in the garden.'

With that brief statement, she turned and left the room.

Pondering his niece's abrupt comment and unusual demeanour, Franklin heard a knock on the door.

'Come.'

Hartman walked into the room. 'You wanted to see me, Judge?'

At that moment, Catherine returned. When she saw who was present she hesitated, but then put the papers on the desk and without a further word, or look, left the room.

Franklin noticed Hartman watch her leave and caught his small sigh. He narrowed his eyes. There was an unwelcome situation developing here that would need his attention, he mused to himself.

'I understand you will be missing tomorrow, Hartman. Who is covering for you?'

'Sergeant Johnson will be with you during the day. Freeman takes the night. Sergeant Johnson again for day duty, and I start nights that evening. Is that satisfactory?'

'Yes, I suppose so. By Friday we should be summing up, and next week should see an end altogether. I presume now is the difficult time, if anything is to happen?'

'If someone had wanted to apply pressure they might have considered it before now, but nothing can be taken for granted, and your cover could remain on alert even after the end of the trial.'

'Very good. I am ready to leave now,' said Franklin, standing and closing his briefcase.

'I'll go and tell Painter.'

The younger man left the room and Franklin sat down again in his chair, rubbing his chin and staring, deep in thought, at the closing door.

*

Catherine heard the Rolls leave and sat where she was on her bedroom window seat with her face up against the cold glass. What was happening in this house at the moment? Everyone was on edge all the time. No, she thought to herself, that's not quite correct. She was on edge, that was the problem. For a moment out in the garden this morning she had felt at peace with herself, and then *he* had appeared, and it had all fallen apart again. Every time she saw the man she felt unable to act in a normal way; and to make matters worse, she was sure he knew it. Her senses were on full alert when he was around, as if she had come alive in some way. Why was she so tongue-tied in his presence, not quite knowing what to do or say, and always getting it wrong? It wasn't as if she liked him – was it?

She realised too late that he had been teasing her out in the garden this morning. Her reaction must have seemed ridiculous to him. She should have known that Sarah would have sent him packing if he had tried anything with her. She was envious of her friend for being able to enjoy an evening in his company. Should she try to apologise, or just leave it? She wasn't sure what to do any more, but mindful of her uncle's warning, and her own uncertain feelings, it might be better if she tried to ignore him – if she could.

CHAPTER 8

The change from days to nights was always difficult as it altered his sleep patterns, but Alex found there was something peaceful about a night sky, even in the middle of London. Out here in Richmond, it was even better. He'd been around the outside of the house and garden, and all seemed secure. As a light drizzle began to fall, he made his way back indoors.

Grace had left him a sandwich on a tray and a note for him to help himself to coffee. He made a cup and munched on the sandwich, looking through the daily paper lying on the kitchen table. He thought that at one point he had heard a sound in the quiet house. He went into the hall and listened for a while. Nothing. Just someone using a bathroom, no doubt. He returned to the kitchen, but stopped again and listened hard. There it was again, more a suggestion of a noise, and difficult to pinpoint.

He moved back to the hall and stood outside the door to the Judge's study. He was sure the noise had been from here. He slipped inside, and sensed a change in temperature, like a draft of cold air. In the moonlight he could see that the room was empty and the French windows were still closed. He moved towards them and looked out at the garden, now wet after the rain shower. He was about to turn away when something on the carpet at his feet caught his eye. He bent down. It looked like a small leaf from one of the garden plants. Picking it up, he found that it was wet. The carpet just inside the French windows also felt damp to his touch. Someone had just been in and out of this door. But how? The door was still locked, the alarm hadn't gone off, and the outside light wasn't on. He unlocked the door and slipped outside, hoping not to activate the alarm – if, in fact, it was working. He inched down the side of the house and glimpsed a dark shape just turning the corner ahead of him. He broke into a run and sprinted after the figure. He heard a muffled oath and saw his target trip and fall to the ground. In an instant Alex was on him.

'For Christ's sake, don't start shouting, Hartman. We're on the same side.' The low whisper was just audible.

Alex hauled his captive to his feet. 'What the hell's going on! How do you know my name?' His voice no more than a hiss.

The other man was attempting to brush himself down, his breathing heavy from his fall.

'I knew it was you here tonight. We know what cars each of you drive. If you must know, I'm doing a job for Francis. We needed to see the contents of the safe.'

'How in God's name did you get past the security?'

In the wash of moonlight Alex saw the other man smile, and reach into his pocket. Quick as a flash Alex had his wrist in a vice-like grip.

'Don't be a fool, Hartman. I'm not armed.' He managed to extricate a small square box from his pocket and held it up. 'This overrides the alarm system. I scarpered when I heard you moving around. I was just about to activate the alarm again when I tripped over the bloody garden. I'll give you time to get back in and then do it.'

'Oh no you won't, young man.' Alex took the device from him and grabbed his arm. 'You're coming back inside with me and we're going to have a little conversation with Francis about this.'

He propelled the other man back to the French windows.

'Are you sure the alarm is still off? I don't want all hell breaking loose.'

'Yeah, its all OK. Don't worry.'

Back inside, Alex pulled the heavy curtains and switched on the desk lamp. He studied the other man for a moment. He was in his late twenties, and seemed relaxed, given his fall and the subsequent scuffle, with no apparent unease at potential exposure as something different to what he claimed.

Alex dialled the number Francis had given him. Would it reach him at this time of night? On the second ring it was answered.

'Yes?'

'Do I understand there was a visit arranged tonight?' Alex demanded.

After a moment's silence, he heard a sigh. 'Ah. Been discovered, have we?'

'A bit risky, wasn't it? Not the quietest of burglars, and he left clues behind.'

'Oh? Such as?'

'Wet leaves from the garden on the carpet. Alright, they would be dry by the morning, but they were there for me to see tonight. I bet I gave him one hell of a start. He tried to make a quick exit.'

'He's with you then, is he? God's teeth… Put him on.'

Alex handed the phone over with a grim smile.

'Your boss wants a word with you.'

After a moment or two when his companion had, it appeared, been treated to a less than harmonious conversation, the receiver was handed back to him.

'You don't need to worry, Hartman. We've done this before and by morning no one will be any the wiser.'

'Do I also assume that the security people did a more complicated job than was thought?'

'Yes, that was tricky. Good idea on your part to have one of your people oversee the job, but it made life a bit difficult for our man. He had a hell of a job getting a copy of the door key, and dealing with the electrics. Handy, though, to have people placed in firms like that.'

'You should still have warned me.'

'Mm, yes, I take your point. Perhaps we should. Let our friend out of jail will you. Make sure he puts the alarm back on, though.'

After his visitor had left, giving an assurance that the alarm would be reactivated, Alex had a close look at the safe. There appeared to be a film of liquid around the keyhole, greasy to the touch. He hoped Francis was right and there would be nothing to see in the morning.

He left the study and stood for a moment in the hall. All was still quiet. He went to check the control box for the alarm system and it appeared to be working as normal. He returned to the study and opened the French windows, closing them again as soon as he saw the warning light for the alarm start to blink. He was about to turn off the light when he saw something lying on the floor under the desk. He reached down to pick it up. It was a piece of paper torn out of a notebook of some sort, on which two dates had been written. He shrugged and placed it on the desk.

It would be as well to check around the house again, he thought. Making his way up the stairs he noticed a faint light coming from under one particular door. This, he knew, belonged to Catherine Franklin. Was she still awake at this time of night? It was past one o'clock. Had she heard anything? Should he risk taking a look? If she was awake she might well scream the place down. He had to take the chance; it was just possible she could be ill.

With caution he opened the door. No sound. He eased through the small gap. She was asleep, but her bedside light was on. She had been reading and the book was still in her outstretched hand. Any moment now it would fall to the floor and wake her. Alex moved over to the side of the bed and, removing the book from her unresisting fingers, placed it on the bedside table. He looked down at her as she slept. Her hair, shining in the dim light, had fallen over her face. He reached down and moved it aside with the tips of his fingers. The lines of her jawbone and slender neck were now exposed and he wanted to… Good God! What was wrong with him? This was ridiculous. He was reacting like a love-sick schoolboy.

He turned out the light and left the room. He checked the rest of the upstairs and went back down to the kitchen. He found he was breathing hard, and forced himself to regain his composure. You're going to be in serious trouble, my boy, if you carry on like this, he told himself. Just keep your mind on your work. However, at times during the rest of the night he thought again of the shadowy room and the sleeping figure.

*

Lionel Franklin looked at his niece, still eating her breakfast at the other end of the table. She was beginning to look more and more like her mother these days. If things had been different... He dismissed the disquieting thoughts. In was in the past; water under the bridge. Things had been dealt with in such a way that no one was any the wiser, but at a cost, and a lot of favours.

With the assistance of Villiers and Hamilton the legal and financial niceties of his brother's estate had been dealt with, to their advantage, but now he was meeting some unexpected resistance at the final hurdle.

'I trust you are still obeying my instructions about conversing with our guardians? I somehow have the feeling you might have become a little relaxed about it.'

Catherine looked up at him, and he noticed the slight hurt in her eyes. Her reaction pleased him.

'I'm just polite to them. I didn't imagine you would mind.'

'As long as that's where it stays. Take Hartman, for instance. You might find yourself interested in him. He is, after all, an attractive man and, in my estimation, very experienced with women. However, this is not the sort of person you have been groomed to associate with. I feel it is my duty once again to make that clear to you.'

Green eyes flashed at him. 'What do you mean, groomed? Why can't I be free to choose my own friends?'

God! Still that sudden show of independence. Franklin felt his temper rising. 'Friends? Like that Jennings woman? Someone else, in my view, unsuited to you.'

'Sarah has been a very good friend!'

'Good friends don't fill people's heads with notions of independent careers, when they should realise that your duty is here. I've seen that you had a good education and learnt social skills to enable you

51

to make a good marriage, and it's my responsibility to see that is achieved.'

He watched with satisfaction as he saw Catherine's shoulders slump, and some of the fight go out of her. 'We've had this conversation before, Uncle. I've told you, I don't like the men I've been introduced to.'

'What about Duncan Hamilton? Good family. It's a while since you last saw him, I believe.'

'Yes it is, and I don't like him either. I don't trust him.'

'Perhaps you just don't know him well enough. You ought to spend time with him a bit more. Maybe you could go up to Scotland for a break, or I'll see if he's coming down to London soon. I'll have a word with his father.'

He noticed she made no further comment, and continued with her breakfast.

Franklin congratulated himself. That had gone better than he'd anticipated. Perhaps he'd speak to Gregory this morning.

*

After a few hours sleep Alex drove in to his office. He wanted to get down on paper the events of last night, just to cover himself. He didn't intend to stay, and his dress was informal. There was a knock on the door and a face peered round it.

'Hi, Alex, heard you were in.'

'Hello, Bob. How are things?'

Bob Patterson was a former colleague still working in the CID. They'd become friends during Alex's time with the Department and from time to time socialised together.

'We've had the lab report on that Franklin letter. No joy, just the Judge's prints. I'm not sure we can do anything more with it. We've hauled Johnny Clarke in for a chat to see if it's anything to do with him; after all, it's one of his men in trouble. Of course, he maintains he's squeaky clean, allowing the law to take its course etcetera!'

'I'll bet he's smarting a bit from Atkinson's gaff. He's going to make sure he's as far removed from any suspicions surrounding the case as he can, so I can't think he would do something as stupid as this.'

'Anyway, wondered if you were free for a spot of lunch?'

'Yes, sure, just finishing off here. I was on nights last night so I didn't intend to stay long. Am I smart enough for you?'

*

They settled themselves into an alcove seat of the pub and started on their ploughmans.

'Is Jenny OK, Bob?'

'She's fine thanks.' Patterson looked rather sheepish and stared down at his plate for a moment. 'Well, I might as well tell you, I suppose. We're expecting the patter of tiny feet in about seven months.'

'Brilliant! Congratulations to you both from me. Tell Jenny, won't you.'

Alex had attended their wedding about six months ago. Now, in no time, they would be a real family. Bob looked tickled pink at the idea, and he realised with a shock that he felt a small stab of envy.

With an uncanny echo of his thoughts, Bob poked his arm. 'When's it going to be your turn, Alex? How about that sexy blonde you brought to the wedding?'

Alex took a sip of his beer. 'Oh, that was over some while ago. I haven't been involved with anyone since.'

'Well, take a tip from me and don't leave it too long. You don't know what you're missing. You're too wound up with this career business. There are other things just as exciting!' He grinned, with a knowing look.

'Yes, sure, I get the picture.'

Alex wanted the topic changed. He was beginning to feel pressurised. Everyone had the same idea about him it seemed. Well, he was doing just fine, a rising career which was what he had striven for, and so far he had never been short of female company if he desired it. Why was it, then, at times he felt unsettled and restless? As thoughts of a particular young woman came into his mind, he knew he had to change the subject.

'How are things in the Department, Bob?'

'Oh, a bit quieter than you, I'll bet. You've settled in well with SB, so I hear.'

'I've had a bit of luck, I suppose,' Alex smiled. 'It must all have started from that tip-off with your brother. How is Ralph?'

Years earlier Alex had been on a protracted stake-out with Bob, and during the long hours spent in a parked car together, Bob had told Alex about his brother, a whiz kid in new electronic fields, who was looking for extra backing to put into his fledgling company. As far as Bob was concerned, this would be a gold mine for anyone investing. Alex had been thrifty in his life so far and had a small amount of spare money. The more he listened, the more interested he became, and in the end put some funds into the company. Bob told him to watch it take off on the Stock Market, and as Alex saw over the following years, it did just that. The value of his shares increased several-fold, but getting cold feet, he'd cashed them in about six months ago for a considerable profit, enabling him to purchase his Porsche.

'I'm afraid I bailed out and cashed in my shares a few months ago,' he admitted, 'but thanks for the initial tip-off. It made me some money.'

'Just as well you got out when you did. The company's taken a bit of a hit at the moment. Annoying, because it's not Ralph's fault. He's been dealing with a couple of suppliers for some time, but one of them has begun to have trouble with duff parts and it's had a knock-on effect with his own supply, a couple of orders have been cancelled on him because of delays and he's struggling at the moment. Ralph says the suppliers are in a jam as well, so it's not just him. Getting their lawyers in on it, so he says. There's even talk of deliberate sabotage. A bit far-fetched, but I suppose that's big money business for you!'

Alex murmured his agreement, conscious that something had started to nag away at him.

'Now you're keeping a watching brief on Franklin, what do you make of him? Some of the lads reckon lawyers hate him being on the bench; he has the knack of coming up with legal points that ruin their cases.'

'He's not someone I would want on my Christmas card list.'

'Well,' Bob finished off his beer, 'you may be at leisure this afternoon but I'd better get back to the treadmill. We'll have to sort out a foursome one night. Go on the town. I'm sure you can find someone out of your little black book!'

Alex watched his friend leave the bar, and then made a sudden decision.

'I say, Bob,' he called. 'I wonder if I could contact Ralph for a chat, for old times sake.'

'Yes, sure,' Bob walked back to him and fished out a small card from his wallet. 'Here's his business card. Give him call. Buy him a beer. Might cheer him up.'

Alex turned the small card over and over in his hand. Was this in any way connected with Francis's theories or was he just grasping at straws?

CHAPTER 9

As Carl was due a day's rest, Alex had arranged with him to reverse their shifts on the Friday of that week.

The Rolls had been playing up on the way back from town and Arthur wondered if they would even reach Richmond. The Judge was taciturn about any other arrangements and they managed to limp home. On arriving, Arthur set to work to see if matters were terminal for the old car.

As Alex went inside he made a mental note to warn Carl that if the Judge required to leave the house that evening before the Rolls was repaired, other transport requirements would be needed, and if this were the case he had better contact him. He had a sudden humorous vision of Carl and the Judge packed into his tiny Mini! With a smile still on his face, he went into the kitchen.

'It's been a good day then, has it?' Grace was giving him a quizzical look.

'No, not at the moment. The Rolls is playing up. Arthur is giving it the kiss of life. I was just having a surreal thought about the situation, that's all.'

'So you mean it's off the road?' Grace asked, her tone of voice sharp.

Alex looked at her. 'Could well be. Why?'

'Catherine is at Sarah's and Arthur had arranged to fetch her home later. He must have forgotten. I'll have to ring her and tell her to get a taxi or something.'

'I'll go and fetch her.' As soon as he said it Alex wondered what on earth had put those words in his mouth. It was a stupid idea from every angle.

'Alex, you're off duty now. You can't go all that way into town and back again. Although it's a very nice offer.'

'I dare say it will make my halo sparkle a bit more!' His remark sounded more light-hearted than he felt. He hadn't even begun to consider Catherine Franklin's reaction. 'I think it might be a good idea if we don't inform Miss Franklin of the change of arrangements beforehand.'

His meaningful look was not lost on Grace. 'She couldn't complain about such a nice gesture.'

'Oh, I wouldn't bet on it. I get the impression she considers me to be an incarnation of Bluebeard.'

'Well,' stated Grace, 'perhaps this is your chance to change that opinion.'

'Mmm, we'll have to see, won't we. What time was Arthur going to collect her?'

'Not until seven-thirty, I think. Look, why don't you stay here and have something to eat. That's the least we can do, otherwise you're never going to get a meal tonight. It's a Friday night and the traffic will be horrendous. Go out now and tell Arthur in case he's panicking about getting the wretched thing fixed tonight, and I'll get the meal on the go. OK?'

'Yes, that's fine, Grace. Thanks.'

*

Grace had been right. The traffic was heavy, and although Alex thought he had timed it right, it was nearly eight o'clock before he turned in to the South Kensington street.

His ring on the doorbell was answered by Sarah.

'Alex! What a surprise. Come on in. I have Catherine with me at the moment. She's waiting for Arthur to come and collect her.'

Alex followed her into the lounge, which appeared to be empty.

'I know Miss Franklin is here, Sarah. I've come to collect her. The Rolls is off the road.'

'You've come to collect her? You mean you're going to do all those journeys backwards and forwards tonight? Did her uncle ask you to do it?'

'He doesn't know. I volunteered. I'm off duty now. Arthur and I agreed it was safer than her getting a taxi on her own, and he wanted to work on the car in case it's needed for tomorrow.'

Sarah's grin was wide. 'Well, this is going to be interesting. I wonder what Catherine will say.' She then saw Alex's tense expression and added, laying a hand on his arm, 'Don't worry, it'll be alright.'

Just then Catherine came into the room and saw the visitor and the closeness of the couple, with Sarah's hand on his arm. Her face appeared to tighten.

'I thought it was Arthur,' she said, her voice cool.

Alex was annoyed at her obvious misinterpretation of the scene. When would this wretched female learn not to jump to conclusions? It was about time she acted her age. He gave himself a mental kick. He must stop getting so worked up about her.

'I'm afraid, Miss Franklin, the Rolls has broken down and I've come to take you home.'

He saw the small face whiten, and her obvious response to his statement made him even angrier.

'Why didn't Grace ring? I could have arranged for a taxi home, instead of all this... fuss.' She waved her hand in Alex's direction.

He was sure he had not misplaced the hint of panic in her voice.

'It wasn't considered safe for you to be alone at this time of night.' Alex was becoming even angrier now. 'Fuss', indeed!

'Inspector Hartman, I remember you telling me the other day that your job is to protect my uncle, and I see no reason therefore why I should be included in your duties. I am quite capable of looking after myself.'

'Oh, I see! Then just consider this. Any person or persons who have threatened your uncle could decide to use you as a target instead, something I've warned him about already. They could have been observing your movements, just waiting for an opportunity to inflict some harm on you which would put pressure on him.'

'That's just rubbish,' she flared back, green eyes flashing. 'What harm could come to me in a taxi? You're just trying to scare me.'

'I hope I am scaring you, young lady! Perhaps you might care to know that the Met Police have just arrested a taxi driver for taking lone travelling females into certain areas of London, on at least two occasions, where they have been accosted by him.'

'How convenient. Well, thank you for the thought, Inspector Hartman, but all the same I will take my chances with a taxi.'

In the ensuing silence, there was an audible gasp from Sarah, who had by this time taken a spectator's position on one of the dining area chairs.

Alex was beyond angry by now. All he'd attempted to do was help in some way. He ignored the small part of his brain telling him that he had an ulterior motive and had been quite looking forward to having her alone to talk to for more than a minute or two.

He stared at her for a long moment and then turned to leave. In a quiet voice, holding his anger in check at the extreme edge of his control, he said, 'Very well, have it your own way. I've had enough of the whole thing. I cease to care what happens to you. I made the offer of a lift in my own time. I was off duty an hour ago, if you're at all interested, but as it seems to me you're more frightened about being in my company than by anything else, I'll make it an easy choice for you and say good night. Just to run true to form, though, before I get home I might stop off and have a drink or two, or even three, and then perhaps ravish a few young girls just to liven the evening up a bit. I would hate to spoil a free Friday night now when I have the chance.'

With a slight nod to Sarah he stormed out and slammed the door.

Catherine almost winced at the sound, and felt a sudden sense of loneliness and loss. She hadn't been sure of her ground in the argument, but something inside her was desperate that she should not be alone with this man. She looked over at Sarah, who just shook her head.

'Don't look at me for any help. You got yourself into this one. What's wrong with you? I've never known you to be so rude. He didn't have to put himself out, did he. What makes you panic so about him?'

Catherine didn't need her friend's obvious censure to make her feel bad. She knew she had been rude but she had felt real fear at the idea of being alone with him in the close confines of his car. She couldn't explain this to her friend, though, or even herself.

'I will apologise to him, I promise. But he's gone now, anyway.'

'Of course he hasn't gone!' Sarah stood up and looked out of the window. 'His car's still there, and whatever he said he wouldn't leave you to find your own way home.'

Catherine put on her jacket, collected her things together, and with a last look at her friend went into the hall. Taking a deep breath she opened the front door. He was leaning against the stair banister with his arms folded. To her consternation he looked even more overwhelming and masculine than normal. The grey eyes regarding her were cool and hard.

'I'm very sorry I was so rude to you,' Catherine managed to say in a quiet voice. 'I would like to have a lift if that is still possible, please.'

Without a word he stood up straight and went off down the stairs with her trailing along behind him.

They had travelled a short distance when he pulled the Porsche into the kerb and turned to stare at her. She was looking back at him with wide, startled eyes.

'What's wrong! What's the matter!'

'Miss Franklin, as sure as I am that the makers of this car did a good job when constructing it, there is always the possibility that parts could fail. I would hate for the door locks to give way and pitch you out onto the roadside. How could I explain that to Sarah? Now for God's sake sit round in your seat instead of trying to get as far away from me as possible. I find I've gone off the thought of molesting young girls tonight, they're just not worth the trouble.'

He waited while she straightened in her seat and then pulled away again. He reached out and switched on the radio. A slow, gentle melody covered the strained silence and cooled his temper as he drove along. This wasn't how he'd thought it would turn out. If she disliked him as much as it appeared there was no point even bothering with her, and yet he was still fascinated by her. Those flashing green eyes earlier had given him the crazy impulse to kiss her, and keep doing so until she gave in to him.

Finally drawing to a halt on the gravel driveway, he switched off the radio. Aware of the awkward silence, he realised she hadn't moved and turned to look at her.

'There you are Miss Franklin. Safe and sound,' and with sudden wicked amusement he leant across to the door lock on her side, 'or are you just a little disappointed?'

Her face was close to his and those remarkable green eyes were huge. With deliberate intent he looked down at her mouth. Her lips parted, and despite himself he felt the reaction in him. He cursed under his breath. What was it that made him want to flirt with her? Taking a deep breath, he nodded outside to where Carl stood in the shadows of the front door, and Arthur was approaching from the direction of the garage.

'The door is open and you will, no doubt, be pleased to see that you have two chaperones. Perhaps you'd better get out now or they might be having ideas!'

She gathered up her belongings with a rush. With a glance at him she murmured 'Thank you for the lift', tumbled out of the car and almost raced inside the house.

Alex nodded to Carl and Arthur and turned out of the driveway, glad to be heading home. He could smell her perfume in the car, and opened the window, as if that would do any good! For weeks now her fragrance was always with him, like a tantalising presence.

As he drove away a curtain closed at an upstairs window of the house.

*

Catherine dumped the shopping bags on her bed and sat down. She felt as if she'd run a marathon. What was it that was making her act like this when he was around? She had been trained to have poise and composure in social situations, but it all seemed to evaporate when she was with him. She wanted him to like her and yet she always caused him to be exasperated with her. What was wrong? Then she knew, and her cheeks grew hot at the thought. In the car she had been conscious of his strong hands on the wheel and his thigh close to hers, and just now for one wild moment she had thought he was going to kiss her, and she knew she wanted him to. Then she had realised that he was teasing her again and wouldn't have done anything anyway, even if there had not been an audience.

She knew her original opinion of him was wrong, but it had been made out of a sense of panic and desperation she hadn't understood. Now she was sure that he would not treat any woman with anything less than respect. Was it possible she could try to change his view of her? She sensed that he didn't have a very good one, and now it was even worse. It was all so confusing. Then again, she remembered her uncle's comments. He wouldn't let her associate with the likes of Alex Hartman anyway, even if they could be friends now.

With a heavy heart she knew she must face the fact that in a short while she would never see him again. The thought was painful, and with an unhappy sigh she started to prepare for bed.

CHAPTER 10

The following day she received an unexpected call from Duncan Hamilton. His father was a friend of her uncle's, and one of her trustees, and on a couple of occasions she had spent some time with the family in Scotland. Duncan ran their farming estate in Ayrshire and came to London when his infrequent duties as a company director made it necessary. She knew he had always professed an interest in her, but she was never that keen. There was something hard and selfish about him, and he made her feel uncomfortable. She knew her uncle would have no objection to any alliance, but she managed as much as possible to avoid any discussion on the matter.

She tried to sound pleasant when, with reluctance, she answered his call. 'Hello Duncan. Are you in town?'

'Yes, my dear, for a day or two. Wondered if you would like to join me tonight. We could have a drink somewhere.'

She could have lied, but knew her uncle would be displeased if he found out.

'Yes, alright then, Duncan.'

'Excellent.' He sounded almost relieved, she thought. 'Shall I pick you up about eight o'clock?'

'Yes, that would be fine. Thank you. I'll see you then.'

She put down the phone and already dreaded the coming evening. She decided not to tell anyone yet that she would be out that night. For some reason she didn't want Alex Hartman to be made aware of it; why, she couldn't say.

She waited until she heard the Porsche pull away and then went through to seek out Sergeant Johnson to tell him that she would be going out. She had the odd feeling that he guessed she had been deliberate in not mentioning it to anyone before. He just raised his eyebrows and hoped she would have a nice time.

By eight o'clock she was ready. She had decided to wear a cream suit with a green fitted blouse. She knew Duncan had arrived but when she went downstairs Grace told her that he was in with her uncle. It was nearly eight-thirty before the two men came out of the study together, both in obvious good spirits. She could feel Duncan's eyes looking over her body, and already she wished she had declined his invitation.

The evening deteriorated further. He took her to a bistro pub and found a table in a secluded corner. She tried to be a polite guest, and asked him about his work in Scotland and anything else she could think of. She asked for a glass of white wine but noticed he was drinking whisky. Making sure he was sitting close to her, Duncan draped his arm on the back of her chair. As she had taken off her jacket she could feel his hand touching her through the material of the blouse. She felt more and more uncomfortable. She drank very little of her wine, but Duncan ordered another drink for himself. She hoped he would be sober enough to drive.

'You know you're a very beautiful girl, Catherine,' he murmured into her hair. 'You could send a man mad if you lightened up a bit.'

'Don't be silly, Duncan.' She tried to extract herself from his arm, but his grip was tight.

'You know I've always fancied you.' He tried to kiss her, but she turned her head away.

'Duncan, not here, please.'

She realised that this was the wrong thing to say when he rose to his feet and held out her jacket for her.

'We'll find somewhere else then, my dear.'

'Duncan, take me home, please,' she said, trying to sound firm, 'or I'll get a taxi.'

'Alright, Miss Iceberg, I'll take you home,' he said with a smile she didn't like.

She was relieved when they reached Richmond and his car turned into the driveway. She climbed out in a hurry, but he followed her round to the front door.

'Don't I get a thank-you for taking you out?'

Before she knew it, he had manoeuvred her back against the brick support of the porch and was pressing his body against hers. He trapped one of her arms against him and held her head while he kissed her. She tried to push him away but his weight was too much. Trying to place his knee between her legs, he pushed one hand inside her blouse, reaching for her breast, which he enclosed in a painful grip. His breathing was heavy, and she could smell the whisky. Then his mouth was on hers, forcing her lips back against her teeth. She managed to free herself enough to cry out for him to stop and tried to beat at his back.

A voice spoke from the darkness. 'Do you need any assistance, Miss Franklin?'

It was Sergeant Johnson. Relief made her feel weak but she managed to push the startled Duncan away from her and heard him swear, hard and vicious, under his breath. She thought for a moment he was going to strike out, but he must have taken in the impassive stare and easy stance of the older man and thought better of it. With another oath he stumbled off to his car and drove away in a swirl of gravel.

'Thank you so much Sergeant Johnson,' Catherine managed to blurt out before doubling over as a wave of nausea washed over her. Her heaving stomach subsided without the loss of that dignity, but her torn blouse was very obvious and she felt embarrassed.

'Come along now, let's get you inside, Miss.'

Taking her arm he led her round the side of the house into the warmth of the kitchen. He made her sit in one of the big wooden chairs near the Aga and disappeared for a moment to return with a glass of liquid and stood over her until she had drunk it. The brandy made her cough and her eyes started watering; whether from the drink or emotion, she couldn't say. She was still finding it difficult to even think straight, and she knew that was the last thing she wanted to do.

'Good job I was about and heard you call out, Miss. Not a pleasant way to end an evening, if I may say so.'

Catherine nodded her agreement, fumbling with her blouse. She knew he had noticed, and with gentle fingers he buttoned up the jacket to conceal her.

'I think it would be a good idea if you went off to bed now, Miss. I'll have a warm drink brought up for you if you like.'

She smiled up at him, tears pricking the back of her eyes. 'Yes, I think I will go up now, and it would be nice to have a drink if it's no bother, Sergeant Johnson… Why don't you call me Catherine?'

He smiled at her. 'Then I think it's fair if I'm calling you Catherine that you call me Dougie.'

She stood up and moved over to the hall door. On impulse she turned and walked back to him and planted a gentle kiss on his cheek.

'Thank you, Dougie,' she whispered, and left the room with as much dignity as she could manage.

Dougie gazed after her, swore loud and hard, and then reached for the internal phone.

Catherine was undressed and ready for bed when Grace knocked and entered with a mug and biscuits on a tray.

'Dougie thought you might like these, Catherine.'

'Thank you, Grace. I'm sorry you were bothered at this time of night.'

She turned away so the other woman wouldn't see the tears springing to her eyes again.

'Dougie told me what happened. Are you alright, my dear? Do you want a doctor or anything?'

'Goodness, no, not a doctor! I'll be fine, just a bit shaken up, I suppose.'

'These men! I don't know what the world is coming to these days. We shouldn't have to put up with it. A pity Sergeant Johnson didn't teach him a lesson.'

'I think I'd have been cheering him on!' Catherine tried to make light of it. She could see Grace was upset. 'Never mind. It's over now and I'm going to enjoy my drink and then I'll get to bed. Thank you, Grace. Good night.'

When Grace had left, Catherine sat on the bed and drank some of the cocoa, but she still felt sick. Why were men always like this with her? There must be a man out there somewhere who could love her with gentleness and caring. Unbidden, a figure with dark hair and grey eyes came into her mind. Her heart told her that if this man loved a woman it would be with total dedication, and for ever. She wanted, no, needed to be that woman, but her head told her that there was no way it could be when he thought so little of her… and with her uncle's commands to be obeyed. With a deep sigh she climbed into bed, but sleep was a long time coming.

*

The Judge surprised Grace in the kitchen before breakfast the next morning, demanding a cup of coffee, and then retired to his study asking that Catherine be sent to him as soon as she was up. Grace decided to refrain from speaking about what had happened the night before.

Dougie had told her that he was going to tell Alex as soon as he arrived, and leave it for him to make any decision. She wondered what Alex would say. She had often caught him watching Catherine, and they seemed to spark something between them when they were together.

To her surprise Catherine appeared a moment later, dressed in trousers and a high-necked angora jumper. She looked a little pale and there were dark circles under her eyes as if she hadn't slept. As she poured herself a cup of coffee, Grace told her about her uncle's request.

'I'd better go and see him then, I suppose.'

When Dougie came in from the garden a moment later, Grace brought him up to date on the movements so far. He too was surprised at the early risers.

'I hope her uncle gives her an easy day today,' commented Grace, then both of them looked at each other in consternation as loud voices were heard coming from the Judge's study.

'I've heard them quarrel before, more when Catherine first came to live here, but then less and less. This is the first time I've heard them now for some time. A pity it has to be today,' said Grace.

'It always happens. Anyway, Alex will be here in a moment, I'd better get outside to meet him.'

As he left, Grace heard light footsteps in the hall and then a door close, and all was quiet. She shrugged, and carried on preparing breakfast.

*

Alex was himself running ahead of time, but as he pulled into the driveway Dougie was already outside waiting for him. He had the distinct impression that Dougie was doing just that, waiting for him. As he approached, Alex looked closer at the other man and began to feel a sense of apprehension.

'We had a little problem here last night, Boss.' Dougie began. 'Miss Catherine went out with a young man and when they came back the young fool tried to take advantage of her. I was in the vicinity and heard scuffling and then she called out. The young man's attentions were not welcome. I made my presence known. I thought for one moment he was going to clobber me, and I would have just loved that, but he beat a hasty retreat once he realised there was no use making an issue of it.'

'Miss Franklin, is she alright?'

'A bit shook up but I kept her in the kitchen at first and gave her a brandy, and when she looked steady enough I sent her to bed and asked Grace to look in on her with a hot drink. Grace said she thought she would be alright.'

Alex felt a build-up of unreasoning anger. 'If it had been me that found them I would have floored him, the little bastard. How far... I mean...'

'He tore her blouse, so you know what that meant, and he was trying something else when I got there. She was attempting to fight but he had her pinned against the brick pillar in the porch. I don't know how it would have ended if no one had been about.'

Alex thought of the girl having to cope with this violation, and was furious now. He could see Dougie regarding him with a wary look. He was well aware his colleague had been around in the past when his temper had almost got the better of him. He must be wondering what his boss intended to do. Alex took a deep, steadying breath.

'Does the Judge know?'

'No one has mentioned it to him yet. I wanted to see you first. He seemed quite chummy last night with the young man in question. His name is Duncan Hamilton. His father is something big in the banking world in the City and is a friend of the Judge. Catherine knows the family. Hamilton and the Judge spent some time together in the Judge's study before he and Catherine went out. It looked as if the young man had a small parcel with him when he arrived, which didn't look like a box of chocolates. He didn't have it with him when he and Catherine left, I noticed.'

He then brought Alex up to date with the events so far that morning.

'God, what a mess! This is all we need. Oh well, I'd better see Franklin, I suppose. Can you hang on here for a bit Dougie?'

'Yes, sure thing, no problem. If he wants a first-hand account I'm happy to speak to him.'

'Thanks, Dougie, and thanks for last night. I think we ought to make a formal note of what happened, and perhaps you can let me have that?'

'Any time, Boss.'

Alex went inside, and on entering the kitchen, Grace informed him that his presence had been requested by the Judge as soon as he came on duty.

'How is Catherine, I mean Miss Franklin, Grace?'

She noticed the Christian name but made no comment. 'Quiet, but I haven't seen much of her so far.'

Alex nodded and went through into the hall and knocked on the study door.

The Judge looked up as he entered.

'Well, Hartman, what have you to say about your colleague's meddling last night.'

'I beg your pardon?' Alex was not prepared for this sort of remark.

'What are your people doing, interfering in private affairs instead of going about their own business as requested?'

Alex was still startled at this line of attack, but managed to retort, 'If by "private affairs" you mean common assault which could even have led to rape, I think my colleague acted with commendable restraint. Your niece was in danger, and as an officer of the law, appropriate action was taken.'

'Rape? Appropriate action? Inspector Hartman, you are a man of the world. You know women. They all understand that it's not the done thing for them to give in at first but that doesn't always mean they are adverse to the whole idea. Another five minutes and things could have been very different.'

Alex couldn't believe what he was hearing. 'So you mean that my officer should have hung back for a while just to see how matters went, and meanwhile your niece could have been in serious trouble?'

'If your watchdogs hadn't been here at all, that's how it would have been.'

Alex's brain was working again and an icy calm settled on him.

'Who told you about last night? I gather you have spoken with your niece this morning. Did she mention it to you?'

'If you must know, Inspector, I received an irate telephone call last night from the young man in question, complaining about his treatment.'

'Complaining about his treatment? If I'd caught him he'd have been nursing a broken jaw this morning. Willing or not, there are certain ways for a gentleman to treat a lady, and in my book he is not a gentleman. I intend to make a report of the whole matter. If you wish to do so yourself then that is a matter for you. I will now interview your niece to obtain the facts from her. You are welcome to be present if you wish.'

'No, I do not.'

'Very well, Sir, may I proceed?'

Franklin just looked at him and then waved him away.

Alex left the room, unable to comprehend the man's attitude to a niece he had helped to raise from a child. It seemed to him as if she was regarded as a chattel, or a parcel. He looked at the closed door of the office and dreaded the next few minutes.

*

Catherine was finding it hard to concentrate. The interview with her uncle had been a worse experience even than last night. How had he known what had happened? Grace or Dougie must have told him; how else would he know? Or had Duncan been in touch with him, putting his side of the story?

Her uncle made it seem as if she had been in the wrong. 'I don't understand you sometimes Catherine. Why make all that fuss? At your age, you should know men do that sort of thing, even more so when pretty girls they fancy are involved. You can't be so naïve as not to know that matters can become a little heated sometimes.

'If I'd had my way you would have been married long ago, and I'm afraid the time has come when you can no longer ignore your responsibilities. I shall have to take steps to see that the situation does not continue for much longer.'

Finding her voice at last, she retorted, 'I don't consider that I am a responsibility, and I will marry someone I love, and who loves me.'

Her uncle just smiled and shook his head. 'It seems you have not yet learnt what happens in the real world. I have spent years grooming you to make a good marriage, and this is what will happen whether you like it or not.'

Although shocked at his words, she managed to reply, 'I think the whole idea is Victorian', and left his study without another word.

There couldn't be any way he could force her into a marriage against her will, was there? After all she was over twenty-one. Perhaps Sarah had been correct all along and she should have left this household years ago.

She heard the knock on her door, and guessed who it was. Her mouth went dry and her knees started to shake, but she knew he would come in anyway.

Turning to face him, she had what she hoped was her composure in place. He was standing leaning against the closed door, just looking at her. She couldn't read his expression and, as usual, had no idea what he was thinking.

'I suppose you've heard everything that has happened. All the lurid details!' That remark wasn't fair, but she had to build a wall between them as fast as she could, otherwise she was sure she would have given in to her instinct to walk over to him and bury her face in his chest, just wanting to be held in his arms.

She saw his expression change, but again it was impossible to gauge what he was thinking. She turned back to her desk and shifted a few papers around.

'I'm rather busy. Is this a business or social visit?'

She wanted to lash out at someone, and he was the obvious choice, but in an instant she regretted her tone.

'Catherine, stop it!' He sounded as if he was trying to keep his anger under control. 'I'm prepared to give you the benefit of the doubt today, so goading me just won't work. I've already spent an uncomfortable time with your uncle and I would just as soon not spend the same with you. I need to hear your side of last night's events in order to make an official report. Your uncle has declined to be present, but if you wish either Sergeant Johnson or Grace to be here I have no argument with that.'

She sat down as her legs gave way beneath her.

'What do you want to know?' She felt too tired to bother any more.

'Tell me what happened.'

As she went through it all, he interrupted her to ask for more clarification on a couple of points. It became more difficult when she had to describe how she had been touched. Then it was over. She hadn't noticed that he had moved to sit on the corner of her desk.

'I'm sorry I had to ask you to relive it all again.' His voice sounded soft.

She looked up at him, the tears ready to spill over. She heard him swear under his breath. He reached out and tucked a strand of hair behind her ear, and then stilled. She could feel his hand on her skin as he turned her face up. He was looking at her neck. He pulled down the high collar of her jumper. She had worn it on purpose when she had noticed the marks on her skin.

'Have you any more like that?' he asked, his voice quiet and controlled.

All she could do was nod. She wanted to turn her head, lay it down on his palm and go to sleep.

He stood, and the abrupt movement startled her.

'You're tired out. I suggest you take yourself off to bed and get some rest. We'll be leaving soon, so the house will be quiet. I'll see you before I leave again tonight.'

'Yes, I think I will go to my room. Thank you.'

He turned to leave. 'I'm sorry for what happened, if that's of any comfort to you.'

She gave him a small smile as he left. She had no way of knowing that he did so before he gave in to an overriding desire to take her in his arms and comfort her.

CHAPTER 11

Alex thought about Catherine for most of the day, and when they arrived back at Richmond he looked around for her. However, Grace told him that she had been asleep all day, and as far as she knew was still in her room. Alex wondered whether just to leave things there, but he had made a promise and wanted to keep his word. He went upstairs and knocked on her door. There was no answer, so he opened the door a fraction. The bedside light was on and he could see the figure in the bed. He had to make sure that she was alright. He moved across the room and looked down at her. She was curled up on her side with one arm flung out over the pillow. Her hair was tangled around her face and, as before, he swept it aside. Her skin felt cool to his touch and he tucked the covers closer around her. She looked very young and defenceless lying there, and he cursed under his breath at the rough handling she had received.

In the short time since he had known her, he was now beginning to realise that thoughts of her were always with him, night or day. He couldn't remember when a female had ever made such an impression on him. The growing protective feeling he had for her was strengthened by what had happened to her last night, and the level of shock and anger he had experienced on hearing the news of the assault still confused him. He must remember, however, that there was a job he had to do, and he couldn't allow himself to become diverted from it. Maybe, when this was all over…? Then again, if her uncle was still involved in his enquiries, any further contact with her would be out of the question. Hell, why did it have to happen this way!

His mind still on the problem, he returned to the kitchen. Grace looked at him in enquiry.

'Miss Franklin is still asleep. It might be an idea if you wake her soon, Grace, or she might not sleep tonight, and start thinking about things again.'

'I'll do that, Alex. It's kind of you to be so concerned.'

He could see the question in her eyes as to his level of involvement, but she made no further comment.

*

He wasn't sure if he was doing the right thing. He turned off his normal route home and headed for South Kensington. During his talk with Catherine this morning he had sensed her loneliness and vulnerability. She needed friends, and this was the only way he could think of to help her.

Sarah answered the door. 'Well what a nice surprise,' she beamed. 'Come on in Alex.' She called over her shoulder. 'Jerry, it's Alex.'

'I'm sorry to intrude. I can't stop long anyway.'

'That's OK. Do you want a coffee or anything.'

'No, I'm fine, thanks. Sarah, I think you ought to know Miss Franklin had a bad experience last night.'

Sarah looked at him, anxiety apparent on her face. 'What's wrong, Alex?'

He went on to tell them both what had happened. To his surprise, Sarah put her head in her hands and groaned, 'Oh, not again!'

'What on earth do you mean, "not again", Sarah?

'We were having a chat a year or two ago…' she looked at the two men for a moment, hesitating, and then went on. 'Catherine told me when she was at her school in Switzerland there was an incident which happened to her, and from what you have said, Alex, it sounds very much like the same thing. She must be wondering what on earth men are all about by now, I should imagine. Do you wonder she's so diffident? How can you reach out when you're afraid of the response?'

Jerry spoke then. 'You know, I've always thought of her like a young animal who doesn't know whether to trust you or not, and you have to be patient and coax them. It took me a while to get to know her.'

On hearing this, Alex recognised her attitude this morning, the underlying need for comfort – from him. It appeared that their relationship had undergone a subtle change since the night he had brought her home. She trusted him more, and the depth of his own feeling for her, which he was now forced to admit, frightened him.

He felt torn and anxious. For so long his mind had been fixated on climbing his career ladder and women had been an occasional, if pleasant, diversion. There had been no real emotional attachment to any of them; but since he had known Catherine he had experienced feelings foreign to him and the need to get to know her better was like a sweet ache inside him. Then his mind moved on to how he would feel if they got to know each other well, but having found her confidence, she didn't need him any more. It would be difficult to let her go. These were all thoughts he had not anticipated, and he needed a quiet moment to work them out in his mind.

For now, though, he had to enlist Sarah's help.

'She looked worn out this morning when I saw her. I don't understand the attitude of her uncle either. He doesn't even seem as if he's bothered about her safety.'

'I've never liked the man. I don't like his eyes. I've told Catherine before that she should get away from the house and live somewhere else, even on her own. I'll have to speak to her again.'

'Don't tell her that I've been to see you.'

'Why not, Alex? I think it was a rather nice thing to do.'

'I just thought it might help her if you knew. I'm afraid I have to go now. I'm changing shifts. I'm on nights from tomorrow, so I've things to do. I'll let myself out.'

Catherine knew she had slept too much, and spent most of the next day out in the garden. She wanted the fresh air and exercise. As usual, she felt at peace just pottering around by herself. She was called in to take a telephone call from Sarah during the morning, and although it was never mentioned, Catherine had the distinct impression that she was aware of what had happened. She wondered who had spoken to Sarah and thought it was certain to have been Grace.

She didn't see Alex Hartman at all during the day. She wasn't even sure what shift he was working, but that evening she heard his car arriving. She passed him in the hall as she was going up to bed, and gave him a small smile.

His polite, 'Good evening. Are you alright?' was formal, but his grey eyes were warm and she could feel him watching her as she went up the stairs.

She woke during the night feeling thirsty, and decided on a glass of milk. She knew they had been warned about moving around the house at night, but it would only take a minute.

She put on a full-length pink robe over her long satin nightdress and decided to go in bare feet. She opened her door. All was still. She crept downstairs and into the kitchen. It was empty.

She reached into a cupboard, retrieved a glass and was just moving over to the fridge when she was conscious of a dark figure coming through the outer door. She gasped with fright and the glass fell from her hand, breaking on the kitchen floor.

She was about to take a step when she heard Alex's voice, sharp and urgent. 'Don't move, Catherine'. Before she knew what had happened she was swung up into strong arms and deposited on the kitchen worktop. His hands were round her waist, she could feel them through her gown.

'You little idiot, you could have walked in the glass with your bare feet. Let me have a look at you.'

He moved away and put on one of the lights. Coming back, he brushed away the folds of her skirts and with care inspected both feet.

It was nice to feel his hands on her skin, and she began to feel a slow mounting excitement.

He let go of her and, pulling her clothes back into position, said, 'They look alright to me. Now stay there while I clear this mess up. What on earth are you doing down here anyway? You were warned about wandering around at night.'

'I just needed a drink of milk.' She knew that sounded quite childish, but didn't want him angry with her again, and added, 'I'm sorry. I overreacted, I suppose.'

'You do quite a lot of that, don't you.'

He didn't sound so angry now.

'Do you realise you called me by my name just now.'

'Did I? I wanted to stop you moving, I suppose,' was his casual answer. 'Do you have a problem with that?'

'No. Can I call you Alex?'

'I don't see any reason why not.'

He was rummaging in the cupboard for a dustpan and brush and she started to get off the worktop to show him where it was. 'For God's sake, will you stay put,' he ground out, locating what he needed.

Catherine subsided back on her perch. It was rather nice to be down here alone with him in the warm kitchen. It was an intimate feeling, but she was not afraid in the least.

She gasped as the door into the hall opened and her uncle stood there surveying the scene.

'I thought I heard a noise. What's going on here?'

'Your niece was getting a drink and dropped the glass. As she has bare feet I'm clearing the broken glass out of the way before anyone gets hurt. Otherwise there's no problem.' Showing no embarrassment at the situation, Alex continued his cleaning up and turned away into the scullery with his pan.

Catherine could feel her uncle staring at her.

'I think its time you were back in bed, young lady, and perhaps it would be a good idea to take a drink to bed with you instead of coming down during the night. I am sure *Inspector* Hartman has better things to do than clear up behind you.'

The meaning was clear in his tone.

For a moment she considered making a comment, but then decided it would be better not to.

Alex came back into the kitchen and, ignoring the Judge, looked at Catherine. 'Do you want me to lift you down or can you manage?'

She knew she could manage, but she wanted to feel his hands around her waist again. She moved forward a little and then held out her hand to him. He stepped to her and, as she had hoped, placed his hands on her waist and with no effort, lifted her down and set her on her feet. His hands, however, remained in place for a second or two longer than was perhaps required. She looked up at him as he released her, not altogether forgetting the other person present, but somehow needing to make her independence register.

'Thank you, Alex. Good night.' With a rustle of her soft skirts she disappeared out of the room.

Alex stood looking at Franklin, waiting for a comment, but with nothing more than a cool glare the other man turned on his heel and also left the room.

It was a pity the Judge had appeared, Alex thought. It would have been nice to have Catherine sitting in the quiet kitchen with him. They might have been able to talk for once.

He then realised that she still didn't have her drink. He contemplated taking one up to her but thought better of it; the situation was becoming awkward enough without that sort of gesture.

CHAPTER 12

As Arthur had taken Grace out shopping the next morning, Catherine was preparing breakfast. Her uncle had left a note that he required her to attend at the British Museum library on Monday to do some urgent research for him and also that he had accepted an invitation to a French Embassy reception on Tuesday night and required her to accompany him. He had been cool and distant since their argument, but she felt that she ought to continue to assist him in his social activities as she was, after all, still living under his roof.

Dougie was on duty. She made him a cup of coffee and sat with him in the kitchen. He was pleased to see that she had regained her composure and was looking happier. He felt she wanted to talk to him and he thought he knew about what, or rather, whom.

'Dougie,' she asked, 'have you worked with Alex a lot?'

The use of the Christian name instead of her more usual form of address was not lost on him.

'I think I've told you before that I've worked with him in the past, and known of him through the grapevine before and since then. He's pretty single-minded and focused on his career, which doesn't always lend itself to being well liked by others. However, I have to say, although a little younger than me, I've always got on with him well enough. The impression he gives me is that he has a strong sense of duty and you can be sure he puts in one hundred per cent of himself. Working with him I've found him hard but fair, as young Carl found out, and you always know where you are with him. He's good at his job. He must be to have reached the position he has now. He's come a long way from his original background, and I mean not the silver spoon sort.'

He shot a quick look at the young woman. She wasn't an idiot and knew what he meant.

'As I've said, the trouble with trying to succeed is that you have to be determined to get what you want, almost to the exclusion of anything else. You sometimes don't have the time or the inclination for other aspects of life, like relationships, etcetera. Or they are, at the very least, not given great importance.'

'Grace says he's not married.'

'I know that for a certainty, but I don't know much more. He has a flat in Kennington and he takes great store by that Porsche monstrosity of his!'

She laughed at that, and it was nice to hear. However, Dougie was worried about her questioning. He could pick up vibes as well as the next person and he was aware that this protection job was not the ordinary run of the mill. Alex's abilities wouldn't be wasted by putting him in charge of something this routine, and Alex's own instructions to both him and Carl was enough to flag up the idea that this job was a little out of the ordinary. Dougie surmised that it was something to do with Judge Franklin. Had he been a naughty boy in some way? He couldn't say that he had made a very favourable impression, and he didn't like the way he treated his niece. It seemed ridiculous to think that Catherine herself was being investigated, and he couldn't imagine Alex making use of any relationship with her to try to get information. He had never impressed Dougie as being that sort of person. Nevertheless, it would be as well to warn her in some way.

'Catherine, I'm a good deal older than you, so is Alex, and we have also seen a lot more of the nastier side of life that's out there than you have. I suppose it makes us have a different view of things at times, and this can be misconstrued. We might give an impression that was not quite the truth. We'll be gone out of your lives in a week or so, and things will get back to normal. In a month or two you'll be laughing about it as a bit of an adventure.'

He could see she knew what he was trying to say, but he also knew from the look in those remarkable green eyes that it was far too late.

*

Catherine made sure she kept out of Alex's way that night, although she would much rather have been able to speak to him. She wanted to prove to him that she was grown up enough to put the problems of the other day behind her; but, mindful of Dougie's warning, felt it better to keep a low profile.

She had no way of knowing that Alex himself was endeavouring to bump into her but resisted the temptation to knock on her door. As Sunday was his day off, it was Monday morning before she saw him again.

She was dressed in work mode in a black suit with a white high-necked jumper. Her hair was caught back in a loose ponytail tied with a black velvet ribbon. She had decided to take her large black leather handbag with her, as she would be bringing back papers from her research at the British Museum. She went into her office to run through her uncle's notes again to make sure that she knew what it was he required. The weather was blustery and rain was promised for later, but she felt she couldn't cope with an umbrella and would have to chance it.

She heard Arthur manoeuvre the Rolls out of the garage and went out into the hall. Alex stood there by the front door, looking his usual handsome self in a dark navy suit and tie. As always, she felt a quick surge of excitement when she saw him. He turned towards her when he heard her footsteps, and his eyes swept over her in a quick, appreciative glance. She was aware of a sense of pleasure inside her that he found her attractive. She felt comfortable under his gaze and not threatened in any way, unlike the other men… but she mustn't relive those memories again.

'Good morning, Catherine. You're looking much better.'

'I'm feeling much better, thank you, Alex,' she replied. All very formal, she thought, apart from the Christian names, but she would settle for that.

The drive into town was quite silent. Arthur dropped her off outside the Museum and agreed that they should pick her up at the same place at five-thirty, and she was told to be on time.

*

The promised rain came with a vengeance and brought the wind with it. The normal evening rush hour traffic was even worse on a day like this, and the Rolls was running late. As they pulled into the kerb, Arthur was looking for Catherine.

'I can't see her anywhere, Inspector. Can you?'

There was an exasperated tutting sound from the Judge in the back seat, then with relief Alex spotted her sheltering from the rain in a doorway, camouflaged in her dark suit. At the same time she saw the Rolls and started to move towards them through the wind and rain swirling around the buildings.

As a security precaution, because the Rolls was stationary, Alex kept a sharp look in the side mirror. It was for this reason he became aware of the situation about to occur. He catapulted himself out of the car and ran the few steps towards Catherine's slight figure, lifting her off her feet. One of London's notorious cycle couriers was approaching, head down against the wind on a collision course, and Alex knew who would come off worse in any impact. At the last moment the courier saw the danger and veered away. Alex's strength managed to save them from falling, and once he regained his balance he looked down at Catherine, still held in his arms. Her eyes were wide with shock and he could feel her trembling. His hands were around her waist inside her jacket and he could feel the heat from her body through the thin material of the jumper. With care he set her down on her feet, still retaining his hold.

'Are you alright?'

He realised she had thought that the dire warnings he gave her the other night about being accosted in the street had come true.

'You were about to be mown down by a damn courier cyclist,' he explained. 'You couldn't see each other in this weather.'

Some of the shock was leaving her face, but she wasn't trying to free herself from his grasp.

In a gentle voice he said to her, 'You know we're getting soaking wet!'

Now pink with embarrassment, she began to pull free.

'Have you dropped anything?'

'Er… no, I have my bag and that's all.'

He steered her to the waiting car and helped her into the back seat. He tried to shake off some of the water from his coat and hair before he got into the front. There would be a few wet patches to be mopped up in the car tonight!

Arthur pulled the Rolls away from the kerb and turned to him. 'How on earth did you see that about to happen. I'd looked in the rear view mirror but I didn't spot that idiot.'

'It's my job, I suppose,' Alex said, attempting to dismiss the whole thing. No doubt the Judge would have another moan about him exceeding his allotted duties, but what the hell!

The Judge did moan, but not to Alex. 'I suppose all my papers are now soaking wet.'

'No, they are safe in my bag. That's why I took this with me.' Catherine brushed the wet hair out of her face and rummaged in her bag and brought out a large envelope and handed it to him. After a moment or two perusing the contents, the Judge smiled and murmured 'Excellent! Excellent! Well done, my dear.'

In the front, Alex and Arthur looked at each other with raised eyebrows. That was a first!

Although Arthur put the heater on in the car, because of the weather it was still quite cool by the time they reached Richmond. Without a further word the Judge disappeared into his study.

Alex turned to Catherine in the hallway. 'I'd get upstairs out of those wet things and have a hot bath if I were you, before you catch your death of cold.'

'Yes, I will. You need to as well,' she added.

'I'll wait until I get home, I think,' Alex said with a calculated wicked smile, and watched with interest as the colour appeared again in her cheeks as she realised his meaning.

However, she gathered herself together enough to meet his gaze, and with a slight smile said, 'Thank you for what you did today.' She then turned away up the stairs.

Watching her go, Alex had to put a brake on his wild thoughts.

*

'Well, as I thought, Geoffrey, we seem to be in luck with my research. I now have all the information in front of me and I'll bring it up at the right time. I think it should do the trick enough for the sentence to be reduced. Not by much, but enough to appease Clarke and keep him on our side and in our pocket.'

'Good work, Lionel.' Geoffrey Villiers breathed a sigh of relief. 'I wouldn't want to report to Clarke with any other news. With this letter business, though, won't it seem funny if you throw a spanner in the works?'

Franklin's smile was without warmth. 'Don't worry, Geoffrey, the courts are used to me by now; this won't seem very much out of the ordinary. Remind Clarke not to tell Atkinson anything yet. We don't want him appearing smug during the rest of the case. Make sure you get Clarke's agreed payment to us.'

'I might contact him tonight, Lionel. Get it over with. By the way, I heard from Gregory that young Duncan got in a mess the other night.'

Franklin sat back in his chair and drummed his fingers on his desk.

'Typical of the young idiot to try something in the wrong place. Hartman became quite out of order about it. Time he was put in his place. When I meet up with you and Gregory at the reception tomorrow night, I'll explain in more detail.'

CHAPTER 13

The night of the Embassy reception was dry but there was a cool wind. Catherine took her time about getting ready. It seemed important tonight for everything to be just right. Grace had offered to help but Catherine wanted to be quiet, on her own. She didn't wear much makeup but tonight she emphasised her green eyes, which made them appear softer. She put a creamy pearl colour on her nails and used a matching lipstick.

Her dress was on a hanger on the wardrobe door. A slim column of pale coffee-coloured silk covered with chiffon drapes in the same colour, edged in satin. The thin straps to the low, square-cut bodice were almost invisible and she was glad the chiffon would cover her. She had never felt confident or at ease with clothes that displayed her figure. A soft cream shawl was lying over her bedside chair.

Her glossy dark brown hair was soon piled up into what she hoped appeared to be an artless creation of curls: her attempt at a more sophisticated look. Looking at her reflection she noticed that it made her neck seem long and slim, and quite liked the result.

Time was now getting on, and she must finish dressing. After a little struggle when she thought she would have to call Grace, she managed to get into her gown. It curved around her slim shape, and the chiffon billowed as she moved, softening the outline.

She heard the sound of the Porsche arriving and felt the sudden quickening of her pulse. What would *he* make of her tonight, she wondered? And admitted to herself that this was the reason for her extra care.

She sat down at her dressing table to put on her silver sandals. She had just put on the small diamante earrings and was applying another coat of lipstick when she heard her uncle calling to her. For a moment she sat still, almost frozen with nerves, then hearing her name called again she scooped up her small silver bag and hurried out of the room before she could change her mind.

*

For someone who was about to experience a pleasant social evening, the Judge seemed to be in a bad mood. Alex arrived to relieve Dougie and found Arthur in a state of exasperation with his employer over certain supposed sartorial shortcomings, which didn't amount to very much at all, it appeared. Alex tried to sooth his ruffled feathers, as he would be driving the Rolls soon in heavy traffic, which he himself had just encountered. He had wasted time by going back into his flat for his dark overcoat once he had experienced the chill of the evening. He suggested Arthur should start up the Rolls and get the heater working.

He was standing in the hall near the front door when the Judge came out of his study in evening dress, looking at his watch.

'Where is the girl? Its time we went!' He moved to the bottom of the stairs and called her name. He paced up and down for a moment, and when there was no response he called out again, 'Catherine, I'm leaving right now!' and stormed off out to the car.

Alex heard a door bang upstairs and turned to see Catherine hurrying down the staircase. He felt as if the wind had been knocked out of him. From the top of her piled curls, through the slim column of her figure surrounded by billowing folds of chiffon, to the small silver feet he saw beneath the hem of her dress, she looked unbelievable – pure loveliness.

She moved past him without a look, although he was sure she

was aware of him. He caught the familiar fragrance of her perfume. Following her outside he held the car door open and saw her seated inside. As he was taking his seat and the Rolls moved off, he wondered why she didn't have some sort of coat. She would be cold on a night like this. It was fortunate that at least the Rolls was warm.

He noticed that the Judge made no mention of his niece's appearance, which was, at the very least, impolite. It was obvious she had taken some trouble to achieve the sophistication she thought right for the occasion. As he knew himself, to arrive at a function with a beautiful woman was always an asset for any man.

The Embassy was a blaze of light when they arrived. Again the Judge annoyed Alex by marching out of the car and heading up the steps, not waiting for Catherine. Alex assisted her out of the car himself, and followed her into the foyer. She turned to him with a small smile of thanks just as what he took to be a junior French diplomat arrived to usher them into the reception. Alex watched the slim figure retreat and regretted the fact that he himself would not be spending the evening in her company.

He went to find the head of the security detail for the Embassy and spent some minutes going over their arrangements. It was then a waiting game. He loitered around the foyer and then went outside to find where Arthur had parked the Rolls and to offer him a break.

On going back to the foyer once Arthur had returned, Alex was surprised to see the Judge coming towards him.

'Inspector, there has been a slight change of plan for the rest of the evening,' began the Judge. 'I will be going with two associates from here back to the Club, and I would like you to take my niece back to Richmond.'

'I should be accompanying you to the Club, Judge,' Alex replied, annoyed at this sudden alteration to the arrangements.

'Well, I'm sure there will be no trouble, as the decision has just this minute been made. Catherine has to get home somehow, and as you seem to have a particular aversion to seeing her travel alone at this time of night...', he smiled. 'Yes, I am aware you collected her the other evening when the Rolls was out of order. I thought you would be the first to assist as an escort.'

Alex wanted to make some retort, but took in the raised eyebrow of amused sarcasm and held his tongue.

'I'll see what I can do about providing you with some sort of cover. What time will you be leaving?'

'Oh, about an hour, I should say.' With that the Judge turned on his heel and walked away.

Alex was seething. What the hell was he going to do? He knew that Carl had a day off and was in Norfolk somewhere. He could try Dougie and see if he was prepared to turn out again; or he could, as the Judge indicated, just leave him on his own. This, however, was the very occasion when something was bound to happen. He asked for the use of a telephone and rang Dougie, who, after he'd explained the situation, agreed to take over the duty again. He told Alex he would get a taxi to the Embassy and charge it on expenses.

When he arrived they discussed between them the best course of action. It was agreed that Dougie, more at his insistence because, as he commented with a laugh, he had gone to the effort of getting dressed up again, should go with the Judge, and Alex would indeed take Catherine home. When Dougie arrived back at Richmond with the Judge he could go home again and Alex would stay until Carl relieved him in the morning. The Porsche was at the house anyway, and Dougie seemed quite happy with the arrangement. He could have another taxi ride home! Alex asked him to brief Arthur about the changes.

In a short while the Judge appeared with two other men. They all seemed very jovial together. It looked as if the hospitality had been exceptional, thought Alex.

As they were getting into their coats the Judge looked at him. 'All sorted out are we?'

'Yes, Judge. Sergeant Johnson will accompany you to the Club and back to Richmond. I will, as you have requested, take Miss Franklin home.'

'Excellent, Inspector.'

To his amazement, an out-of-character broad smile was bestowed on him. The hospitality must indeed have been splendid, thought Alex once again; but then, it was the French Embassy. He'd made do with a snatched cup of coffee.

As the Judge and his party departed, it seemed that everyone was heading home. He wondered if Catherine had been told of the change of arrangements and what she thought. After a few moments he saw her coming down the main staircase on the arm of a distinguished grey-haired man. With a sick feeling in his stomach he acknowledged how appropriate she looked in this kind of setting. Her beauty and natural poise were made for this grand living, and all her education had been geared to it. He experienced an empty coldness building up inside him, like the sun going behind a cloud. He realised that he had to face it: she was not meant for the likes of him, however much, he now admitted to himself, he wanted it otherwise.

Nowadays she never left his thoughts, and he longed for more of her company. The truth was now obvious to him. As his mind registered the fact, the pleasure of that knowledge was bittersweet. He could never have her. He must stop thinking along those lines, now, before it was too late. He had to attempt to carry on as before and concentrate on his duty, however hard he now knew it would be.

She came towards him, still on this man's arm, whoever he was. Despite all his efforts, Alex felt an almost physical wave of envy against the man for having had the pleasure of this beautiful young woman's company all evening.

As if echoing his thoughts, the man spoke to him in accented English. 'It is with great regret that I hand this charming lady over to you. I too would be glad to escort her home.' He kissed one of Catherine's small hands and placed it on Alex's arm, and then retreated back up the staircase. Startled, Alex looked down at the hand on his arm and then looked up at her face. She seemed quite calm, but her eyes were very bright.

With an effort, trying to regain his composure, he managed to stammer, 'I... I'm to take you home. Are you ready?'

Catherine just nodded, and they walked to the main door. There were plenty of taxis milling about and a member of the Embassy staff hailed one for them. Alex felt her shivering in the cool air.

'You needed a coat, Catherine.'

'I know, but I left my shawl behind. I was in a hurry when we left.'

Alex took off his overcoat and put it round her slim shoulders as their taxi pulled in.

'Who was the attentive gentleman?'

'The French Ambassador.'

It was stated in such a matter-of-fact way that he wanted to laugh. Any other young woman who had just hit it off with an important French diplomat at a prestigious social event would have been falling over herself with excitement and self-congratulation. The whole thing seemed to have left Catherine unmoved. Perhaps another example of her upbringing, was his sudden unhappy thought. For one stupid moment he considered suggesting that instead of going back to Richmond they could go on somewhere – it wasn't that late yet. But he found he didn't quite have the courage to face her predictable refusal, and in view of his earlier discovery it was maybe just as well. He did, however, want to regain that sense of friendliness that had begun to build between them over the last few days.

'Did you enjoy the evening?' He was desperate in his search for something to say to her. She was just sitting there, silent, staring out of the taxi window, looking small, enveloped in his coat.

'It was a bit of pressure having to speak French most of the time, out of courtesy. Unless you use something like that every day you can soon get rusty.'

'I'm sure you can. I've never had a go at languages. English can be a trial at times!'

She did turn her head and smile at this remark. He wanted to hold that smile but could think of nothing more to say. Sitting in the enclosed confines of the taxi, smelling her perfume and looking at her sweet face, he knew that talking to her was the last thing he wanted to do. All her worst fears would be realised if she could read his mind, he thought.

They arrived at Richmond far too soon for him. He paid off the taxi and led her inside, closing the door behind them before the alarm could go off. The hall was lit by one small lamp on a table at the foot of the stairs and it created a warm, intimate glow. He watched her as she moved away and placed his coat on a leather chair near the stairs. With one small foot on the bottom tread she turned back to him, her dress billowing about her slim form. 'Thank you for the loan of your coat, and thank you for bringing me home Alex.' She then turned to go.

He crossed to her side. It was important for someone tonight besides her gallant French escort, to tell her how beautiful she looked, and he wanted it to be him.

'Catherine?'

She turned back and registered surprise at seeing him standing next to her at the bottom of the stairs. He looked at her, from the shining curls, the creamy skin and soft green eyes, to the slender curves of her body under the wafting folds. He brought his gaze back up to her face. Her eyes now seemed like dark green velvet and her mouth with its covering of gloss glowed wet in the dim light. His hand reached up to smooth away a tendril of hair which had curved onto her cheek, and he felt her tremble at his touch. He tried to calm his rioting senses and, in a deliberate move, lowered his hand to the banister between them.

'You look so beautiful tonight, Catherine.'

Then, ignoring a subconscious warning to remain detached, he lowered his head and brushed her lips with his. The merest butterfly touch, but it started a fire within him. Hearing her murmur his name brought him back to his senses. He drew back from her.

'Get up to bed, Catherine. Now!'

His voice sounded sharp and loud in the silent house. He reached for his coat on the chair, uttering an oath. He thought he heard her gasp and, with a soft rustle of skirts, she ran up the stairs.

Damnation, he was in an impossible situation, feeling the way he did about her but knowing she was out of his reach. He reminded himself that he had a duty to concentrate his full attention on his professional duties; but it was beyond him tonight. Swearing with uncontrolled violence he left the house, threw himself into his car and drove away at speed. To hell with waiting until Dougie arrived, or any of them for that matter, he needed to get away fast because if he stayed in that house tonight he might do something he would regret.

Who was he kidding? He knew he wouldn't regret it at all.

CHAPTER 14

Grace sat at the kitchen table, her hands toying with the pile of placemats in front of her and every few moments she looked up at the kitchen clock as the minutes crawled by. Where was everyone, and what should she do when they returned? Then, as her anxiety grew, she heard the Rolls in the drive. She rose and started to prepare a supper tray in case any refreshments were needed. It startled her when the Judge burst into the kitchen.

'Where are my niece and Hartman? His car is not here.'

Grace made a decision. She replied in quiet tones, trying to appear calm.

'Catherine is asleep in bed. I have just helped her to undress and given her a nightcap and Inspector Hartman left the premises as soon as he arrived with Catherine.'

'Left? He was supposed to be here.'

'I couldn't say, Judge. I didn't speak to him.'

The Judge swore and stormed upstairs. Grace watched him go and prayed he wouldn't try to wake Catherine, but he went straight into his room.

She hoped she'd done the right thing! A couple of hours earlier she had heard what sounded like a car returning, and moments later the Porsche leaving, but it was the sound of someone in distress which made her leave her room to investigate. She found Catherine lying on her bed, sobbing and almost beside herself. After a while she managed to quieten the girl, but dare not upset her again by trying to find out what had happened. Grace never thought for a moment that Alex would mistreat her in any way, but something had occurred. With Alex gone, she knew there was no cover at the house; but no one else appeared to be home, so the Judge was still out. There must have been a change of plan. What should she do when the Judge did return? Should she mention anything about Catherine?

She had helped the still distraught girl out of her clothes and into bed, and then took her up a drink together with one of her own sleeping tablets. Risky, but in this case she thought, necessary, and after all they weren't that strong.

With relief she saw Arthur come into the kitchen. She would tell him what had happened. To her amazement, Dougie was with him, and both were looking puzzled.

'Has Alex gone, Grace?' asked Dougie.

'Yes, he has.' She was reluctant to say any more, even to him, just yet.

Dougie shrugged his shoulders and then sighed 'Oh well, it looks as if I'm here until the morning. Have you any strong coffee going?'

*

Catherine had woken to a grey dawn, and the thoughts of the night before swamped her again. She recalled how, when she reached her room, she stood in the middle of the floor not knowing what to do next. How had it gone so wrong? He had kissed her, so soft and sweet. If she could have somehow shown that she wanted him to continue, his kisses would have been everything she had ever needed. She had tried to tell him, but then he had been angry with her. How else could she have shown him? She would much rather have been out with him alone all evening than being fawned over by some Frenchman. Was there something wrong with her attitude, for men to behave this way with her? If so, she didn't know what it was. The tears started to come again, and she turned her head into the pillow and allowed them to fall once more.

*

Dougie, having received official notification that Inspector Hartman had been moved to other duties, was instructed to continue the Richmond detail under his own control. The case had now concluded and, although it made the papers for a day or two, after it quietened down, Franklin declared that he felt he no longer needed his protection, and requested it be ended.

On Dougie's last day, Catherine asked for a word with him and they sat together again in the kitchen. He had studied her over the last few days and thought that she looked almost ill. There was no longer any glow to her. He was sure something had happened between her and Alex the night of the reception. Although Grace told him Catherine had remained silent about the events of that night, something had distressed her. He was almost sure he knew what it might be: Alex had told her that there was no future between the two of them, and she hadn't taken it well.

Then another thought occurred to him. Grace had indicated that when the Judge arrived back he demanded to know the whereabouts of his niece and Alex, in such a way that it made her suspicious, even more so when he seemed angry to find the situation normal. Dougie gave the matter a fair amount of consideration. After making a lot of fuss about going on with friends to the Club, the Judge had, in fact, asked to be driven home less than an hour later. Catherine could have remained in the car with Arthur for this short time and saved everyone a lot of bother. It began to occur to him that it had been the Judge's deliberate intention to set up a scenario that night whereby Catherine and Alex would be alone at the house, and then be found in a compromising situation. Alex had either foreseen this happening, or he himself didn't want it to happen, which was why he left in a hurry. It was, after all, pretty obvious to everyone in the household that there was some sort of attraction between the two of them. He felt sorry at the outcome,

96

but that was always the trouble, working in close proximity with members of the public.

He looked again at Catherine. She didn't want to talk about Alex, he was pretty sure, but something was bothering her.

'How can I help you, my dear?' He tried to be as gentle with her as he could. She seemed so fragile.

'Dougie, you know the trial and how it ended, the historical law information brought up at the end? That was research which my uncle had asked me to do for him. He told me what to look for, and in the end I found it. If I hadn't, the outcome would have been a little different, wouldn't it?'

Dougie glanced at her again. 'It's possible.'

'Have I changed the course of justice by digging it out?'

He took a deep breath. 'Written law information is there for anyone to find. It depends how hard you want to look for it, I suppose. You haven't done anything wrong, you know, my dear, if that's what's worrying you. You were asked to do something and you did it.'

'It's not the first time it's happened, Dougie. Maybe not in such a public way, but I believe things I have been asked to research before have made a difference. I've seen correspondence from barristers. Why does my uncle want to bother so?'

'I couldn't say, my dear. I shouldn't let it worry you any more.'

She smiled her thanks at him, opened her mouth to say something else, then thought better of it and left him alone in the kitchen.

Dougie began thinking. As he had suspected, was that what all this was about? Was the Judge being investigated for possible abuse of his position? Did Alex know the truth? Well, it was all over now, and none of his business any more from tonight.

CHAPTER 15

Lionel Franklin stretched to ease his stiff shoulders. It had been a long day in Court. As he shrugged out of his robes his thoughts turned yet again to the recent weapons case. During his summing up he had brought in the information sourced for him, and the jury had returned the verdict he had sought and anticipated. Guilty, but with a recommendation for a reduced sentence due to mitigating circumstances.

At the sentencing hearing he had handed down the requisite term, but with a small reduction. There had been the usual murmurings on the benches, some positive by Defence Counsel, the other side less so. He had quite expected to be paid a personal visit for feelings to be aired. It wouldn't be unusual – but so far he had received no such approach. Today though, for the first time since that trial, he knew both he and Raven were in the building.

There was a knock on the door, and one of the Court messengers entered.

'Mr Raven is asking to see you, Judge.'

Franklin smiled to himself. Right on cue!

'Ask him to come in.'

Anthony Raven was a tall, imposing man, and used it to effect in commanding attention in Court. He was still dressed in his robes, which accentuated the impression, but Franklin had long ago ceased to be influenced by these theatrical figures with their inflated egos. Having said that, Raven was smart and Franklin had already born the brunt of one or two skirmishes with him. He was no fool.

'I wondered if I might have the pleasure of your presence, Raven.'

'Then I needn't waste my time explaining the reason for my visit. I think you know my views on the timing and dubious relevance of the information you supplied to the jury. If it hadn't been brought to their attention, I wonder if they would have agreed to the recommendation you suggested.'

He came further into the room, and Franklin had to recognise the force of his presence.

'As I made clear, Judge, my clients were engaged on an important investigation observing who was involved in illegal arms trading. Vital information for counter-terrorism purposes. As admitted in evidence, Atkinson was known to my clients as having made a purchase, being observed by an undercover officer during the negotiations. In his client's defence, Mr Metcalfe suggested the police might have warned Atkinson of their knowledge and offered him a chance to assist them, rather than apprehend him by later posing as potential buyers. This point was then accentuated by your comments regarding similar situations that had occurred in the past. In my view, this swayed the attitude of the jury as to Atkinson's position and the supposed activities of the police.'

'Everyone was well aware of all the facts, Raven. My outlining of scenarios in other similar cases was to assist in clarifying the views of the jury.'

'Circumstances which didn't fit the immediate facts, and none of which were relevant to the severity of the weapons on offer here. Plus, if I may say so, brought up at such a late stage in the case that little proper consideration could be given to their merits in apportioning any blame.'

Franklin settled a cool gaze on the other man. 'Weapons are weapons, Raven. I might make the comment that I felt neither you nor Mr Metcalfe covered yourselves in glory as to the representation of your respective clients in this whole matter, in the end relying on my intervention.'

Raven stared at him in astounded silence for a moment, appearing to control himself with some effort.

'Judge Franklin, I, and indeed others, are at times unhappy with the way you conduct your Court.'

'Mr Raven, might I remind you that I run my Court as I see fit, and I will make that apparent to any barrister who comes before me. In the end you obtained your guilty verdict, and should be satisfied. However, if you, or any other person has any complaint then they should take the matter up through the correct channels. Now, if that is all? If you don't mind…'

He turned his back and sat down at his desk. A moment later he heard the door slam. He was well aware of the attitude many had towards him. To hell with what they all thought, he was still a Judge, and still in control!

*

As Dougie was leaving headquarters one evening he bumped into Alex; although on reflection he suspected that the other man had contrived the meeting. There had been no contact between them since the night of the Embassy reception. He rather doubted the story of Alex being moved to other duties. There were rumours flying around of an almighty row with his superiors; understandable, when he had walked off the job.

'Hello Dougie. Are you in a hurry, or do you fancy a drink?'

Dougie studied Alex. He looked pretty strained and tired, he thought, not full of his usual energy.

'Yes, sure. Why not.'

They didn't speak again until they were settled at a secluded corner table in the nearest public house. Dougie had asked for a beer but he noticed that Alex chose a whisky.

Alex cleared his throat. 'I just want to get something out of the way first, Dougie. I'm sorry if I dropped you in it that night. Circumstances… changed.'

'Didn't make much difference to me, apart from lack of sleep. It all wound up after a few more days anyway.' He sensed this wasn't the reason for Alex waylaying him and so he just drank his beer and waited.

'Dougie, I've been asked to take on a special duty. I need someone to work with me, and I thought about you. What I'm going to tell you is confidential, in a big way. I'm not supposed to mention it to anyone, but I can't expect you to get involved without knowing what you're doing. I won't insult you by asking for your word of honour not to breathe a word, but you get the idea.'

Dougie looked at Alex, his gaze steady. He knew this man played fair and here was a good example. Good detective work was a team game, so Alex was breaking the rules to allow Dougie to see the full picture.

'Fire away, Boss. I'm on board so far.'

In a quiet voice, Alex began to outline to him the content of all the discussions so far between Sir John and Mr Francis. As he listened, Dougie thought about it, and came to the same conclusion as Alex: that the wrong people in certain positions could cause trouble. Alex told Dougie as much as he knew about Richmond, but confirmed that he was still unaware of just what was wrong there.

'Catherine thinks something's wrong, Alex.'

Dougie watched the other man turn a little pale and down the rest of his drink. He's got it bad by the look of him, he thought. Poor sod.

'What do you mean?'

Alex waved to the barman for a repeat order. Dougie didn't want another, but said nothing.

'She had a word with me on the last day I was there. She's worried that by doing research on these obscure cases she's somehow perverting the course of justice. I told her not to worry about it.'

'Damn the man for getting her involved,' Alex ground out, and took a long swallow of his replenished drink.

Dougie felt he had to say something. 'You need to go easy on that stuff, Boss. It doesn't cure a thing, I've found.'

'I've found the same thing.' Alex pushed his now empty glass aside with a tired sigh. 'Do you fancy coming in on this, Dougie? I'd like to have you with me.'

Dougie thought about what had happened at Richmond, and knew he wanted the chance of, just maybe, exposing the truth about certain upholders of the law.

'Count me in, Boss. How do we play this?'

'Now I can give Sir John the green light, he'll set things in motion by getting us transferred to Anti Terror and giving us a cover story, I understand, of setting up a small-scale enquiry into policing organised gang crime and terrorism. We might also be given other normal duties from time to time. We'll have to do a lot of the paperwork ourselves to keep it confidential. What are you involved with at the moment?'

'Relief on a long-term stake out. My part should finish in a week.'

'OK. I'll get it sorted out, if you're sure?'

'I'm fine with it. Glad to be aboard.'

*

Alex was heading for his car, trying to stamp out memories that his discussion with Dougie had evoked, when he felt a tug on his arm. Turning, he was surprised to see Lucille Prentice standing beside him. She was a prostitute he'd met a year or two earlier when, still with CID, he'd worked on a joint operation with the Vice Squad to crack down on the use of under age girls in Soho. She seemed, on the face of it, a decent girl, drawn into her career as a consequence of drug problems; but he suspected the start of those problems lay with others. He hadn't seen her for over a year.

'Hello, Lucille. Are you well?'

She smiled and nodded, but he noticed she was giving nervous glances up and down the street and seemed on edge.

'I've been hanging around, hoping to see you. Is there somewhere we can go for a chat?'

Intrigued, he motioned to the pub he had just left. 'Will this do?'

He saw her seated in the corner he had just vacated with Dougie, and bought her a drink.

He watched her twist the glass round and round, and then she glanced up at him, her blue eyes serious.

'Can you sit nearer and pretend that we're... getting... you know...?'

Alex slid nearer to her on the bench seat and laid his arm along the back.

'What's the trouble, Lucille?'

'You may know I'm a bit of a favourite with Johnny Clarke at the moment? I'm often at his house. He's taken a bit of a shine to me. He pays well, but the more I know about him the more frightened I'm getting, because I know what he's capable of. I'd like to get clear of him, but I'm not sure how I can. The other night he had a visitor, late on. I needed the bathroom and was crossing the landing and heard them talking. It wasn't intentional. They looked up and saw me and afterwards Johnny warned me in no uncertain terms to keep my mouth shut about anything I might have seen or heard. I didn't want to get into his bad books. He's still pretty worked up about this court case and I've heard him talking to some of his cronies about losing face and maybe having some fun 'stuffing Ellison', whatever that means.'

She took a gulp of her drink. 'Anyway, that night he was rough with me, more so than normal, and I've had enough. I want to tell someone what I saw and heard, and I thought of you.'

'What did you hear?'

'Johnny and this visitor were talking together, sounding quite upbeat and cocky. The visitor said something like "Money well spent, eh?" and then they both started laughing. I saw Johnny hand him a small package and he said, "Well worth it, for his sake." That's when they looked up and saw me. When Johnny asked me about it later I told him I didn't hear anything. I don't think he believed me.'

'What did this other man look like?'

'Oh, what I'd call the successful businessman. Fifty-ish, suit and tie, dark overcoat. Well-spoken, like a professional man, a banker or lawyer. Look, I know I'm taking a bit of a risk, but I'm not letting this one go. It may be nothing, but at least I've done something. He's a bastard!'

In an unconscious gesture she rubbed her arm, and Alex saw the faint outline of bruises around her wrist.

'You need to make a formal complaint, Lucille. You can't let him get away with this sort of thing.'

She looked at him with a sad smile. 'I told you – he pays well.'

Alex shook his head. 'OK, it's up to you. I appreciate you telling me about this. I can't promise, but I'll see if I can make any use of it. I'll give you something for your trouble, but for God's sake be careful. Don't show you've come into some money. I'm serious. Drink up, we'd better leave now.'

For the sake of cover, he kissed her cheek as they both got up to leave. After walking a little way down the street, Alex put his arms round her and kissed her again, and at the same time put some notes in her coat pocket. As he watched her walk off he knew, with regret, what the money would be used for. Such a shame. She was a pretty girl. She ought to treat herself to something nice.

*

Harry Fowler watched the Prentice girl leave with the man. Clarke was right to be suspicious. He followed them out into the street and saw the 'tender goodbye'. His practiced eye also saw something else: a pay off for information obtained? He watched the man walk away. Thirties, good-looking, smart dresser. He didn't have to follow him. He knew what he was, and he needed to keep an eye on the girl. He set off after her.

As he walked he smiled and gave himself a mental pat on the back. He knew he was right about the man. He never failed to spot the law. He had a sixth sense as far as they were concerned, a sense which had kept him under their radar all these years, and clean as a whistle. As far as anyone knew, he worked in a betting shop, one of many owned by Johnny Clarke. The other 'work' he did for Clarke was something different altogether. His irregular absences both from work and home were never queried – and they paid well! He wasn't stupid enough to flash the money about, and he had a nice little nest egg tucked away. Something else his wife didn't know about.

He knew he was good at his extra job. Not for the first time, he pondered on how other people might have a hobby like sport, art, music or good wine... but he enjoyed his own special hobby and derived enormous satisfaction from honing and crafting it to perfection. It was fortunate that people that Clarke always had trade for him; they were often too careless in their dealings and needed him to get them out of trouble. Then, take Jack Ellison. He was a different breed. He had the brains to keep himself, and those working for him, under control, and Fowler admired that. Pity, though: it meant Ellison never had work for him.

He watched Lucille Prentice cross the road. She was heading back to her flat, by the look of it. Then she stopped in front of a classy shop selling shoes and bags, hesitated for a moment and walked in. Through the window he observed her purchase a pair of shoes and hand over cash taken from her coat pocket. Dear, dear, silly girl! Clarke was going to be annoyed when he heard; still, it served him right. He should have learnt to keep his whores well away from his business.

He looked around for a phone box, and was soon breaking the bad news to Clarke. By the end of the call he had received his instructions, to be undertaken at his discretion.

CHAPTER 16

Things moved on at a fast pace after Alex informed Francis that he was ready to proceed. Within days Sir John Fraser informed Alex's Superintendent that he would be required for other duties, and outlined his requirements.

When Alex was contacted about the matter, it was embarrassing for him to pretend that this was all unknown to him when, in fact, he knew more about it than his superior did. The interview was made worse because Alex still remembered the lecture he'd endured on being forced to report his actions at Richmond. He'd been called all sorts of a fool for jeopardising his career by walking off a detail. Somehow he'd managed to avoid explaining the real reason. The two things that saved him were: one, the fact that Dougie was in actual attendance on the Judge anyway; and two, his superior's annoyance that he'd been detailed to be involved with the job in the first place. He was now less than pleased to find he was to be removed yet again, and also that Alex had requested Dougie Johnson to assist him. The knowledge that he could have them back if needed went some way to mollifying him and so, with a good deal of reluctance, the transfer was agreed. However, the matter still left Superintendent Charles annoyed that two of what he considered to be his best men were being taken out of circulation on what he viewed to be something of a whim by the outgoing Commissioner; but he was in no position to say so.

A room was put at Alex's disposal, and when Dougie was free the two of them set to work trying to sort out a plan of campaign. They decided the best thing to do was work from normal police procedures relating to a known situation: try to identify the actual crime committed, its motive and how it was executed. With this starting point they might then be lucky enough to spot a possible pattern.

*

Lucille Prentice walked into the entrance hall of her block of flats. She had pressed the call button for the lift when she sensed someone behind her. She turned to see a dark-haired man in his late twenties regarding her. She wasn't on duty that night, so she had no intention of doing any business. The man smiled, but she noticed the smile didn't reach his dark eyes.

'Good evening, Miss Prentice. I have a message to deliver from Johnny Clarke.'

*

Dougie glanced over at his companion. He was becoming concerned about Alex and his state of health. He appeared none too well, almost gaunt, and it was pretty obvious to Dougie that he was drinking far too much. It didn't appear to affect him workwise; in fact he was already in the office when Dougie arrived each day and was the last to leave at night. He wondered whether to say something to him, but didn't want to run the risk of provoking that latent temper. Perhaps he would just bide his time. He had a good idea what was causing the problem, and had no solution. They were both grown up people and could make contact with each other somehow if they wished to, couldn't they? It was a great pity. Nevertheless, work had to come before anything else.

'Seems as if the word's out that there are rumblings in the underworld, Boss. Clarke and Ellison. I bet Jack Ellison is watching. He wouldn't like it if Clarke started to gain on him. How about this

107

for a thought: with the change here in top brass coming up, it would be a good time to start a turf war and keep the Force off balance and tied up trying to contain it. Even more so, if what you said a while ago about influencing police appointments is true.'

'Good point, Dougie. I think I'll ask around and see what information there is on the street. If Johnny Clarke's involved, there might be something worth knowing.'

Dougie watched as Alex played with a small business card, then appeared to make a decision.

'You remember that we're working on the premise that people are put in place to cause disruption of some kind, or someone is manoeuvred into a particular specific role.'

'That's what we're leaning towards at the moment, Boss. It would be a help if we had a bit more explicit information to go on. I've been trawling the papers for anything that leaps out at me, but let's face it, most of the news is bad at the moment. I've been putting some feelers out in the unions which could prove interesting, if we get the right answers.'

'Good idea. Umm… Dougie, there's something I'd like to run by you. I know of a firm that's in trouble because their regular suppliers have had problems, and its causing a bit of suspicion. Am I just clutching at straws in a desperate attempt to start finding something, or is it worth a look?'

'It wouldn't hurt to take a closer look. I'd go for it if I were you. Who are they?'

The phone rang and Alex picked up the receiver. Watching him listen to the person on the other end, Dougie saw him close his eyes for a moment and give a deep sigh.

*

He was getting unfit, Alex thought. He was already working up a sweat and he'd been on the weights for less than ten minutes. Perhaps he ought to make an effort and come to the gym more often than he did. Running was alright in its way, but it wasn't the same as a real workout.

The owner of the small gym in Lewisham was known to him since schooldays. They had both been caught up in the same dubious associations, and when Alex was put in the Army, Joe Fenton went into professional boxing as a middleweight, doing well enough over a number of years in a minor way to get him started in his current premises. The undesirable element knew better than to approach him for protection money. They valued their health!

Although not a regular contributor of information, Joe was aware, with some amusement, of Alex's profession and had on occasion mentioned the odd useful titbit to him.

'You're out of condition, Alex. About time you put in some more work.'

Alex took a breather. He needed it, Joe had set his work rate up a bit high today, he thought. 'I was just thinking the same thing.'

'The room's clear if you want to do some horse exercises.'

This sounded interesting, thought Alex. 'Yes, that's fine by me.'

The upstairs room was used for boxing training, but when the ring was removed there was a clear area which could be covered with soft matting. They moved the pommel horse into position and Joe, no mean gymnast himself, worked Alex through some routines. It was good to be back doing this sort of work, Alex thought. This discipline had always been his first love.

When Joe called a halt after about fifteen minutes, he grinned at Alex's exhausted grimace. 'It's still there, but it could be better if you trained more.'

He then went across to the door and looked out into the corridor. Locking the door, he came back to where Alex was just about getting his breath.

'Ellison and Clarke are getting ready to spar a bit. One of Clarke's men was in here the other day, bragging about a job coming up that Ellison would not like one bit. I told him to clear off and keep away from my premises.'

'What do you think, Joe?' Alex wiped away the sweat running down his face.

'Well, they hate each other's guts, and they both want to be top dog, so there's got to be a winner and a loser. Perhaps it's the old smoke screen trick: doing a job and blaming someone else. Given the choice, I'd prefer Clarke not to get the upper hand. He's a maniac, pure and simple. Nothing's beyond him. Ellison at least has a brain.'

'I think I tend to agree with you, Joe. Can you get a quiet word out to Ellison?'

Joe looked at Alex for a long moment. 'I would imagine he's already aware of something, but I'll see if there's anything I can do. Are we wavering in our resolve, Alex? Is the other side looking greener? I must admit I'd be disappointed in you if it was.'

Alex grinned at him. 'Don't worry, I'm still on the side of the good guys. Thanks for your help, Joe, but watch yourself. I don't want to get you too involved. I'm just thinking that it would be nice if we didn't have World War Three breaking out any day soon.' He stretched to ease his aching muscles. 'I'd better get back downstairs for a shower before people start clogging them up.'

As he showered and dressed he wondered if he would be able to get through the rest of his day without falling asleep!

On arriving home Alex knew there was no way he could face another night in with his own company and thoughts, but he also knew he'd better stay off the drink. He had noticed Dougie watching him, and was sure he would soon say something. What he needed was the respite of the normal, cosy world out at Sunbury for a few hours.

*

The logs blazing in the fireplace filled the comfortable lounge with their pungent outdoor smell. Alex felt as if, at last, he was beginning to relax. They had just finished a delicious meal. Maria was clearing up in the kitchen and he and Luigi were on their second cup of coffee. They were both silent for a while, gazing into the fire, but then Luigi spoke.

'What's wrong, boy? And don't try to deny it, either; I know you too well.'

Alex realised he would have to say something, and admitted to himself that perhaps, in his subconscious, he had wanted to come here tonight to try to get his thoughts straight.

'Things have been a bit difficult of late, Luigi. I've had some hard thinking to do, and I'm nowhere near finding any answers. Now, on top of that, someone I used to know has... died... in less than pleasant circumstances.'

'That is indeed a shame. I can always listen, Alex, even if I can't give you any answers.'

Alex leant forward in his chair and put his elbows on his knees, looking down at the carpet. 'I'm wondering if I've had my priorities all wrong, Luigi. I don't want to rake over the past, but because of what happened, as you know, I've tried to push on and make something of myself. I thought I still did, and to some extent I do, but with recent events I've begun to wonder if other things are more, or just as, important.'

'Such as?'

Alex cleared his throat. He was finding it very difficult to voice his innermost thoughts. They were still new to him, and by saying them out loud he was afraid it would make them real before he was ready to acknowledge them.

'The possibility of a home and a family.'

Luigi leant over and patted the younger man's knee. 'You don't know how relieved I am to hear you say words like that! Mama and I have been hoping that one day your thoughts would turn to these kinds of things. A career is commendable, and you have worked harder than most, but it isn't everything. We know why you have tried so hard to compensate for your earlier years but—'

'Damned right I have. I've told you before, Luigi, no one's going to leave me in a mess again.'

Luigi ignored the interruption. 'Alex, we've been through this so many times. Michael thought he was doing it for the best. Don't let the harsh feelings I know you still have colour the rest of your life.'

Alex ran his hand through his hair. 'I don't want to talk about all that any more, Luigi. It's in the past.'

'I hope what you say is true. If you have been thinking about family life, does that mean you have at last found someone to share that idea with?'

For a moment Alex was silent, then with a heavy sigh he murmured, 'In a perfect world, yes, but life doesn't seem to be like that. There are too many obstacles. She isn't for me, and I'm not right for her, for many reasons. It's just the way it is. Perhaps another time it will work out.'

'In my experience, Alex, what we may consider as insurmountable problems can sometimes be overcome with the will and effort of all parties and, most important of all, with love. If you have that you're halfway there.'

At this point Maria came in to join them, and by mutual silent agreement the topic of conversation was changed. For the rest of the evening, however, Alex thought about what Luigi had said, without finding any further answer to his dilemma.

CHAPTER 17

Geoffrey Villiers was becoming irate. Franklin had been ranting on the other end of the phone for the last ten minutes.

'For God's sake, Lionel, calm down. There's no problem.'

'No problem! You pitch up at Clarke's place unannounced, you get spotted by one of his women, she's seen speaking to the police, and now, from what you tell me, it's obvious that maniac Clarke's lost his head! And you say there's no problem?'

Villiers winced and held the receiver away from his ear. 'Who's going to suspect anything? It's an occupational hazard with that sort of girl, they know the risks they run. Clarke says his man is good, never been caught yet.'

'I don't suppose anybody thought to question her about what she said and to whom, so we can do some damage limitation if we have to? Clarke's man could have frightened her enough to get some information and make sure she didn't talk to anyone again; and not this way, either. Did anyone stop to think what her contact might do now? No, of course not! Of all the...'

'Lionel, it might not have been the police she spoke too, just an old client who owed her some money. I doubt the authorities will find out much about it anyway, for the reasons I've already mentioned.

I'll update you on what I can find out when we meet with Gregory as arranged.'

'I just hope you're right, Geoffrey. I just hope you're right.'

*

Jack Ellison hadn't been to a boxing match for quite a while. The invitation which reached him a day or two ago came out of the blue, but he quite liked the idea. The fact that it was a handwritten envelope and delivered to his mail box at the gates overnight was another interesting point.

The hotel where the event was being staged was busy. Amateur bouts were always quite popular. A bit hit and miss sometimes, but participants, for the most part, gave their all. His minders were keeping a close eye on proceedings, so he settled back in his seat. An attractive young lady was moving along his row, handing out programmes. She would give his Lizzy a run for her money, he thought, eyeing her with pleasure. She pushed a programme into his hand and moved on. He began to open it out and then realised that there was a piece of paper inside. Under cover of a handkerchief he slipped the paper into his pocket, and then settled down for the night's events.

*

A post-mortem is never the best way to spend any time, and Alex was glad to be out in the fresh air. Although requesting to be present, he'd found it disturbing, knowing Lucille was being dealt with in that fashion. He still remembered her cheeky grin and animated conversation from his time with her all those months ago. He also remembered the concern in her eyes when she'd spoken to him in the pub, and the bruises on her skin.

Her body had been spotted at low tide by the crew of a river barge. She was dead when she was put into the water, with the cause of death confirmed as strangulation, but there were also multiple bruises – those on her wrist now indistinguishable from all the rest. She could have been just one more unfortunate victim of the sort of dangerous life these girls led, but somehow he didn't think so. He was certain that someone had found out about what she'd done. Had she been seen to have come into a bit of money, despite his warning? Had Clarke put two and two together, and was this the result?

Whatever the circumstances, it was a frightening way for a young life to end. His colleagues would make their enquiries and he had already informed them of what he knew. He'd keep a close eye on things; he owed her that.

*

Sarah was pleased to escape the lecture hall for an hour. Opthalmics was not her first love, and there was the whole afternoon to go. A breath of fresh air and a coffee seemed very welcome. She left the main hospital entrance and headed towards a café just across the road. She saw Alex just ahead of her.

For the last six weeks they had heard nothing from him. She had wondered whether to try contacting him. Jerry had warned her against doing so, but something had to be done. Catherine would be ill soon, she was sure of it.

'Alex!'

He turned, and after a moment saw her. She was close enough to see his expression change when he realised who it was. The closed face and hard eyes might have deterred her, but she steeled her own resolve. She was doing this for her friend.

'Hello there, long time no see! How are you?' The remark sounded casual but Sarah could see now that he looked no better than Catherine. He appeared to have lost weight and his face looked strained and tired.

'Hello, Sarah. I'm well, and you?'

Liar, she thought, but kept the smile on her face. 'I'm just going for a quick coffee between lectures. Have you time for a cup with me?'

She saw the hesitation in him, and then he shrugged and she took his arm and hurried across the road before he could change his mind.

When they were settled with their coffee, which he insisted on paying for, she asked, 'What brings you to Brompton?'

He stirred his cup with obvious deliberation. 'I've been to a post-mortem.'

'Oh Lord, never the nicest things. You could do with more than a coffee, I suspect.'

He looked up at her with a slight smile and she could see the pain in his eyes; not altogether, she judged, from his recent experiences. As a gesture of comfort she put out her hand and covered his.

'What happened, Alex?'

It was obvious he knew what she meant, and with something like a sigh he removed her hand.

'Don't start, Sarah, please!'

'Alex, I must. I love Catherine like a sister, and I'm worried about her.'

'Worried? What do you mean, worried?'

She could sense his immediate concern and this gave her courage to continue. 'I think she's ill, both physically and mentally.' She put up her hand to stop his incredulous retort. 'Yes, I know that's putting it a bit strong, but she does need help. There's been something wrong since… that night.' She watched him and saw the reaction in his grey eyes. 'Catherine is living with me at Kensington now. Did you know?'

'Know? How on earth could I know that, for God's sake?'

She heard the exasperation in his voice. He was by no means as detached as he pretended to be.

'It was about a week after that reception. She called me and asked if my previous suggestion of us sharing the flat was still convenient. I was delighted. Grace had rung me to say that she thought Catherine was very unhappy, and I ought to know. I was glad of the chance to get her out of that place, and living with me so I could keep an eye on her. Jerry has gone back to staying with a workmate of his.'

She noticed Alex was looking at her with narrowed eyes.

'What did her uncle have to say about it all?'

'It was strange, because Catherine said that he made very little fuss. Knowing him, I can't understand his sudden change of heart. But within a week we had the move completed, and she's been with me since then. It's worked well. I get help with all the chores and expenses. I gather Catherine has agreed to still help her uncle when or if he requires, but she's also enrolled on a correspondence course for a history degree. I wasn't able to get her to enrol anywhere in person, she seems to be happy working on her own. She has, though, agreed to be part of the hospital's volunteer group of translators, and I know she's proved to be an asset there. She seems to have a natural empathy for people in emotional circumstances. I think it's because she understands how they feel.'

She paused and looked up at the man opposite. 'I know she cries a lot, although she tries not to let me see it.' She saw the muscles in his jaw tighten but knew she had to go on, whatever happened. 'Alex, she's lost weight, although she assures me she's eating. She doesn't sleep well. I often hear her up in the night. More than anything, though, it's her total calmness that worries me. She doesn't show all her emotions any more, as she used to do, but I know that it's all welling up underneath and I'm frightened about what might happen one day. I'm thinking of having a word with one of the psychiatry consultants about her.'

'She's just going to take time to adjust to her new freedoms after so many years.'

'She isn't free, Alex. That's the trouble.'

Sarah held his eyes with her own. He broke the contact first, moved his coffee cup away from him and looked out of the cafe window.

'What do you want from me, Sarah?'

'Talk to her, please, Alex.'

'What am I supposed to say to her?'

'Grace said that she found Catherine in a distressed state that night of the reception. She thought you had brought her home. Something must have happened. Catherine won't talk about it.'

'What do you think happened? That I molested her?'

'No, of course not, we both know you would never do that.'

'I came damned close!'

Sarah sat back in her chair and just looked at him. She hadn't expected that vehement retort.

He ran his hands through his hair and looked up at her. 'She looked so beautiful and sophisticated that night. I wanted to let her know what I thought, but without frightening her. She seemed so innocent and vulnerable. I didn't touch her, Sarah. I just kissed her the way you would kiss a child you loved goodnight. I felt her respond, and I knew that if I stayed it would become dangerous in that quiet house, so I sent her up to bed and left, cursing myself for what I'd done. I didn't mean to hurt her, but it was for her safety that I went.

'I shouldn't have left the house, Sarah. I deserted my duties and paid hell for it with my superiors. I was lucky not to be suspended. I thought about telephoning her and trying to explain, but in the end decided it was better to leave things as they were. I hoped after a while everything would settle back down again.'

'Alex, will you tell me something, and be honest?'

He looked at her, his grey eyes steady. She could see that he was bright enough to know what was coming, but he wasn't shirking the question.

'Are you in love with Catherine?'

'Yes.'

Although she was hoping to hear it, the instantaneous simple reply caught her off guard for a moment.

'Please go to her, Alex, and tell her that. I'm sure she feels the same about you.' Sarah was almost pleading.

'It's not that simple, Sarah. Our backgrounds are so different. She's been brought up to marry into a different social class, one she's suited for; I'm not so much of a fool I can't see that. I have a responsibility to her, as I'm older than she is. I've been on my own for years now and I've done all manner of things and had experiences. Catherine is now free to have a chance to enjoy all this, she doesn't need to be tied to me. Anything you say she might be feeling is because she now trusts me and considers me a pair of safe hands as far as a romantic liaison is concerned. She wants to explore this, but I don't want to be her teacher and find later on she decides to spread her wings in another direction. I don't think I could cope with that. So its better left as it is now, with no further harm done.'

'Alex, I'm sure that Catherine doesn't desire to be married into aristocracy or want numerous relationships. She just wants someone to love her. I think deep down you want the same thing.'

For a moment Sarah wondered if she'd gone too far. Alex was looking at her with a touch of annoyance on his face.

'Sarah, I have my career to think about. That's important to me, more than you think. Up to now I haven't needed, or wanted, to look for anything more permanent by way of a relationship. This situation has come out of the blue, and at the moment I'm at a loss to know what to do for the best. There are other matters involved as well. I'm sorry, in other circumstances it might have been different.'

'Well, I don't know about all that, but if you ask me, I think you should just get to know one another better. It would be good for both of you. I'm sure at the end of the day all Catherine needs is a home and children; much more than I do, if I'm honest.' With a start, Sarah realised that she had never mentioned this to anyone else, even Jerry. What a day for revelations.

This time it was Alex who covered her hand and squeezed it. 'I'm sure that's not true, Sarah. You would make a marvellous wife and mother. Don't sell yourself short.'

'Maybe not, but I think I'd better start giving it some serious thought.'

She looked down at her watch. She was late for her afternoon lecture, but this was far more important. She could always crib someone's notes.

'What are we going to do, Alex? I am worried about her. Will you just go and talk to her? Jerry and I are going to Scotland next weekend from Friday lunchtime, so Catherine will be alone.'

'I can't promise, Sarah, but I'll think about it.'

'All right, Alex. Thank you for speaking to me. I must dash off to my lecture now and face the wrath of the professor!'

She planted a quick kiss on his cheek and raced off. Alex watched her go, and then ordered another coffee.

*

Lionel Franklin pushed his plate out of the way and leant back in his chair.

'Well, at least Aubrey has agreed to my plans for the Scottish route. When I've finalised my arrangements I'll let Duncan know in good time.' He looked across the table at Gregory Hamilton. 'That was a pretty stupid idea of his, taking Catherine back to the house when the police were around. It's caused me to review my plans for her somewhat.'

'He didn't know anybody would be patrolling around, or would interfere even if they were.'

Geoffrey Villers, still smarting from his tongue-lashing a few days earlier, couldn't resist making a point. 'In fairness, Lionel, I noticed your little plan didn't work too well either.'

Franklin stared at him for a moment, then answered, his mild tone surprising Villiers who had been anticipating another roasting. 'I'll grant you that, Geoffrey. For whatever reason, Hartman didn't take the bait, but I haven't finished with him yet. He may prove a useful catalyst. I've decided to give Catherine a free rein. She's gone to live with that Jennings woman.'

The other two looked at him in astonishment.

'What on earth made you agree to that? I thought you said she was a bad influence.'

'Yes I did, Gregory, and I still think so. This time, though, it may work to our advantage. If I'm not mistaken, Catherine has formed some schoolgirl romantic attachment for Hartman and Sarah Jennings is just the sympathetic type who might encourage that to continue. Hartman has been around, and given different circumstances might well take advantage of that. Catherine could find herself in trouble, with no one to fall back on, and no choice but to ask me for help. Then she'll be even more compliant to my wishes.'

'It's a hell of a long shot, Lionel.' Villiers's sceptical tone was matched by the look on his face.

'We'll see. It's amazing what a bit of old-fashioned romance can do. I'll just leave it for a bit and see what happens. I shall, however, be keeping a closer eye on her than she might think.'

CHAPTER 18

Alex thought long and hard about his conversation with Sarah, going round and round the problem, trying to decide what would be for the best. Being unable to tell Sarah the whole truth had made the situation seem simple to her. He knew better, and also knew he should just forget all about Catherine and immerse himself in his work. But he'd been trying that, and it wasn't working. He found it difficult to sleep and was beginning to enjoy the taste of whisky. He even looked up one of his former girlfriends and endured an evening in which he found he had no interest at all, and it was obvious the lady in question realised his attitude and made it plain that he need not contact her again. He couldn't get away from the fact that a beautiful green-eyed girl had managed to find a place so deep inside him that he would never be the same again.

What was the future? Should he see Catherine again, and at least set things straight between them... and then, for her sake, walk away? Perhaps. It was possible that by seeing her again, just once more, he could draw a line under the whole thing. Wish her well for the future and then get on with his life, however hard that might be. The danger was that he might find it impossible to walk away. It was certain, though, that he couldn't go on doing nothing. He had to make some sort of decision.

He was still wrestling with the problem as he neared South Kensington that Friday evening. He parked outside the flat and sat in the car for several moments, trying to prepare himself. He had come this far and he must go through with it. As long as he didn't touch her, he might keep control.

As he reached for the door bell he noticed the slight tremor in his hand.

*

Catherine had wondered how she would occupy herself this weekend with Sarah away. She decided physical activity was a good start and began by giving the flat a good clean and changing the bed linen on both beds. She then treated herself to a long soak in the bath. As it was already late in the evening she slipped into a comfortable shirt and trousers and, tying her damp hair back with a ribbon, made herself a coffee. Even after all that effort she still couldn't face anything to eat.

She sat down on the settee with her course books and tried to concentrate, but as usual when she was alone, her mind kept wandering to things she would rather forget. She reminded herself yet again how she'd been strong enough to make the break away from Richmond to try to start a new life. However, the truth was that although no longer living with her uncle he still had some control over her until she was twenty-five. If she went against his wishes he might still cause problems for her… but there was no point even thinking about doing so, was there?

Alex had made it plain that night that he didn't want her and she had to try to accept the fact. She must keep her thoughts focused on the future, however hard it seemed at times, and stop feeling sorry for herself. The ache started to grow inside her again as she acknowledged just how much she still missed him. Then the door bell rang.

*

The door opened and Catherine stood there. Alex was overwhelmed at the sight of her. For a moment he thought she was going to faint, but she held herself together. With the immediate shock of his

122

unexpected presence leaving her, he saw that she was marshalling all her defences to deal with the situation.

'Sarah isn't here, I'm afraid.' Her voice sounded unnatural and forced.

'I know, Catherine. I've spoken with her. May I come in, please?'

After a moment's hesitation she opened the door wider and he slipped inside before she could change her mind.

He moved through into the lounge and turned to face her. He sensed the strain in her, and saw that Sarah was right: she had lost weight. She was even slimmer than he remembered.

'Sarah is worried about you.'

He thought it better to start with the truth. She would never believe that this was a casual visit.

With apparent calm she regarded him for a moment.

'You don't have to worry about me, if that's the reason you came.'

'I'm glad to hear it.' He could hear the edge in his voice. That calm stare was beginning to affect him. He decided to press on. 'I thought it might be a help if I explained about... that night.'

She turned away from him, then. 'I'm sure I don't know what you think there is to explain.' Her voice sounded almost bored, and he wondered if he'd imagined the further tenseness in her body.

He was beginning to feel rising anger in him now. This wasn't the response he'd expected. What had he expected, though? That she would throw herself into his arms? Yes, he knew that's what he had hoped for.

'Catherine, I left that night because otherwise I would have ended up in your bed!'

She turned to face him again and he could see the sheen of tears in the green eyes.

He forced himself to go on. 'I told you that you looked beautiful, and any man would have been tempted. I think you felt that now you trusted me you had a chance to widen your experience, and the scenario that night was ideal, but you deserved better than a few stolen moments. Catherine, believe me, I would find it no hardship at all to be the first to instruct you in the art of love... but one day, when you have enough confidence to move on… I'm not sure if I want to handle that.'

He put up his hand to silence her as she made to speak. 'It's no use pretending that it wouldn't happen. I'm older than you, I've had more experience in these matters. You have a chance of freedom now, to do what you want in life. The last thing you need is to be tied down again. I want you to be happy. You are a very beautiful, accomplished young lady and you'll find someone who is meant for you.'

He started to move across the lounge towards the hall. He knew he had to leave. Now. 'Please take care of yourself.'

'Alex!' Her cry halted him. Against his better judgement he turned back.

She was standing there with her arms wrapped round herself, as if she was in pain. Tears were running down her face.

'Please don't go, Alex. Can't you understand? I don't want anyone else. I want you! You're all I've ever hoped for.'

'Catherine', he sighed, 'how can you know that? Haven't you heard what I've just been saying?'

'I heard it, and I don't believe it …and I don't think you believe it, either!'

All his good intentions went out of the window then, as he crossed to her and took her shoulders.

'Catherine, don't make it any harder than it is already. Believe me, its best this way, for any number of reasons.' He couldn't tell her of one particular reason.

She started to undo her shirt buttons and pressed her body close to his. 'Alex, please love me. I need you.'

He pushed her away from him. He felt his anger spiralling out of control, but he knew the anger was against himself and his reaction to her.

'Don't you dare offer your body to me, or any man! There's no way on earth you have to resort to that. You're a lady, act like one!'

She was sobbing now. 'How else can I make you understand?'

'I understand that we're making each other unhappy, and it has to stop. I'm going now, Catherine. Goodbye.'

He found his way outside into his car and was pulling away down the road before he realised just why his eyesight seemed to be blurred. He ran a shaking hand over his wet eyes. Christ, what a mess!

A few streets away, Alex found somewhere to pull in and rested his head on the steering wheel. He could feel himself trembling.

It had been worse than he thought, and he knew that it would continue. He would see those green eyes for the rest of his life. Had he been wrong? Could it work, or was he just deluding himself? Was it worth taking the chance that she was speaking the truth, that she wanted him? Perhaps he could keep her with him after all. He imagined with longing the life that they might have together. He could feel that slim body pressed against him, and he groaned and put his head back down on the wheel.

His dilemma still remained. He knew that he wanted to be with her, but the fear returned to him of what might happen if she had to be told about his investigation of her uncle's affairs. His uncertainty of her reaction washed over him again. Would any relationship between them be strong enough to overcome a revelation like that? Could he believe that, when the time came, there would be a way to convince her that his work was in no way related to their personal feelings? She might, of course, never have to know.

After a moment or two he knew his decision was made. He squared his shoulders, started the engine and drove away.

*

Catherine stood in the darkening room, listening to the sound of the Porsche recede into the distance. How had she not heard him arrive? Her ears had always been listening out for his car, just hoping!

Now it was over. Just like that. Had she done something wrong again? Could she have made him stay if she hadn't made that stupid gesture? It was too late now, anyway.

She became aware of a pounding ache behind her eyes, and tears threatened again. Fetching a bottle of painkillers and a glass of water, she sat on the settee. If she took something, she might sleep. As she sat alone in the empty room she felt the tears splashing onto her hands.

There was so much unhappiness inside her that it felt as if they would go on for ever. Her worries regarding her uncle no longer mattered. She knew Alex was the man she loved, and now he was gone. Her life seemed to stretch before her like an eternity. How could she cope without him?

She lay down on the settee, buried her face in one of the cushions and wept until, worn out, she fell asleep.

*

Alex stood on the pavement for a moment, still irresolute. The flat was in darkness. Had she gone to bed? Well, there was only one way to find out.

He reached the door and was about to ring the bell when he noticed the door stood ajar. He couldn't have closed it when he had left before, and Catherine hadn't checked it. He went into the hall. Everywhere was dark and quiet. As his eyes adjusted to the pale light coming in through the windows, he made out the figure lying on the settee, one arm hanging down by her side. Then he noticed the bottle and glass on the table, and a cold fear possessed him. Oh God, no! No, she couldn't!

He went down on his knees beside her. With a trembling hand he reached for her wrist to feel for a pulse. Yes, there it was! Steady and strong. He placed his hand against her neck and the pulse there told the same story. With a sigh of relief he laid his forehead on the settee for a moment and said a silent prayer. He was now certain that he never wanted to be parted from her, and no matter what might come in the future, there would have to be a way of dealing with it.

With a gentle hand he stroked her face. He could feel her skin was wet. She had cried herself to sleep, but he had to be sure.

'Catherine.'

She made a whimpering sound, like a small hurt animal, and he gathered her up into his arms. As she came awake, he stroked her face again. Heavy eyelids lifted and he could just make out pain-filled green eyes swamped with tears.

'Don't cry any more, my love. I'm here, and I'm not leaving you.'

126

She lifted one small hand and touched his cheek, as if to make sure that he was real. He turned his face into her hand and kissed the soft palm.

'Alex?'

'Don't worry any more, Catherine. But I must know… did you take any of these?' He held up the bottle of tablets. She removed her gaze from his face and looked with slight confusion at the bottle.

'What?'

'Did you take any Catherine?'

'No. I had a headache, but I didn't…'

He stood up, and she cried out in distress. He took off his jacket and flung it down on a chair, then came and sat beside her on the settee, folding her into his arms.

'I told you I wasn't going anywhere!'

'Alex? Why did you come back? How did you get in?'

'So many questions for such a little person!' He was feeling quite light-headed with relief after his shock. 'The door was open. I couldn't have shut it when I left.'

'You still haven't told me why you came back.' She touched his face. 'I thought I would never see you again. Alex, I couldn't bear it.'

He could feel her agitation and held her face against his chest, stroking her hair with a gentle hand.

'I couldn't bear it either. I found I didn't have the strength to walk away from you. I love you, Catherine, and I want to be with you.'

He heard her give a sigh of pleasure, and her body relaxed. After a few moments he realised that she had gone to sleep again. He held her close and let her sleep. Everything else could wait for now.

The room was quite dark when she eventually stirred in his arms, and he saw the glitter of her eyes as she looked up at him.

'Feeling better now?'

'Much.' She struggled upright. Running a hand over her tangled hair, she seemed awkward and shy. 'I'm going to wash my face.'

'I could do with something to drink. Can I make myself a coffee?'

He sensed she needed time to collect her thoughts.

'Of course. I'll have one too. What's the time?'

He looked at his wristwatch. 'About midnight.'

'It can't be!'

'What's the problem? Are you going to turn into a pumpkin or something?'

She smiled at him then, and he watched as she went through to her bedroom. He busied himself in the kitchen, hunting until he found everything he needed.

By the time she came back he had made the coffee and brought it through to the lounge. He switched on one of the table lamps near the settee and turned on the radio. Soft music filled the room.

She came and sat by his side, looking at him as if she still couldn't believe he was there. He noticed with pleasure that she had left her hair loose, and her face had regained some of its colour.

Taking her hand in his he rubbed her soft palm with his thumb. Neither of them said a word, just looked at each other. After a while the sound of the music and the soft lighting relaxed her and she laid her head on his shoulder, their coffee still untouched.

Realising she was becoming sleepy again, Alex whispered into her hair, 'It's time for you to be in bed, young lady. I'll come and see you tomorrow and we can talk some more.'

She sat up and stared at him in consternation.

'You... you said you wouldn't leave me!' The fear was back in her voice.

'Catherine,' he sighed, 'you know I mustn't stay.'

He watched as she made to say something and then changed her mind, and he saw the green eyes fill with desperation. This time she was frightened of making any sort of move. Alex was then certain that he couldn't leave her, not tonight. He would be too worried about her here on her own. He gave a sigh of resignation and saw the change in her eyes as she recognised his decision. It wasn't triumph, just a look of deep relief and contentment.

He stood up, and brought her with him. Taking her hand, he walked through to her bedroom.

'Catherine, you must go to bed like a good girl, and get some more sleep. I'll make myself comfortable on the settee and I'll see you in the morning.'

'Alex…?'

He slid his arms round her slender waist and looked into her eyes, soft as green velvet. It would be so easy… but no, not yet! He shook his head, kissed her soft lips, and left the room, closing the door behind him.

CHAPTER 19

Lionel Franklin looked out over the garden, bathed in bright sunlight. It was a beautiful Saturday morning, all the more so because of the phone call he had just received. Perhaps with the news from Kensington, things were working out his way after all. Excellent!

*

Catherine awoke, and the events of the night before returned to her. She listened, but everything was quiet. For one terrible moment she thought Alex had gone, but then she heard sounds from the kitchen. She relaxed back on to the pillows and thought about what had happened to her over these last hours. How could life change from total despair one moment to total bliss the next?

She slid out of bed, brushed out her hair, dressed in her best long pink robe and went into the kitchen. Alex was busy laying out plates, and when he glanced up at her she saw the appreciative look in his eyes.

'I've made use of your bathroom facilities, if that's OK. Breakfast's ready. I was about to call you.'

He had dressed in his trousers but was bare-chested. She wanted to touch his smooth skin, to feel the well-toned body beneath her fingers. She became alarmed at her thoughts. In an effort to distract herself she moved over to him to see what he was doing, and then, realising that he had shaved, on impulse ran her fingers down his cheek.

He smiled at her. 'I always keep an overnight bag in the car, as I never know if I might need it.' Her face registered her thoughts, and seeing her expression Alex amended with a laugh, 'For business purposes. Well, sometimes!'

She was about to make an appropriate remark, but her eyes were diverted by the apparent mountain of toast he was placing on the table.

'How ever much toast have you made, Alex?' she laughed at him.

'I'm hungry,' he replied, his gaze steady.

It sounded a simple statement, but looking into those grey eyes she felt warm from head to toe, and remembered how he had been very deliberate in leaving her alone last night. She sat down in a hurry and then found a plate of fluffy scrambled eggs being placed in front of her, together with a quick kiss on her neck.

'Eat up. You need to put on some weight.'

Ignoring the remark, she found that, in fact, she was ravenous and soon the eggs and mound of toast were devoured between them.

'You see, I told you! Perfect planning on my part,' Alex grinned at her.

'I must say, those eggs were very good. I don't think I could have done any better.'

'High praise from a cordon bleu cook! Don't forget, I've spent a lot of time looking after myself.'

Catherine looked at him and placed her hand on his arm. 'I'd like to look after you now, Alex.'

He didn't reply, but just kissed her hand.

Taking the empty dishes over to the sink, he turned back to her. 'It's a nice day. I could do with some fresh air. How do you feel about having a walk in the park?'

Catherine had the odd impression there was an ulterior motive here somewhere, but was quite happy to go along with his suggestion. At his insistence she left him to deal with the dishes, and went for a shower. She dressed with care in a green pleated skirt which swung around her knees, and a cream jumper, with her favourite gold chain. She hunted out a pair of knee-high tan boots and a matching bag. As she came out of the bedroom into the lounge she shrugged into a soft green suede jacket, tossing her plaited hair back from the collar.

Alex was about to button up his shirt. He looked up and stopped still, his eyes wandering over her.

'What's the matter?' she queried, wondering if something was wrong.

'Nothing at all,' he said, grabbing his tie, and coming over to her. 'I think you look beautiful. I'll just be a moment,' and headed for the bathroom.

When he reappeared, fully dressed, several minutes later, she took a cheeky look at her watch and shook her head in mock exasperation. 'You men, you take such a time to get ready!'

As she turned for the door, Alex gave her a playful smack on her small behind and, laughing, she danced out of the flat ahead of him.

They found a parking place for the Porsche, and walked for a while, hand in hand, mingling with the Saturday morning joggers and dog walkers, talking about everything and nothing in particular. Finding an empty seat, they sat in companionable silence.

Alex was the first to speak. 'Now we have the chance to talk, tell me a little about yourself, Catherine. I know your parents died when you were young.'

She turned her face up to his for a moment, her eyes registering indecision, then she looked away again. He placed his arm across her shoulders. After a moment she spoke.

'My mother had connections to a well-to-do Irish family. She met my father when he and Uncle Lionel took a holiday in Ireland during the time they were students at Cambridge together. My father was studying Classics and Uncle Lionel the law. My mother herself came over to England to study at Cambridge and they all met again, and the romance between them blossomed from there. I can't remember seeing much of Uncle Lionel until after their death.'

She looked up at him again, hesitant. 'I'd like to tell you something.'

He placed his lips against her hair. 'You can tell me anything you want, Catherine, you know that.'

'I've never spoken of these things to anyone, except Sarah, and even she doesn't know everything, but I'd like to tell you.'

She paused, took a deep breath and began. 'On one occasion, Uncle Lionel informed me that he would be coming out to Switzerland to see me during one of the school holidays. I was quite pleased about that as it was something he had never done before. He contacted me and told me to meet him at a Geneva hotel. That evening I found there was another guest for dinner, an older Italian man, who uncle described as being an industrialist. The evening was just polite conversation, but I was encouraged to practice my Italian language skills. I didn't like uncle's guest, and I was glad when the meal was over and he left. Uncle Lionel accompanied him out and was gone for some time. When he returned, he was in an unpleasant mood. He said he was going to his room and I was free to return to my school the next morning. I didn't understand what had gone wrong, so I did just that. Nothing more was ever said about the matter between us. I remember feeling as if I'd been interviewed for a job, and failed.'

Alex listened to her story in silence and came to his own conclusion as to the reason for the meeting: her uncle had used Catherine as marriage bait. His already low view of the man went even lower. He wasn't sure what to say, and sensed there was still more to come.

After a moment or two, she started to speak again, and he realised she was talking about the incident which Sarah had mentioned to Jerry and himself.

'There was always a grand ball held at the school for the girls who were finishing that year. That night I was passed a note, which even today I swear was in my uncle's handwriting, asking me to meet him in a particular room in the school buildings. I complied with the request but found it was a young male student who was waiting for me.'

Catherine hesitated in her narration at this point, and went quiet for several moments. Alex reached out and took her hand. She looked at their fingers linked together, and then went on with her story.

'It became something like the situation with Duncan Hamilton at

133

Richmond. It was lucky that a member of staff found us. I was sent to my room and I learned later the boy was expelled from his college. The next morning the school Principal interviewed me and made it clear that she did not believe my story, but because of my good record I would not be punished and I would still achieve my passing out certificate. No one told me whether Uncle Lionel was informed. Afterwards I could never find the written note, and I have no idea what happened to it. It was hurtful not to be believed. I never dared mention it to my uncle, and he has never spoken of it to me. I still don't understand what that was all about. One thing I do know is that Uncle Lionel wants to marry me to someone he chooses, and I'm frightened in case he could do it.'

Alex picked up her hand and kissed it. He kept his own thoughts to himself. Had her uncle staged the other meeting, too? Had the Italian turned down his offer, judging Catherine to be too young and inexperienced, and had her uncle then sought to take steps to educate her? It was manipulation of the worst sort, and almost amounted to sexual grooming; all for one purpose, it seemed. If he never met the man again, it would be a blessing, he thought.

Stroking Catherine's hand, he said, 'I realise now why you're a little unsure around men. I'm glad you felt you could tell me about all this. But you must now try to forget it. It's in the past, and your whole future is before you to enjoy and explore.'

'As long as it's with you, Alex.' Anxious green eyes looked up at him, asking a question.

Still wracked by indecision, and unable to give her an answer, Alex changed the subject. 'Shall we have a sandwich and a coffee at the park kiosk?'

After lunch they carried on with their walk. Alex found an empty bench in a more secluded area of the park, and suggested they sat together in the sun.

By this time Catherine had started to feel that he had something on his mind. He seemed more withdrawn, deep in thought. At one point she was going to enquire if something was wrong, but thought better of it. Had he changed his mind about staying with her? Had she upset him again in some way? Perhaps she shouldn't have told him about the things that had happened to her. She began to feel afraid, but resolved that this time she would not let her emotions show, no matter what. She must try to prove to him that she was grown up.

Startling her, Alex rose from the bench and walked a few steps away, then stood looking out over the vista for some time. He then turned and regarded her for several moments. His grey eyes were serious, and there seemed a sudden tenseness about him. She sat still, returning his look, trying not to let him see her fear. He came and sat beside her again, and took one of her hands in his. She felt herself begin to shake.

'Catherine, will you marry me?'

There was no way Alex could interpret the various emotions he saw cross Catherine's face, and her continuing silence unnerved him. Was it too soon for this? Had he been a complete fool, or had she just not understood him the first time?

'Will you marry me, please?'

To his relief, with a happy cry, she threw her arms around his neck. 'Oh yes please, Alex. I thought… I thought you'd changed your mind about me.'

'There was no chance of that, but I had to be sure I was doing the right thing. For us both.'

She planted a loving kiss on his cheek. 'I'll do all I can to make sure you never regret that decision. I love you, and I want to spend the rest of my life with you, looking after you.'

He held her close and kissed her, feeling her response.

'I suppose you want the white dress, church bells and all the rest?' he queried, rather breathless, several moments later.

She snuggled up to him. 'No, I'm not bothered about that at all. I just want to be your wife, as soon as possible. I would marry you today if I could!'

He laughed down at her. 'I think that's a little bit too quick for everyone, including me. I'm flattered, of course, but there are certain formalities. If you're sure, I'll see what I can do about it when everywhere opens up on Monday.'

135

After a while, still wrapped in each other's arms, they walked back through the park. Alex was amused as every now and then Catherine broke away from him, to dance off down the path ahead of him, and then rush back to either plant a kiss on his cheek or snuggle herself in his arms again. It was an exuberant display of pure happiness, and although he felt an immense happiness himself at the idea of a lifetime in the company of this remarkable young woman, he still felt uneasy about not being able to be honest with her.

Back at Kensington, after a light meal, they sat close together on the settee with their coffee, sometimes talking, at other times quiet, music playing in the background. As their intermittent idle conversation died away, Alex could sense the atmosphere changing and evolving into one of sweet anticipation. He looked down at Catherine curled in his arms. She had changed into a soft green shirt and black jeans and he could see a gold chain glinting at her throat. He wanted to kiss the soft skin beneath it, but he was afraid of frightening her. Yet as she looked up at him, her eyes suggested that she also wanted more.

However, he had to be sure that she was ready to take this next step. If he recognised there was the slightest doubt in her, he would have to stop – somehow!

He put his hand against her neck and let his fingers slide under the heavy gold links before letting them fall back against her skin. There was a slight tremor in her body as he moved his fingers along her shoulder under the soft material of her shirt. With his eyes intent on her face he let his hand glide down until it reached the soft curve of her breast. She made no sound, and was lying relaxed under his touch. He cupped the small breast in his hand and saw nothing but pleasure reflected in her eyes. He lowered his head and kissed her mouth, long and hard. Picking her up in his arms, he carried her through to the bedroom. Throwing back the covers he laid her on the bed and turned on the small bedside lamp, angling the light away from her eyes. She was trying to undo the remaining buttons on her shirt, but he stopped her with a gentle hand.

'Leave that to me, my sweet,' and he kissed her again.

CHAPTER 20

Catherine didn't want to be disturbed from the warm comforting cocoon surrounding her, but the gentle touch and soft voice were becoming more insistent. With a slight protest she lifted heavy eyelids, and looked straight into soft grey eyes, full of desire.

'I've been waiting for you to wake up, sleepy-head!'

His voice was warm and indulgent, his hand light on her cheek.

As her mind replayed the recent events, despite herself she felt warm colour flood up through her skin. There was no way his sharp eyes missed her reaction, and he gave her a quick kiss.

'Oh yes, it happened alright!'

She remembered not being conscious of him removing her clothes, all her senses absorbed by the feel of his lips and hands on her body. At one point he left her and she thought he had changed his mind. She cried out, but then he was there with her again, calming her agitation, and she realised that he had removed his own clothes. He held her for a while, letting her become used to the feel of their bodies against each other. With music still playing in the background, he began to arouse her to a degree she had never thought possible. It reached a stage where she felt that she might scream if she couldn't find a way to release the pressure building inside her. She remembered pleading with him for help of some sort, and his soft, soothing replies. Then his body joined hers, and after a small moment of discomfort she knew that this was her answer, and allowed her instincts to take over. It seemed a long time before she was able to even think again. Alex had held her close, and she felt so warm and relaxed that she had curled herself tighter against him as she slid into sleep.

Her thoughts still dwelling on her delicious memories, she heard Alex murmur, 'I think we might try that again, don't you? I have the feeling we both enjoyed it the first time. I want you to remember tonight, my love.'

Full of some nameless emotion she lifted a hand to run her fingers down the side of his face and touch his mouth.

'Yes please, Alex.'

Without another word, he worked his magic on her again, coaxing those same feelings in her, but she sensed that this time there was more urgency in his movements, and when he came into her she felt his full power and realised that before he had shown great consideration for her first time. Unafraid now, she matched his passion, and they both reached their peak together in a breathless tangle of arms and legs. As she drifted into sleep again, held in his arms, she was bathed in the warmth of pure happiness, something which she knew she had been longing for all her life.

*

The red glow of a cigarette penetrated the darkness between the pools of light from two street lamps. The man stamped his feet in the pre-dawn chill. Soon it would be time to leave and make his report to Clarke, he thought. The Porsche was still parked outside and the man had stayed the night again. Alright for some. They'd be a damn sight warmer than he was.

*

The sun in her eyes woke her, and Catherine stretched with pleasure as she remembered last night's events. Turning her head, she found Alex already awake and studying her, a smile hovering round his mouth.

'I'm used to waking at this time each morning,' he said, reading her unspoken thoughts. 'I should be out running by now, but somehow I don't have the energy this morning!'

She pretended to ignore his remark, which made him chuckle with amusement. 'Anyway, my love. Did you sleep well, after all your exertions?'

'I had a wonderful sleep, and I'm not sure what exertions you're referring to.'

She wasn't going to rise to his teasing banter, despite the wicked gleam in his eyes which did strange things to the pit of her stomach, as did the memories that flooded back, but she was never going to let him see that.

'That's a pity. I was hoping you'd remembered something. Perhaps we'll have to keep repeating it until you do!'

His grin told her that he had seen through her deception. He buried his face in her neck and kissed her.

She ran her hand down his cheek. 'I didn't imagine it could feel like that, Alex. I know you were kind to me, weren't you.' She wanted him to understand that she had realised this.

'A man should have consideration in such circumstances.'

'I'm not certain it would be true in all cases,' she murmured, feeling a sudden coldness at the thought of how it might have been. Some of the men her uncle had encouraged her to associate with she now knew would not have shown her such consideration.

'Catherine?' Alex was looking at her, searching her eyes and reading her fear. He held her close again. 'It won't happen. You're mine now.'

She pressed herself against him and reached up to kiss his mouth. 'I love you. Do you know?'

'Yes, I think I do.' With gentleness he turned her on to her back. 'Shall we practice some more?' She knew it was an attempt to divert her earlier unwelcome fear and again she felt a warm glow of gratitude to this man for his understanding.

Breaking into her thoughts she heard the telephone ringing, and trying not show her embarrassment Catherine slipped out of bed, put on her robe and went to answer it.

'Oh… Sarah.' She listened for a moment or two. 'That's a shame for you. So you're not going to be back until Monday now… OK. I'll see you then at some point.' She listened again. 'Yes, I'm just fine, Sarah. See you soon.'

Putting down the phone she returned to the bedroom. 'Sarah and Jerry have been caught up in traffic by an accident and they won't make it back to London tonight. They're going to put up somewhere overnight and drive on tomorrow morning.' As a sudden thought occurred to her, she climbed back on the bed. 'That means you could stay tonight, couldn't you? Please!' She smiled at Alex and placed her arms around his neck.

He slid his hands around her small waist and pulled her close to him. 'I think you're leading me astray, young lady, but I must admit the idea appeals. I'll have to leave at the crack of dawn, though, to get back to my flat and change before I go into work.'

Catherine gave him a coy smile from underneath her lashes. 'We seem to wake up at that time of the morning anyway!'

Alex looked at her, his eyes steady but turning darker. 'So we do. Now, I wonder how we can fill in the time?'

The rest of Sunday passed in carefree talk, passionate interludes and contented sleep. After a late meal they ignored the washing up and curled close together again on the settee. Alex apologised to her for wanting to watch a TV news broadcast, and Catherine realised with a start that the weekend was almost over. Tomorrow, Sarah would be back; and what would happen then?

Before too long Alex's attention turned from the daily news to an overwhelming interest in the soft skin at the neck of her gown and he turned off the TV and carried her to the bedroom.

*

Alex woke and sensed she was not beside him. He listened, but everywhere was quiet. Some premonition that all was not well made him slide out of bed and pad through into the lounge. In the dim light he could see Catherine standing at the window. He moved over to her and placed his arms round her waist. He felt her jump as he caught her unawares.

'What's wrong, Catherine?'

She sighed, and he held her closer.

'I woke and started thinking and realised that I'd been stupid and not behaved in a grown up way, yet again! I should have been more sensible. I'm wondering if, after a while you might find things like that about me irritating: not behaving the way an adult should. So I would quite understand if you wanted to change your mind about marrying me. I could maybe find a place of my own and be with you whenever you wanted. I would still like that.'

Her statement shook him. He wondered if he had misheard her.

'Catherine, come back to bed and talk about it in the warm. You're getting cold, and I'm freezing. Please.'

After a moment she turned in his arms and faced him.

'Alright,' she sighed. To his ears she sounded despondent, and he didn't understand this sudden change in her.

He picked her up in his arms and placed her back in the bed, drawing the covers around her, and when he lay down beside her he made sure that they were tucked down between them. He knew that just at this moment he should not touch her further.

'Now then, talk to me.'

'When we made love I know you took... er... certain precautions. But Alex, it's something I should have thought about as well. I should have been more conscious of my own situation, but I wasn't. I was so overwhelmed by the whole wonderful experience. I shouldn't have relied upon you to do the right thing... but, dear Alex, it's made me love you so much more because you took care of me. You must be thinking you deserve someone more mature than me. That's why if you want to change your mind I shall understand...'

Her voice died away, and from the look on her face, he realised that he must have registered the emotion he was feeling, a mixture of disbelief and anger.

He took a deep breath and in slow, measured tones said, 'Catherine Franklin, listen to me. I am going to have this discussion with you now and I never want to repeat it again. I love you, more than I could ever describe. I'm aware that modern women like to take charge of their own lives, but men should still be responsible for their actions. I knew there was no chance you were on the Pill, so I took appropriate precautions. I don't think anything less of you for not reacting to the situation. Catherine, I want you as my wife, and to know that we can be together for the rest of our lives. I have asked you once to marry me and you have accepted. I will now ask you one more time. Will you marry me? And if you don't say "Yes" I'll keep you in this bed and kiss you to distraction until you do!'

She strained against the covers to be in his arms but he held her away, still wanting her answer.

'Oh please, Alex. Please let me marry you. I was so afraid for a moment. I love you so much.'

He pulled back the covers and brought her against him. 'That's that, then. Can we get some sleep now, please?'

He could feel her smiling as she burrowed into his arms, and he held her close until she was asleep.

*

Alex had no desire to leave the next morning, but he knew he had to, there were things – important things – to be done. He stood and watched Catherine, still fast asleep. He thought of the events of the weekend and the complete change in his life.

He remembered the confidences Catherine had disclosed to him, and again his anger grew at the conduct of her uncle. As if aware of his scrutiny, Catherine stirred and opened sleep-filled eyes. Noticing that he was dressed, she struggled up in the bed.

'Is it time for you to go?'

Alex came and sat on the side of the bed. He ran a light finger over the soft skin of her shoulder.

'I would very much like to stay,' his tone was rueful, 'but I must tear myself away, so cover yourself up, young lady!'

'You will come back tonight won't you?' pleaded Catherine, gathering the covers up around her chin.

Alex thought that it didn't seem to matter if she was uncovered or not, he still wanted to remain with her. He heaved himself off the bed with a sigh.

'Barring any accidents, I'll come and see you. Any problems, and I promise to ring you. OK?'

'I can't wait until tonight.'

Alex looked back at her from the doorway. She was sitting there in the large bed, swathed in rumpled covers with her slim arms wrapped round her knees. Her hair was a tangled mass of glossy brown, but he thought she had never looked more beautiful. He crossed back to her and planted a quick kiss on her lips, but before she could trap him with her soft arms he straightened up and left the room.

If he hurried he could make it back to his flat, shower, change, and deal with his important errands before going to the office. He patted his pockets to confirm that he had everything he needed, which he had been fortunate to find while Catherine had still been asleep. If it all went according to plan he would have a surprise for her when he saw her tonight. He smiled to himself, happy at the thought.

CHAPTER 21

Catherine considered going back to sleep, after all it was only six o'clock, but she felt restless. She showered and dressed, and while eating her cereal she thought about the weekend. What was Sarah going to say? What might she think about Alex having stayed in the flat all weekend? After all, it was her flat, or rather, it belonged to her parents. Perhaps she ought not to say too much. She would have to think about this. Maybe she should have asked Alex what he thought. She felt he would have told Sarah the exact truth. If Sarah preferred her to leave, she would beg Alex to let her go and live with him before they were married.

Just in case, she thought she had better change the linen on her bed, and was just coming back up from the basement laundry when she met Sarah on the main stairs.

'Oh goodness, you're back! I didn't expect you until nearer lunchtime.'

'Jerry wanted to get into work so we had to get up at some atrocious hour this morning. Good job I'm not on duty until tomorrow.'

Back in the flat, Catherine went into the kitchen to make her friend a drink while she unpacked.

'Was the laundry free? I've got some stuff to be done.'

144

'Yes, I thought I'd get down there myself before everyone else. Shall I take yours down for you?'

'In a while, I'll have my coffee first to wake me up a bit.'

Sarah sat down at the kitchen table and regarded her friend. 'You're looking much better, poppet, almost glowing!'

Catherine brought over their coffee and sat down opposite her.

'You spoke to Alex, didn't you, Sarah?'

'Yes, I did. I saw him outside the hospital one day and we had a talk. I told him about you and that I was worried and asked him to speak to you. He looked as unhappy as you did, and I told him so. I asked if he would come and see you. He said he would think about it. Did he come?'

'Oh yes, he came!'

'And...?'

Catherine took a deep breath. 'He stayed the whole weekend and we are going to be married.'

If Catherine had announced she had proof that the world was flat, Sarah could not have looked more surprised. 'You are joking, aren't you?'

'No, I'm not. Alex is coming back tonight and you can ask him yourself.'

'But... but you don't even know each other! I thought that the two of you could spend some time together, as friends, but not to go this far, so fast. Has he told you anything about himself? Does he know anything about you? Are you sure you know what you're doing, Catherine? Marriage is quite a step, you know. Don't you think that perhaps Alex was just being a gentleman and doing the honourable thing?'

'I thought you liked Alex.'

'I do. I like him a lot, and I know he would be good for you... given time.'

'I understand what you're saying, Sarah, but I'm certain, and so is Alex. We want to be together as soon as possible.'

'You say he's coming tonight? I think I'd better have a word with him.'

'Sarah!' Catherine's tone was sharp. She realised she had never spoken to her friend in this way before. 'You can speak with him if you want, but it won't change our minds. Please be happy for me, Sarah.' The last words were almost a plea for her understanding.

'I want to be happy for you, that's why I'm worried. I don't know what more to say to you.' She shook her head. 'I think I'd better get on with my laundry.'

That remark set the tone for the day, and very little more was said between them.

As Catherine tidied herself up in her bedroom that evening, she resolved to beg Alex to take her back to live in his flat. She couldn't understand Sarah's attitude. She had imagined her friend would have been happy for her.

When the doorbell rang she raced through to the hall and wrenched open the door, and almost fell into the strong arms she loved.

'Well, that's some greeting, I must say. How's my girl?'

Alex moved them both inside the flat and shut the door behind him. He took one look at Catherine's woebegone face and stood with her against the wall in the hall, shielding her with his body from any possible onlookers. 'What's wrong, my sweet? Tell me.' He tried to turn her face up to his.

'Please take me home with you, Alex', she whispered into his neck. 'I've told Sarah, and she seems very unhappy about everything.'

'There's no reason for her to be. I'll speak with her. Nothing will change, so don't worry. I'm sure everything will be fine. Let's go through and have a word with her. I've something to show you, anyway.'

They moved into the lounge. Alex made sure that his arm was round Catherine's shoulders. He looked over at Sarah seated at the dining table.

'Hello, Sarah. Did you have a good weekend?'

'Yes, thank you, Alex. I hear you had an even better one.'

He noted that her tone was cool. Well, there was nothing like coming to the point, he thought.

'Indeed we did. I'm glad I took your advice.' That's at least apportioned the blame, he though to himself, not understanding her hostility. 'This beautiful young lady has consented to become my wife and I have never been happier. I'd like to think, neither has Catherine. I trust you approve?'

'I must admit the speed at which things have moved has surprised me a little.'

The edge was still there, but Alex decided to ignore it. He looked down at the anxious face beside him and, smiling, reached into his jacket pocket and brought out an envelope.

'I've something you might want to see in here.'

He put the envelope in her hands. She looked at him for a moment and then opened it. The first things she saw were her passport and birth certificate.

'How did you get these? Did you take them?'

'Yes. Grand larceny, I'm afraid. Have a look at the paper with them.'

His eyes were intent on her face as Catherine opened the paper and read the contents. He held his breath, just hoping.

Catherine's gasp of surprise and the glowing smile she bestowed on him were the exact reactions Alex had wanted to see.

'Friday! This Friday? Oh Alex, how wonderful.'

'I had to work very hard to achieve that, young lady. The trouble was that you're registered at Richmond, not here. I could have done it through my own area, but I thought this would be nearer for you. I'm sure the Registrar thinks that I'm up to no good, so you might have to prepare yourself for some close questioning before the actual formalities. I cheated a bit by impressing on him that my professional duties were fluid and time was critical. I hope you approve?'

'Approve? Of course, I approve. I told you to make it as soon as you could, and you have!'

Catherine stretched up and placed her mouth against his, and ignoring Sarah's presence Alex folded his arms around her and held the kiss for as long as he dared. They were both a little breathless when Catherine turned to Sarah and beamed at her.

'We're going to be married on Friday at Chelsea Registry Office! Alex has a Special Licence.'

'There's not much I can say then, is there? I hope everything works out for you both.'

Alex still sensed the edginess in her. He needed to speak with her alone. He turned to Catherine.

'I'm afraid I can't stay long, but I wondered, if you sorted out some of your stuff, I could start taking it away with me.'

'Oh yes, of course, what a clever thought. I haven't even unpacked some things yet. Shall I go and sort some out now?'

'A good idea, I think. Maybe Sarah will make me a cup of coffee?' He looked over at the other girl, who nodded, having picked up on his meaning.

Catherine raced off to her bedroom and Alex followed Sarah into the kitchen and closed the door. He sat down at the kitchen table.

'It's obvious you don't approve. Why?'

'Alex, it's so quick! You don't even know each other. I didn't expect you to… well, you know… after you made a point of not taking advantage of her before. Are you marrying her because you're afraid she could be pregnant? She's not on the Pill, you know.'

'It's disappointing you don't credit me with the attributes of a gentleman. I love Catherine and I would never have considered treating her in the way you're referring to. I want her as my wife so that she can be with me as soon as possible, and I can take care of her. I can't explain it, but I have this urge to protect her in any way I can, and by marrying me she will have legal protection as well. Sarah, when I came to see her I tried to give all the excuses I mentioned to you the other day. I did manage to walk away from her that night, but it almost killed me. For the first time in my life I shed tears.' He looked up at Sarah. 'Do you understand me? I cried at the thought of being without her. Then I made up my mind that somehow we would make it work between us. So I came back.'

He kept his gaze on her and saw the shock register as he recounted the sight he had discovered on his return to the flat.

Sarah sat down at the table and grabbed his hands. 'Alex, had she taken anything? She didn't tell me this!'

'The tablets were because she had a headache, she told me later, but in the end she hadn't taken any. She had cried so much she had sent herself to sleep. Can you imagine my relief? How would I have lived with the knowledge that because of me she had done herself some harm?

'Her fear of dealing with men had been reinforced, because despite telling me she loved me, I had still walked away. There was no way I was leaving her again, Sarah. The first night I slept on the settee, but after I made my decision to propose to her, and she accepted, well… neither of us wanted to wait. I felt it had to happen for her to be sure.

'It's been a revelation, Sarah. It's as if a door has been unlocked in her. I know it's the right thing. You can see how happy she is. I know there will be problems, there are in any marriage, but I'm sure we can get through them. She still needs your friendship Sarah. She's very upset that you're not happy for her. Can we be friends again?'

'I hadn't realised it would affect her so, or I wouldn't have suggested you call when I was away. Thank God it wasn't what you thought, Alex!' She managed to smile at him. 'I know you love her and will take care of her, and that's all I can ask. I'll recover from the shock of all this some time, I suppose.'

'Thank you, Sarah. I'd rather have you on my side than against me.' He stood up and grinned at her. 'Well, I suppose I'd better see just how little space I'm going to have left for my clothes now, I suppose.'

It wasn't as bad as he thought, and he soon had the couple of bags stored away in the Porsche.

'I'm afraid I shall have to be going now,' he told a crestfallen Catherine. 'I seem to have so much to get out of the way this week. It might be difficult to see you again until Wednesday evening, but before I go, there's one more thing. We need witnesses for Friday, and with your agreement I wondered if…', he looked over at Sarah. 'Would you and Jerry do the honours for us?'

'Oh, please, Sarah. Please say you will. That would be perfect.'

Sarah looked from one to the other and then smiled and nodded.

'I think I should be free, and I'll see what Jerry's doing. I'll let you know for sure tomorrow.'

Catherine dashed over and hugged her friend, then she danced back to Alex. He smiled down into her happy face. 'Come and say goodbye to me, wife-to-be.'

CHAPTER 22

'But Jerry, you must agree with me that it's all gone too fast.'

Sarah had called an emergency meeting with Jerry in the hospital cafeteria. After explaining her news to him, she was amazed at his enthusiastic response.

'Where's the problem? They love each other, that seems very clear.'

'But they still don't know each other. They need time to be friends and find out about each other.'

'I'd have thought after one weekend together they've found out quite a bit about each other.'

'Jerry!'

Sarah's shocked response brought a wide grin to Jerry's face.

'You know very well what I mean, Jerry.'

'Look, Sarah, stop being so prudish. One thing is for certain. Alex and Catherine will never be friends.' He held up his hand as she made to interrupt him. 'Some relationships work in a different way to others. Theirs will no doubt swing between drama and making up, that's the kind of personalities they have. Laughter, tears and love. Alex is experienced and, as he said to you, already knows how it will be, but he loves Catherine enough to forgive her most things. Catherine needs to look after someone who she is certain loves her, but I think she will also hold her corner on something she wants. It will be interesting to see who wins. Then you take us…'

Again Sarah tried to speak but he took her hand and continued. 'We have known each other now for, what… three years? We've come to know each other well over that time, in every way.' His smile was soft. 'You know what I'm talking about. That doesn't mean we love each other any less than Alex and Catherine, just in a different way, because we're different sorts of people. What we mustn't do is get trapped in our comfy world. I've been meaning to have this sort of conversation with you for some time now, but in a more appropriate place.' He looked around the busy room. 'Sarah, I would very much like to marry you. I want to know that we can be together and start to build a proper life. I realise that your job is important to you, and I understand that, and I'm proud of your achievements, but I would like to think that we could make a proper home and have children together. Will you think about it for me, my dear?'

Sarah just sat and stared at him. This was the first time she had heard him speak quite like this. Marriage had always been something that was going to happen, but somewhere hazy, in the future. Jerry was right, though. How much more in the future could it be? She knew that she loved him enough to commit herself to him, and had always realised that at some time she would have to give up work if children came along. In the course of that work she knew how tragic events could take over a life. Was she wrong to deny not just Alex and Catherine, but also herself and Jerry, the enjoyment of a full and complete life now? With sudden insight, she realised that she was.

She looked at the man sitting opposite her in this crowded room and knew that there was no one else she would rather be having this conversation with.

'Jerry, are you proposing to me?'

'Well, yes I suppose I am, but I'm damned if I'm going to go down on one knee in here.'

'It would cause a riot!'

'Alright, damn it. If that's what it will take.'

To her absolute amazement and confusion Jerry moved off his

chair and went down on one knee in front of her. 'Sarah Jennings, it would give me the utmost pleasure if you would agree to marry me.'

A hush descended on the room, and all eyes were on the pair.

Ignoring them all, Sarah put her hand in Jerry's and in a clear voice said 'Yes, Jeremy McIntyre. I would be delighted to become your wife.'

The whole room erupted with whoops and yells and clapping. Sarah was swamped in hugs and Jerry was slapped on the back by helpful males all prophesying his ultimate doom.

As they struggled hand in hand out of the cafeteria and into the comparative calm of the hospital corridor, Jerry turned to her and said, 'Well, you'll have something to surprise Catherine with tonight.'

'I think she must have some sort of terrible disease, and it's catching.'

Laughing together, they went back to work.

*

Jack Ellison had decided to take a holiday! With his wife still reeling from the shock, Ellison put out the word that all operations would cease until his return. He also made sure that the news found its way to other quarters.

If what he had learnt from the paper passed to him at the boxing match was true, with his operations closed down for a while, there would be a lot less opportunity for the opposition to undertake anything which might be attributed to him. Not foolproof, but more difficult.

Besides he might even enjoy some sun. He'd enjoy looking at the girls, anyway!

*

No one dared go near their boss. Johnny Clarke had been in a foul mood since hearing about the temporary amnesty issued by Ellison. Just as he was ready to do something big, this had to happen. It was almost as if Ellison had been warned. Now, there was a thought! He turned it over in his mind. Who might have had the opportunity?

153

He remembered hearing that one of his men had been thrown out of a gym in Lewisham for shooting his mouth off about the opposition. It was Fenton's place, he was sure. He didn't think Fenton ever became involved one way or the other, but just suppose that on this occasion he had decided to pass the information on. How?

Then he remembered the latest round of photographs showing Ellison attending a boxing tournament in a local hotel. Fenton had been a boxer. He was bound to have been involved in the organisation. Was that how it was done? He also remembered another photograph. This one showed that policeman he was told to keep an eye on going into the gym a few days before. He knew that he used the gym from time to time, and that he and Fenton went back a long way. Now this was making sense. Was Fenton keeping his ears open for the police, but also thought he could make some money by warning Ellison? Either way, it looked as though Fenton would have to be dealt with. Serve him right for coming on hard with one of his men. Yes, thought Clarke, this would show him who was boss. If Fenton considered he could handle himself and play the big man, it was up to him to show how it should be done.

*

The gym had closed but Joe Fenton was working late, going through his books. Although he had an accountant, he still liked to know what was going on. It was quite pleasing. He was doing well. He looked around the small crowded room which acted as an office cum storeroom. He might even have to start looking around for bigger and newer premises.

He gave a slight shiver. The old paraffin heater wasn't making much impression on the chill of the evening. He'd get away soon. At one point he thought he heard a noise outside, but decided it was cats going through the bins in the alley. It wouldn't be the first time. With a shrug he turned his attention back to his figures.

*

Harry Fowler stood in the darkness, cursing under his breath at one of his companions for blundering into the waste bins. All was still quiet, with just a dim light showing from the room which he knew was Fenton's office. With gentle pressure he tried the handle to the side door and, much to his astonishment, it opened. That was a stupid mistake for a start, he thought. Fenton must fancy his chances, not to take even simple precautions. Well, this would teach him. He smiled to himself, and motioned one of his companions forward.

*

Fenton was making a final note of his calculations when the door to his office burst open and he saw a man standing in the shadows of the corridor, brandishing what appeared to be a wooden club. He smiled to himself. He'd dealt with situations like this before. As he rose to his feet and was about to make a move, two more men came into the room, both of them also armed in a similar fashion.

This was a different proposition, and Fenton felt a frisson of fear run through him. Nevertheless he feinted a move towards the first assailant, but veered in the opposite direction and seconds later had one man on the floor. However, the blow that caught him on his back sent pain throughout his body, and he found it difficult to move his left arm. He attempted to sidestep away from the next anticipated blow, but another caught him round his knees and he was on the floor. He felt one more, and knew that to survive he must somehow get back on his feet. But he couldn't make his legs move. With the next blow the darkness started to close in. He had to do something, but it was difficult to...

It was an unequal struggle, and after a few moments a crumpled body lay on the floor. Fowler motioned for his two companions to leave and, glancing around, laid a trail of papers from the desk over to the body. He then kicked at a pile of boxes, which spilled over, taking the paraffin heater with them. He waited until he was sure that the fire was well alight. With another quick look at the body, the dark creosoted beams in the low ceiling above and the flames already consuming the paper trail snaking through more close-packed boxes, he left, shutting the door behind him.

*

'It went like clockwork. I waited until the fire brigade came but by then the old building was well alight. They won't find a lot.'

'Good. Payment as usual?'

'Fine.'

Clarke put down the receiver. That had sorted Fenton out, once and for all. This would show his posh friends that he was capable of coming on strong when he had to. Might keep them thinking too!

*

Alex had the office to himself all day, as Dougie was called away on other duties. He had spent the last hour looking through the first reports of the investigations into the death of Lucille Prentice.

None of her colleagues remembered her mentioning any particular client she was nervous about. Johnny Clarke himself queried her whereabouts with them. When interviewed by the investigation team and informed of the situation, he appeared quite distressed, indicating that she was a particular favourite, and made veiled promises that he himself would find out who had done such a thing. He had a cast iron alibi for the whole time frame involved. When questioned about his treatment of any female company, he admitted to sometimes enjoying the more extreme side of that particular form of entertainment, but stressed that it had to be consensual, and he always offered a substantial extra payment. All a bit too coincidental and convenient, Alex thought, but there was little else that could be done.

With a heavy heart, he took over the daily job of trawling through news items and company financial reports of various kinds, making notes. A meeting had been arranged for tomorrow with Francis and he hoped to be able to give him some information. He had also arranged to see Ralph Patterson tonight for a meal and intended questioning him about his company's problems in detail, to confirm whether or not his hunch was correct, that they might fit the pattern they were looking for.

During the day he found himself thinking about Catherine and the events of the last few days. He wondered what she was doing, and had to stop himself from picking up the phone to ring her. He

156

continued to be amazed at the effect she had on him. No one in the past had come close to eliciting the same feelings in him. However, he decided against contacting her. He wanted to keep her as far removed from his daily work involvement as possible. All the same, he couldn't wait for Friday.

His pleasant train of thought was interrupted by Dougie coming into the room.

'I didn't expect to see you today.'

'It turned out to be a bit of a red herring, and I was told that my services were no longer required. I didn't need to be told twice. Picked up the evening paper on my way in.' He pushed it in front of him, pointing to a particular article. 'Another company in trouble, by the look of it.'

Alex glanced at the other man with a frown and then down at the paper on his desk. It had been folded back and an article ringed in pen, but it was a headline at the foot of the page that caught his eye, and his blood ran cold.

'Oh my God!'

Dougie turned, arrested by the look of horror on the face of the other man.

'What's up, Boss? Trouble?'

Alex gazed up at him and there was a tortured look about the grey eyes. 'Dougie, I think I've killed a man.'

CHAPTER 23

Dougie stood for a moment just staring at Alex, who seemed to have lapsed into something of a trance. He took the paper from his unresisting hands and read the article.

A small gym in Lewisham had been burnt out, and the owner found dead in the rubble. It was thought that a paraffin heater had ignited papers in an office cum storeroom and, as the building was old, the fire had spread and engulfed the whole premises, which had later collapsed. The owner was identified as Joe Fenton, an ex professional boxer.

'What do you know about this, Alex?' Dougie used his Christian name in a deliberate effort to break through the dazed look on his partner's face.

Alex slumped back in his chair. 'I knew Joe from the old days before I went in the Army. I've used his gym for years. He is.... was... one of my contacts. Nothing regular, but one or two useful bits. Despite his past connections, he took a hard line with the gangs, wouldn't deal with them and wouldn't tolerate any business done on his premises. Because they knew he could look after himself, everyone accepted it and gave him a wide berth. Dougie, I was there the other day for a session. He told me he had turned one of Clarke's men out of his premises for boasting about a plan Clarke had in store for Ellison, which would stitch him up.'

Dougie looked at the article again. 'If we work on the supposition that this fire wasn't as accidental as they seem to think, it looks as if Clarke took a dim view to him rousting out one of his men, and thought he would deal with him. Knowing that maniac, he wouldn't just stop at giving him a hell of a beating.'

Alex was looking at him again with that funny expression on his face. 'There's more to it, Dougie. I asked Joe if he could warn Ellison about what Clarke was planning. You know what we said about not wanting a gang war to break out on top of everything else happening at the moment. He said he would see what he could do. He must have done something, and that's why Ellison has left town in a hurry. Just suppose that Clarke worked out who warned Ellison, and Joe was paid a visit? Dougie, if I hadn't asked him to get involved, this wouldn't have happened.'

'It could just be a coincidence.'

'Do you believe that?'

Dougie shook his head. 'No, I don't suppose I do. Alex, it's not your fault. Fenton knew the score in dealing with these people. He could have refused to help.'

'That doesn't make me feel any better. What else do they know, Dougie? Do they know about me? I was there, don't forget. You don't suppose for one moment that Franklin's mixed up in all this?'

Dougie stared at Alex in astonishment. 'You think he's giving Clarke orders? Come off it, Alex. I think you're just letting everything rattle you. He isn't going to get involved in things like this fire. It's just Clarke going off like the maniac he is because his game has been spoilt.'

Alex ran a hand over his face. 'Perhaps you're right, Dougie.' He looked at his watch. 'I'd better leave now to see Ralph Patterson. I'll catch up with you tomorrow.'

*

'Well, one thing's for sure, they do a mean steak here, Alex.'

Alex didn't feel much like eating, but he needed information and he forced his mind to concentrate.

'Glad you enjoyed it, Ralph. I've had no complaints.'

They had been able to find a corner table in the restaurant, away from the other diners. Having both declined a dessert, over coffee Alex began his questioning.

'Tell me a bit about your problems, Ralph.'

'I'm gutted about it, Alex. Everything was going so well, and now we're in a spot. I've had regular suppliers since I started and we've all done well out of the contracts I've obtained, even the government ones. As you know, my factory finishes off electrical components, with parts coming in from two other sources. The trouble began about a year ago. Some parts from one particular supplier started to fail on testing, squeezing my deadlines. We complained, of course, and the other firm at first was at a loss to explain the problems.

'They started to investigate at their end, and to begin with there didn't seem to be any reason why there was a problem. Then someone spotted that certain batches had a small fault that for some reason had gone unnoticed by quality control. It meant going through all their machining and technical data from scratch to check everything. Staff were questioned about it and then they discovered that the faulty batches started about the time a particular employee was engaged, working in the engineering department. That person was with them for about nine months and left about six months ago before anything was suspected. As the pre-made parts filtered through to us and we started to notice the problem, it was found that the fault had not reoccurred in the time since he left.

'It seems it wasn't easy at first glance to work out what had gone wrong. It was when the whole matter was looked at in depth that discrepancies in some of the tooling records were found. I gather the person thought to be involved was approached by the company's legal people, but denies any wrongdoing. The directors are wondering whether to call in the police to see if there is any question of deliberate sabotage.

'It appears that, for some reason, the faulty parts were confined to those destined for us on the work sheets. It's a good job we have spot checks in place at our end, which found the problem before they reached the end user. The point is, because I've defaulted on orders, these have been placed elsewhere, and finances are now critical. It's had a knock-on effect down the supply chain, too. I'm trying to do damage limitation by contacting in person all those involved to reinstate confidence and offering initial sweeteners for orders. Something else that's eating into the profits.

'I just hope I can salvage things. I've put too much work into the company to lose it all, through no fault of mine. I can't understand why it looks as if my company is the one to be targeted.'

'It must be a worrying time for you. Is your supplier certain of all these details? The likelihood of it being deliberate action? The problem couldn't have occurred in any other way, like pure carelessness?'

'Not according to their Engineering Manager. He's furious about it. Sees it as a slight on his department. He's adamant that it was deliberate action. Just as a precaution, all my departments have double-checked their technical records. We're starting to get some stuff computerised, which will make it easier. One of my technical guys is on the ball as far as that's concerned. It's the coming thing. I can imagine, with your job, that you'd benefit from a record-keeping point of view.'

'It's coming Ralph, but not fast enough.'

*

It was Wednesday already and Alex was desperate. He looked again at his watch; time was running out. He had left Dougie in charge at the office, covering for him. He hadn't explained the exact need for him to leave far earlier than required for his meeting with Francis; he'd felt embarrassed at the reason.

He was due in Whitehall in two hours, and he had yet to achieve his goal of finding Catherine an engagement ring. It should have been easy, but he was looking for something special. He sensed that she wasn't a flashy, sparkling diamond kind of girl. She needed something more subtle. Everything he had seen so far was, in his view, unsuitable. He would have to make a choice soon though, or give up and buy something for her after they were married. He didn't want to do that. He wanted to follow convention and place his ring on her finger before then.

He turned off the main street into a Victorian arcade of small shops. The second shop was a jewellers. There was nothing much displayed in the window. In truth it looked a bit run down, and without much hope Alex went inside.

An old-fashioned shop bell tinkled as he entered, announcing the presence of a customer – to an empty shop! Just right for a robbery, Alex thought with a grimace. A curtain was pulled aside from a doorway in the rear, and an old man shuffled into view.

'Can I help you, sir?'

Alex regarded the man. Should he say anything?

'You ought to keep your door locked if there is no one in the shop. I'm a police officer, but I could be someone with other ideas.' He tried to be as gentle as he could in deference to the old man's age and obvious frailty.

The man regarded him, then smiled and waved his hands in the general direction of his stock. 'There isn't much to steal, Officer.'

'Nevertheless, an intruder is not to know that, and you could get hurt,' Alex reminded him.

'Yes, I understand you. Thank you for your suggestion. Is that all?'

'Um, in actual fact, I'm not on duty. I came in as a possible customer.'

'Ah, even better!' A smile appeared on the lined face. 'How can I help you?'

'I'm looking for an engagement ring, but I want something special, and to be honest with you I've been searching and I haven't come across anything yet, and I'm running out of time. I know the sort of thing I require but I don't seem to be able to find it.'

'What sort of thing are you looking for? You say you want something special...'

'Yes. I don't want something bright and flashy, and it seems this is the modern style. I know my young lady would prefer something more understated. Everything I've seen so far seems to be wrong.'

The other man regarded Alex for a moment, his clouded eyes showing a spark of interest. 'Tell me about your young lady.'

Alex sensed the question had been asked in all seriousness, so he took a moment to collect his thoughts and then, almost half to himself, murmured, 'She's small and slender with shiny dark brown hair and gorgeous green eyes you feel you can drown in. Her skin is creamy and so soft, I want to touch it all the time. She excites my senses, one minute as a child and the next a woman… and I love her very much.'

Alex had been concentrating on answering the man's question and was unaware that he had revealed so much of his inner feelings.

The old man smiled and nodded, and then went back behind his curtain. For a moment Alex thought he was refusing to serve him and, feeling annoyed, made to leave the shop. Then the curtain swung back again and the old man returned, carrying a small wooden box. He placed it on his counter top and seated himself on a stool. He motioned for Alex to bring up a chair nearer the counter.

'What is your name, sir?'

'Alex. Alexander Hartman.'

'And your young lady?'

'Catherine.'

The old man beamed. 'Perfect. I knew it would happen one day!' He didn't explain his meaning, but went on, 'I am going to show you something which I have kept for many years just in case the right occasion would arise. I think this might be the time.'

With stiff fingers he opened the box and lifted out a leather bag and placed it on his counter top. He undid the cord at the neck of the bag and brought out two smaller bags of soft material that might have been velvet.

'You say your lady has green eyes? As green as this?'

He opened one small bag and drew out a ring and handed it to Alex.

As soon as he saw it Alex knew that this was the one. The rich gold gleamed in the light and the three square-cut emerald stones, set flush in the band, shone with their own muted fire. The ring looked old, and even to Alex's untrained eye it was obvious that it must be very expensive.

'It's perfect, I'll grant you that, but I have a feeling it will be out of my price range.'

He rang a finger over the emeralds and it was like touching her face. With the greatest reluctance he handed it back to the old man, who regarded him with a solemn look.

'I wish to tell you a story and then we can speak of money.' He settled back on his stool. 'My father was a jeweller in St Petersburg before the Revolution. He was beginning to attract commissions from some important people. He made a set of jewellery, hoping that it would sell and make him money. Then the troubles of the Revolution came upon him. He would not have been thought of with favour by the new class because of his association with the nobility. He found a way for himself, my mother and myself to leave Russia through Finland, but had to pay for assistance by using part of the jewellery. He came to England.

'He started again as a jeweller, but his eyesight was failing. He taught me his trade. It was unfortunate that I did not have his gift and I have made a meagre living. I never married, and none of my family is alive any more. Out of the original set of necklace, bracelet, ring and earrings there is now only this ring and... these.' He opened the other bag and took out a matching pair of earrings. 'I have no one to leave them to but somehow I have been reluctant to put them up for sale before now. I think I have found that time. I can see that you love your lady and care about her. I also sense that she is beautiful and will grace the jewels. You will, of course, need a wedding band?'

'Yes, and I think I would like to wear one too.'

'Yes, in my view it should always be so. If you would care to purchase the wedding bands and this ring from me, I am sure we can reach a suitable arrangement.'

'We don't even know if it would fit. Would you be able to judge from this?' Thanking the good fortune which had prompted him to remove a ring from Catherine's jewellery box when he had also taken her papers, Alex handed it over to the old man.

The jeweller went back behind his curtain for a few moments, leaving Alex still worrying about the impending costs.

The final figure agreed made Alex wince, but he knew his purchase was perfect. It was a fair price, and the little man had been generous to him. Catherine would be enchanted not just by the ring but also by the story attached to it.

Before Alex left, with his purchases safe in an inside pocket, the old man smiled at him. 'I will keep the earrings for a while. Perhaps when the first child arrives you will bring your lady back for them?'

Alex smiled at him and just said, 'Perhaps. Thank you very much.' He knew he would have to get a new bank manager before he could afford that.

The old man's voice stopped him as he was leaving the shop. 'Would you care to know my father's name? It was Alexander Fedorovich and my mother's name was Katherine.' He smiled once more and disappeared back behind his curtain.

Alex left the shop feeling as if he had just emerged from a time warp.

CHAPTER 24

When he arrived home much later that evening, Alex was almost punch drunk with the events of the day. After the strange meeting with the old jeweller, he had found it difficult to drag his mind back to his meeting with Francis. Over the course of two hours they discussed the possible new leads uncovered by Alex and Dougie, and Francis himself filled in some information. He seemed interested in the manufacturing problems Alex had unearthed, and the significance of the company being involved in government contracts was not lost on either of them.

Once again, Alex refrained from telling Francis about his decision to inform Dougie of everything they were supposed to be doing, and why. He understood the directive that he shouldn't do so, but couldn't for the life of him work out a way of conducting this investigation without making Dougie aware of all the circumstances. He trusted his colleague to keep his confidence, and felt that Dougie in turn respected the trust that Alex had put in him. This was why, in his view, they worked so well together.

Alex had also decided not to mention to Francis anything about his forthcoming marriage. Once the formalities were over, he would think again about telling him, but not before.

On returning to the office he brought Dougie up to date with the discussions. On the spur of the moment he decided to tell Dougie his other news.

'What the hell…!'

Alex was amused to see his startled reaction.

'Well, you're a fast worker and no mistake, but I couldn't be more pleased. I can see the difference in you. I was beginning to get a bit concerned before, I must say. Is that little girl happy too?'

'She seems very happy, Dougie, and I intend to do all I can to keep her that way. It was quite a shock, I must say, when Sarah told me about her moving out of Richmond. Part of me wonders if that old bastard is up to something. Still, I'm not going to dwell on that at the moment.'

'I'll make sure I keep you out of the loop from Friday until Monday morning, Boss.'

'It would have to be a national emergency to drag me back here, Dougie!'

Alex then rang Sarah's flat. It was Catherine who answered, and her obvious delight at hearing from him warmed his heart.

'I'm coming over to see you in a little while, but I can't stay, I'm afraid. Can you meet me downstairs when I arrive? We can go for a walk, perhaps. If you have any more of your possessions to be transported I can take some if you bring them down with you.'

Catherine agreed, and when later he parked outside the flat, raced out to meet him carrying a couple of bags. He put them away in the Porsche and, enjoying the pleasure of being with her again, took her arm and suggested they walk up to the small garden square at the end of the road. He sat her down on one of the benches and held her hands in his.

'I want to tell you something.' He then proceeded to repeat the tale the little jeweller had told him that afternoon. He could see her fascination building as he spoke, and knew for certain that he had done the right thing. As he told her the name of the St Petersburg jeweller and his wife and that two pieces of the set remained, he brought out from his pocket the small velvet bag and placed it in her hands. 'There is one piece left now, as the other is here, for you, with all my love, my darling.'

He watched Catherine undo the drawstring at the neck of the bag and draw out the small parcel of tissue paper. She unwrapped it and gazed down at the ring gleaming in her hands. She looked up at him and the look of pure pleasure and love in her eyes was all he needed. He removed the ring from its tissue paper bed and, holding his breath, he took her left hand in his and placed it on her finger. The fit was perfect, and it looked perfect. Alex brought her hand up to his mouth and kissed the ring on her finger.

He knew she was crying, but he also knew that they were tears of happiness.

'Don't cry my love. We'll soon be together.'

'Oh Alex, I'm so happy. It's a beautiful ring. However did you find something so special?'

He laughed down at her. 'Oh, it took all my training as a police officer to track it down.'

He held her and they kissed, but he knew that he would have to leave her now.

Back at his car, he once again held her close. 'I'll see you and Sarah at Chelsea Registry Office at twelve o'clock on Friday. If you don't turn up I'll have the whole of the Met Police out looking for you.'

'I'll be there, Alex. I promise.'

Alex had one more errand to do that evening. He parked the Porsche at the rear entrance to a restaurant near Chelsea Bridge, and waited until it closed. After everyone seemed to have left a figure emerged, saw the car and came over to him. The man looked around for a moment, then climbed in beside Alex, who drove off.

'Sorry, Alfredo, to meet you like this, but I wanted to see you. I'm a bit pushed for time to arrange our usual meeting place. At least you'll arrive home in style.'

'I'm sure it will be alright, Mr Hartman.'

'How's Mrs A?'

Alfredo was one of Alex's longest-serving informers. He was a freelance waiter, and by moving around all the city's eating places he was well placed for seeing who met who.

'She's doing well, thank you. What can I do for you?'

'Can you keep an extra eye on what a couple of the gangland bosses are doing and who they might be meeting? If you hear of anything, can you let me know?'

'What, you mean the likes of Ellison and Clarke?'

'That's the ones, Alfredo.'

'I don't like to get too close to those sort of people, Mr Hartman. They're bad news.'

'I appreciate that, Alfredo. Don't try to be clever about it and don't get yourself in trouble; but if you can, just give me a nod, OK?'

'I'll think about it, Mr Hartman.'

'Good man.'

Alex dropped him off a street away from his home and then, with a thankful sigh, set off for Kennington.

*

Catherine woke with a start. She thought something had disturbed her, but could hear nothing. Looking at her bedside clock, it said just after nine a.m. With a shriek she leapt out of bed. She had remembered now: this was her wedding day, and she was getting married in three hours time!

She rushed through into the lounge and heard a noise from the kitchen. She found Sarah filling a glass vase with water.

'Sarah, why didn't you wake me sooner? It's nine o'clock!'

'I'm aware of that,' Sarah seemed much too calm for Catherine's satisfaction. 'I thought I'd let you sleep. There's plenty of time, after all. I'm sure you don't need three hours to dress.'

'No... perhaps you're right,' Catherine subsided onto a chair at the kitchen table. 'I just got in a panic, that's all.'

'Right, well, now you're up, you can sit there and have your breakfast.'

'Oh Sarah, I don't think I could eat a thing.'

'Well, I'm sorry, but you're going to. I don't want you fainting

169

away at the appropriate moment in the formalities. Now get yourself some cereal and I'll make some toast when I've done this.' She turned back to the sink.

'Have you been given some flowers?'

'I haven't, poppet, but you have. Go and look in the lounge.'

Catherine went into the other room. Lying on the dining table was a large bunch of long-stemmed cream roses.

She called to Sarah. 'Where have they come from? There isn't a note.'

Sarah came in, carrying the vase. 'Alex brought them just now.' She grinned at her friend's expression. 'He went out to the Flower Market at the crack of dawn this morning to get them. He prayed you wouldn't answer the door when he rang the bell.'

'Alex has been here, this morning? Why didn't you wake me up?'

'Because it's bad luck for the groom to see the bride on her wedding day before the ceremony. He just thought you might like them. They're a beautiful colour.'

Catherine ran her finger over one of the creamy heads and was overcome with emotion that Alex should have thought of her in this way.

Sarah saw the emotion but wanted no tears this morning. She put the roses in the vase and went back into the kitchen, returning with some aluminium cooking foil.

'Just a suggestion, but I wondered if we shortened some of the stems we could wrap several in some of this and tie it up with something pretty, and you will have a bouquet. What do you think?'

'I think that would be marvellous, Sarah. What a good idea. I'll look out some ribbon.'

'Come and eat your breakfast first.'

Later, dressing with immense care, Catherine realised that she felt quite calm. She was about to marry the man she loved, and who, she was sure, loved her. She had chosen a soft cream georgette dress she had seldom worn, but knew fitted her well. It had pintuck pleats down the front of the bodice and on the short sleeves. There were pale green buttons on the bodice, matching the thin belt around the waist. The skirt was smooth and swirled around her knees. She had even found a pair of pale kid sandals and a bag. It was lucky she had kept them back from her recent removal of belongings to Alex's flat. As her mind began to register the idea that in a short while she would be living there alone with him, as man and wife, she felt less calm and butterflies began to form in her stomach.

Sarah came into the bedroom, smart in a pale blue suit, the colour matching her eyes.

'How are you doing? We've got about twenty minutes before the taxi comes. Oh, and I mustn't forget to keep hold of your make-up case until later.'

'I'll be ready.' Catherine swept her hair up into a loose coil secured on either side with green and gold trimmed combs. She then fastened plain gold studs to her ears and placed her engagement ring back on her finger.

She looked up at Sarah. 'What do you think?'

'Stand up and let me have a look at you.'

Catherine did so, and Sarah thought she had never seen her friend look more beautiful. The understated cream emphasised the glow of her skin and the various points of green echoed the shining eyes.

'You look beautiful. Alex is going to be bowled over.'

'I hope so,' Catherine whispered, the butterflies inside her even worse.

The taxi was on time and it was just a short ride to the Registry Office. Waiting outside was Jerry, resplendent in a smart navy suit, his wavy light brown hair almost tamed.

'Well, I'm glad you've arrived.'

'Why?' said Sarah looking at her watch. 'We're not late. If anything, we're ahead of schedule.'

'I have one nervous bridegroom in there. If we don't get this thing under way soon I'll be administering to a coronary. Mark you,' he looked Catherine up and down, 'when he sees you he might have one. You look ravishing!'

'Please take me to him, Jerry.' Catherine's quiet voice was evidence of the nervous tension inside her.

Jerry took them to a small anteroom where they found Alex pacing up and down, his dark good looks accentuated by a charcoal grey suit and cream silk tie. Catherine walked towards him and the look she saw in his eyes was everything she had hoped for. He said nothing at all, but he didn't need to, she thought. He just took her hands and kissed them, taking note, she was sure, of her small bouquet.

'Thank you so much for the flowers, Alex. It was a wonderful thought. Do you like what we've done?'

He just nodded and for one moment Catherine thought she detected a sheen of moisture in his eyes.

The Registrar's assistant came over then, and asked Catherine to accompany him for some final formalities. Alex squeezed her hand and let her go.

Catherine tried to concentrate on the questions being asked, but found it very difficult. What the Registrar must have thought, she had no idea. Then it was done and she was allowed to return to her party. She hovered in the doorway for a moment, looking over at Alex standing talking to her friends. With her nervousness growing, she realised that she knew very little about this man, and in a moment she would be pledging her life to him. She comforted herself by once again remembering that she loved him, and he had seemed so sincere in his love for her. That had to be enough for now. Then, any doubts she had were swept aside as, sensing her gaze, Alex turned his head and looked at her with such wondrous love in his eyes that her fears melted away. He held out his hand to her, and without any further hesitation she crossed to his side.

They were called through to start the ceremony, but first Catherine whispered to Alex, 'Please take my ring and keep it until later.' He looked at her for a moment and then took off the engagement ring and placed it in his inside pocket. 'Near to my heart,' he whispered back to her as they took their seats.

The exchange of vows seemed almost a blur to Catherine apart from Alex's strong hands holding her own. She was filled with emotion when he slipped the wedding band on her finger and more so when she realised that he also would wear a ring.

When the Registrar pronounced the ceremony complete, Alex reached into his pocket for her engagement ring, placed it back on her finger, and brought her hand up to his lips and kissed the rings. 'Together for always,' he whispered.

Sarah was close enough to hear the whispered exchange, and was overcome with emotion. She reached for Jerry's hand and he twined his fingers through hers and murmured, 'It will soon be our turn, my love.'

CHAPTER 25

After the final formalities were dealt with, but before leaving the Registry Office premises, Sarah produced a camera from her bag and insisted that a record should be made of the occasion. Jerry proceeded to shepherd his rather embarrassed subjects into a small flower-filled corner, and snapped away.

Outside in the warm May sunshine, Alex turned to Jerry. 'I know you're tight for time but can we at least grab a cup of coffee together before you go?'

After consulting his watch and receiving a nod from Sarah, Jerry grinned and said he would be delighted to help escort such beautiful ladies. Alex walked them to a small Italian coffee house nearby, his arm through Catherine's. She seemed almost in a daze.

When they were seated, Alex took her hand and squeezed it. 'Are you alright, my love? You're quiet.'

She looked at him and smiled. 'I'm sure I'm in a dream and I'll wake up and find all this isn't real.'

Alex grinned at her. 'Well, if you do, just tell me and we can do it all again! I do have a piece of paper to prove it to you, though.'

Jerry queried, 'I suppose you two will be jetting off somewhere exotic for a honeymoon?'

Alex took Catherine's hand again. 'I'm afraid circumstances don't permit at the moment, but you never know in the future. However, if my wife agrees I might have a surprise planned for her.'

Catherine looked at him with a question in her eyes, but he just smiled and said nothing more.

Sarah was relieved that Jerry didn't make any inappropriate comment as to the nature of the surprise planned, and she decided it might be as well to remove him from the situation before he did. 'I think it's time we were going, Jerry.' She looked at her watch and nudged his ankle under the table.

Taking his cue, Jerry stood up. 'Yes, indeed. No doubt my adoring public is awaiting my healing touch.'

'Do you want a lift anywhere, Sarah? I don't have my car but we could share a taxi.'

'Thank you, Alex, but I'll go with Jerry back to Brompton and then either walk home or do some shopping. Thanks for the offer.'

Before she climbed into the hailed taxi, Sarah handed Catherine's small make-up case to her and then whispered, 'Enjoy yourself!' With a quick hug for both of them, she waved goodbye.

For a moment Catherine felt lost and embarrassed about what to do next. As always, Alex was sensitive to her mood. With his arm around her slim shoulders he hailed another taxi and murmured to her, 'I think I would like to take my wife home, if she has no objection.'

Catherine was intrigued to see where Alex lived, and gazed with interest at the large double-fronted Victorian villa.

'My flat's on the first floor. The landlord, Jake Turner, lives in one of the ground-floor flats. He's an anglicised American. A bit brash, but I get on with him well enough.'

'Does he know about you getting married?'

'Oh yes. I've suffered nothing but gentle verbal abuse since then. Jake's the product of two failed marriages!'

They made their way up to the first floor and Alex took out his key and opened the door.

'I suppose you want me to carry you over the threshold.' The resigned tone belied the amusement in his eyes.

'Of course,' Catherine twinkled back at him and felt herself swung up into strong arms.

He set her on her feet in the lounge. She put down her make-up case, bag and flowers on a small table.

'Have a look around and see what you think.'

She knew he was watching her as she moved in and out of the rooms. She liked what she saw. Nothing like as big as Sarah's, but the rooms had nice proportions. Everywhere was spotless. Alex must be very good at looking after himself, she thought. She must keep up his standard.

When she came to what was the main bedroom she hesitated for a moment before pushing open the door and walking in. Her eyes were drawn to the bed. The pale green spread complemented the basic cream colour scheme and made the room feel light and airy. For a moment she felt a little short of breath as visions came into her mind, and she made herself walk over to the window. It looked out on to the garden at the rear and would get the morning sun.

The thought came to her that now she was Alex's wife, might he act in any different way towards her? From the start she had always been touched and soothed by his gentle consideration for her in their love-making, but would this change?

She turned back to the room and saw, lying on the bed, a single cream rose of the sort Alex had brought her this morning. Catherine picked it up and touched the soft petals. She now knew it would be alright. Just a small thoughtful gesture like that was typical of the man she had come to love. Placing the rose back on the bed she went into the lounge where he was waiting. He hadn't moved. She walked over to him and, reaching up, kissed him on the cheek.

'I like your home, Alex.'

'I'm glad. It's yours now, too. You can change anything you like. I've hung up some of your clothes and you can sort out the rest when you like.'

'Thank you for doing that when you're so busy. Thank you also for the rose. It was a kind thought. You're very good to me. Was this the surprise you mentioned?'

'Lord no, I should be able to do better than that, my dear.' He smiled down at her and placed his hands on her waist, but said nothing further.

She gave him a playful punch on his chest. 'Don't be so secretive. Are you going to tell me or not?'

'In a moment. I have something else on my mind.'

He bent his head and kissed her mouth for the first time that day. As always it felt so good to have his arms around her and she relaxed against him. It was a long while before he released her but kept his hands on her waist.

'Would you like to go away for the weekend? Some people I know run a small bed and breakfast in Sunbury near the Thames. They would be pleased to see us. We can leave later this afternoon and come home on Sunday night.'

'That would be nice, Alex, but I don't mind anything at all as long as we're together.' She nestled her head against him, soaking up his warmth.

'I'll take that as a "Yes" then, shall I?' he murmured against her hair. 'Of course we have an hour or two yet before we need to leave and I have …an idea to pass the time.'

Catherine smiled to herself, guessing his meaning, but she didn't want to make any mistakes, however, by saying anything.

Alex turned her face up to him and the look in his grey eyes, now almost black, told her everything.

'I would very much like to take my new wife to my bed if she had no objection.'

'I don't think she would mind,' was all she could think of to say in reply.

She found herself gathered up into his arms again and carried into the bedroom. He laid her down on the bed and for several moments just sat, looking at her.

'I've waited so long to have you here. I can't tell you how many nights I've lain in this bed during all those weeks since I've known you, wishing you were here with me.'

There was no doubting the sincerity of his words.

177

'I'm here for you now,' Catherine whispered.

With great care he began removing her clothes. The undoing of the small buttons on the front of her dress seemed to take a long time to achieve, and she could feel the familiar excitement mounting as her breathing became shallow and uneven.

'You look so beautiful today, it seems a pity to spoil it all.' His words were spoken into her throat.

She stroked one hand through his dark hair, down the side of his face to his mouth. He kissed her fingers and then transferred his attention to her breasts.

As usual, time dissolved into a haze of pleasure and sensation.

*

The sound of Alex's voice woke her, and for a moment she wondered where she was.

'Catherine, my love, wake up. If we're going to go away we'll have to leave in a little while.'

As her senses returned, she found him sitting on the bed beside her. He had changed his clothes and she realised she had never seen him dress in such a casual fashion.

'I have no desire to prise you out of my bed, you know. If you would rather we stayed here, it would be alright. The trial run seemed to go OK!'

Pretending to be put out by his words, she threw back the covers and slid out of bed. 'Just for that remark, I'm getting up and we will go away. How much time do I have?'

'There's no set time, but say forty-five minutes?' Alex turned away with a grin on his face. 'Shall I make you a coffee as a peace-making gesture?'

During the drive to Sunbury, Alex told her about Luigi and Maria. Catherine picked up from his words that he had a great affection for the couple.

'Do they know you're bringing me?'

'I've said I will have a lady with me, but I didn't say anything else, so we'll surprise them!'

She began to feel apprehensive about the forthcoming introductions, and noticed Alex glancing at her. As usual, he sensed her unease.

'My sweet, I'm certain they're going to love you.'

Catherine hoped so, but by the time they arrived at their destination she was feeling rather nervous.

Their arrival had been observed, and they were met in the entrance hall by a man in his fifties, his face wreathed in smiles. Catherine watched as the two men embraced, and then Alex took her arm and brought her forward.

'Luigi, I'd like you to meet someone. This is Catherine, my wife. We were married earlier today.'

She had already felt the dark eyes studying her, and hoped that she looked smart enough in her cream blouse and green trousers.

'Married!' Luigi looked at her again. 'Alex, you are telling me the truth?'

'Catherine and I were married at twelve o'clock today at Chelsea Registry Office. I thought she might like some pampering for a day or two and I could think of nowhere better than here. And I was proud to bring my wife to show you. I warn you, she speaks Italian!'

Luigi studied Catherine anew, then, making a slight bow, he spoke in Italian. 'This is a pleasant surprise. Welcome to our home Catherine. Alex has found himself a beautiful bride.'

He took her hand and placed a kiss on it and then looked up with a mischievous smile. 'We had better give Mama a shock also!'

He turned and called over his shoulder, 'Mama, Mama, hurry! I have a surprise for you.'

A bustling figure with apron and floury hands burst into the hall. 'What is the urgency Papa! I'm busy baking. I'll see Alessandro in a moment.'

However, she held her arms wide and was enveloped in Alex's embrace. 'It's good to see you again.'

Bright dark eyes flickered between Catherine, Alex, and then to her husband.

'Mama, this is Catherine. Alessandro's new wife.'

'Wife!' She looked again at her husband. 'But… Luigi?'

'It is true, Mama,' he said, 'they were married today. She speaks Italian too.'

He watched in amusement as his wife looked from one to the other in total amazement, lost for words. With a chuckle he added, 'That must be the first time in a long while that Mama has had nothing to say!'

She retaliated by smacking his arm, resulting in a cloud of flour drifting down to the carpet.

'Now look what you have made me do. Make yourself useful and show Alessandro and his wife to their room while I clean this up.' She smiled at Catherine. 'We will talk much together later on.'

Luigi, beaming in approval, turned away to lead them upstairs. 'Mama has put you on the top floor, Alex, so you will be on your own.'

The self-contained suite, constructed in the roof area, was light and airy, with a good view over the large garden and through trees to the river beyond.

Luigi showed them where everything was and then turned to leave, looking back at Alex with a raised eyebrow, 'Settle in, and I will see you downstairs for a drink?'

Alex nodded, then crossed over to the window where Catherine was standing looking at the view. He wrapped his arms around her and pulled her close. 'You see, I told you they'd love you. Take a minute to unpack by yourself, and join us when you're ready.'

Alex bounded down the stairs, whistling under his breath.

'I'm here in the back,' called Luigi from the patio area. 'I have a drink ready for you.'

Alex joined him at the large table. 'Thanks, Luigi. Do you have water or soda or something to put in it? I've had enough of strong drink for the moment.'

'That's a first, isn't it?' chuckled Luigi, passing over a jug of water. 'I thought you were a master at heavy drinking. Has your new wife forbidden it?'

'No she hasn't, Luigi. Its more that the last month or so has been a bit rough and I've done all the drinking I want for quite some time.

I only trained myself to do it in the first place because it comes in handy. Its amazing what someone will tell you over a drink.'

Alex drowned his whisky with water, making Luigi wince at the sacrilege. He regarded the younger man, his face now serious.

'Well, you have your drink, so perhaps you would like to talk some. Are you sure about this, Alex? She seems very young.'

Alex looked at him, his gaze steady. 'I've never been more sure of anything in my life, Luigi. I know she seems young for her age, and it worried me too at first, but it's because of... circumstances... she's been through. And given time, when she finds her feet, she'll be a force to be reckoned with. Then I'll be in real trouble.' His grin was rueful.

Luigi still didn't look too convinced. 'What do you mean by "circumstances"? Am I to take it that Catherine was the dilemma you were speaking about a while ago? I think I need to know the whole story, my boy.'

CHAPTER 26

Luigi watched as the other man settled back in his chair, making an obvious attempt to marshal his thoughts. Then they both heard the sound of a door closing, and Catherine came out into the sunshine. He watched with interest as Alex stood up and slid his arm around her waist. The young woman looked up at him and their light kiss was natural and spontaneous. The whole effect was quite charming. He realised he had never seen Alex so tender in his actions before.

'Maria is in the kitchen preparing dinner,' he said. 'You are welcome to visit her there, or you can stay and charm us with your presence.' He smiled at Catherine and patted the chair next to him.

'It doesn't seem fair for Maria to be working while I'm sitting about. I would like to go and see her if that's alright.'

'Catherine!' Alex's tone was sharp. 'I brought you here for a rest, not to work preparing meals.'

Luigi was amused to see the young woman turn to this very masculine male and, in a firm voice, reply, 'I would find it very impolite to leave Maria preparing the meal on her own with me sitting out here like royalty. I will, however, make sure not to contravene your wishes by assisting in any way.' With great dignity, she turned and left them.

Luigi smiled into his drink and waited. Alex sighed and then chuckled, 'You see, Luigi, you don't have to worry about her. It's me you need to pity!'

'Tell me about her.'

Accepting that Luigi wasn't going to let up, Alex began relating what he knew of Catherine's life. When he began to describe his own involvement, the emotion he was feeling was very evident to the man sitting opposite him, and very revealing.

'From what you have told me, Catherine has been through some unfortunate experiences which no woman should have to. I would suggest that this uncle has failed in his duty towards her, for his own purposes. You might think that he now has no control over her, but I can't help feeling, Alex, that you should still be careful of him. If this man has been making plans involving Catherine for several years, he will not be too pleased to have all his time and effort come to nothing.'

Alex had tried to ignore his own worries on this score, but to have them realised by another was something else, and caused him even greater concern. What would Luigi say if he knew of his ongoing investigations into Lionel Franklin? At the end of the day, though, Alex had come to the conclusion that other than the administration of her parents' finances, the man had no legal hold over Catherine. And what could he do, anyway? However, it was one of the reasons why he had wanted to make Catherine his wife as soon as possible.

'I will do all I can to protect Catherine,' he stated.

'I am sure you will, but look to yourself also; I feel this man could be dangerous.'

Startled by the remark, Alex looked over at Luigi and could see the seriousness in the older man's face.

He was about to reply when Maria bustled in to prepare the table, and Catherine came back and sat down.

Alex took one of her hands in his. 'Did you enjoy yourself? Does Maria know all my secrets now?'

Catherine smiled at him. 'As I don't know any myself, how can I pass them on?' She leant closer to him, still smiling. 'Do you have any secrets Alex?'

She turned her head away to smile at Luigi before the agonised expression crossed her husband's face. Luigi was watching the exchange, and when he picked up Alex's expression his worries increased.

Much later, after a pleasant evening, Alex looked at his watch and suggested to Catherine that it was time for bed. With a shy smile, Catherine wished Luigi and Maria goodnight, and took her husband's outstretched hand.

Alone in their room, Alex folded Catherine into his arms, then picked her up and placed her with great care on the bed. Without putting on any lights he removed their clothes and lay with her. Soft moonlight caressed her body, turning the creamy skin to ivory, and for long moments he let his eyes move over her. Then his lips and hands retraced that path, and soon their emotions carried them both away to their special place of pleasure, where no worries existed.

*

The light knock on the door woke them both. Alex looked at his watch. It was just after nine o'clock.

'Alex? Who is it?' Catherine was struggling to extricate herself from his arms, and out of bed. 'We mustn't be… like this!'

He looked down into her shocked face with amusement. 'It's Mama with some breakfast, no doubt. And why on earth shouldn't she find us in bed together? We are married.'

'I know, but…' Catherine was still struggling to free herself. 'I don't have anything on. Let me go to the bathroom, please.'

'I don't have anything on either, and you're going nowhere.' He pinned her down in the bed and called out 'Come in, Mama', trying hard not to laugh.

Maria appeared with a loaded tray which she placed on a small table. 'I thought you might be hungry.'

She then turned and observed what was happening. Catherine was trying to wriggle deeper under the covers which Alex seemed intent upon removing. There was a broad grin on his face, and even Maria had to admire the subtle play of muscle across his back and arms.

'Alex, please, don't be a beast. Let me go.'

'If I let you go, the covers come too!' Alex laughed back.

'No, Alex, please!'

'What's it to be then, to be found in bed, in my arms, in a state of undress, or to bare all?'

'I hate you!'

'No you don't, at all.'

He kissed her, then wrapping the covers up round her chin he turned his smiling face to Maria who had been regarding the scene with both amusement and consternation.

'My wife is still a little shy about some things, Mama.'

'You shouldn't tease her, Alex.'

'Don't worry, I'll make it up to her later, if she's good.' He received a blow around the head from a pillow for that remark.

Laughing with delight, Maria left the room. It was good to see them enjoying life together. She knew somehow that her breakfast would be cold by the time it was needed, if at all.

It was well after twelve o'clock when Alex came into the kitchen with the empty tray. Even though the toast and coffee had gone cold, he and Catherine had found they were hungry, and consumed it all.

'Thank you for the thought, Mama. It was kind of you.'

Dark eyes twinkled back at him. 'I hope you behaved yourself after I left. You're far too big a dose of manliness at times for anyone to cope with.'

'Oh, I didn't hear any complaints.' He laughed as he dodged out of the way of a well-aimed slap with a teacloth. 'You can ask my bride when she comes down, if you like. Where is Luigi?'

'He is out in the garden somewhere. I'm just starting lunch, so if you find him you can tell him.'

Alex wandered outside into the sunlight and down the steps into the garden. He felt a great peace and contentment within himself, and knew the reason for it. Being with Catherine was everything he had hoped for, and more. The sweet and innocent pleasure she had given him was, for the moment, keeping at bay the darker thoughts of his working life. He must do all he could to try to keep her innocence untainted by the other world he knew.

He found Luigi in the greenhouse. 'Mama says she is just preparing lunch.'

Luigi looked up and took in the carefree smile and relaxed manner of the younger man. 'I will be there at any moment Alex. You have had a good sleep?' His smile was broad.

Alex answered with his own smile, knowing full well that his leg was being pulled. 'Yes, marvellous, thank you. I needed the rest.'

'I hear you were having fun earlier at Catherine's expense.'

Luigi was interested to see a slight flush in Alex's complexion. 'I think I have given her cause to forgive me by now, Papa.'

Luigi turned with him to walk back to the house. 'Do you talk together in a serious way about your lives? Have you spoken about your career, a home, children? You know about Catherine's earlier life, but have you spoken to her about your own?'

Alex stopped walking, and Luigi turned to face him.

'What are you getting at, Luigi?' The sharpness of the tone betrayed a sudden flash of annoyance.

Luigi considered him for a moment. 'Is Catherine aware of the trouble in your younger days, and what you are now seeking out of life? Is it what she wants as well? My boy, by your own admission you have moved fast in your association. You appear to be delighted with one another and your marriage is very new and exciting... but not all things can be decided in a satisfactory way in bed.

'Since you have been here I have observed your caring attitude towards Catherine. I will just say to you, Alex, that as much as you care for Catherine you must let her grow with her own thoughts as an individual person. Do you understand what I am trying to say, my boy? As you are older and more experienced than she, it is you who must take the lead, no matter how else you may feel. I have said all this before to Vincenzo. It was up to him whether he listened to his father's advice, and you have the same option, but I feel it is my duty to have brought it up with you.' His smile was sheepish. 'Well now, boy, my sermon is over and I think we could do with our lunch, eh?'

He sauntered off up towards the house, leaving Alex thinking hard. At first when Luigi had started speaking he was angry, then he realised with honesty that Luigi was right. Come Monday morning their married life would start for real and they had to have some idea of where they were going in the future. He also acknowledged the truth that Catherine was ignorant of his life up to now. He owed her the honesty of telling her about himself, however reluctant he was to do so. He had one secret which she must not know, but he ought to make sure that she was aware of the rest.

He hurried to catch up with Luigi. 'I understand what you're trying to say Luigi. I'll make sure we have time for a talk together.'

Luigi said nothing, but patted him on the back.

*

After an afternoon stroll, they arrived back in time for dinner. As there was no one around when they returned, Catherine suggested they ought to change for dinner. She had brought one dress with her and she might as well wear it.

Alex was in the bathroom. She sat on the stool in front of the dressing table, wrapped in a bath towel, and regarded herself in the mirror. Why did she still feel so shy when they were in the bedroom together? It wasn't as if she was unaware of what he looked like! He had a nice body, and she loved the feel of it when they were making love. She came to the conclusion that it must be because, in some ways, he was still a stranger to her. The short time since Alex had come back into her life had gone by in a daze, but from now on, she realised, it would be the real thing. From Monday morning the normal routine of their life would start.

What did Alex want from her? How much did he want her to do around the flat? She felt it was still very much his, and there were some things he might prefer to do himself. Did he want her to find a job and help share the expenses? What about a family? This, she knew, would give her more happiness than anything else.

The magic of these last few days would always be in her memory, but real life was very different and could create its own problems. She needed to speak with him about it all.

He came back into the bedroom, and catching sight of his almost naked body in the mirror, Catherine found herself averting her eyes. There was no logical reason for her to behave like this, she told herself, and she tried to carry on dealing with her hair and face, but she couldn't resist the occasional glance.

Now dressed in navy trousers and white shirt, Alex came and sat on the end of the bed. She could see him watching her in the mirror.

'Did you enjoy it?' There was laughter in his voice and eyes.

'Enjoy what?' Catherine didn't understand the joke.

'Watching me get dressed. I saw you, looking at me in the mirror.' His laughter was bubbling just under the surface now.

'I was doing no such thing!' Catherine denied, colour flooding into her face.

'You're quite within your rights, you know. It doesn't always have to work one way.'

He reached out and ran a finger over one bare shoulder. Despite herself, Catherine felt a tremor run through her at his touch. Why did he always have this effect on her senses, and achieve the desired reaction? She felt annoyed at herself for being so transparent with her feelings, and even more annoyed at him for teasing her.

She stood up and reached for her dress. 'I'm putting my dress on now and I don't care if you look or not.' She wanted to be cool and calm, but she knew she sounded like a petulant child. She threw off the towel and pulled on the green jersey dress.

'I'll zip you up, my love. I need to get some experience of doing it this way round.'

There was still laughter in his voice as he accomplished his task. She felt his fingers against her skin. He pushed aside the loose hair from her neck and placed his mouth against the pulse beating there.

'Remind me to practice the reverse procedure later tonight.' He turned her round to face him, and she knew he noted the high colour she could feel in her cheeks. 'I'm going to kiss you, and then you can repair your lipstick, and then we'd better go down.'

He touched her mouth with the briefest of kisses and, despite her annoyance at him, it left her wanting more. She saw him watching her with a slight, knowing smile, and knew that he guessed her feelings, but for some reason he was denying her. Holding her emotions in check, she said nothing, but did as he requested. Underneath, her body was a whirl of sensations and anticipation. Why was there always this instant, almost electric, physical reaction to each other? She sighed. It was confusing, and at times unsettling. She didn't understand this sort of game.

CHAPTER 27

Alex took her hand as they came out onto the terrace. Catherine was glad they had changed their clothes, as Maria had dressed the table with candles and flowers. Luigi was dealing with a bottle of wine.

'Ah, there you are. I was just going to call you. I will tell Mama we are ready to eat.'

He offered them both a glass of white wine and looked at Catherine's slim figure, draped in soft folds of green jersey, held close to her husband's side.

He spoke to her in Italian. 'You are a very beautiful woman, my dear,' and in a gallant gesture raised his glass to her, then disappeared back into the kitchen.

Throughout the meal Catherine was aware of Alex watching her, and turning to him on one occasion she encountered the same inner laughter in the depths of his grey eyes as had been evident when they were changing earlier. He seemed intent on keeping her senses at fever pitch, and she was very conscious of him beside her, although she tried hard to ignore him. It was beginning to agitate her. Tonight, for some devilish reason, he seemed determined to generate a response in her. She must try to build some sort of wall as a foil against him, or, as always, she would just give in and allow herself to be taken into his arms, and yet again he would win this game he was playing. However, the tension was beginning to build inside her and she was finding it difficult not to say something to him.

In the end it was Maria who provided the catalyst by asking Catherine, 'What will you do all day when Alex is at work, Catherine?'

Before Catherine could make a considered reply, Alex answered for her. 'Catherine must realise that now we have had some fun together, I have other responsibilities which will take up a lot of my time. She must be prepared for this. Other wives, I am sure, have the same problem. We'll find something for her to do, no doubt.' He flashed what she considered to be a patronising and superior grin in her direction.

Her emotions boiled over. She leapt to her feet and swung round on him, green eyes blazing. 'How dare you presume to know what I think! I'm quite capable of answering questions that are put to me. I'm not an idiot. I do manage to think about things myself, you know. I am well aware of the changes that will have to happen, and I'm sure I will be adult enough to deal with them. You will have to make up your mind what you want, Alex. You like me to be a woman enough in your bed, and when you feel the need to play with me, as you have been doing all evening. On the other hand, you seem to consider I'm too much of a child to be able to have an adult conversation.'

Alex had by this time stood up and reached out for her.

'Don't you dare touch me!' Catherine was beside herself now with all sorts of emotions. 'I'm not prepared to be your plaything any longer.'

She turned and ran off down into the garden, ignoring Alex's urgent call.

There was silence for a moment after Catherine had left, and then Alex made to follow her.

'Sit down, Alex!' Luigi's voice was sharp. 'Let her be, she needs to have time alone.'

'I must go to her Luigi. I never meant to upset her so.'

'No doubt you didn't, but it's happened. What will you do when you find her? You will take her in your arms, and even if she fights you at first, you will be stronger than she is. You will kiss her until the anger leaves her. Nothing will be resolved, as I said earlier today. It's obvious that Catherine has been worrying about the situation herself. We will leave her for a moment or two longer, and then I will go and find her. What did she mean about you playing with her tonight?'

Alex ran a hand through his hair. 'I don't know, Luigi. I thought there was a playful mood between the two of us, but perhaps I came on too heavy. I forget that she's still inexperienced in banter of a... particular kind. She's let it unnerve her, perhaps.'

Maria had been silent, watching the events unfold, but now reached over and took Alex's hand. 'I'm so sorry, Alex. I never thought this would happen. I wish I hadn't said anything now.'

Alex squeezed her hand. 'Don't worry, Mama. Don't blame yourself. I'll sort it out.'

Luigi shot his wife a wry smile. 'My dear, if it's any consolation, I was about to make the same sort of comment.' He finished the rest of his wine and stood up. 'I'll now go and find your little wife, Alex.'

Catherine was leaning against the trunk of an old apple tree when she heard someone coming, and guessed it was Luigi. If it had been Alex, she would have heard nothing until his arms were round her. She could feel the tears coming now as she thought about her words to him. What had made her talk to him in that way?

'Catherine?'

She walked out from under the tree and confronted the older man. 'I must apologise to you and Maria for my bad manners. Is Alex very angry, Luigi?'

'No, my dear, he is just concerned and worried.'

He came close to her and observed the sheen of tears in her eyes. He put his arm round her and let her head fall on to his shoulder.

'It is all so confusing for you, is it not? Listen to me for a while. I have known Alex all his life and seen him develop into a man. He has overcome many things, things I know he wants to tell you about, and I am proud of what he has achieved. Mama and I can see that Alex loves you very much, and it is obvious that you love him also. He seems happy and this is clear from the mischief he seems to wish to make with you. My dear, it is part of loving you. He means no harm, no dominance of you. The look on his face as you ran off just now was eloquent of his feelings. I had a hard job to stop him following you, but I felt you needed time to be quiet and think.

'You are quite right to be concerned about the future together, and he is also. You need the time to talk, and I am sure this will be easier when you are in a less emotional atmosphere than at present.

'I must say that I was amused to see you standing up for yourself, Catherine. Alex can be an intimidating male when he puts his mind to it. He mustn't be allowed to have it all his own way. I might suggest that if you wished to use your feminine charms on him, he wouldn't stand a chance!'

Catherine broke away from Luigi then and stared at him.

'I can't imagine that for a moment!'

'Oh, believe me, it is quite possible. You are inexperienced at the moment, but you could perhaps try your power in a small way now and again.' His grin was impish and full of mischief. 'Shall we go back now? Perhaps Mama has made some coffee. All that talking has made me thirsty.'

Catherine put a hand on his arm. 'Thank you for being so kind to me, Luigi. It's so nice to have someone to talk to.'

They walked back arm in arm to the lights of the house.

In the gathering dusk, Catherine could see Alex still sitting on the patio. Luigi left her, saying he was going to find Mama, and Catherine hesitated at the foot of the steps. She needed to apologise, but didn't quite know how to start. After all, was she the one at fault?

Alex spoke first. 'Do you feel better now? Come and sit down. Maria is making some coffee.'

Catherine's ears couldn't detect anything untoward in the even tone of his voice. He sounded very calm and controlled. Perhaps he was angry and she would find out how much, later, when they were alone. She started to shake inside, but decided not to think about that. Was it possible she could try the idea Luigi had suggested? Did she dare?

Before she could give herself any more time to think, she walked up the steps and, in a deliberate move, sat down on his lap. If he was surprised, he didn't show it. He said nothing, and just looked at her. Catherine couldn't discern any particular expression which would help her in any next move. His grey eyes were calm and steady. She laid her head on his shoulder, and after a moment placed her lips against his neck. He still didn't move. She raised her head and looked at him. There was still no expression. She looked at his mouth. Could she...? Yes, she could, and she wanted to so much. She kissed him and his lips felt soft under hers, but there was nothing of the usual response. Almost desperate now, she broke the kiss and looked at him again.

'You asked me not to touch you, remember?' His voice was very soft, as if he didn't want to speak.

'I'm sorry. You know I didn't mean it, Alex.' She laid her head back on his shoulder.

'Perhaps you need to prove that to me.'

She sat up again and looked at him. There was still no visible expression, but he now appeared to be holding his breath. She looked again at his mouth, and then back to his eyes. Did she imagine that they seemed to have darkened? She bent her head to his again and touched his mouth with hers. She felt his arms come around her, but they were gentle. She moved her mouth against his and tried to convey to him all the love and pent-up emotion within her. There was still no response, and almost in frantic desperation she lost all control. She placed her hands in his hair to hold the dark head against hers and poured all her feelings through the touch of her lips.

At last, his emotion broke through and it ran like a fever through her blood. His hands were in her hair, holding her own head still under the onslaught of his kiss. She felt on the point of fainting when he broke free, his eyes glittering in the dim light.

'If we take this any further right now, we're going to be in trouble.' His voice sounded rough and unsteady. He picked her up in his arms and with great care placed her in the chair next to him, smoothing down her tangled hair.

He looked deep into her eyes. 'My little bird may just be learning to fly?' The look on his face was one she had never seen before, full of pure joy. Then it changed to one of amusement. 'Please be kind to me for the rest of the night, my love. I'm not sure my blood pressure can stand any more!'

When Luigi and Maria came back with a steaming coffee pot the two were sitting side by side, not talking, just holding hands, but the look of love was clear on both their faces.

CHAPTER 28

The fine weather broke overnight and the wind and rain lashed against their bedroom window. It woke Alex and he decided to get up, and encouraged Catherine to do the same. The night before, Luigi had told him that he was going to accompany Maria to Mass that morning, no doubt with the idea of giving the two of them the possibility of a quiet moment together.

The kitchen felt warm and cosy, despite the change in the weather. As they sat together at the big wooden table, Alex let Catherine finish her breakfast before he spoke.

'Catherine, I want to apologise about last night. I never meant to upset you. I went a little mad with happiness, I think. I forgot that you take things to heart. My teasing was meant with love, my darling. I also made a mistake in speaking up for you. I wanted to save you the embarrassment of suggesting how we will live together as husband and wife when we haven't discussed it ourselves. I know we must talk together about this. Most couples would have done so by now, but our situation has been rather different. I don't want you to worry about it, though; let's take it day by day.

'Catherine, I know you'll say that this doesn't matter, but I would like to tell you a bit about my life so far. You were brave enough to tell me of your problems, and I'm glad you did. It's helped me to try to understand you. Do you mind listening to me?'

Catherine reached out and took his hand. 'You're right, Alex: I love you, no matter what you tell me, but if you feel you would like to talk, I'm quite happy to listen.'

Alex looked away from her, out to the rain-soaked garden, and tried to gather his thoughts.

'My grandfather came over from Europe before the Second World War, probably Holland, but I'm not sure. He must have sensed something bad was going to happen and wanted to get his family away.' He reached for her hand and touched the rings. 'Something like the Russian jeweller, perhaps.' He released her and settled back in his chair.

'I think the idea was to take his wife and son Michael to America, but the war started before he could achieve this. He was a doctor and took a job in the East End. He was working in an aid station during one of the night raids on the docks and was killed, along with many others, in a direct hit. My grandmother did all sorts of jobs to make ends meet and right from a young boy my father also ran errands, amongst other things, to pick up the odd pennies. Later, he drifted as far as a job was concerned, until my grandmother suggested he try for the police force. He was accepted and started well. He was commended for bravery on one occasion. It was a pretty rough time for the police just after the war, but he knew how to handle himself, as I found out later on!

When he was nineteen he had become infatuated with a girl, and after she was found to be pregnant, he decided to marry her, against his mother's wishes.' He looked over at Catherine. 'I learnt from Luigi that it was a disaster right from the start. It seems that once I was born, my mother never had much to do with me. She liked the good life and made sure she got it. My grandmother brought me up, but when she passed away in a flu epidemic, it left my father to take over. Maria used to look after me when he was on night duty and my mother was out.

'When I was about five years old, my mother left for good, leaving

197

behind a pile of debts. My father tried to pay them off but it was all too much for him. He started drinking and began to mix with the sort of people a police officer should not associate with. By then I was at school and had to put up with verbal abuse from my classmates, who knew him and what he had become. They used to call him things, like "Mick the Nick" and other less savoury names. I had a temper even then, so of course it used to lead to fights. My father had taught me how to take care of myself and I made a bit of a name.

'Other people heard about it too, and I began to be involved with the criminal elements at that time in the locality. Sometimes I even accompanied the so-called "heavy men"… and I saw things I should not have seen at that age.'

He knew he had to make something clear. 'I swear to you, Catherine, that I never laid a hand on anyone myself. My father was furious when he began to hear the rumours about me. I had more than one beating from him. One day I went home and found my bags packed, and he boarded me out with Luigi and Maria. He took me down to the nearest recruiting centre, and before I knew it I was signed up in the Army. He said he was going away for a while, and they would look after me.'

Alex found he had to pause for a moment. It was difficult, recounting his past life. As much as possible he had tried to wipe it from his memory. After a moment or two he went on. 'I have never seen or heard of him since. He just left me! Dumped me, without any explanation! I understood later from Luigi that he had resigned from the police force and emigrated to Canada. I couldn't bring myself to try to make contact, I was too shocked and angry with him. Luigi told me that for a year or two they corresponded, but then he heard nothing further. I've just concentrated on trying to pick up my life, and over the years I've done that to the exclusion of everything else.'

He stopped talking for a while, reassessing his emotions from the past. As the initial anger had begun to subside and he had started to make something of his life; if he ever allowed himself to think about the past, it was always tinged with a sense of loss. It was something he had never understood, and over time he'd taught himself not to dwell on it.

He noticed that Catherine remained silent, waiting for him to continue.

'The Army must have seen me as a right tearaway, at first. I was in trouble more often than not, but over time I began to see sense. It was easier, in more ways than one, to go along with the flow rather than fight against it all the time. I started to enjoy my time then. Being good at sport earned me privileges. My speciality was gymnastics and I had the chance to train with the Army team. I also went on all sorts of courses. I became good at field craft, in particular night exercises. I earned a commendation once from my Commanding Officer for helping to ensure my section took top honours in a multi-regiment exercise. I received promotion after that. When my initial service time was up, I was encouraged to stay in. They dangled eventual promotion to Sergeant in front of me. I did consider staying in as a PT instructor, but I wanted to try something new. I was still young and I didn't want to be tied down. For some reason, I thought about joining the police. I've never looked back. I've worked hard for my success, though, studying and learning my job over the years. In return, it's given me companionship, and a steady wage.'

He turned to Catherine and smiled. 'If you're wondering where the Porsche came from, I got lucky with some money from a Stock Market tip-off. I saw the car, it was reduced as a repossession and also a non-fashionable colour, so I negotiated a deal. I was single, so the money didn't seem to matter. I don't know how much further I can go up the ladder with my job, but now things are different. I have a wife to consider.'

He turned away from her again. 'You come from a different world and it must be hard for you to appreciate the more sordid aspects of my life, both personal and professional. I don't want you involved in the latter anyway. So… there it is. You know I've been a bad boy. I hope you can see that I've tried to redress the balance. To be quite honest, my love, I'm nervous as to what you might think of me.'

After a moment, Catherine reached out and took his hand. 'I

think I love you more than ever, if that's possible. Nothing you've said will change that. The future is what matters now – our future. Whatever you want to do, I want to be by your side. Alex, despite what you may think, I'm sure your father would be very proud of what you have achieved.'

He looked down at her hand linked together with his, and brought it up to his lips.

'Someone else said the same thing a little while ago,' he murmured. 'I'm not bothered. Anything I've done in the past has been for myself, but now there's you.'

Catherine took hold of both his hands and he noticed that her whole body was trembling. Alarmed, he was about to comment when she spoke in a tiny voice. 'Alex, I want us to be a family.' She hesitated. 'More than anything, I would love us to have a child.'

He drew in a sharp breath, shocked by her words, and was about to make an incredulous denial of the idea, but then he looked into her sweet face and saw the earnest pleading in her eyes.

Before he could say a word, she went on, 'I know what you're thinking, Alex, but with everything you know about my life so far and after hearing about your experiences, somehow... oh, I can't explain it, but I just know that it's important, for us. Can we, please? It would make me so happy.'

Alex found it difficult to speak, and when he did his voice sounded strained and hoarse, even to his own ears. 'Would it make you that happy?'

She nodded, hope in every beautiful inch of her face. He let out a sigh as if he'd been holding his breath. Remembering his earlier thoughts about a sense of loss, he now realised that the loss he had felt was a lack of real family. The whole idea was something to which he had just begun to give any serious thought – since he had met Catherine. With total certainty he knew that this was what he now hoped to regain, with this wonderful young woman sitting by his side.

He smiled at her then, his eyes soft and warm. 'Well, maybe it's something we'll have to think about. Perhaps you'd like to come and sit on my lap and try some more persuasion.'

Catherine had just begun the task of achieving her aim when they both heard a car. They looked at each other for a moment in consternation, and then started to laugh.

The laughter was heard by the couple entering the hallway, shaking off the rain from their clothes. They exchanged a surprised look and stood together, somehow reluctant to break in on the happy scene.

Maria caught her husband's arm. 'Oh, Luigi, I never thought this would happen. Alex seems so happy, and she's such a nice girl. She loves him, and I know she will be right for him. The beginning of a family; what he needs. We must help them all we can.'

Luigi took his wife into his arms and held her. 'If he's as lucky as I've been, he will indeed be a fortunate man.' His kiss was soft. 'Let's leave them alone for a moment or two longer, shall we? Come, my dear, we'll get out of these wet clothes.'

PART TWO

CHAPTER 1

Catherine looked around the lounge with pleasure. She had spent the day cleaning an already spotless flat, and it was now just as she wanted it: immaculate. The dining table was laid with precision, the meal was almost ready, and all she had to do was change. Tonight, Sarah and Jerry were to be guests at their first dinner party.

Although she knew Alex was a little impatient at the impressive attention to detail she was giving to the event, he had said nothing to her, except to raise his eyebrows when, at one point, he had found her busy making a table arrangement.

Over the weeks since their marriage, her thoughts had often returned to the things Alex had told her about his past life. She was certain that if Luigi and Maria had not given their support to him during those difficult times after his father had left, the outcome might have been very different.

Now, having experienced the happiness he brought to her with his unfailing care and consideration, more than ever she knew that she wanted to provide a happy and secure home life for him, and tonight would be an example of that.

To her surprise, Alex gave her complete control of the household and made sure she understood their financial situation. She decided to keep meticulous track of everything by noting down all their income and expenditure in an exercise book. Alex was amused by her diligence and, peering over her shoulder one evening when she was making some notes, enquired whether she would allow him pocket money!

She began to welcome all the laughter and teasing, content in the knowledge that it was the sweet expression of their ever deepening love for each other.

Alex rang to say he had been detained, and as time went on, for one terrible moment she thought he might not even make it home at all. Dressed and ready for the evening, she was beside herself with frustration. He arrived with half an hour to spare before their guests were due. She could tell that he knew she was upset, and he allowed her a few minutes to vent her fury on him before taking her into his arms.

'My sweet love, please calm down. The flat looks beautiful, the food smells wonderful, and you look ravishing. I did everything I could to get away on time. I know how much this evening means to you and I wouldn't spoil it for the world. What I do want, though, is for us to enjoy the experience. Now, I've still plenty of time to have a shower and change, and I'll even clean the bathroom!'

True to his word, he was ready with three minutes to spare; or longer, as it turned out, with Sarah and Jerry arriving late because of traffic.

After dinner, when they were settled with their coffee, Sarah looked over at Jerry. 'Shall we tell them our news?' She sounded excited.

'By all means,' Jerry grinned back at her.

Catherine, sitting on the settee curled up against her husband, looked from one to another. 'Come on, then, what news?'

'I have a new job,' Jerry announced. 'I'm going to work at St Thomas's as junior to a consultant in paediatrics. I was lucky, there were a lot of other applicants.' His obvious pride at the achievement was mirrored in his wide grin. 'I start in a couple of months.'

Sarah then added, 'I'm trying for a Sister's job at the same hospital.

It would be nice to work together again, if we could. We've also sorted out our wedding arrangements. We're going to do what you did. It's been an uphill struggle convincing Jerry's parents, but they've now come round. We're going to be married in September at the Chelsea Registry Office. My parents are going to make it home for a few days, and Jerry's are coming down from Scotland. We've agreed that at Christmas we'll go back to Scotland, and maybe have some sort of blessing in their local church.'

Catherine looked up at Alex, her face wreathed in smiles. 'We seem to have set a trend.'

'This is all marvellous news,' agreed Alex. 'You must be so pleased.'

'The one nuisance is that it will be farther to travel from Kensington,' said Jerry. 'Sarah's parents will be back in the UK some time next year, so we'll have to think about finding somewhere else to live. I've put a lawyer friend of mine on notice that we'll need his services. With an eye to business, he's even suggested that when we're married we should make Wills, of all things!'

Catherine looked up at Alex. 'It sounds a little morbid, but is it something we should think about?'

'It might be. Is your friend good, Jerry?'

'I'd trust him, without a doubt. He was at med school with me and then dropped out to do law. He always has a dig at me that he'll make more money than I will.'

'He's right, if he drums up business like this. All the same, it's not a bad idea, something to keep in mind. We'll give it some thought.'

CHAPTER 2

Alex and Dougie were into their second hour of a review of the lines of enquiry they had set up, to search for information which might be useful. They had come to a consensus of opinion that there was still merit in trawling through newspapers to pick up any reports of manufacturing glitches or industrial unrest.

There were already occasions which, when followed up, appeared to fall into their suspected pattern. Dougie looked up an old acquaintance in one of the unions who promised to keep his ear to the ground. They also began to check on what cases Judge Franklin had presided over, and made notes of the people involved. One particular case, about two years ago, provided some interesting information regarding one of the defendants, and they were making some further enquiries.

The telephone ringing interrupted their train of thought, and answering it, Alex's voice showed his irritation. 'Yes!'

However, once he realised who was on the other end he modified his tone somewhat. 'Yes, of course. No, it's quite alright.' He listened for a while. 'So, tonight, you say.' After a moment's thought, he said, 'Can you book me in? A table for two, say seven-thirty?… Fine. Thanks a lot for that.'

He put down the phone, but then Dougie watched him pick up the receiver again and dial a number.

'Hello, my sweet.' Dougie made to leave the room, but Alex waved him back. 'What do you say to going out tonight for a meal?… Mmm, I thought you might. Can you be ready for seven o'clock? Dress up, we're going somewhere posh… Yes, that's what I said. See you later my love.'

Putting the phone down with a sigh, he glanced up at his companion. 'I hate getting Catherine involved, but I can't think of an alternative. I've just been told that Johnny Clarke has booked into La Gioconda tonight for an important business meeting. It seems too good an opportunity to miss. It would be interesting to see who he's meeting.'

Johnny Clarke was still high on their list of priorities, attention-wise. Alex would love to be able to nail him on some misdemeanour. He remained certain that Clarke was behind what had happened to Lucille Prentice; and although he never raised the matter again with Dougie, he had a notion that Joe Fenton had also been on the receiving end of his particular warped sense of violence.

'I'd like to join you, and save Catherine the trouble,' Dougie chuckled, 'but I don't look good enough in drag, that's the problem.'

Laughing together at the idea, they turned back to their deliberations.

*

Catherine decided she would take her time getting ready for tonight. It might be an opportunity to practice a few more feminine wiles, and with that in mind she took out a garment from its protective wrapper. It was, at first appearance, just a plain sleeveless dress, but it was the material which had caught her eye when she had first seen it. The silky fabric appeared bronze, but changed its colour to gold as it moved. She had tried it on once at Richmond but thought the styling of the dress moulded too much to her body, and made her nervous of wearing it in public. Now she had more confidence – and a husband to impress!

She had bathed and was drying her hair when Alex arrived home. He had a quick shower and then dressed in his best charcoal grey suit. He kissed her on one bare shoulder and looked at her in the mirror.

'In case we're caught up in traffic, I'd like to get away on time. Is that alright with you?'

Catherine smiled at him. 'That's fine. I'll be about ten minutes.'

As Alex took in her state of undress, she could tell from his expression that he thought it unachievable, but he said nothing and left the room with a smile.

Feeling better at having to face a tight deadline, Catherine didn't have any time to worry or become nervous. As her hair had grown over these last weeks she was able to draw it back and curl it into a chignon at the nape of her neck, then she added small gold earrings and her favourite gold chain. Zipping up the gown, she noticed that the material still moulded itself to her figure and accentuated her curves, but that's what it was supposed to do, after all, she told herself. Looking in the mirror, she felt quite daring. She had never viewed herself like this in the past, but that was before... Alex!

With no time to change her mind, she put on high-heeled shoes, picked up her cream shawl and small bag, and left the room with as much bravado as she could muster.

Alex was standing in the lounge, fastening his watch strap. He glanced up at her, returned his attention to the buckle, but then in slow motion looked up at her again, and Catherine was delighted at the look of complete shock registering on his face.

She sailed past him out into the hall. 'Well, come along then, if you're ready. We don't want to be late!'

Without a word, Alex followed her down to the car and maintained his silence during the drive, although she could feel him giving her one or two sideways glances.

When they arrived at their destination, it was her turn to glance at her husband. 'La Gioconda! Alex, it's very expensive!'

'Just the right setting for my beautiful wife.'

By this remark she had her confirmation that he liked her appearance.

Catherine soon found herself being fussed over by the head waiter, and a second waiter summoned to answer her every whim, much to the amused resignation of her husband. She thought she heard Alex refer to this second waiter by his name, as if he knew him, which made her wonder if Alex had been here before.

It was a coincidence that when they had ordered their meal and wine, he asked her, 'Have you been here before, Catherine?'

'Yes, once, some time ago. I came with my uncle for a business meal. There was his lawyer friend, another man, and their wives. In actual fact it wasn't too bad an evening.'

They had just been served their starters when two other diners entered. Catherine made a small sound which Alex heard, and he glanced at her. Her face registered consternation.

'What's wrong, my love?' He placed his hand over hers.

'One of the men who has just come in, Alex. He's Geoffrey Villiers, the lawyer friend of my uncle and one of my trustees. I don't like him very much. I hope he doesn't recognise me.'

CHAPTER 3

There was no chance that any man could miss the sight of a beautiful woman, and it was only a moment or two before the man in question saw her. His dark face registered total surprise – almost alarm. Then, much to her horror, he spoke to his companion, stood up and came their way.

'Alex, he's coming over!'

'Don't worry my love. It's no problem,' said Alex, his voice soft and soothing.

The man stopped beside their table and surveyed them both.

'Good evening Catherine. This is quite a surprise to see you here. I gather you are no longer with your uncle. Would you care to introduce me…' His voice tailed off as his gaze transferred to Catherine's fingers around the stem of her wine glass. Her rings were shining in the low table light.

In a sharp tone he questioned her. 'Catherine?'

For a moment she was tongue-tied and then found her voice, 'Geoffrey Villiers, this is Alex…'

Alex, displaying good manners, stood up at this point and finished for her. 'Alex Hartman, Catherine's husband.'

For a moment Villiers looked astounded.

Then, with a slight sneer on his face, he commented, 'Hartman? You were the policeman keeping watch over Lionel Franklin at Richmond. Keeping a watch on other things too, it seems!'

The veiled insult behind the remark and its delivery was obvious. Catherine looked up at Alex. He appeared unmoved and just regarded the other man with a steady gaze.

Villiers was enjoying himself now. 'This place is a little above the expenses budget, I would have thought? Still, you have married into money, so perhaps that is no problem.'

The inference was obvious and Catherine was about to interrupt this rude man in her husband's defence, but some instinct warned her to remain silent.

In a quiet, level tone Alex replied, 'As we have two reasons for celebrating, Villiers, we thought it would be nice to do it in style. If you will excuse us, our meal is spoiling, and as you have pointed out, it is expensive!'

He sat down again and began to eat. He appeared quite relaxed and composed, but Catherine sensed the tension in him. Villiers turned on his heel and rejoined his companion, who appeared to be very interested in the exchange.

Catherine felt as though her throat had closed up. Alex glanced at her.

'Eat your food, Catherine, before it spoils. Don't worry about anything. It's quite alright.'

She knew it was anything but! Her intuition told her that Alex was wound up like a coiled spring, but one coated in velvet. It was obvious that he had been insulted. However, he had not risen to the bait and had held his temper; in deference to her and the public situation, she was sure. If the exchange had been in more private circumstances she was not certain how it would have ended.

However, she owed it to her husband to do her part in normalising the evening, so she began to talk about the first thing she could think of, and described to him some of the jokes Sarah had perpetrated at their school. He appeared to enter into the humour, but Catherine knew it was just on the surface.

When what would have been a superb meal ended, and Alex asked for the bill, Catherine excused herself for a moment and hoped that in her absence no further problem would arise. To her relief, when she returned moments later everything appeared to be normal. She noticed Alex watch her come towards him across the room, and with a loving smile he wrapped the shawl around her shoulders and with his hand at her elbow they left the restaurant, not before having made a promise to the head waiter that his restaurant would indeed be graced again by 'such a beautiful lady'.

Outside, the night air was still warm.

'Can you walk at all in those ridiculous heels?'

The remark took Catherine by surprise, and she answered with an immediate retort. 'Of course I can!'

'I wondered if you would like a walk by the river before we went home.'

Sensing that Alex still hadn't yet regained his full composure and needed a breathing space, she couldn't refuse him. Stifling a groan as best she could, she pasted on a false smile. 'That would be nice. I'd like that.'

They managed to park the Porsche and started to walk. Neither of them said a word for some time, but Catherine judged that the tension was easing. She put her hand in his and Alex brought it up to his lips and kissed it. She knew it was in silent thanks for her sensitivity.

After about half an hour, they leant against the stone wall looking out over the water. Alex pulled her close against him.

Catherine knew that she had to talk about tonight. 'You know he will tell my uncle now, don't you.'

'Yes, I know, my dear. It had to happen sooner or later. We might as well get it over with now.'

He was quiet again. Catherine wanted to comment on the insulting remarks but didn't feel brave enough.

'What did you mean, Alex, when you said we were celebrating two events?'

He turned to her, his face transformed with a huge grin. 'You

214

don't look at the calendar, do you? It's two months – well… over since we were married.'

Catherine thought about it for a moment, and was amazed at how he had remembered. 'You're very clever, you know, Inspector.' He chuckled, but then she gave him a playful prod on the arm. 'What was the second reason, then?'

He looked down into the water for a moment, then said, 'It's my birthday.'

Catherine was frozen in horror for a split second. 'Alex, why didn't you tell me this morning? When I've asked, you've always said you don't celebrate your birthday, and you would never even tell me a date. Oh, my dear, I'm so sorry, and the day's almost over!'

She wriggled into his arms and placed her mouth on his. 'Happy birthday, my dear, dear Alex.'

'Mmm… that was nice.' Alex held her close and placed his own lips against her hair. 'Perhaps we ought to go home. There's still time for my birthday present.'

Catherine drew back from him, puzzled at his words, until his soft smile made her realise their meaning.

'Oh, I see!' She put on her most innocent face. 'I suppose something could be arranged, although it's very short notice.'

'That's kind of you, my dear. Of course, I'd hate to put you to any trouble.'

The laughter was bubbling up in him now, and Catherine knew that she must keep things as perfect as she could for him.

'Let's go home, Alex.'

She reached up and kissed him again with all the promise she could instil. She felt his arms tighten around her and a tremor ran through his body.

Later that night they lay in each other's arms, sleepy, but not yet ready to let go of the emotion generated between them earlier. There had been a fierceness about his love-making tonight that Catherine had never known. It was as if he was reaffirming his ownership of her. She knew it was in part due to the events of the evening. She had to be honest with herself, however, and admit that she enjoyed the wild and free sensation.

Alex spoke, his lips against her skin. 'I'm sorry. I was rough with you tonight. You didn't deserve that. I had too much emotion bottled up inside me. I've wanted to make love to you since I saw you dressed up tonight. For the first time, you've acted as a woman who was aware of her charms and wasn't afraid to show them off. Everyone else tonight, as well as me, got the message! Do you realise how many people looked at you? Most of the men were envious that you were with me. I was so proud that you were mine, and I was the one who would take you to my bed and have the pleasure of your body.'

Catherine heard the pride in his voice and realised that her being with him tonight had meant a great deal to him and his self-esteem. She hadn't realised that her appearance, a definite departure from her normal style, had aroused so much attention. As a woman, this made her feel elated. It also gave her the confidence to run her hands over the body of this man who lay almost asleep in her arms, staking her own form of ownership.

'Please don't stop, Catherine.'

The sleepy tones had gone and she heard the urgency now in his voice. His mouth touched her breast and emotion took over again for them both.

CHAPTER 4

'Is Clarke sure about this, Geoffrey?' Franklin's tone was harsh and cold.

'Oh, he was sure. He quizzed me about Catherine first, seemed to be quite taken with her. I must admit she looked a little different to when I last saw her. Very grown up and sophisticated. Married life must suit her!

'When I got back to our table and explained the situation, Clarke took a longer look at Hartman and confirmed that he was the person in the photographs going in and out of Fenton's gym. And his special operator, who has also seen the photographs, says that he was the person with that Prentice girl. He was sure at the time that he was police.'

'So it's probable that Hartman did have something to do with the Ellison thing as well? It seems he's getting quite involved with our affairs.'

'I'm getting worried about the same thing, Lionel. Clarke's not impressed, and wants to get even.'

Franklin almost screamed down the phone. 'Keep that stupid bugger away from him! Hartman's mine! Oh, yes, he's mine alright!' Then he went on in calmer tones. 'I hadn't expected Hartman would go so far as marriage, but it might just work even better.'

Catherine smiled to herself as she sipped her coffee. Alex had just left for work. They had both overslept. The look in his eyes when he kissed her goodbye told her that he remembered with pleasure, as did she, the events of last night.

She stood and moved over to the calendar on the wall, picked up a pen and marked in Alex's birthday. Then she counted up the weeks. Yes, he was right, they had been married over two months already. Then a thought struck her. She counted up the days again.

No, she hadn't made a mistake. Was it just possible…? What would Alex say? She tried to calm herself. It might be best to wait a little longer. It could be just one of those things, after all.

The phone started to ring. She went to answer it, her mind still busy with her new discovery.

'Catherine?'

'Hello, Sarah.' Should she tell her? No, better not.

'Catherine, I've just had a call from your uncle, trying to contact you. He sounded pretty mad. He wants you to go and see him.'

Reality came flooding back and banished her other thoughts.

'We thought this would happen, Sarah. Alex and I went out for a meal last night and we saw a friend of my uncle. We had to tell him about us being married. It was obvious he would pass it on… but this quick? I suppose I'd better see him. I ought to tell Alex first, though.'

'Yes, Catherine, you must tell him. He would want to go with you, I'm sure.'

'Yes, I'll do that, then. I'm sorry you were bothered.'

'Don't be so silly, it's no bother. When are we going to have our shopping trip, poppet? Jerry says he feels it's only fair that if we're going to do that, he and Alex should have a pub crawl, and he'll be in touch with him.'

Catherine laughed. 'Yes, it does sound fair doesn't it? I'll tell Alex.'

They fixed up a possible date for their shopping trip, and then after replacing the receiver, Catherine looked at her watch. Would

Alex have reached his office yet or ought she to leave it until he came home tonight? She felt cold and sick, needing the warmth of his strong arms around her. Pull yourself together, she chided herself. You're a married woman – and maybe more – it's about time you faced up to life and coped on your own.

She had never rung Alex at work before and was diffident about ringing the number he had given her, but his calm voice on the other end settled any apprehension.

'Alex?'

'Yes, my love.' His voice now betrayed the surprise at her call. 'Is anything wrong?'

'I've just had a call from Sarah—'

'Ah, now I know something's very wrong,' he interrupted, but she could hear him smiling. 'I can feel my bank balance groaning already.'

'No, Alex. Please listen a moment.'

For a second or two there was silence, then he said, 'What is it, Catherine?'

'Sarah's had a call from Uncle Lionel this morning. He wants to see me, and she said he sounds angry.'

'Don't worry, Catherine. We'll both go and see him tonight. He'll just have to wait until then. Perhaps you could ring Grace and tell her to pass the message on, but Catherine, please don't speak to your uncle at all before tonight. Do you understand me?'

'Yes I do, Alex. I'll… I'll see you later on.'

She wanted to tell him about her new suspicions, but now was not the time.

*

Alex replaced the receiver and looked over at Dougie. They had been discussing the events at the restaurant last night.

'Things have moved fast. Her uncle wants to see us. A royal command!'

'Well, now, that can either be because he's not keen on his friend being spotted by you, dining with an undesirable, in public or not; or he's just upset at the lack of a wedding invitation.'

'I doubt it's the latter. I'll bet he's more upset that his golden goose has well and truly flown the nest.'

'Going back on what we've discussed,' mused Dougie, 'do we suppose that the dinner invitation was a thank-you for getting an employee a lesser sentence than might have been the case? Or a chance for client and solicitor to discuss new or old business?'

'Whatever it is, I still can't get my head around why a prominent lawyer would want to dine in public with a known hoodlum. There are plenty of other places they could have gone which would have been more private. Who's trying to impress who, I wonder? The trouble is, because the guest turned out to be Villiers, it's going to look pretty suspect that I just happened to be there at the same time.'

Dougie looked over at the other man. 'I think you ought to watch yourself tonight, Alex. It could turn nasty, and I don't trust Franklin an inch.'

'I'll try to make it as short a stay as I can. He can rant all he wants, he can't change a thing.'

'Just watch it, that's all I say, Boss.'

Alex smiled his thanks at his colleague and tried to turn his mind to the other matters of the day.

CHAPTER 5

It was a silent ride out to Richmond, neither wanting to start a conversation. As they walked towards the familiar front door, Alex took Catherine's hand and gave it a squeeze.

Arthur showed them into the Judge's study, with a grimace concealed behind his hand. The Judge looked up at them as they stood in front of his desk. Like naughty schoolchildren, Alex thought. They were not asked to sit down.

'Well, I understand you have something to tell me.' The voice was cold.

Catherine spoke first. 'Yes, Uncle. Alex and I were married a few weeks ago. We've been quite busy, but we were going to come and tell you.'

'How kind.' The snide remark was not lost on either of them. 'I heard the news first from Geoffrey Villiers.'

Alex put his arm around Catherine's shoulders. He could feel her trembling. This had to be nipped in the bud as fast as possible, for her sake.

'Catherine is quite correct in what she has said, but in any case you are now aware of the situation.'

The cold, pale eyes settled on him. 'Oh yes, I'm aware of a situation which is of considerable benefit… to you.'

'Perhaps you would care to explain that.' Despite himself Alex could feel his anger starting to rise.

The Judge gave a small smile, as if he sensed the discomfort in the other man. 'Perhaps Catherine would care to renew her association with my staff, while we have a little chat?'

Catherine looked up at Alex. 'I want to stay Alex.'

'It's alright, my dear. You go and have a chat with Grace and I'll be through in a minute.'

He kissed her and ushered her out of the door. He turned back to face the other man.

'Well, what is it you want to get off your chest?'

'How charming a scene. I must admit you are a class act, Hartman.' Franklin was still smiling in that superior way. He leant back in his chair. 'I could see something developing between the two of you while you were in this house. Nothing too overt. Just enough to stir romantic notions in an inexperienced girl. I wondered why someone of your rank was involved in the day-to-day workings of a simple protection operation. Were you aware of my niece and thought this might be a useful opportunity? Masterful, my dear Hartman.

'Then, of course, your very clever rouse to remove her from my immediate control. I never did trust that girlfriend of hers, either. It took no time at all for you to achieve the desired result, did it? You must be a very accomplished lover! Still, the lure of a pretty girl and money can drive most things.'

Alex felt cold fury sweeping through him. He clenched and unclenched his hands. 'Just what are you getting at?'

'Oh, I must hand it to you for taking advantage of an opportunity when you became aware of the money my niece will inherit. It's obvious that you have expensive tastes. You appear to like fast cars, dining in classy restaurants and, of course, you would also have the added luxury of being seen with a beautiful woman. Does she live up to your... ah... expectations?' The smile was even broader. 'You have made sure to teach her very well, no doubt.'

Alex was teetering on the edge of control now, incensed at this man's insinuations. 'Are you suggesting that I married your niece as a way of gaining access to any monies she may inherit?'

'Oh, come now, Hartman. Do you expect me to believe that it was all an innocent love story? You saw a naive girl who you could manipulate for your own ends, and to your credit, you have achieved your aims.'

Alex couldn't believe what he was hearing. This man had the nerve to be accusing him of the very thing he himself had tried to do. To keep control of his temper, he knew he had to stop listening to any more of this sort of talk, and he turned to leave.

'I'm not staying here any longer. You can think what you like. Catherine is now my wife, and needs nothing more from you.'

Sounding quite calm, Franklin spoke again. 'I realise you still have to keep up the pretence, but you're not fooling anyone. Now, let us not be too hasty in our judgements, Hartman. We perhaps need to talk about the situation and see how it can be... er... used to our mutual benefit, shall we say?'

Franklin's smile was still in place, but Alex noted his eyes were cold and hard. Despite himself, he wondered what the man meant by that statement, and against his better judgement felt compelled to stay and listen to what he might say next. What he heard rocked him to the core.

'I was wondering if we could come to some arrangement whereby Catherine was returned to the fold, as it were. I'm sure we can arrange an annulment or a quickie divorce. You would be well recompensed for any outlay expended so far, and it would save you the expensive bother of keeping a wife in a certain class of luxury. Always a drain on any man's purse!' The jocular tone further sickened Alex.

'You would then be free to play the field again, but with cash in your pocket. I would be able to rekindle my own ideas as to Catherine's future. However, on the other hand, if you are now accustomed to her... charms, and feel you should benefit from the effort in this direction' – again, he seemed consumed by his own amusement – 'you could retain ownership, shall we say, but make her available if required at any time for other purposes. For a fee of course. I would not expect you to make a charitable donation! What do you say, eh? Man to man, with none of this romantic nonsense.'

Alex was finding it difficult not to reach over the desk and throttle this smug, superior bastard. How dare he sit there discussing his own niece – his wife – in this way. Alex felt his skin crawl at the thought of other hands running over Catherine's body – and worse!

Just managing to hold on to his emotions, and through clenched teeth, he grated, 'You are suggesting that I sell my wife back to you for a sum of money, or at the very least rent her out to you for your own twisted ideas? I've never heard anything so warped and perverse in my life. If you were any sort of man at all I would have knocked your teeth out by now, but I don't even want to dirty my hands on something as low as you. If there was any proof of this conversation I would drag you through every Court in the land.

'I warn you, stay away from my wife from now on, or I will seek some sort of injunction against you. You are sick and depraved to even harbour any such notions, and I feel insulted that you could consider I would be a party to it. I can assure you I have no wish, or need, to see a single penny of any monies Catherine will inherit, and if you don't accept my word as a gentleman I'll agree to sign a paper saying so.'

With no hint now of a smile Franklin reached into a drawer and pulled out a sheet of paper. 'In actual fact I have such a letter here which, if you are serious about your intent, you could sign.'

Alex heard warning bells in his head, but he was past listening. He was appalled that Catherine had been forced to live in a household such as this, and was even more grateful that she was now under his love and protection. His resolve to fight to keep it that way was even stronger. This creature, studying him with fixed concentration, like an exhibit, wasn't worth any more of his time. He wanted to get Catherine away from him as fast as possible. He moved over to the desk.

'Where do you want me to sign?' He scanned the content of the letter, which seemed to acknowledge his disclaimer of any funds going to Catherine, and with angry strokes he signed his name at the bottom and threw both pen and paper on the blotter in front of the other man, then turned on his heel and left the room.

As the door closed behind him, Franklin looked at the signed letter in his hand, and settled back in his chair with a satisfied smile.

'Dear, dear, Hartman,' he mused to himself, 'you're not as clever as you thought! I knew the way to get under your guard was through the girl. It was all too easy. Now I have the means to make sure you will regret your interference.'

CHAPTER 6

Catherine knew that something dreadful had taken place between Alex and her uncle as soon as he came into the kitchen. Everyone had heard their angry voices. She was aware of his hard, closed face and heavy breathing. With just a brief word of acknowledgement to Grace and Arthur, he took her arm in a firm grip.

'We're leaving.'

She found herself propelled out of the house and into the car. He drove in silence, with intense care and precision, but Catherine could tell he was exerting extreme control over himself to do so. She did not dare speak to him.

When they reached the flat, he changed into his running gear, and with the words 'I'm going out for a while' left the flat again, slamming the door on his way out.

Catherine worried about the situation during his absence. She didn't know what had happened today, but knew that she must try to make it up to him. All she could think of was to show him that she loved him.

It was late before he returned. She heard him run the shower, and soon he got into bed beside her. Pretending to be asleep, she waited for his arms to curl around her, as they most often did. But not tonight. After a while she turned over. He was lying on his back with one arm behind his head, eyes closed. However, she sensed he wasn't asleep. He didn't acknowledge her movement or pull her close, and she could still feel his tension. Rather tentative about her move, she curled her body into him.

'Go to sleep, Catherine.'

She recognised the warning tone, but tonight she had to make amends. Running her fingers over his chest, feeling the muscles under the skin, she placed her lips where her hand had been, and, bolder now, repeated the same process until she had reached his waist. His skin smelt fresh and clean from his shower, and she found her own senses heightened.

He had made no sound, but she could feel a slight trembling in his body. Continuing her exploration, across his flat stomach and still lower, she was much more unsure now. However, her actions were creating a feeling inside her that she had never experienced before. Could she arouse him as he had done her so many times? Her body needed him now and this thought blotted out all her preconceptions of what was permissible. She lowered her head, and then found herself swept up in strong arms.

Much later, as she lay curled into his shoulder, Alex stroked her hair as it fanned out over his chest. 'My sweet love, I never knew I could need anyone as much as that.'

He turned her face up to him and smiled down at her. 'I'm sorry I spoilt your voyage of discovery, but I couldn't hold out any longer.'

She smiled back, feeling a little shy. 'I wanted to show you that I loved you.'

'Oh, you did that,' he whispered against her hair. 'I think my little bird has flown solo.'

She reached up and kissed him. 'Do I get a certificate or something?'

'Oh, you'll get something much better than that,' he murmured against her mouth.

Before they settled down to sleep some while later, Alex held her face between his hands and looked deep into her eyes. He was serious now, she could tell.

'Will you promise me that you'll not have any contact with your uncle unless I'm present, Catherine? It's important. Will you do this for me please, my darling?'

Catherine wanted to ask questions, but knew he would not give her the answers. She must show she trusted him.

'Yes, of course I will.'

He kissed her with such tenderness that it overwhelmed her. Basking in his love, as never before, she was left with no illusion as to how precious she had become to him, as he had to her.

*

In the sweltering heat of the July day, Alex was glad to be out of his airless office. As the Porsche was in for a service, he had decided to get away so that he could walk home, and relished the fresh air on his face. He took off his jacket, slung it over one shoulder, and with his other hand in his trouser pocket he strolled along.

He had been on his own all day. Dougie was called away on other duties. It gave him time to think through the information they had obtained so far. No more than leads to possible other leads at the moment, but already some disquieting possibilities were emerging. He would have to arrange another meeting with Francis soon.

The voice was quiet, very close behind him, but loud enough for him to register the finality of the tone, broking no argument.

'Mr Ellison would like to see you. Please get in the car.'

As his mind registered the situation, a Jaguar pulled in to the kerb. The man standing behind him opened the rear passenger door and waited for him to enter. Alex noted the driver had now alighted and was blocking the opposite side passenger door. Very professional. They were leaving him no option to scramble through and out the other side.

With apparent calm he put on his jacket and climbed in, sliding along the back seat while the other man took his place beside him. The car glided back out into the traffic. No one spoke.

Alex was annoyed he'd not been in a position to defend himself, but it had all happened so fast. He'd just been unprepared for it. Then he remembered his instructor in the Army, saying that if one opportunity for action goes by, ride it out until another presents itself. He settled back in the seat and prepared to do just that.

So Jack Ellison wanted to see him. Why? Ellison had been involved in the same East End crowd all those years ago. He was about ten years older than himself, Alex remembered. Now, after making his way up the pecking order in the London underworld, he controlled a substantial network involving the usual prostitution, drugs, extortion, etcetera. However, to Alex's knowledge, Ellison, unlike some, had never been involved in violence for its own sake, and for the most part remained outside the clutches of law enforcement. The fact remained, however, that he was still a powerful man in London, the sort of person you ignored at your peril.

What did he want? Alex knew you didn't decline this sort of invitation. The good thing was it had been cordial enough… so far! They appeared to be travelling north. Alex was aware Ellison had a home somewhere in north London and perhaps that was where they were heading. At least it was better than a warehouse near the docks.

The car turned into an affluent-looking road and at the far end entered the driveway of a detached mock Tudor property. Alex was ushered from the car into the main reception hall. He was still accompanied by his companions, but not, it seemed to him, in a threatening way. As he was directed into a downstairs room, Alex thought he saw someone out of the corner of his eye on the main staircase. The two men withdrew and Alex was left on his own. He crossed over to the windows but found them locked. No escape that way! He came back towards the centre of the room, intending to try the door, when it opened and a young girl entered.

In deference to the heat of the day she was wearing very little, and what she was left nothing to the imagination. She was about nineteen or so, Alex estimated. She circled around him, eying him up and down, her hands with scarlet painted nails smoothing down her curves and then touching her full red lips.

'I saw you come in. You're nice! Would you like to play with Lizzy?'

She came close to him and laid one scarlet-tipped hand on his chest. This was not the sort of household in which to cut up rough with one of its occupants, so Alex just kept still and tried to ignore her.

She stood on tip toe and planted her mouth on his. Disappointed at the lack of result she started to undo his tie and open his shirt, placing her hands on his skin. He began to feel anger at her unwelcome touch, but he kept himself in control. She kissed him again and pressed her body against his chest, her hands getting bolder on his skin. Now, it seemed, even more annoyed at the lack of response, she moved her hand down below his waist with one obvious intention. Alex moved like lightning and caught the roving hand in an iron grip and moved it away from his body.

Neither person had noticed the door opening again, and the man who entered stood for a moment, observing the scene.

'Oh for God's sake, Lizzy, put him down. He could eat you for breakfast if he wanted. Anyway, he's spoken for. Now scram!'

The young girl flounced out of the room, rubbing her wrist. Jack Ellison held up both hands in apology.

'Sorry about that. She's got a one-track mind that one. I'll have to do something about it before her mother complains to me again.'

The smile was rueful. He watched Alex straightening his clothing 'That wasn't the reason you were invited here, I assure you.' He took a handkerchief out of his breast pocket and handed it to the other man. 'You might need this. That colour doesn't do anything for you.'

Alex scraped at his mouth with the handkerchief and went to hand it back.

'Keep it, why don't you. Unless it can be construed as a bribe, eh?'

Stuffing the stained handkerchief into his trouser pocket, Alex looked at Ellison, his face calm and expressionless.

'What do you want, Ellison? I haven't got all night.'

CHAPTER 7

The older man waved Alex to a chair and offered him a drink, but was refused. Turning to his desk, Ellison reached for a small envelope and took from it a set of photographs, handing one to his companion.

'I like to keep an eye on things that are happening which might be of interest to me. In light of this, I felt I needed to have a word with you. I told the boys to look out for an opportunity.'

Curious now, Alex was unprepared for the content of the photograph. It was of himself and Catherine leaving La Gioconda the other night. Despite his serious situation, Alex could not help the feelings that flooded through him, looking at the beautiful woman in the photograph. This was his wife, and his body remembered the events of later that evening. He looked up at Ellison, and found himself being regarded with keen interest.

'I'm sure you haven't brought me all the way here to show me that.'

'You're quite right. It wasn't until I checked on just who the lady might be that I began wondering.'

He passed another photograph over to Alex. It showed Geoffrey Villiers together with Johnny Clarke.

This was more like it, thought Alex. Johnny Clarke was the

opposition, and he could understand his movements being of considerable importance.

Ellison sat back in his chair. 'Now, the interesting part comes when, on the same evening, in the same restaurant, we have dining a business opponent of mine, a lawyer who is a friend of a certain High Court Judge, the Judge's niece and her new husband, who is a police officer. Add to that the fact that the Judge has just tried a case which had a good outcome, connected with an opponent, and you might begin to wonder if anything is going on. Is it, Mr Policeman?'

Alex relaxed his stiff shoulders. 'I couldn't say. I took my wife to the restaurant that night as it was my birthday. Who else happened to be dining there at the same time was pure coincidence.'

'I'm not sure I believe you, Hartman, but that's by the by. What I don't like is the idea that Clarke appears to have friends in high places in the judiciary; and I wonder, does he also have friends in the police force? In other words, Hartman, are you going back to your roots and branching out into areas more lucrative? Was the Judge's niece a present for you having been a good boy at some time in the past – or future?'

For Alex, this suggestion was too close to the content of the recent conversation held at Richmond and his blood boiled. He stood up and looked at the other man, his grey eyes cold.

'You can make all the inferences you want, Ellison, and they'll all come out wrong. I married my wife because I love her and I warn you now, stay away from her, or I'll come back here to find you, and I won't be afraid to be on my own. I intend to leave here now, and anyone who stops me will be in trouble.'

'Oh sit down, for God's sake,' sighed the other man. 'I know very well you can handle yourself. That's why I asked the lads to invite you… with care. I needed to find out if you'd changed horses again. You've gone from poacher to gamekeeper in your life and I wondered if you had reverted back, playing games on Clarke's team. If you were, I was going to offer you more to switch sides. I know your capabilities and I would rather have them working for me than the opposition. Speaking of which, now you have expensive family obligations, I could offer you more than the police force pay, if you were interested. You'd be far more useful than a lot of the dossers on my payroll at the moment. We both remember how it was done in the old days.'

'Thanks for the offer, but no thanks. Is that all?'

'Not quite. I understand you used to frequent the late Joe Fenton's place. You've been observed, not only by my colleagues but, so I'm told, by others who also appear interested in photography.'

So, Alex thought, his suspicions of being watched had been correct.

'I used the gym when I felt like it.'

'Was Fenton telling you stuff, and was that why he was nailed?'

'I told you, I used the gym. I knew Fenton, like you, from the old days. It was a great shame, what happened.'

'I'll bet you know as well as I do that Clarke was behind that little caper. Sore because his little prank to hurt me was spoiled. I'm damn sure it was Clarke, it has his handiwork written all over it – or at least the person who does these things for him.'

'Handiwork?'

Ellison grimaced. 'Yes, the ability not to get caught! You know it's strange, isn't it, that you're in the mix with that Fenton thing too? If I didn't know better I'd say you had something to do with that warning. Trying to keep the peace, eh? Needless to say, don't think I'm not grateful.'

Alex shrugged. 'If I knew what you were talking about, I might be able to make a comment.'

Ellison gave him a disbelieving look.

'What's your take on Judge Franklin?'

Although surprised at the question, Alex attempted to keep his face expressionless. 'How do you mean?'

'If you've married his niece, you must have come to know him, how he operates?'

'I didn't have a lot to do with him.' For old times sake, though, he added, 'If I'm honest, I didn't warm to him. What's your interest, anyway?'

'One or two unsubstantiated rumours are starting to circulate that maybe favours have come from him, in his official capacity. I want to make sure that the opposition are not getting an unfair advantage. Something your side of the pond might like to poke around in, perhaps?'

Alex pretended to think. 'Yes, you may be right. If you hear anything, I might be interested.'

'I'll consider it.' Ellison stood up. 'Now, I must let you get back to your new wife. I think it would be fair to say that you're fond of her, considering your expression when you saw that photograph. A bit too revealing, Hartman! Someone with bad intentions could have used that knowledge for their own ends. You're getting soft and letting your guard down, boy. Remember the old days. Keep yourself and your emotions buttoned up.'

He walked back to his desk and picked up the photograph. 'Here, have this one on me. Should look nice in a frame.'

Alex was ushered out of the house and into the car. He was taken back over the river, but at his insistence was dropped about a quarter of a mile away from the flat. He needed another walk and time to think.

It felt warm and comforting to turn his key in the lock and hear Catherine's soft voice calling his name. He knew he was now late and she must have wondered where he was, but she met him with a smile. He went to her and, much to her surprise, folded her in his arms and kissed her, hard. He looked into her beautiful face and thought how clean and innocent she was, and once again vowed to do his best to keep his life's more unsavoury experiences away from her.

*

'I'll have to take some stuff to the dry cleaners today. Do you have anything to go?'

Catherine's call arrested Alex just as he was leaving. He was on duty at Heathrow today and that meant setting out earlier.

'Yes, my navy suit could do with a clean. Can you manage it all?'

'Yes, that's fine. If not I'll get a taxi.'

Later, sorting through the pockets of the clothes she was taking,

Catherine pulled out a handkerchief from the trouser pocket of the navy suit. She knew all her linen by now, and this item was strange. For a moment she thought it was stained with blood, but when she looked closer she realised what it was. Bright red lipstick! Nothing like any she owned. Her hand started shaking.

For quite a while, Catherine sat on the bed, staring at the livid red stain, her insides churning. Where had it come from? Then it came to her. Alex had worn the suit the other day when he was very late coming home. She hadn't questioned where he'd been. She tried not to. His was not a nine to five job. He did his best to let her know if he was ever going to be extra late.

Then she remembered that on arriving home he had come to her and, without a word, kissed her almost as if... he felt guilty. No, she mustn't think that way. She must trust him. She would get rid of the wretched thing and try to forget it. With that intent she pushed it to the bottom of the waste bin, but it wasn't quite so easy to dismiss the question in her heart.

*

The sickness each morning was becoming quite severe. Catherine now made a point of not getting up until after Alex had left for work. He questioned it at the beginning, but she laughed it off as just being lazy. There now seemed little doubt as to her condition, and she knew she must have it confirmed, one way or the other.

Would Alex be pleased, or not? Although he had agreed to the idea in principle, she couldn't explain the reluctance she felt to speak to him about it. She should have been brimming with joy, and eager to tell him, but somehow she was uncertain as to his reaction. If, however, she was honest with herself she knew it was because of her recent discovery of the handkerchief, which still hovered in the back of her mind.

She also knew she had become a little hesitant about their love-making. She realised she was quite naive about the whole pregnancy process, and needed to learn about what would happen to her body as time went on.

The telephone ringing startled her out of her thoughts.She moved through into the lounge to answer it.

'Hello, is that Catherine Hartman?'

She had seldom been called by her married name, and it still sounded strange.

'Yes, it is.'

'Hi Catherine, its Andrea Brown from Brompton Language Liaison. I was wondering if I could ask a favour?'

Although living too far away now to assist the hospital in language problems in an emergency, Catherine had still offered to help if they required any sorting out of long-term paperwork.

'Yes, of course, Andrea. How can I help you?'

'Well, it's not for us, and I don't know if you'll agree, but I've had a call from a colleague of mine at Fulham General. They have a French national with them who's causing some bother. Their main French speaker is on holiday and the other one is not very fluent and is having some problem with the dialect. They're in a bit of a panic and rang me wondering if we had anyone more experienced who might be able to help out. We've sort of assisted each other in the past if needed, and I just wondered if you might be free. They have agreed to pay for your expenses, by the way. Can you help out at all?'

Catherine thought for a moment. There was no reason why she couldn't. It ought to take about an hour or so, if that.

'Yes, that's OK, Andrea. I'll help out. Can you give me a little while to sort myself out at this end? Who do I contact when I get there?'

They made their arrangements and Catherine wrote down a few details. She washed and dressed with care, and when she considered that the sickness was passing off, called a taxi.

In fact, the whole problem took most of the morning. The elderly man was in an emotional state and it required all of Catherine's knowledge to help him through the various departmental questions. After he was settled in a ward, Catherine was offered a cup of tea by the Ward Sister, with her grateful thanks for the assistance. Somehow Catherine started to tell her about her pregnancy suspicions, and before she knew it, she was whisked to Maternity.

236

Sitting in the taxi on her return journey home, Catherine found it hard to contain her happiness. It was definite, the results were positive. Now she was sure, she must tell Alex. Tonight, if she could. She hugged herself and thought about the miracle taking place inside her.

CHAPTER 8

The taxi passed through a parade of shops and turned right, opposite a church, into a pleasant tree-lined road. Catherine was gazing out of the window, still dreaming, when she saw it. A house for sale. Her eyes fixed on it as the vehicle passed by. Without conscious thought she asked the driver to stop and wait. She walked across the road and up to the gate. It was a 1930s red brick and pebbledash semi-detached with bay windows top and bottom, as were all the houses in the road. The garden looked a little overgrown, as if it had been unattended for some time, but the house itself seemed well cared for from the outside. For some unaccountable reason, Catherine knew that this would be the right home in which to start their family. Noting the estate agent's details, she walked back to the waiting taxi and requested to be dropped off outside their offices.

Caught up in her dream of the future, she lost all track of time. She was informed that the property had just come on the market. It was being sold by a widowed lady so that she could live with her daughter in the West Country. It needed some updating, but this was reflected in the price being asked. As the property was empty the young salesman, eager to please his attractive client, offered to show her round. He was at pains to assure her that a female member of staff would accompany them.

Once inside the property, Catherine was even more certain that this was the right house. Despite its old-fashioned décor it felt light and airy and welcoming. The back garden would be a delight for children to play in.

The agent warned her that the property would be snapped up and advised her, if she was interested, that a decision would need to be made as soon as possible. He asked if finance was in place and she had to admit to him that nothing had been discussed. Before she knew it he had conducted her back to his office and began to offer advice on the various options. Listening to him, Catherine was still unaware of time passing by. When she climbed into the taxi to head for home, clutching a folder full of paperwork, she smiled to herself with pleasure. She would have so much to discuss with Alex tonight.

*

The flat seemed rather silent as Alex let himself in. He called out, but there was no reply. He went into each of the rooms but they were empty. Where was Catherine? He looked at his watch. It was nearly six o'clock. There was no message left anywhere. He wracked his brains. He didn't remember her saying she was going out with Sarah today. She'd still been in bed when he left this morning, something she now seemed to do regularly, and that caused him some disquiet.

He waited another fifteen minutes and then rang Sarah's number. There was no reply. He looked down at the pad by the telephone and saw Catherine's writing. Something about Fulham General, and a Sue Potter, with a number. Becoming alarmed by now, Alex decided to ring the number. After a long wait he was put through to someone who remembered that Catherine had been at the hospital that morning but had left just after lunch. Putting down the phone, his anxiety grew. It was now after six-thirty.

Might she have gone to Richmond to see her uncle? Alex was aware that Catherine had a soft heart and wouldn't feel comfortable with the strained situation as it had developed. She had promised him she wouldn't see her uncle alone, but Alex had experienced her impulsive behaviour, and something could have changed her mind.

He grew afraid. If she had gone to see her uncle, was he capable of spiriting her away? He could deny he had done anything, other than speak to her, and then seen her on her way home.

Alex rang Sarah's number again, but still no reply. He paced up and down the room, trying to think what to do for the best. Should he ring Richmond on the off-chance? No, better not to admit to a problem if there wasn't one. Was Jack Ellison involved somehow? Had Catherine had some sort of accident, and needed him? There were so many possibilities running around in his mind, none of them good.

Then an even more disturbing idea came to him, which might explain her slight reserve of late. Had his worst nightmare come true, after all? Was there someone else? But if there was, where could she have met this person? He began to feel sick. He stamped down on the idea as ridiculous, but now it had registered in his brain it kept gnawing away at him.

He decided to wait another ten minutes and then consider ringing the hospitals and even reporting the matter to his Duty Officer. He was just about to pick up the receiver when he heard the sound of a car door slamming, and ran to the window. A taxi was just pulling away. Catherine was walking up the driveway.

With various emotions churning around inside him ranging from relief to anger, Alex raced out of the flat and down the main staircase. As Catherine came through the entrance door he caught her by the arm, startling her.

'Where in God's name have you been? Do you realise what the time is? I've been out of my mind wondering where you were.'

She smiled up at him, amused at his concern, which angered him even more. Didn't she realise how worried he'd been?

'Oh Alex, I'm glad you're home, I've so much to...'

'I should think you have young lady!' he interrupted her.

He was shaking with anger now, and half dragged her upstairs into the flat, where he rounded on her again.

'Suppose you tell me just where you've been all this time, and even more important, with whom! It's nearly seven o'clock. I was home an hour ago. I rang Sarah but there was no reply. I saw your note about Fulham General. I rang them and they told me you had left by lunchtime. I was about to start ringing round the hospitals!'

He was stupefied that Catherine looked so surprised at his fury, as if she was wondering what was wrong.

'Oh, sorry, I didn't realise it was so late. Anyway, you're very often late, and I don't get all worked up.'

Alex was now beside himself, and shouted at her, 'You know very well it's different for me if I'm late home! It's my job!'

He should have read the warning signs in Catherine's flashing eyes, but he was far too angry. She threw her bag and a file of papers on the coffee table and turned on him.

'Oh, of course, I forgot, its quite alright if you're out and about somewhere to all hours without me knowing where, or with whom! Very convenient to say it's your job. I have to believe that, don't I. Are you sure it's always your job, Alex? There isn't something you have to tell me? About someone with red lipstick...'

Alex had no idea what she was talking about.

'Well, two can play at that game!' The words were now spilling out of Catherine's mouth in a torrent. 'I've been in the company of someone who has been very kind and attentive and couldn't do enough for me. I might be going to see him again!'

Alex felt as if someone had kicked him in the stomach. So it had happened. She had found someone else. He grabbed her by the shoulders.

'You're my wife, damn you! I'm not letting someone else get their hands on you. Some raw, spotty youth who wouldn't know the first thing about how to handle you.'

She went very still under his hands. 'So that's how you see it, is it? You know how to "handle me"? I'm your possession, am I, to be moulded into some living art form by the Master? To be kept as a plaything? The obedient wife. Always waiting for you to return, whenever you fancy – and from whom. No doubt your great experience told you that this innocent girl was so besotted with you that she would agree to your every whim.'

She broke away from him. 'What was going to happen soon, Alex?

241

Were you going to introduce me to some less savoury ideas of sexual behaviour? You've no doubt learnt a lot during your job!'

He started to raise one arm towards her, and she shrank back.

'First comes the physical violence does it? Well, go on, hit me. See how masterful that makes you feel. Is this how you do things in the East End?'

Her last remark penetrated down into his inner being, through all the anger in him. The social chasm had opened up between them. It hadn't seemed to matter, but now he knew better. She had met someone in her own social class, and realised the difference. Well, so be it. To hell with her. Whoever she had found, she could go to him.

He turned from her, grabbed his coat and strode to the door. 'You'd better return to your new lover, my dear. I'm sure he's far more suited to your aristocratic needs. Meanwhile, I'll seek out my own recreation. Don't wait up!'

The door slammed behind him.

Catherine stared, unseeing, across the empty room. What had just happened? She had come home brimming with happiness and exciting news, and now... this.

She hadn't realised how late it was. She could understand that Alex might be worried, but why should he assume that she was with another man? That had confused and shaken her, but what then possessed her to make all those wild statements? And to her horror he had believed them! Why should he assume that she would even want to look at another man? Hadn't she shown him just how much she loved him?

Oh God! Catherine wrapped her arms around herself. Nothing could happen now, of all times, please! No, of course not, she told herself. He was angry at the moment but he would soon cool down and in a while he would be back, they would say sorry to each other and he would take her to bed. It would be alright. She could tell him then.

But time dragged on. By eleven o'clock, as something to do, Catherine made ready for bed. Had she driven him to the one with red lipstick? She tried not to think about them together, but the idea became too vivid as she lay in bed, tears welling up inside her, but struggling to remain calm for the sake of the baby.

As the hours continued to pass and the dawn light filtered through the window, the sickness inside her was for more than one reason.

CHAPTER 9

Alex drove like a maniac for mile after mile. He must be breaking every speed limit in London, he laughed to himself – but the laughter was more like a sob. So this was it, the realisation of all those torments. The knowledge that his world would have to carry on without its centre. That beautiful girl, just turning into an even lovelier woman, would no longer be part of it. The ache inside him was immense. Braking hard, he pulled the Porsche into the kerb. He felt as if he was suffocating. He climbed out and started to walk.

What had gone wrong? It was almost laughable that it had happened so soon, just a matter of weeks. Everything had seemed perfect. Had he been unreasonable to expect her to be waiting for him each night? If she was unhappy about it, why didn't she say something? He didn't mind what she did, as long as he knew she was safe.

They were good in bed together, even more so now that she was losing her earlier inhibitions. Although, of late, he remembered, she had been a little less enthusiastic. Was that a warning sign? Should he have seen something coming?

What had she meant, inferring that he might have been having a secret liaison? All that 'red lipstick' nonsense. There was no way on earth any woman could interest him after her. If he couldn't have her, he didn't want a poor substitute.

He kept walking, and walking, and after what seemed a lifetime, he rested against a stone balustrade near the river, questions swirling around in his mind, mirroring the dark water below. How had he ever been stupid enough to tell her that she could leave him for another man? He must tell her he wasn't prepared to let her go at any price… but what would that achieve? It was like imprisoning a bird in a cage, watching it day after day, fluttering against the bars. His little bird, who he had taught how to fly! No, he couldn't do that to her. If she would be happier with someone else, he loved her enough to let her go and be happy. Whatever it cost him.

He sighed. He might hand in his resignation. Start a new life, maybe even in a new country. But who would take over his investigations? Dougie would need some help. Was there someone else the Commissioner could trust to carry on? After all, he wasn't irreplaceable? It was just that he and Dougie had begun to glimpse the faintest thread in their enquiries of what had been going on; would someone else spot those same clues? Did his duty override his personal problems?

He was back to the same dilemma he thought he had resolved at the beginning when realising his feelings for Catherine. He had made his decision then and never regretted it for one moment – until tonight! Even if he let her go now, the investigation would bring a daily reminder of her. The way he felt at the moment, he doubted he was strong enough to cope with that. He leant his head on the cold stonework.

'Are you alright, sir?'

Alex straightened and turned to see a uniformed police officer standing a few feet away.

He just about managed a smile. 'Thank you, officer. Don't worry, I'm not going to do anything stupid.' He'd already done that, he thought to himself.

'That's alright then, sir.' The officer moved closer.

Alex could see he was a mature man, not far from retirement.

'Been celebrating, sir?'

Alex gave a hollow laugh. Celebrating? How did you celebrate the end of a marriage! 'No, officer. I'm stone cold sober, but I'd like to be very drunk indeed.'

He turned back to his contemplation of the water, running a hand through his dark hair.

The officer was near enough to catch the slight glint of the new ring on the man's hand.

'You know, sir, my old lady and I have had some real corkers of rows over the years. Always talked it through in the end. Someone has misunderstood the other in some way. It's worth a try.'

Alex turned back to the other man with a rueful smile. 'Thank you, officer, for your interest. I take your point, but I'm not sure it will help in this instance.' He looked up at the lightening sky and sighed. 'I'd better be on my way though, I've a job to go to.'

'Where do you live, sir? Do you have a car?'

Alex stood up straight. The car! Where on earth had he left the Porsche? Where was he anyway? He knew he was near the river, but where?

'You won't believe this, but I did have a car tonight. I remember parking it, but I don't know where. I don't know where I am now, but I'll have to walk or get a taxi back to Kennington. Someone will find the car at some time, I suppose.' With a mirthless laugh he added, 'What a good headline for tomorrow's papers, 'Detective loses own car.'

The officer looked closer at him. 'You're on the force, sir?'

Alex produced his card and handed it to him.

The officer sprang into action. He brought out his pad and took down details of the Porsche and where Alex thought he might have left it. 'For your information, sir, we're in Southwark. I'm waiting to be picked up. When the car arrives we can go back to the station and set up a search. Someone will spot it. I dare say we can arrange a lift home for you. If I may, sir, I'll take the liberty of indicating that you had to abandon your vehicle whilst in the course of pursuing a lead. Sounds better, eh?'

Alex just managed to smile his thanks. He felt cold and numb.

'If you care to leave your car keys at the station, I imagine we could have the car dropped home for you if you like. Someone is sure to fancy a chance to drive a Porsche!'

True to his word, after a few minutes a police car came to a halt near them. Two police officers alighted and all three conferred together for a moment or two.

'Right, sir, ready to go?'

Alex straightened up from the wall and headed for the car.

'Thank you, officer, for your assistance.'

'That's alright, sir. Don't forget what I said, now.'

Alex slumped into the back seat. So he was in Southwark. It would have been quite a walk home. Home! Did he think of it like that any more?

It was a grey dawn, and just starting to rain, when he let himself into the flat. There was no sound. He moved through into the bedroom. He could see the figure in the bed. Was she asleep?

'Catherine?'

There was no answer, but he was sure she had heard him. He moved closer to the bed. She was lying on her side facing away from him. He walked around the bed and sank down to the floor near her, leaning back against the mattress. He felt ill, and old, and tired. But he had to go through with it.

Catherine remained still and quiet. She didn't know what to say or do. She would have to take her lead from him. He was so close to her, sitting on the floor, that she could have reached out and stroked his hair.

'We must talk, Catherine.'

She turned over and sat up, drawing her knees under her chin, the covers wrapped around her. Alex didn't move.

'I thought from the beginning that this might happen, but hoped it wouldn't. If you've now found someone else you feel is more suited to your idea of life that you would rather be with, I must let you go. I just want to know that you're happy. I hope he loves you and takes good care of you. I won't make a fuss, just let me know what

247

arrangements you want to make and I'll do my best to oblige. I can't say fairer than that.' He paused for a moment and then went on in a whisper. 'I'll miss you.'

Catherine was in tears. He had said he loved her, and now he was prepared to let her go if she wanted someone else – just to make her happy.

'Alex, I don't want to go.'

'For God's sake, Catherine, you can't have both. I'm not prepared to share you!' He sounded angry again.

'Alex, please listen. There is no one else to go to. I love you. I didn't mean what I said before. I don't know why I said it. I was just angry that you assumed because I was late I had been with another man, with no thought that there might have been another reason.'

Leaping up from the floor he stood beside the bed, looming over her, almost menacing. 'What on earth did you say all that rubbish for if it wasn't true!'

Although afraid of his cold anger, she found herself becoming annoyed again. 'Because you didn't give me a chance to explain anything, you just assumed!'

She could see him trying to keep control. He took a deep breath. 'Alright. Now's your chance. Tell me!'

She had to gather all her courage, and prepare herself for the reaction she knew would come, her happy dreams now shattered.

'I went to the Fulham hospital because I was asked to help in a one-off translation job. I was to be paid for my expenses. On the way back in the taxi I noticed…' She took a deep breath. 'I noticed a house for sale. I stopped and looked at it, and I loved it. I went to the estate agent's, and they took me back to have a look around inside. I loved it even more. With some work it could be a wonderful house. We went back to their office and talked through some financial options…' She tailed off as she glanced up and saw the look of shock and total disbelief on her husband's face.

CHAPTER 10

Catherine watched as, almost in slow motion, Alex seated himself at the foot of the bed and stared at her, his face pale. When he spoke, it wasn't with the blistering anger she had expected, but in such a quiet tone that it was all the more unnerving.

'Are you telling me that all… this… has been because of a house!'

What could she say to explain? Yes, that was part of it, but the rest wasn't, but she dare not tell him, not now.

In a small voice she said, 'Whatever the reason, you still didn't trust me, did you?'

He ran a hand through his hair. 'I hadn't expected you not to be here without any idea of where you were. I couldn't reach Sarah. The hospital hadn't seen you since lunchtime. I even wondered if you'd gone to Richmond.'

'Alex, you made me promise not to. Do you think I would disobey you?'

'I hoped you wouldn't, but I was running out of options by then.' He ran a shaking hand over his face. 'I was frantic about you being hurt, and I didn't know how to help you.'

She could hear the distress, but also the residual anger in his voice. 'Catherine, if you were sitting in an office brimming with telephones all this time, why didn't you call either my office or here? Didn't you care that I might be worried?'

She realised now that this was obvious, but at the time she just hadn't thought about it. 'I'm sorry. I should have done that, I know now.'

He exploded then as his anger poured out, his fists thumping the bed in frustration. 'God Almighty, Catherine, why do you do these crazy, impulsive things without stopping to think? I've been through hell and back tonight. I've driven or walked half over London just trying to think it all through. To do the best... for us.'

Catherine put her head down on her knees. When she saw the house it all seemed so right, at the time. Her heart told her it was meant to be. But now... And he still didn't know her other news. Then her inner spirit rebelled. She wasn't going to let him put all the blame on her.

She lifted up her head. 'So your lady friend wasn't available tonight, then?'

He reached out a hand and she recoiled, thinking she had pushed him too far. With a muttered oath he stood up and walked to the window. He turned back to face her.

'Whatever you might think to the contrary, Catherine, I have never yet been so angry that I would strike a woman. I wasn't going to before, although you thought so. I don't intend to do so now. I'm angry, yes! That will pass with time, I've no doubt. Whether I can ever get over what's happened tonight is another thing. To answer your question, your inferences about another woman are about as insubstantial as my suspicions of you. There is no one else, Catherine. I don't want anyone else. I thought I had found all I wanted in you.'

Catherine looked at him. She wasn't finished yet. 'What about that handkerchief?'

'You keep going on about that. What in God's name are you talking about?'

'When I turned out the pockets of your navy suit for dry cleaning the other day I found a handkerchief covered in red lipstick. I didn't speak to you about it. I just threw it away in the bin. I tried to believe in you.'

He stood quite still. She could see him thinking, and then saw some of the anger draining away from him and he almost smiled. 'Ah, yes, I remember. A certain young lady made unwelcome advances to me. Her father – yes, her father – proffered the handkerchief for me to remove the evidence. I must have put it in my pocket.' He glanced at her with a wry expression. 'You should have mentioned it after all, Catherine. That would have been one problem out of the way.'

He came and sat down on the bed again. 'The question is, what are we going to do now? We can't keep on like this. Perhaps Sarah was right, we've tried to move our relationship on too far, too fast. Maybe we still don't know each other well enough yet.'

Catherine reached out for his hand. She couldn't bear him looking so tired and defeated. 'Alex, I love you. I always have and I always will. I don't want to be anywhere but with you. I know I do stupid things at times. I'm sorry. It's just me, I suppose. I must try to think first. Don't bother any more about the house. It's not important. We'll manage somehow.'

Too late, she realised her slip. It was testament to how tired Alex was that he didn't pick up on the statement and query it. He turned her hand over in his and studied it as if for the first time, twisting the rings around on her finger in an absent-minded gesture, then he gave a weary sigh.

'Catherine, you exasperate and infuriate me as no one else has ever done, but despite all that, as God is my witness, I love you. I suppose it's one of the reasons why I do love you. You excite my senses. I want you to be here for me all the time, but I must learn that you have a right to an independent life, away from this flat. I would just ask you, please, please try not to put me through the worry of wondering where you are again. I do trust you. I promise I won't make any more wild accusations. I'll try to listen to what you have to say before I start to shout. I'm sorry.'

He reached out and touched her cheek. She took hold of his hand and pulled him towards her. He came and sat against the pillows and held her against him. They sat there together in silence. Too much emotion had been expended over the last few hours for their embrace to lead to anything more; it was just a gesture of shared relief and comfort.

The silence continued for a while and then Alex stirred and stood up. 'I'd better get changed and ready for work, I suppose.'

'Alex, you haven't slept. You can't go to work.'

Turning back at the bedroom door, he said, 'I'm used to nights without sleep. I'll manage. I'd appreciate a coffee, though.'

Knowing that moving around at this time of the morning might be a problem, Catherine was very cautious, afraid that she might yet give herself away. She was sitting at the kitchen table with a pot of coffee when Alex returned, not looking any fresher. He drank a few mouthfuls, and then pushed the mug away.

'I'll have to get the Tube in today.' He glanced at her. 'I parked the car somewhere last night, and I can't remember where. The lads are looking out for it. They have the keys. They've promised to deliver it back here.' He stood up, keeping his eyes averted from her. 'Stupid, or what!'

All Catherine could do was bite her lip and try not to burst into tears. She couldn't say a word, and didn't dare look at him.

Alex walked past, ruffling her hair and murmured, 'See you tonight.'

The door closed behind him, and she raced for the bathroom.

It was just before lunchtime when Catherine heard the sound of the Porsche outside. A few moments later the doorbell rang and when she answered it a young police officer stood there, beaming, holding out the keys.

'Thank the Inspector will you for letting me have the chance to drive his car. It's great!'

The young man loped off down the stairs, muttering to himself how some people had all the luck. Rank, a sports car, and a wife like that!

*

Alex was facing another day in the office on his own. He would have preferred Dougie to be there, just to help him keep awake. He drank what seemed to be gallons of coffee, and had the window wide open, but there was no way he could concentrate.

It was only because of a note on his blotter that he remembered he had arranged to meet Jerry McIntyre at lunchtime for a drink. He left the office well before time, for the chance of some exercise and fresh air he told himself.

When Jerry arrived, apologising for having slept in on his day off, he gave Alex a considered look.

'You look a bit frayed round the edges.'

'I don't think it's just the edges, Jerry. I feel about ninety all the way through.'

'I'd say you can add about twenty to that, my friend. What's been happening? Are the criminals gaining on you, or shouldn't I ask?'

There was a pause. 'It's not work, Jerry.'

'Ah!' Jerry kept his eyes on his drink. 'Bad is it? Or do you want to keep it private? Don't forget, I'm a doctor, I can hold my tongue.'

Alex swirled the remaining liquid around in his glass. Perhaps if he discussed the situation with someone else he'd have a better perspective on the whole thing.

Jerry listened in silence. He took particular note of Alex's embarrassed comments about Catherine's recent odd behaviour.

'Well, you sound as if you've sorted most of it out. A touch of misinformation by the look of it. At least you both know there's no third party. What do you want to do about the house? Forgive me for saying this, but had you considered that even though Catherine likes the flat, she might feel that it's still your flat, rather than somewhere belonging to both of you. Nest-building and the like can loom large to a feminine mind. Catherine has always lived in someone else's property, rather than a home in a family sense. There would be no harm in taking a look at this property that she's found. If it's not the one, it could start you on the road to finding something. I've got the card of that solicitor friend of mine here somewhere,' he added, fishing in his inside jacket pocket, 'yes, here we are.' He handed Alex the small printed card. 'Give him a call when you're ready and tell him I've recommended you. I might get commission.'

Alex took the card and studied it. 'You've got a point, Jerry. I never thought about Catherine's attitude to the flat. She seemed happy enough. I must admit it would be nice to have somewhere to put down roots together. Why is it, though, that I get this feeling there's something else wrong? Something she still isn't telling me.'

Jerry grinned to himself. Even the great detective hadn't worked it out yet. Boy, was he in for a shock!

*

Alex was glad to see the Porsche had arrived back. He walked round it to see if there were any dents or scratches, but it all looked fine. Seeing it again brought back some of the feelings of the previous night, and he was a little apprehensive as he let himself into the flat.

Catherine was doing her history course work at the table, but she looked up and smiled at him. He went over to her and placed a quick kiss on her hair. He still felt too raw inside to be able to cope with more.

'Are you busy? I was just wondering, as you'd done all that investigating yesterday, if you wanted to have another look at that house?'

He noticed that she made a point of not meeting his eyes.

'I told you that it didn't matter.'

'Catherine, I've been thinking today that it's something we should perhaps give some consideration to. Get your coat on. We'll go and take a look.'

She did look at him then, and some of the sparkle was back in her eyes.

'Do you mean it?'

'Of course, I just said so. Come on, hurry up!'

She raced off to get a coat, and he felt better than he had all day. The bridge had been spanned, and whatever happened regarding this house, there was now a shared idea as to their future.

Catherine, as usual, worked her innocent magic and the estate agency allowed them to have the keys to view the property on their own. Following Catherine's directions, as soon as he turned into

Church Road, Alex knew what had attracted her to the area. The tree-lined road and well-maintained properties were a good first impression. The property they had come to see looked a little more unkempt than the others, but, he thought, from a first glance, nothing major.

As they went from room to room inside he was quite impressed. Catherine had been thinking about the interior and suggested to him some internal changes that could be made. The kitchen and bathroom needed some updating, otherwise it appeared to be just cosmetic work required.

Catherine said she would leave him to have a further look around inside while she went out into the garden. A clever move on her part, he thought. It gave him time to think about things on his own. He knew very well that this was the first property they had looked at together, but like Catherine, he was beginning to feel something for this house. He went upstairs and stood at one of the back bedroom windows watching her out in the garden. She was walking around, looking at the various shrubs and bushes, and even pulling up weeds. In her mind she belonged here already, he thought. The question was, did he?

He searched around in his inner self for an honest answer. Since he'd met Catherine there had been a shift in his attitude to many things. The whole idea of marriage and a home had been alien to him such a short time ago, but now he felt an irresistible urge to continue the journey with her. Yes, it was time to make the next move in their lives.

He went downstairs and out into the garden. Catherine saw him coming and he could sense the apprehension in her.

'Doing some gardening already? You might need some help. You'll have to teach me, there's a lot here to do.'

He watched her face, the hope coming into her eyes. He took a deep breath.

'I like the house, a lot. Perhaps we could shave a bit off the price, as there's work to be done. Anything we can save will be a help.' He reached out for her and she came into his arms. 'Would you like to make this our home Catherine, to start building our lives together?'

She buried her head in his chest, and he heard her whisper, 'Yes please, Alex. I would like that.'

'We'll have a go then, shall we?'

She lifted her head and he saw, to his surprise, her eyes were serious and apprehensive. His felt his stomach tighten.

'Alex, even if we don't get this house, it would be nice if we could find one as soon as possible. You see… we're going to need some extra space soon.' She was looking up at him, anxiety clear on her face. 'Do you understand?'

Then he did! My God, he had been so slow not to spot it! This would explain her odd behaviour of late.

'Are you sure? When did you know?'

'I've suspected it for a week or so, but I had some tests when I was at the Fulham Hospital and they confirmed it, although it's not far along.'

'Catherine, when were you going to tell me?' Then he realised, and looking at her face, he knew. He sighed. 'You were going to tell me last night. That, and the house. And then… Why didn't you tell me earlier today?'

He saw her head go down. 'I didn't want to put pressure on you to make any decisions because of that,' she said in a small voice.

He put his hand under her chin and lifted her face. He looked deep into her eyes. 'Supposing that I did have someone else to go to, what would you have done then?'

He felt the trembling in her body and saw the green eyes cloud over with tears. 'I would still have had the baby, just to remind me of you. I'd have managed somehow.'

Alex knew that it was the truth, and for a moment was overcome with the depth of his emotions. He bent his head and kissed her soft mouth.

'I love you, Catherine. You, and now our child.'

He gathered her close in his arms, and for some while they just stood there together in the darkening garden, letting their mutual love heal the wounds they had inflicted on each other.

CHAPTER 11

Their first introduction to Simon Kingsley, Jerry's solicitor friend, was very favourable. He steered them through all the initial legal formalities, and suggested that if everything went as he anticipated, the whole matter could be nearing completion within a few weeks.

At the conclusion of their interview he suggested it might be a good idea if they thought about Wills. Alex had to work hard to hide his grin, and didn't dare glance at Catherine.

'I always feel plans should be made for the future as soon as you start owning property and having a family. I have a checklist here you can work through for ideas. I think you ought to give it some thought at least, and when you come to sign the papers perhaps we can talk about it again.' He rummaged in a tray on his desk and handed them a printed sheet.

Alex looked over at Catherine. It seemed a bit over the top to think about something like this, but then again he could see the logic.

'I take your point, Simon, and I suppose it is a good idea.' Alex knew he had to bring something out in the open. 'There's also the matter of money to which Catherine will be entitled when she's twenty-five.'

Simon looked interested at this news. 'Lucky girl! How long do you have to wait for this, Catherine, if I can ask a delicate question of a lady?'

'It will be next year, September 1976.'

'Do you know how much will be involved?'

'I have no real idea of total value. I've never bothered to find out. I believe there are proceeds of sale from areas of farmland in Ireland which came from my mother, and also an extensive portfolio of stocks and shares. I remember my uncle commented once that it was a considerable sum. The trustees are my uncle and two of his friends; one is a banker and the other a lawyer.'

'If you let me have their details I'll get in touch and see if I can find out some up-to-date information.'

Alex cleared his throat. 'I would like to make one point about this, Simon. Can we indicate in some way that none of Catherine's money from this fund comes to me; it should go straight to any children?'

'Alex?' He could feel the green gaze on him. He glanced at Catherine's distressed face.

'I mean it, my love. It's your money, and I want no part of it. Do what you want with it, give it to a cat's home if you like.' He couldn't keep the edge out of his voice.

He saw that Simon was looking from one to the other with a slight frown, no doubt realising that there was an issue here.

'Well, as I said, talk a bit about your affairs and we'll sort something out next time you come.'

As they left the offices Alex knew he could well hear more about the point; however, he would never tell Catherine what had passed between him and her uncle. He would just have to remain firm on the matter even if she was upset. To his relief, Catherine didn't refer to the issue. She must have guessed that he had a reason and wouldn't change his mind.

After further discussion over the next few weeks, they found their deliberations and thoughts on any executors and guardians always came back to the same people, Sarah and Jerry. Another lunchtime drink between Alex and Jerry settled the matter between the four of them.

It was with a smile that Alex later passed on to Catherine Jerry's parting comment that if Simon was drumming up business with this much success, his remark about making a fortune was scheduled to come true.

*

Lionel Franklin reread the papers in front of him. It was a report from one of Clarke's men who had been keeping an eye on the Hartmans. He noted several attendances by them both to a local GP, and a solicitor. He was beginning to form a disturbing idea. What if that wretched girl was going to have Hartman's brat and they were thinking of getting a house? Damn the man! It was happening again!

He could feel the old resentment building in him. Like her mother, Catherine was causing his plans to be thwarted. It was frustrating. The chance to get back at Hartman was starting to eat away at him, but it had to be done with care, and he must learn patience. He'd been ready to move ahead, but decided it was better now to wait and see what developed. With the possibility of a child, a new idea was forming. Long term, but worth the wait, and so much more satisfying.

*

'She's turned into this demented harridan overnight. I feel sorry for the workmen. I keep out of the way, I'm too embarrassed. Likewise shopkeepers. I don't think she's bought anything full price yet.'

Laughing, Alex ignored the glare directed his way. Jerry and Sarah were at the flat for a meal. Catherine was busy in and out of the kitchen, and Alex was bringing them up to date on all that had happened over the last month or two. The house had been purchased in record time with Simon working his magic, and builders were at the moment finishing off Catherine's requested alterations.

'Despite some serious sickness in the mornings, Catherine seems to be a going concern for the rest of the day. Although I think she does too much. I have to put my foot down from time to time, especially about her course work.'

'When do you think you'll be moving?' Jerry asked, glancing at Sarah.

'Within a week or two, according to the builder. They're just finishing off the decoration, and then it's carpets, and furniture.'

Alex looked from Jerry to Sarah, sensing something more in their questioning.

'Did you rent this flat furnished, Alex?' It was Sarah's turn for the query.

'Pretty much. I'll be taking one or two pieces. The old desk over there came from my father's house. Luigi stored it until I found this flat. Why the interest you two? Out with it!'

'Since Sarah obtained the Sister's post at St Thomas's we both have much further to travel from the South Kensington flat, plus Sarah's parents will be back in the UK soon. Do you think your landlord would be interested in renting this flat to us? It's just right for what we need at the moment. We'll no doubt go down the house-hunting route in the near future ourselves, but just for now this would be fine.'

'Jake hasn't said he has a new tenant lined up, so I can always ask him. I'll make a point of seeing him, and let you know what he says.' He saw Catherine coming in from the kitchen with some food, and raised his voice so she would be sure to hear. 'Perhaps I should ask The Fixer to have a word with him. She'll no doubt flutter her eyelashes at him and the poor devil won't know what's hit him.'

Catherine maintained her dignity as she waved her guests to the table. 'Well, it seemed to work on you, didn't it.'

Alex came and put his arm around her and patted her bump. 'And then look what happened!' he murmured.

He kissed her on the mouth to silence her gasp of embarrassment, and then, with a wicked smile, saw her seated at the table.

*

Sarah was full of her observations of the evening during their journey home.

'Have you noticed, Jerry, how different they seem now with each other? That electric excitement is still there, but it's more mellow. They can tease each other without mercy but the bottom line is always their love for each other. Perhaps that's what a home and a baby can do for you!'

Jerry commented, 'That's the normal progression of any relationship I suppose. You're more sure and comfortable with one another.'

'Catherine says how good Alex is to her in the mornings when she's feeling unwell. He's made arrangements with his colleague that he'll arrive later in the morning, and stay later at night. I think that's fantastic, don't you?'

Jerry grinned at her. 'He's my role model, is he?'

Sarah smiled back at him. 'In a short while we'll tick the first box by being married, but I think I'd like to wait a little longer for anything else. What about the New Year?'

'Sounds good to me, sweetness. Did I mention at all that I love you very much?'

*

At the end of a wonderful, but pressure-filled day, Alex felt relieved to come back to their new home. He had felt honoured when Jerry asked him to be best man at his wedding, and endeavoured to discharge his duties as well as he could, both before and during the actual formalities. He was thankful that everything appeared to have gone off without a hitch.

Compared with the number at his own wedding, the Registry Office was crammed full with relatives and friends. Sarah made a charming bride, and Alex was so proud of Catherine. In his mind, she was the most beautiful women there, still elegant in a loose green outfit, despite her growing difficulties. He saw other men's eyes on her, but felt no threat, secure as he was in the knowledge of her love for him. It had been agreed between them that her twenty-fourth birthday would not be celebrated in any special way, but by using the wedding as a double event.

As he helped Catherine out of the Porsche, not for the first time, Alex faced the fact that it was no longer an ideal vehicle for them. As much as he loved it, changes would have to be made. He must give it serious consideration.

'I'm going to mark down on the calendar when we have to put provisions in the flat for when they come back off their honeymoon. We're bound to forget otherwise.' Catherine walked over to the calendar hanging on the kitchen wall.

'It was a wonderful day. Sarah's parents are still quite high-powered, aren't they. I remember them from the odd holiday I had with Sarah when we were at school. Her mother was interested in how I was getting on with my pregnancy. A pity they couldn't have stayed in the UK for longer. I think Sarah would have liked more time with her mother before the ceremony. I liked Jerry's parents. Very Scottish. You were talking to his father for some while weren't you.'

Alex felt a sense of guilt. He'd mixed business with pleasure. Jerry's parents lived on the Ayrshire coast and his father, who'd been in the Navy, talked about all the small bays and harbours along that western coastline, and how there were always rumours of irregular happenings over the years. Once he was aware of Alex's profession, he commented that it must be very hard to police the area all the time. Something at the back of Alex's mind started to bother him, and then he remembered: the book in the Judge's library about the western Scottish coastline. Also, the parcel brought by Duncan Hamilton and left with the Judge. Brought from Scotland? He then remembered the piece of paper he had picked up from the study carpet that night, with dates and times. Delivery arrangements? Delivery of what, and from where? Ireland? It wasn't that far across the Irish Sea. He would get a map next week and he and Dougie could study the area. Perhaps they should contact the local police forces to see if there were reports of any unusual happenings. He couldn't say any of this to Catherine, of course.

In answer to her question, all he could think of was, 'Oh, he was quite interesting, talking about his old Navy days.'

'Do you want tea or coffee, Alex? I'm just putting the kettle on.'

He walked up to his wife, put his arms around her thickened waist, and turned her into the dining area.

'Go and sit down, my love. I'll make the tea. You've been on your feet a lot today.'

Seated in old leather chairs draped with colourful blankets – a money-saving idea of Catherine's – they chatted about the wedding for several minutes, but it became obvious to him that Catherine was hesitating in saying something to him.

'Reverend Jones, the Vicar of St Luke's, you know, at the bottom of the road, came to see me the other day. Mary next door had suggested to him that I might be interested in a project the Diocese is attempting.'

Their neighbour was a retired history teacher and had been of assistance to Catherine in her studies.

'Catherine, you've enough on your plate at the moment. I'm not sure I want you taking on anything else.'

'Let me be the judge of that, thank you.' The green fire sparked at him and he knew there would be a battle.

'Catherine, please!' He tried once more.

Her smile was now warm for him. She was asserting her independence, but also acknowledging his concern for her.

'I understand it's just a case of translating some old documents. Reverend Jones said there was no time consideration as this project has been talked about for some while now.'

Alex knew from Catherine's face that the idea had sparked her interest. If time wasn't a problem, he was a little happier about it.

In the end, by amicable agreement, Catherine decided she would work on the church documents one day a week. Alex could see that she was keen to be involved, and from a wider angle he felt that it would help her get to know local people who attended the church. He was conscious of the fact that even though she would be busy when the baby arrived, with no family around, and the hours he sometimes had to work, she might welcome other company.

All in all, he felt their move was working out as well as they had both hoped. But however pleasant life was for him in other areas, his thoughts were never far away from his continuing investigations.

CHAPTER 12

It was a brisk late October afternoon as Alex walked down the road to the church. The leaves were already starting to fall, and crunched under his feet.

He had left work as soon as he could today, and was keen to show Catherine his surprise. He decided he would go to meet her and they could walk home together. He let himself in the side door of the vestry and followed the sound of voices. He knocked on the office door and it was opened by Edith Jones, the Vicar's wife. She was helping Catherine to sort through all the old documentation.

'Hello, Alex. I can guess who you've come for!'

Catherine looked up at him and then at her watch. 'I didn't think you'd be home yet.' She walked to him and planted a kiss on his cheek. He wanted to turn his head and capture her mouth, but then remembered where he was, and thought better of it.

'I managed to get away, and I thought I'd come to meet you. I can wait if you're not ready.'

'No, that's alright, I can come now.' She reached for her coat, and Alex helped her into it, buttoning her up like a small child against the chill evening.

Edith watched the scene and marvelled again at the tenderness this man always showed to his young wife. With his job and rank, she knew that he must have seen all the worst side of human frailties, but this he appeared to keep within himself and, she sensed, it did not pervade his home life or attitude to others. Both she and her husband considered that the young couple had proper views on life and would make good parents, and also be an asset to the neighbourhood.

'I'll take this one letter home if I may, Edith, and see if I can start working it out. Bye for now.'

Putting the papers in a plastic bag and tucking them inside her coat, Catherine followed her husband out into the dusk. Alex drew her close to his side and tucked her arm through his.

'Warm enough?'

She smiled up at him and nodded. For the hundredth time he thought that the pregnancy made her look even more beautiful. Her eyes were clear and sparkling and her creamy skin appeared to have an almost translucent glow. His glance landed on her mouth and he couldn't wait any longer. He turned her into his arms and covered her mouth with his. For a long while they just stood there, oblivious to everything around them. He deepened the kiss and, feeling an answering response, wished they were already at home. With reluctance, he lifted his head. Catherine's eyes were closed and her mouth was full and red.

His voice was unsteady as he whispered, 'I think we ought to get home now, don't you?'

The soft green eyes looked up at him, 'Yes, Alex. Please take me home.'

Putting his arm around her shoulders, they continued up the road to their gate.

'I've something to show you,' he told her with a diffident smile, and pointed to the driveway, where a Volvo estate car was parked. 'This is our new car. The Porsche was becoming impractical in the circumstances. When you've had the baby and you're feeling fit, you can have driving lessons from a former police driver I know who has set up his own driving school. This will mean that you'll be mobile for all your daily requirements, with plenty of space for things for the baby. It's big, but reputedly safe. What do you think?'

Catherine turned to him, speechless. 'But... but you loved that Porsche, Alex!'

'I love you and the baby even more. It was just a car, after all, and I'd had a chance to own it. Guess who I sold it to?'

Catherine shook her head.

'Jake Turner. He's always admired it and said that if I needed to sell it at any time he wanted first refusal. He gave me a good price for it too.'

Alex had never seen so much money in cash. Jake told him he preferred to do some of his transactions that way, and it wasn't his place to query why.

'But Alex, what are you going to use for transport if I'm to have this?'

'Oh, there's some money left over. I can get something else for myself in the future. It's what we want now that counts.'

Catherine put her arms around him and stood on tip toe. With her mouth inches away from his, she whispered, 'Did I ever tell you how much I love you, how glad I am that I married you, and that I'm having your child? Also, how very much I want to go to bed with you?'

Feigning indifference, and suppressing his smile, Alex whispered against her mouth, 'Well, I suppose that's some consolation for losing the Porsche.' Then in a more definite tone he added, 'Can we go to bed right now? I'm not sure I can wait any longer.'

Arms around each other, they went into the house and straight upstairs.

*

Christmas, in two weeks' time, was intended to be quiet, first and foremost because Alex refused to accept anything else. Sarah and Jerry were going to Scotland, so they wouldn't be around. However, after much persuasion, of a kind which Alex enjoyed very much, he relented and agreed that Luigi and Maria could be their guests for Boxing Day.

Catherine was in town with Sarah for the day. She had strict instructions not to be on her own, and to get a taxi straight home. They were having a pot of tea together before Sarah left to meet Jerry.

'I don't know how you found it, Catherine, but being married somehow alters a relationship. I feel so much more part of Jerry's life than I did. We were just individuals going along the same path before. The flat and the jobs are working well, and I can't believe it's a fortnight to Christmas. These last weeks have flown.'

Catherine grinned at her friend. 'In answer to your question, Alex and I didn't have any time together before we were married. All our learning about each other has been since then, and some of it hasn't been too easy.' Her face lost some of its radiance and Sarah wondered at her thoughts, and guessed that they were unpleasant.

'But look at you now,' she said, 'a house, a baby – well, almost! – and, its all too clear, a close and loving relationship. For those who know you both, the changes are quite noticeable.'

'We seem to have things worked out, for the most part. As to your observation about time, I know all too well what the date is. I can't deny that I'm finding my size gets in the way a bit now. I'd like to see my feet again at some point. I'm starting to get a little nervous, though, when I think of what's to come.' Catherine's glance at her friend was tinged with apprehension.

Sarah squeezed her hand. 'You'll be fine. Alex will be there, and I'll be around. I've been told that nature seems to take over. Perhaps you'll be able to let me know!'

Still laughing together, they left the café. Sarah hailed a taxi. 'Now, do as Alex said: get the next taxi and go straight home. Be a good girl. I'll be in touch with you before we leave for Scotland.' She kissed her friend and waved goodbye.

Catherine waited until the taxi was out of sight and then turned in the direction of Bond Street. She had an errand to do.

She found the arcade Alex had talked about, and then the jewellers shop. Alex had been right when he said it looked a bit run down. She opened the door and went inside.

*

Pytor Fedorovich had now accepted that enough was enough. The Christmas trade was almost non-existent and he would struggle to pay his rent. He felt old and tired. He heard the shop bell. It was almost too much bother to see who it was, but he forced himself out of his chair in front of the gas fire and pulled the curtain aside.

The young woman standing there was a beauty. Her dark brown hair curled on the fur collar of her green coat, a green which almost matched the colour of her eyes. It was obvious that she was well advanced in pregnancy, with one gloved hand supporting her unborn child.

'Please take a seat, madam.' The little jeweller indicated the seat near the counter. The girl came forward and sat down, her movements still graceful despite her advanced condition. He looked again at her face, and in particular those green eyes. Then he remembered a visitor of some time ago. He looked at her gloved hands resting on his counter.

'Would madam be so good as to remove her gloves?'

With a slight smile, she did as requested. So he was right! There on her finger was the ring, gleaming in the shop lights.

Speaking in a quiet tone, the girl said, 'Thank you for my ring. It's perfect. I'm never without it.'

'Your husband was quite right, madam. This was the ring for you. Both very beautiful.' He smiled at her. He was feeling better now, he realised. 'How can I be of service to you?'

'I would like to buy my husband a wrist watch for Christmas. I missed his birthday, and I would like to combine the two. What can you suggest?'

They discussed the sort of watch that might be suitable, and he brought a small selection for her to consider.

'Would you care to do me the honour of sharing a cup of tea, madam?'

He saw her hesitation, and for a moment was disappointed. Then she appeared to change her mind, and accepted with a smile. He trotted off to find his best cups.

Over their tea they settled on a watch with a stainless steel expanding strap. The girl said she had observed her husband's irritation trying to fasten the buckle on his existing watch. The jeweller wrapped the item and placed it in a small box.

'Will you tell your husband where you made your purchase, madam?'

'I don't see any reason why not.' She was puzzled by his comment.

'Perhaps you would remember me to him, and remind him about our conversation as to the other... ah... item.'

'Yes, of course I will. I must be going now. I'm expected home and I don't want to worry anyone.'

He was sad to see her leaving. She had brightened up his shop with her beauty. She had reached his shop door. 'Madam, if I'm correct, your name is Catherine?'

She turned and nodded.

'God speed to you and your child, Catherine.'

Her smile was sweet. 'Thank you. Goodbye.'

Yes, perhaps he could keep on going a little longer. There was a chance that the final piece of jewellery might yet be sold.

*

Catherine was pleased with how the house looked with its Christmas decorations. She knew that, although he had said little, Alex thought it wonderful and was proud of his home. This was all she ever wanted, to give him a proper home and a family.

She arrived downstairs on Christmas morning to find a large bunch of cream roses waiting for her. She had wondered why Alex said he had a last-minute errand to do yesterday. With a grin, he told her he had kept them in the garden shed overnight to keep them cool and fresh.

After thanking him, which took some time, Catherine retrieved the small parcel from its hiding place and handed it to him.

'Catherine, I thought we said we wouldn't buy presents for each other this year.'

'Yes, I know, but I missed your birthday, so it's a sort of double present. Anyway, you bought me my flowers. Go on, open it!'

269

He did so, and she could tell that he was pleased. 'Brilliant! No more fumbling with buckles. Thank you, my darling. I'll put it on right now.'

After a simple lunch and a short walk, as Alex insisted she had some exercise, they curled up together on the settee in the front room. In quiet contentment they listened to some of Alex's favourite Rachmaninov pieces playing in the background, and watched the dancing flames in the fire reflected in the glittering tree decorations.

'Alex, can you guess where I bought your watch?'

'No, my love. Is it important?'

'It's not important, but I would like to tell you.'

He kissed her on the temple. With an indulgent smile he murmured, 'So tell me.'

'I went to the little jewellery shop where you bought my ring.'

That appeared to catch his attention. He sat up straight and held her away from him. 'Why on earth did you go there?'

'I don't know. I was just intrigued to see your little man. He's quite sweet. You were right about his shop being run down. It looked very empty, as if he had nothing to sell. He insisted I had a cup of tea with him.

'Do you know, I believe that somehow he knew who I was. He asked me to take off my gloves before I had even introduced myself, so he must have guessed about the ring. He said you were right, that it was the perfect ring for me. He seemed pleased. He asked me to remember him to you, and then he said something about telling you not to forget about the other item. What did he mean, Alex?'

'I don't know my, love. He must have been mistaken.'

Alex was quite happy to lie to his wife on this occasion. No doubt the jeweller had remembered his description of Catherine. Yes, perhaps he ought to do something about the last item of jewellery. The little man was old, anything could happen, and the chance to buy the earrings would be lost for ever. He made a decision to deal with the matter after the holiday, whether he could afford it or not. He'd thought of waiting until after the baby was born, but there was no reason why he couldn't make the purchase now. He still had some of Jake's cash. Perhaps Sarah would keep the item safe for him so that Catherine wouldn't discover it.

CHAPTER 13

Boxing Day was a wonderful day for Alex, Catherine and their guests. Luigi and Maria had seen the house after it was purchased but they now took delight in seeing the final transformation. As the ladies cleared away, the men indulged themselves in a Christmas after-dinner brandy in the front room.

'You have found yourself an excellent wife, my boy.' Luigi smiled with pleasure at Alex. 'Beautiful, and a good home-maker. When the child arrives you will be a complete family.'

'I know, Luigi. I just hope everything goes well. I think Catherine is a little worried about things now. In a way, I wish it was all over.'

'It's understandable, for the first one. I can remember when Vincenzo was due, I would never let Maria out of my sight. It's amazing how these women cope, though. There must be some inbuilt mechanism for dealing with it.'

He swirled the remnants of his brandy around in his glass and looked over at the younger man. 'Have you had any dealings with that uncle of hers since you were married? Does he know about the child, Alex?'

'We had a royal summons when he found out from one of his friends that we were married. We had intended to tell him, but I suppose neither of us wanted to rush to see him about it. He became a bit heated and I had to send Catherine out of the room while we dealt with it between us.'

Luigi's eyes narrowed, and he leant forward. 'How do you mean, Alex? What trouble is he making now?'

The old familiar worry returned to him, the pleasure of the day now spoilt. He realised Alex must have seen the concern on his face, as he now attempted to dismiss the matter.

'Oh, it's no problem, Luigi.'

'Alex, tell me.'

As he listened to the account of the heated exchange between the two men, Luigi saw the emotion flooding through Alex.

'I felt like throttling him, the bastard. He seemed so calm, just sitting there, looking at me, smiling, with all this… filth, pouring out of him. I told him if I could have proved anything of what he had been suggesting I would have taken him to a Court of Law.'

Luigi watched as Alex stood and paced up and down. It was obvious he was reliving the feelings he'd had at the time.

'He started to go on once more about the money, but I'd had enough. I told him for the last time that I wanted no part of it, and I would be glad to sign something to that effect. He produced a letter which, he said, took care of this. I read it and it seemed to say what I wanted, so I signed it, and threw it at him, and left the room. I collected Catherine and took her away from that house. She knew that something bad had taken place between us, but she said nothing, and as God's my witness Luigi, that night she calmed all the anger out of me and replaced it with her love. Luigi, I love that girl with all my heart!'

Luigi looked at Alex's anguished face and didn't doubt for a moment what he had just heard.

'Have you told anyone else about this, Alex? Have you told your lawyer about this paper?'

Alex came and sat down again. 'No – and no, Luigi. I thought about telling Simon, but you know what he would say: that I shouldn't have signed anything under such provocation. He's no doubt right, but I swear it did say just what I wanted.'

'Mmm… I just wonder why that man had something already prepared. It's almost as if he expected the outcome.'

'It was obvious that I might feel that way. Well, it was to me, anyway. In any case, Luigi, Catherine and I have made our Wills. I've covered the matter by making sure that any of her monies bypass me and go to our children, and I feel happier now the money question has been dealt with.

'When Simon found out about the legacy he told Catherine he would approach the trustees for more information, but he doesn't seem to have got very far. He says he'll give them a little more time and then lean on them a bit. However, it doesn't seem to be bothering Catherine at all.'

Luigi thought for a moment longer. 'You know, boy, I'm no Einstein, but I begin to wonder if these people have been using Catherine's monies for their own purposes, which is why they are a bit reluctant to give too much information away.'

'I'm sure you're not wrong, I've been thinking much the same. I have a feeling that Simon is beginning to suspect something too,' Alex admitted.

The door opened and the two women entered with the coffee. Luigi watched as Alex stood and walked over to his wife, relieving her of the coffee pot and then seeing her seated in a nest of cushions on the settee. When he sat down beside her he bent and placed his mouth on hers. He then took hold of her hand and they sat there together, almost in a shared world of their own. After what he had just heard, Luigi felt his sense of worry deepen.

*

The Christmas break over, Alex had to prepare for his next meeting with Francis and Sir John. He and Dougie settled down with cups of coffee and they talked through their conclusions so far.

'Following on from what we've started to look at, if we thought about the financial side and were to suppose for a minute that funds were being misappropriated for subversive acts, what sort of things should we look for? Do we go for small? For example, as we've discussed before, monies being used to pay off, or employ a person or persons to carry out disruptive acts in some way, to put glitches into the country's economic base. Long-term instability could be the name of the game. With Franklin's knowledge of the court system and insiders there too, he could be informed about vulnerable people who might be persuaded to assist him. We know we've found out quite a lot of interesting information on these points already.'

Dougie nodded in agreement.

Alex went on, 'Now, then, if you want to upscale the whole thing, you could play with the big boys. Bribery for information in government circles, for instance. I know Francis thinks the same. Take defence procurement, for example: find out where your contract is going to be placed, and then put someone in a factory being used to manufacture just a small part, and using the disruption idea, if you multiply it enough, you could then start having delays in defence contracts. MPs start to get worked up about the delays and rising costs, and you end up with unrest in Parliament... and if you wanted to get unreal, you could even think of it bringing down a government, or at the very least influencing personnel changes within the various parties.'

Dougie was warming to the theme now. 'If we're talking about using the big boys, by that, meaning organised crime, you might also consider that you could play with those lads over the water.'

Alex nodded. 'That's why I'm wondering about the Scottish link. We ought to try to obtain information from the various forces in that area as to any comings and goings they might have been interested in. Can you give that some of your time, Dougie? Spin them the old national security line if they get a bit stuffy. Francis said that he would give us some clout if we needed it.'

'OK, Boss. I'll look up the forces covering that area and start doing a bit of leaning. Do you think this is why Franklin was so keen to keep Catherine under his control, so that they could keep on using her money? If so, what does he do when she's entitled to it?'

'Yes, I know, Dougie. My thought is that Catherine's money was a small portion of what he might control. If one avenue dries up, he could go on to use monies from elsewhere. Don't forget the possible sources the other two might be able to lock onto, with one a lawyer and the other a banker: pretty endless!'

'Would it pay to get bank accounts looked at?'

'I don't for a minute think they've got the stuff sitting in a current account with a bank under their own names, Dougie. Again, with Villiers and Hamilton on board it could be buried in all manner of dummy companies. It will take more manpower than we have between us to do that sort of research. It might be worth a check with Companies House, though, to see what they might be involved in.'

'Sure thing, Boss. I'll start on this Scottish thing, I think.'

'When I bring Francis up to speed, I'll see if he has any thoughts.'

*

Alex arrived at the Whitehall office to find that Sir John was once again present. He didn't look a well man, and Alex wondered if he would even reach his retirement date. He and Francis listened while Alex put forward the ideas he'd discussed with Dougie earlier in the day. Francis soon caught on, but Sir John was a little more sceptical.

'All this disruption business sounds like a lot of bother for very little result. If you've got money for sale, get it out there for use by the professionals. Get big results. That's what I'd do.'

'Fair enough,' agreed Alex, 'but what if you have ideological principles? What if you want to change political thinking in a big way, or just do enough to make some people nervous, make them change tactics, or even sides? Keep Parliament in a state of agitation, and you might be able to slip ideas or amendments through, because no one wants to object enough and be the person who upsets the status quo.'

Sir John still didn't look too sure of this train of thought. He'd been brought up in the old school tradition where a man's word was his bond and you stuck with your principles. Any exposure during his career to the harsh reality of crime appeared not to have altered his vision.

Francis looked at Alex. 'What about this Scottish thing? Do you think they are organising some sort of trafficking?'

'It's a good bet. What, and how much, I don't know. My Sergeant is contacting the local forces to see if he can pick up any pointers.'

'If you come up with anything concrete, let me know, and I can have some of my side do some investigating over the water.'

'I'd rather keep this a police thing, Francis, if it's all the same to you.'

Sir John sounded quite huffy, and not for the first time Alex thought that his ultimate boss was turning this investigation into a crusade for personal glory. He was looking to end his career on a high note, with a massive and successful policing operation. Not the soundest of reasons for embarking on an enterprise like this. Alex was well aware that it would do himself no harm career-wise either, but he'd gone into this seeing the bigger picture from his country's point of view. The fact that Catherine's uncle was involved, and he disliked the man, he tried to keep well apart from his overall objective.

'Keep in close touch with me on this, Alex.' Francis stared hard at the younger man, conveying to him that he was just as unsettled about Sir John's attitude. 'I'll leave it to you, Sir John, to use your resources to keep eyes and ears open for anything happening elsewhere.'

'Of course.' Sir John sounded affronted that he had even been questioned on the point.

Alex felt irritated. He'd seen and heard enough. For some reason he had an overwhelming desire to be at home with Catherine, seeing that young smiling face, hearing about her news, and most of all, capturing those soft lips under his. He made to leave before any of his thoughts became visible.

'I need to get back to see my Sergeant before he goes off duty, if that's OK by you, Sir John?'

'Yes, yes. Run along, my boy. Keep up the good work.'

He sounded like an affable headmaster, Alex thought, glancing at Francis before he turned and left the room. Francis's return look told the same story.

*

Dougie had been quite lucky with the Scottish approach so far, he told Alex. 'Once you can understand what on earth they're talking about!'

Already, information re one or two incidents was being sent down to them, together with Coastguard records, and three forces had now promised to keep them posted on any developments.

'You did impress on them about the confidentiality aspect, didn't you, Dougie? I don't want too many people either up there or down here wondering why we're interested.'

'I did indeed. Up there it will look as though someone in London is just being a nuisance again, and anything coming here will be marked personal and confidential to you.'

'OK. If I'm not here, open it up, Dougie, will you.'

Dougie sent him a sly look. 'What if it's from a ladyfriend.'

Alex chuckled. 'If you fancy her, you have my full permission to take her over. There's just one lady I'm interested in.'

Dougie reached for his coat. 'Well, don't stay here too long tonight. I'd get home to her, if I was you.'

'Don't worry, Dougie, I'm intending to do just that.'

As Dougie left, Alex knew that he wouldn't be leaving just yet. Acting on a worrying thought which had come to him some weeks ago, he had begun to make use of the time he was alone in the office to copy the gist of any new evidence gained on any particular day; therefore, in effect, making an almost complete copy of all their records. From the beginning he had insisted that any typed reports by either of them should be made in duplicate. Unknown to Dougie he had retained these copies and was keeping everything in a folder marked 'Expenses' at the back of the bottom drawer of one of their filing cabinets.

All the filing cabinets were kept locked, and only he and Dougie had keys, but the locks weren't the most robust of their kind. Every night before he left he placed small strips of clear tape on the drawers in such a way that they would be removed if the drawers were opened. He judged, from experience of watching them at work, that the cleaners wouldn't be a problem. Dougie knew of this precaution, and if a problem was ever found they would have to discuss how to deal with the matter between them.

After completing his task for the night, he set out for home.

CHAPTER 14

It was time to sell the Richmond house and perhaps discuss with Bonetti moving into the Club full time, thought Lionel Franklin. Now that the Painters had retired, he made do with a cleaner once a week and either made a light meal himself or dined at the Club. The large house was now pointless, and expensive. If Catherine had still been here it might have been different. If that was the case, he thought the Painters might well have stayed on longer too. Why was it that people never seemed to follow the path he expected, or demanded of them? No matter, to hell with them all! He must still continue with his plans, although there would have to be changes.

He would start with Scotland first. It would be nice to go out with a little victory in winding things up. Time to teach Aubrey's Irish friends a lesson. He picked up the phone and ordered a taxi. A few discreet phone calls were required and, as always, he made those calls from the pay phone at The Grosvenor.

There just remained… Hartman. This was the special one, the one that would give him most pleasure. It would have to be crafted with care, but he had now settled on what he considered to be a perfect outcome. However, he would have to be patient yet. As suspected, information had reached him that Catherine was pregnant by that upstart, but in the long term that could work in his favour. He thought for a moment about what he had in mind. It would be a pity... but then he smiled to himself. No, don't think of it like that. It would be more like exercising justice. He would have Hartman then, and it would be worth it. Yes, he was going to enjoy himself.

*

'Morning, Boss. I've just taken a couple of phone calls that will interest you.'

Dougie had the air of someone just bordering on excitement, Alex thought. He took the notepad Dougie was holding out to him, sat at his desk and started to read.

He looked up at his colleague. 'Are they sure about all this?'

'It seems the letter came in last night, hand delivered somehow, not through the post. The information given sounded very positive. Something happening Saturday night by boat.'

Alex glanced through Dougie's notes again. A anonymous letter had been received by the Ayrshire police to inform them that an Irish courier would be landing by boat at Ardrossan some time on Saturday night for a collection from Glasgow Airport, and returning the same night. Could be identified by a red shoulder bag. No more detail. Just that. It appeared that a Chief Inspector King had put on his thinking cap and reviewed the information already supplied on their earlier request. This included a report of a fishing boat having been seen in the locality of Ardrossan on several previous occasions.

It was possible, Alex thought. A fishing boat coming across from Ireland. Not that big a surprise in that area. What made this interesting was that the boat was always seen in the late evening, but by the early morning it was gone.

'Why the tip-off, Dougie? If it's about who we think it is, you have to be a brave man to upset these people. Is it a diversion of some sort?'

'They seem to be treating it as serious, Boss. King wants to know if we need to be involved. He's ex Met. Went up north for a quieter life!'

'It would have to be Scotland. I'd better find out from Francis if he wants us involved.'

As Alex picked up the phone, Dougie hung around in the corridor outside in case stray ears might be listening.

Francis was enthusiastic about their involvement. 'I think we'll run with this one, Alex. It might be the break we're looking for.'

'Or it could be nothing at all,' Alex countered. 'A long way to go for nothing. The locals can deal with it themselves. We can see what they get, if anything, and take it from there.' In reality he was not that keen about being away from home.

'The local forces will deal with it their way, sure, but they may miss something that we could be looking out for. I'd rather have your presence there in some capacity. You can take your Sergeant with you. Make it look important. Do we know where in Ireland is the jumping-off point?'

'Nothing known. One would assume they use a harbour in a direct route, unless there's a transfer out at sea.'

'Mmm… pity. I could have asked someone on the other side to have a look around. Never mind, we must work with what we have. Tell Chief Inspector King that you will be joining him, and then get yourself and your Sergeant up there as soon as possible on Friday. Keep me informed.'

*

Alex broke the news to Catherine when he reached home. She was busy preparing the dinner but she seemed to be quite calm about the matter.

'It's best for you to be away now rather than in a week or two, isn't it. Don't worry, Alex, I'll be fine. There are plenty of people here I can call on. I'd better sort out what you'll need to pack. How long will you be away?'

'I hope to be back sometime on Sunday. I'll push for that as much as I can, even if I leave Dougie up there.'

He came up behind her and wrapped his arms around her bulk. It didn't seem possible that someone so slight in stature could carry all this extra burden, but she still seemed to move around with elegance. He placed his lips on the nape of her neck.

'I'll miss you both,' he whispered.

She turned in his arms and smiled up at him. 'You can't fail to miss me at the moment. I might be even bigger when you get back!'

As he lowered his mouth to hers, he murmured, 'Whatever size you are, you still delight my soul, and I need you.'

Moments later, she gave his cheek a pat, and released herself. 'Let me finish getting our meal, and perhaps we'll see what we can do later, hmm?'

'That's a promise!'

*

Liam O'Dowd left the Belfast public house in a bad humour. Out of the blue, he'd just been informed that he was to travel to Larne for a trip by boat to Scotland, and to be at Glasgow Airport on Saturday night to collect a package. He'd been told no other information, except that he would be picked up by car when he landed. This wasn't his usual line of work. He wasn't a courier; his expertise was in something very different. He preferred to blend into the background, do his job and move on, and he didn't like jobs arranged in a hurry. He hadn't survived to thirty-six years of age in his business without being calm and controlled. Taking care of the small things. No rush. It always paid off.

He'd been chosen for this job as someone available in the right place. In his case, he thought, the wrong person, in the wrong place, at the wrong time. His instinct, honed over years of experience, told him there was a bad feeling about all this. It sounded a simple enough job, but they were often the ones that went wrong. There was no chance to review the options. Just wait for a car when he arrived, and he would be taken to the airport. Another sort of place he preferred avoiding; and there were too many people involved. Not good at all. He would have to keep his wits about him.

*

John Kerry was surprised when he received the phone call about another trip. It was always more risky at this time of year. The Irish

Sea could be tricky, but the payment promised was higher than usual, and would pretty much pay off all his accumulated debts; then *Patsy* would be his again.

When he had landed up in Court for non-payment of tax and other monies, he had been amazed to come out of it without being declared bankrupt. His solicitor said that some charitable organisation had stepped in with a lump sum payment which kept the creditors happy, and would give him time to pay the monies back on his own terms. When he was asked to do trips from time to time which would help to decrease the amount owed to his benefactor, in truth he wasn't surprised. The phone calls were from an English-sounding person, but you never could be sure of anyone in this country any more.

He had no particular political affinity. He just wanted to get on with his fishing, and sometimes in the summer take sightseers out from Larne round the headland to watch the seals. His deckhand, Fergal, was sixteen and had the fire of ideology in him. He was good enough at his job and willing, but Kerry made sure he was kept away from anything controversial, even more so when they had certain visitors.

This latest visitor would be arriving at any moment, and they were to make sure they had him over the water in time for him to be taken to Glasgow Airport and back on the Saturday evening. The rest of the arrangements would be explained to him when he was picked up.

Perhaps when *Patsy* was his again, he could refuse this type of job. Perhaps!

*

'I think I'll get a paper to read on the flight.'

Alex handed Dougie his bag to mind, and went into the stationers. He bought the first paper he saw. His mind was still with Catherine.

She had appeared quite calm and controlled when he said goodbye to her earlier. She no doubt thought he was fussing, but he didn't like leaving her alone. He knew she had Sarah and Jerry, and Mary next door, to call on, but it just wasn't the same. When he handed her the piece of paper with his contact number she gave him that serene smile he now knew so well, meaning she would remain unruffled by anything he said. All he could do was kiss her, pick up his bag and leave. He would call her as soon as he could when they arrived in Glasgow.

They boarded the flight and settled down. There was nothing left to discuss about the forthcoming operation until they reached Scotland and could liaise with the local Ayrshire force. Chief Inspector King had said he would meet them at the airport.

Dougie retrieved a paperback from his bag and Alex prepared to settle down with the newspaper.

'You know, Boss, this may be pay-back time. If this Scottish thing works out well, we might chalk one up to the good guys for a change.'

'Yes, you're right. I don't like leaving Catherine, but I'm beginning to have a feeling that this is something important and needs all my concentration. Everything else will have to wait.'

*

Catherine had been very careful to conceal from Alex her slight anxiety, and, until he left, maintained an air of apparent casualness. He had a job to do; important, he told her, and it was just unfortunate that it was in Scotland. She had made a deliberate point of not mentioning to him that Mary was away visiting friends in Eastbourne.

The restlessness she had experienced most of the night she put down to her knowledge of him going away. Now that restlessness had turned into the odd cramp or two in her stomach. She hoped she didn't have a bug of some sort. To take her mind off it, she tried to keep herself busy during the rest of the day, and managed to eat something without any repercussions, although she still felt odd. She was glad when the phone rang in the late afternoon and she heard a familiar calm voice.

'Hello, my love. I'm here safe and sound. Are you OK?'

Now was her chance to say to him that she wasn't, that she was on her own and wanted him home. However, she said none of this. She wasn't going to play the hysterical wife.

'I'm fine, darling. A bit of indigestion, that's all.'

'You'll have to keep off those pickled gherkins, you know.'

She could hear the smile in his voice, and it warmed her heart and made her feel better.

'Now he tells me!'

'I'm not sure when I can ring you next, it all depends what happens at this end. Don't forget to lock up tonight, will you. I love you both, and I can't wait to get back. Sleep well, my love.'

'Goodnight, Alex. I love you. Take care.'

As she put down the phone that slight cramp hit her again. Perhaps it might be better if she had a lie down.

CHAPTER 15

Chief Inspector Roy King turned out to be a small, wiry man, with quick movements and bright black eyes which missed nothing. He had spent some time with the Metropolitan Force but decided he no longer liked London and had always enjoyed Scotland. He told them he had never regretted the move.

They were taken to a commandeered office in the airport, and over coffee and sandwiches, in company with a representative from the Glasgow force, King showed them the letter. Alex noted that it was written in childish block capitals, and confirmed for him the details already known. King indicated that no fingerprints had been found. Working on the assumption that this wasn't some sort of hoax, coupled with the reports about the fishing boat, the information received seemed coincidental enough to make it an almost certainty. It now had to be decided how best to approach the matter.

'I'm of the opinion that we should nab him as soon as he lands. The Coastguard can take care of the fishing boat. If we lose him during transition to the airport, he can be away and gone.'

Alex looked at the other men, wondering how he could make his objections known. They seemed approachable and cooperative enough, but this was their patch. King also outranked him. Alex knew that he had to try to be diplomatic, but at the same time he needed to put on the pressure.

'I'm afraid I see it differently to you, Roy. I take your point, but I consider that it's worth taking the gamble and letting him have as much rope as we can give him. We need to see who he's going to meet and what he's picking up. I know there's a risk in doing it this way. We have to keep the airport open, or we might as well all go home. If we have enough personnel and we're dealing with nothing more than a courier, there shouldn't be too much public risk. We've been given this opportunity to find out more, and I think we should use it.'

Roy King stared hard at him, and Alex returned his look.

'Perhaps we ought to start off on the right foot, young man. Have you been sent to take charge of this operation? Is there another agenda of which we're unaware? For example, the information you have already requested… it seems to fit in too well with what we've got here.'

Alex had asked the same questions of Francis before they left London that morning. What authority did he have, and how much should he tell them? He had been told to liaise, and to offer his expertise if he felt it was needed. As to how much to tell them: as much as he felt was required. Which was all a great help! Alex knew he had to be careful. He needed willing assistance, but in his view the job had to get done, either way.

'Roy, we need as much information from this as we can. It could be linked to something else we're working on. That's why I would like it to run as far as we can let it. In official terms, I'm to liaise and offer my thoughts if I consider them needed.' He looked at the other two men. 'If you would prefer a clear chain of command – me, you, and your men – that's fine by me, and I'll carry the can at the end of the day.'

King looked at him for a moment, then broke into a smile. 'I'd forgotten how ruthless you London bastards were! I know you're supposed to be a hot shot, Alex.' His smile broadened at Alex's slight frown. 'Oh yes, laddie, your intelligence network isn't unique. I've found out a lot about you. Now let's see how good you are.'

Alex returned King's smile. He knew, with relief, that he would be able to work with these men.

'Right. The first thing I would like to do is familiarise myself with the layout of the airport and how people move around. If we need to keep observation on this person, we need places to do it. Supposing he's a professional, he'll be keeping his eyes open. I'd like Dougie to take a look at Ardrossan first thing in the morning, and we can work out our cover there. What manpower do you have for this, Roy? We're going to need personnel for Ardrossan, the route in, here in the airport and vehicles, unmarked ones.'

'We can get you all of those. All leave is cancelled this weekend, with people standing by. We can organise most of that tomorrow morning while your man is on the coast, and then fine-tune it. We can give a full briefing to everyone later in the morning.'

'OK. Can you find someone to show Dougie and I around the airport now, so we can liaise with the airport security and work out some placements? Then we pick up again first thing tomorrow.'

'No problem. I'll ask one of our more English-speaking Sergeants to show you around, and then you won't need an interpreter!'

His wicked smile was in no way malicious, and the men grinned at each other. It was always the same in any operation. As the adrenalin started flowing, if everyone worked well together, the camaraderie increased.

It was late before Alex was happy with the information he had gathered, and he was tired. He and Dougie were sharing a room at a nearby hotel, and with an early start the next day both of them tried to get some sleep in the few hours left. Before Alex managed to doze off, he thought about Catherine. He was glad he had been able to ring her as soon as he landed. Would he have a chance to call her tomorrow? He would have to see. He missed not being able to put his arms round her and hold her close while they slept. He kissed her goodnight in his dreams.

*

It was definite, thought Catherine: something was wrong. Her night's sleep had been interrupted and from time to time her tummy was aching. She didn't feel like any breakfast, but she made herself have some toast and coffee. If this carried on, perhaps she would try ringing the midwife, or even Sarah.

By mid-morning she was experiencing bouts of definite sharp pain. She must contact somebody. It couldn't be possible that things were starting yet, there were still another two weeks or so to go.

She tried the numbers for both the midwife and Sarah, but no reply. It was typical, wasn't it, when you needed someone they were never around. Still, she mustn't get herself worked up. It could just be a false alarm, and it would all stop as soon as it had started.

After another hour, she tried the numbers again, with the same result. She was getting anxious now. The pain when it came was quite intense. Should she call her GP? On some instinct she decided to ring the hospital and speak to someone there.

She was put through to the Duty Maternity Sister who listened to her description of the symptoms she was experiencing. The Sister seemed to take on board the fact that she was on her own, and although Catherine wasn't booked in for a hospital delivery, it was decided that she ought to come in so that they could assess her situation. She also offered Catherine some gentle advice on what she should bring in with her, and to remember to secure the house before she left.

Catherine sat in front of the phone. She had just tried her midwife again, but still no reply. The same with Sarah. Where was everybody! She gasped as another bout of pain hit her. Please don't let anything be wrong, she prayed to herself.

She must let Alex know she was going to hospital. She dialled the number he had given her. After a while a soft Scottish voice answered. Explaining who she was, and the reason for her call, to her dismay she was told that neither Alex nor Dougie were available to come to the phone but a message would be passed through as soon as possible. The voice on the other end sounded concerned, but at the same time comforting. She was doing the right thing in going to hospital, she was told, and not to worry, they would take care of her there, and wished her good luck. She thanked the unknown person and hung up. Then she rang for the taxi.

Sister Judy Mason beckoned over a junior nurse.

'Do you know where Dr Newman is, Nurse?'

'I think he's in with Mrs Gibson, Sister.'

'Would you tell him that when he has a minute, I would like a word with him.'

The Nurse hurried away to do her bidding. Sister Mason sat and thought. She was sure this was the same person. She recognised the soft, young voice. As far as she remembered Andy had said that this should be a hospital birth, not a home birth!

Within a few minutes a tired-looking Andy Newman walked up to her. 'What's up, Judy?'

'Andy, do you remember you had a look at a young girl as a favour some months ago? She was here doing a translation job for the hospital. We confirmed that she was pregnant.'

He thought for a moment or two. 'Oh, yes. Pretty little thing. Lucky husband. Yes, I think we said that she ought to go into hospital for the delivery. She's a bit tight on space; there might be a problem.'

'Well, she's just rung in. She now lives in Fulham. She thinks things are happening and she can't get in touch with her midwife. Her husband is away, and she doesn't have anyone with her. I've told her to come in to us. Andy, she was put down for a home birth!'

'What! That's not a good idea. Yes, I think you're right, Judy. When she gets here I'll take a look at her.'

*

If she'd been feeling better, Catherine thought, it would have been quite comical to see the look of consternation on the face of the taxi driver when, on arrival, he noticed her condition, and their destination of the hospital. It was obvious that he was scared to death she would have the baby in his cab. They arrived without mishap, but Catherine disguised from him during the journey that she had experienced the sharpest pain so far.

She presented herself to Maternity Reception just as another bout hit her. She was given a chair, and a Sister she thought she recognised appeared, took one look at her and whisked her away to a side room.

This looks like the real thing, thought Sister Mason. Andy had specified that she was to be taken to a room which had most of the usual delivery apparatus but was kept for possible difficult births. It was also handy if a dash had to be made to the operating theatres.

Catherine had just been settled on to the bed when the Sister returned together with a doctor she recognised as the one she had seen the day she was working at the hospital. It was a relief to have a familiar face amongst all the strangers.

'Mrs Hartman, I'm Andy Newman. I believe we met before, right at the beginning, when we first tested you. I want you to tell me what's been happening and then I'll have a look at you.'

She described to him how she had felt over the past few days.

'Very wise of you to get in touch, my dear. From what you've told me I don't think this is a false alarm. Baby seems to be in a hurry to arrive. I'll just have a look at you and then the girls can make you comfortable and do the dreaded paperwork.'

A short while later, he requested a conference with Sister Mason.

'I haven't changed my mind, Judy. I think there could be trouble. I'm wondering whether we ought to do a C section anyway.' He paused, and thought.

'I think I might just give her a little while longer. Perhaps you could have her sorted out and ready. I'll be back in a few minutes. Let me know if you need me.' He turned to leave and then halted. 'As she's on her own, and it's her first, perhaps we could arrange for someone experienced to be with her? I don't want her too worked up. She seems to be coping at the moment, but things are going to get a whole lot worse.'

'I was thinking the same thing, Andy. I'll ask Margaret to stay with her. There's no one on duty at the moment better suited.'

'Yeah, good thing, Judy. I'll be back soon.'

*

At breakfast, with Alex already making notes, Dougie was called away to the telephone to find Chief Inspector King on the other end.

'A car is on its way to take you to Ardrossan. Sergeant Baird will be with you. Tell Alex I'll be along for him in a while.'

Dougie went back to the restaurant.

'My car's on its way. King says he'll be along for you in a bit. I'll see you later Boss.'

'Fine, Dougie,' murmured Alex, still concentrating on his notes.

*

Much later, Alex had a picture in his mind of both the airport and Ardrossan. Dougie had returned from his visit to the harbour and reported the situation. Alex outlined his conclusions.

'The B780 runs right by the harbour. Good for being picked up in a car. We'll need someone covert in the harbour, on one of the vessels moored there. We also need people monitoring the road both ways to identify any possible vehicle. We'll then need vehicles on the move to shadow into the airport.'

Alex looked up at Roy King. 'We'd better sort out manpower for all this, Roy. Everyone needs to dovetail with each other.'

'I'll get Sergeant Baird in to help us work out who we need, and the vehicles, and then liaise with each force. Where do you want to be?'

Alex looked at Dougie. 'I'd rather have you at the harbour, Dougie. I'll take the airport.' He looked again at King. 'As soon as you know the personnel, I want a full briefing for everyone. I'm going to impress that if this person is from where we think, then he's a pro. He'll have a sixth sense for trouble, and I don't want him spooked in a public place like an airport.'

'OK, Alex. We'll say eleven o'clock for the briefing. I've got the Coastguard involved as well, and perhaps they can send along a representative.'

Alex nodded. 'Thanks, Roy. I'll leave that to you.'

Dougie stayed with Alex, going over the plans again, but after a while he saw Chief Inspector King beckoning him over. They moved outside into the corridor.

'You know you mentioned to me that Alex's wife was expecting their first baby any time soon.' Dougie nodded, apprehensive about what he might hear. 'We've had a message come through from her to say she was going into hospital as she thought the baby had started. We've heard nothing further. Can Alex handle this news now, or should we keep quiet? You know him better than I do.'

Dougie gave a silent whistle. This would blow Alex's mind if he knew, being so far away. He took a deep breath.

'This caper means a fair bit to him, for various reasons. I think he needs all the concentration he can get. I'll take a chance on not saying anything. Catherine's in hospital, she has a doctor and nursing sister as close friends. She's in good hands. Alex couldn't reach her in time even if he left here now. Let's hope the next thing we hear is good news.'

'Right, we'll leave it like that. I'll make sure that any news that comes through goes by me and you, and not him.'

When Dougie went back into the room, Alex was sitting where he had left him, scribbling notes in a pad. Yes, he needed his concentration, thought Dougie; and hoped he'd made the right decision.

CHAPTER 16

Catherine had just experienced another bout of pain. A mature nurse was with her throughout, reminding her of what she had been told for coping with the pain, and offering words of comfort. Catherine was very grateful for her calm, steadying presence.

'Let's make sure we secure your jewellery before we go any further. It's such a beautiful ring.'

'Yes, I love it too. I'm never without it.' Catherine looked at the ring and thought of Alex so far away, but the feel of it around her finger helped her to pretend that he was still close to her.

'If we wrap it up in gauze and then put a piece of tape around, that should keep it safe, dear. Now, then, some of my ladies like to have music playing. I have a tape player and some tapes. Is there anything you would like to hear?'

'Alex always likes to listen to Rachmaninov. He says it calms him down. Perhaps it will do the same for me, Nurse!' Catherine tried to laugh, but found it difficult to generate any real humour.

'I'm sure we can sort out something you like, my dear.' The nurse squeezed the girl's shoulder, sensing her sudden anxiety. 'My name's Margaret, by the way. I don't want you to worry about a thing. You'll be fine. Andy won't let anything happen to you, and I'll stay with you all the time. We're still trying the telephone number for your friend Mrs McIntyre, but so far no luck.'

Andy Newman was in and out, examining her, and having murmured conferences with the Sister and Nurse. Catherine had no idea of the time, it felt as if she'd been in hospital for a lifetime already. Another pain hit her, and she wished Alex was there. She gripped hold of Margaret's hand, and the soothing words she heard were just as Alex might have said. This calmed her, and she hardened her resolve once more.

Out in the corridor, Andy was speaking to Sister Mason and a Staff Nurse.

'It's not ideal, but it's near enough, and I think we'll have to give it a go. We'll see how she copes. If it's all too much, we'll get to theatre. Judy, you'd better warn Dave he may be needed.'

'Already done, Andy.'

'Right, shall we go for it, ladies?'

Catherine saw them come back into the room and sensed some sort of decision had been made.

Andy grinned at her. 'Well now, my dear, I think we'd better get this show on the road. About time you saw this baby of yours, I think. Next time when you feel a contraction coming, sing out, and we'll give you instructions from there on. OK?'

*

Catherine wasn't sure how much more she could take. The effort of pushing when told, and coping with the pain, was beginning to take its toll. The gas and air helped, and Margaret's soothing instructions, but at times Catherine felt she would pass out.

She heard Andy call out, 'Catherine, you're doing fine. Have a rest for a moment, but when the next one comes along try to push for all you're worth. Can you do that for me?'

Catherine managed a rather weak smile and nodded. She felt Margaret bathing her face once more.

'Let's have some more music shall we, dear.'

The soft strains of the melodies Catherine knew so well from the quiet evenings at home, curled up in strong arms, filtered through to her mind. She always felt so safe when he held her. She needed those arms around her now, but they weren't here! Somehow, she gathered her strength once more, and told herself she must use make-believe if she couldn't have the real thing. She let the music fold around her, and imagined his warmth enveloping her.

Andy spoke in a low murmur. 'We'll give it a try, Judy. She's starting to tire, and babe is getting stressed. If it's no go, she's straight into theatre. OK?'

Catherine called out and everyone took their positions.

'Come on, sweetheart, you can do it for Margaret. We all want to see baby, don't we? One mighty push and Andy will do the rest. Hold on to me as hard as you like.'

As the pain came again, Catherine gathered up reserves she didn't know existed. It almost defeated her, then she felt a sudden sharper pain which made her cry out, followed by a feeling of release. As her mind drifted away, she thought she heard a thin wail.

*

Sarah rushed into Maternity Reception, still in uniform. 'I need to see Catherine Hartman please.'

'I believe she's about to give birth. The doctor is with her at the moment.' The interested nurse surveyed the different uniform. 'Are you medical staff?'

'My name is Sarah McIntyre. I'm a Nursing Sister at St Thomas's.'

The young nurse sprang to attention and rushed off. She came back a moment later.

'I think it's just happened. Sister Mason says if you can wait a moment she will come and see you.'

Sarah stood where she was. It was over? Catherine had done it? Well, good for her!

She saw a uniformed figure coming towards her.

'Sister McIntyre? I'm Sister Mason. I'm glad we've made contact at last. Mrs Hartman has just given birth to a baby boy. The baby is fine, but it's been a difficult birth. The doctor is still with her at the moment, dealing with some procedures. She's going to feel uncomfortable for some while, I'm afraid. She's a plucky girl, it couldn't have been easy for her on her own. Were you aware that her husband is away in Scotland?'

'No! I had no idea. Poor Catherine, and even I couldn't be here.' Alex would be horrified, she thought.

'As soon as the doctor has finished we can make her more comfortable and presentable.'

'Can I see her, please? Just to let her know that I'm here at last.'

The other woman hesitated, and then smiled. 'OK, as you're in the profession, but keep it quiet. No celebrations just yet!'

Sarah followed her into the room. She moved over to the figure in the bed.

'Catherine, my pet, it's Sarah. I'm so sorry I wasn't with you. You've been fantastic. You've got a little boy they tell me.'

The dark head turned towards her, and tired green eyes smiled at her. 'Please tell Alex, Sarah.' Then the eyes closed again.

Sarah looked back at the nursing staff. The doctor was still busy and didn't acknowledge her presence. A nurse on the other side of the bed spoke to her.

'Don't worry, Dr Andy's good. She's a bit battered, but she'll be OK. She did very well.'

'You can say that again.' The doctor had now finished his work, and looked at Sarah. 'One of the competition, eh?' taking in her uniform. 'Your friend will be sore for a while, I'm afraid. We'll keep an eye on her as she's lost a bit of blood, but with a rest she should soon make that up.' He turned away. 'Right, I'll just check Junior over, and then I'll have a mug of tea, please, Judy. Do you want to have a peek?' He beckoned Sarah over to a small cot. 'Well, what do you think of that?'

Sarah looked down at the scrap of pink wriggling around in the covers. 'He's just marvellous. I do wish Alex was here. Has Catherine seen him yet?'

'No. She went out like a light just afterwards. She'll be back with us soon, and I'm sure Margaret will help them get acquainted. Do you want to let the father know?'

'Oh yes. Can I use a phone somewhere?'

'Sister will let you use her phone, I'm sure,' he turned to the other woman in query.

'Yes, come on. I need to arrange for that cup of tea anyway.'

Sarah followed her back to a small room off the main reception.

'Your friend was lucky Andy was on duty. He's the best, and she needed him. How anyone thought she could have had the baby at home is beyond us. She would have been in all sorts of trouble. Now, where's that contact phone number. Oh yes, here we are. I'll go and sort out the tea. Would you like one? Have you just been on duty, or are you going?'

'No, I'm finished. I've just done a double shift. That's why I wasn't around when Catherine was trying to ring me.'

Alone, she began to dial the number. She was told that Inspector Hartman wasn't available but the message would be passed through to him, and best wishes were to be delivered to the mother. The person on the other end sounded quite excited.

Nothing to how Alex would be, thought Sarah!

*

Catherine wasn't quite sure where she was. She moved her legs, and felt a sharp pain.

'Try to keep still my dear,' said a familiar calm voice. Margaret was still with her.

'Margaret, what's happening?'

'What's happened, my dear, is that you've had a little boy, and if you promise to keep quiet I'll bring him over to see you.'

Catherine remembered then. A moment or two later a small shape wrapped in a soft blanket was placed on her shoulder. The little pink face was screwed up, but seemed to be making happy snuffling noises. Full of emotion, Catherine touched the little cheek with one hand, the skin felt warm. She looked up at the other woman.

'Is he… is he alright, Margaret?'

'He's fine, my dear. Dr Andy has checked him over. We'll let you have some more rest and then we'll see about getting him his first feed. I gather your friend is passing the message on to your husband.'

For a moment Catherine felt very sad. Alex was missing all this, and she needed to see him. Margaret must have guessed her thoughts, as she patted her shoulder.

'I'm sure it won't be long before your husband is with you. Now try to get some more sleep. We'll put baby in our nursery so you can have some peace.'

Catherine soon slid into an exhausted sleep. When Sarah came back from her phone call she indicated to a rather weary Margaret that she would stay and watch over her.

*

The briefing room was small, and people were packed in tight. Alex had decided to let Roy King and the local force representative lead the briefing, as these were their people; a gesture that was appreciated.

After a general outline of the whole operation, King explained the duties to be undertaken and allotted specific roles. Two people were to be placed on vessels moored in the harbour, to give advance warning of any movements. Traffic along the road couldn't be stopped, but it was to be patrolled by four unmarked cars. A dog handler had been brought in to walk his dog in the general vicinity. Once the subject was identified and moving, the unmarked cars would follow. Plain-clothes police would be patrolling the drop-off area at the airport. The car would be tailed as it moved off again. Its passenger would be watched inside the building from various vantage points already identified by Alex. Any pick-up would be observed, and on leaving the airport building the arrest would be made, thereby causing the least disruption to members of the public.

At this point the Ardrossan end would also be closed down. The Coastguard would deal with the fishing boat. King informed them that extra assistance in identifying the fishing boat involved would be coming from an Air Sea Rescue Sea King helicopter, doing training in the waters around that part of the coast. At this comment, Dougie looked over at Alex, who gave a slight nod, and he surmised that such assistance had come via the man named Francis, who must have some clout with the Ministry of Defence. He knew Alex had been on the phone to him this morning.

King then introduced Alex and Dougie. 'Some of you may already know that we have with us Inspector Hartman and Sergeant Johnson from the SB in London. They've an ongoing situation linked up with what we're trying to do today. Perhaps you'd like to say a few words, Inspector?'

Alex stood, and looked around the room. 'We're working on the premise that this is not a hoax. I'll be much happier, though, when things start happening. From then on you all know your individual roles. If this is who we think, I don't need to remind you that he is a professional. He's been around the block a few times. One whiff of anything out of the ordinary and he'll be off, so remember, act casual, but when you're told, go in hard.' He grinned at them. 'I'll buy the beers afterwards!'

King looked over at Dougie, who shook his head. Not time for a celebration yet, it seemed.

He took over again. 'Right, people. Take your places, and we just sit and wait, but keep alert. Let's show London we know how to do this as well as they do!'

CHAPTER 17

It was early afternoon before a message came through that a fishing boat had been spotted out at sea, heading for the Ardrossan part of the coast. The message was passed around all units to stand ready.

Alex was sitting in the Manager's office at the airport, going over the planning once more in his mind, in case there was anything vital that had been overlooked. He didn't think so. He felt better now that it appeared things were moving. He looked once more at the plan of the airport, visualising possible entrance and exit routes, of which there were several. He wanted this end buttoned up tight, not have someone running around loose with possible danger to the public. He also had a good look at the layout of the airfield itself, and its outbuildings. He drank another cup of coffee. He must be awash with the stuff, he thought, but he needed to keep awake.

It was another two hours before the word came from the harbour that an outboard dinghy had just landed one male passenger, who was making his way up to the road.

*

It was a calm journey across, according to the skipper, but Liam O'Dowd was a land person, and anything above a flat calm was akin to a force ten gale to him. He kept himself to himself on the journey.

The skipper didn't seem to want to talk that much anyway. The young deck hand looked at him in awe and fascination, as if he was some alien, just arrived from outer space. He did learn that they did this run several times a year, which was some sort of comfort.

At one point he thought he heard the sound of a helicopter, and went out on deck to look. The skipper bundled him back into the wheel house.

'It's just an Air Sea Rescue helicopter. They often do training out here, sometimes with the local lifeboat. Nothing unusual. Another hour or so and we'll be there. I'll moor a way offshore and get the inflatable out, and Fergal can run you in. He'll wait there until you get back. I'll stay with the boat.'

The idea of going anywhere in a small dinghy was not to O'Dowd's liking, but if the boy could do it, so could he. He just nodded his understanding.

It was almost dark when, with some relief, he set foot on dry land again. The transfer to shore had been the worst part yet. As he moved along the quayside, all seemed quiet. There were no lights anywhere, and all he could hear was the sound of the water lapping against the harbour wall. He climbed the steps and made his way up to the road. Nothing could be seen except a dog walker in the distance. He waited. He knew he was on time; he had checked before scrambling into the dinghy. A car came past, but kept going. Another car was coming, and he watched as it slowed down. The driver beckoned him over and O'Dowd crossed the road, settling himself into the passenger seat as the car moved off again.

*

King put down the phone. 'He's mobile. Blue Ford Cortina, heading for the A78. Got to be making for Glasgow. Let's get in place everyone.'

He grinned at Alex. Things were moving now, with that news. He'd also heard some other news, but now was not the time to disclose it. Boy, would there be a party tonight if this all went off well!

Alex had decided he wanted to be on the ground. He positioned himself near a small exit door, but it also gave him a good view of the main concourse. The Cortina was being tailed and appeared to be making steady progress towards the airport. As soon as the man entered the terminal, he would be identified. Alex hoped everyone would keep on their toes, alert, but not make any sudden moves. The waiting around was always the worst part, and people being too keen for action was just as dangerous.

*

The car driver told O'Dowd that he was to enter the terminal and wait outside the WH Smith book shop, where contact would be made. He would return in ten minutes to pick him up again. He was handed a red shoulder bag to use as identification and also for the package.

After a quick look around, O'Dowd left the car and walked into the terminal, glancing about in a casual manner. It all seemed quiet enough. He turned towards the shops and identified WH Smith. He pretended to look in the windows for a minute, and then turned to face the passenger area, checking his watch. He put the bag between his feet and waited.

*

'He's here. Six foot, dark hair, mid-to late thirties. Casual black jacket and black cords. Red shoulder bag. WH Smith.'

The alert was passed around the waiting men.

Five minutes went by and no apparent approach was made. The man looked at his watch again, and his gaze searched the area around him. He was getting jittery, thought Alex. And then it came to him. There was no package. This man had been set up.

Someone else was coming to the same conclusion. Alex could see it happening, in the change of attitude and stance. The man was now wary, watching. It was never clear afterwards whether someone or something made the man suspicious, or whether he just decided to get out, but without warning he started to run through the building, leaving his bag behind.

A shouted command rang out. 'He's moving! Close in!'

Alex waited to watch the man's line of flight. He found one of the exit doors, and, thrusting aside a startled young officer placed there, disappeared out into the night. Christ, they couldn't lose him now!

Alex burst out of the door at his side and raced off down the length of the terminal building, dodging luggage containers and other pieces of equipment. He saw the figure not too far ahead, sometimes silhouetted in occasional pools of light. Where was he making for? Alex discarded the heavy coat he was wearing, even though the air was cold. He needed to be free in his movements. He could hear sirens and shouting behind him, but ignored it. He kept his eyes on the black shape and tried not to look at any of the lights. The man was still moving between the machinery, then a roller door screeched up and, for a moment, he was bathed in a pool of harsh yellow light.

Alex moved from his hiding place and pounded forward. The man sensed him coming and turned away into the darkness. Disorientated for a moment, Alex looked around. Which way had he gone? He then made out a dark shape moving across one of the aircraft parking areas near the terminal. He followed after him. The man appeared to be heading for the airfield itself. Was he hoping to hide until first light, and then find another way out of the airport?

Alex felt grass under his feet. The figure was moving quicker now, and Alex upped his pace. It was cold, dark and quiet out here. All the sirens and shouting had faded away. Alex tried to visualise the plan of the airport. Where on earth was he? He saw moving lights to one side, and then realised: the man was making his way towards a runway, and there was a plane coming in! The figure ahead must have become conscious of the situation as he further quickened his pace. As Alex followed him he felt the tarmac of the runway under his feet. The lights were closer now and he could hear the scream of the jet engines. He hurled himself forward and fell on his face in damp grass. He kept his head down as the wind from the passing jet buffeted him, spitting dust and dirt.

After several moments, half deafened by the noise, he raised his head, breathing hard. Where was his quarry? Had he lost him? He looked around in desperation, and then made himself calm down and look again. Yes, he had him: just a dark moving shape. He tried

303

to visualise the airfield plan again. There were some buildings on the far side of the field where, perhaps, the fugitive was hoping to find a hiding place.

Alex could see in his mind's eye that if he circled round to his left, he might be able to intersect with the path the figure was taking. He raised himself into a crouching position. He would have to take a chance and stand up to run, but he doubted the man would be looking behind him. Alex set off at a steady trot; no use expending more energy than he needed at the moment. At one point he thought he had twisted his ankle when he tripped over a divot left by grass-cutting machinery and fell flat on his face. He stood up again, testing himself, but there didn't seem to be any damage.

He completed his flanking circle and came to a small brick building about eight feet high with a flat concrete roof. If his quarry was heading in the direction he thought he was, he would have to pass this way, with any luck making use of the cover of this very building. If he could get on top and lie flat, there was a chance he could drop on the man as he came by.

Alex looked around, but could see nothing to enable him to access the roof with ease. He would have to take a run, grab for the concrete edge and try to haul himself up. His first try ended in failure. He took a deep breath and tried again, reaching as high as he could. His feet scrabbled for purchase on the brick wall, and little by little he managed to inch his way up until his forearms were over the edge. Using the strength of his arms he hauled the rest of his body up on to the roof. He lay there panting. This was doing his suit no good at all, he thought!

Keeping himself in a prone position, he scanned the area. He orientated himself with the way he had come and where he had last seen the man. At first he saw nothing, but after peering into the darkness for a few moments he made out what appeared to be a more solid shape heading his way. That must be him. Alex breathed a sigh of relief. Now, if he stayed lying flat on the roof until the man was almost beneath him, he would be able to carry out his plan to leap down either on him or near him, with height and surprise as his advantage.

He calmed his breathing and tried to concentrate his mind. He turned up the collar of his navy suit jacket to cover the pale outline of his shirt. What if this man was armed? It was possible. He himself had no weapon at all. From what he had seen of the man in the terminal, he was about the same height and build, so there would be no advantage there. He decided not to think about the situation any further. He was here alone and would have to do the best he could.

The moving shape was nearer now, still coming his way. The closer he came to Alex's position the better. He could hear the sound of sirens, but they were in the distance. King was no doubt still hunting for him around the terminal area.

The shape was close now. Alex pressed his body into the roof as flat as he could, and lay still. There was no reason for the man to look up and spot him.

Keeping as relaxed as he could and his breathing steady, Alex became conscious of the figure moving below him. He gathered his legs up underneath him until he was in a crouching position and then launched himself off the roof. This one's for you, Joe, he thought.

With his feet braced together, he hit the man in the back. They both tumbled in the grass. Alex was up first. The other man was on all fours, still half-winded, attempting to draw great gulps of air back into his lungs. This is the one chance I'll get, thought Alex. He dived at the figure and with his shoulder had him prone on the ground. He felt his hand connect with something hard in the grass, and with the stab of pain knew he was injured. It had to end in a hurry now, or he would lose the advantage he had. He swung a blow at the man's head and then struggled to pull his jacket down his arms to try to trap them. The man was kicking out, attempting to connect with some part of Alex's body. Trying with his own weight to keep him on the ground, Alex lay over him, managing to avoid the blows.

He became aware of lights and voices coming towards him. He called out and heard an answering shout. He found himself being picked up by several pairs of hands, and Chief Inspector King's worried face came into view.

'That was a bloody stupid thing to do, boy! Are you alright?'

Alex looked over to where half a dozen of King's men had surrounded the fugitive. There was no way he was going to get away again.

He gave Roy King a shaky grin. 'I am now, Roy, apart from my hand.' He looked at the blood running down his fingers. 'I saw him take off across the field and I couldn't let him get away.'

'Good job a pilot radioed into the tower that he saw figures running across the runway in front of him as he was about to land, otherwise we might have taken some time in finding you. Christ, laddie, you gave me a fright! I wished afterwards that I'd told you!'

'Sorry, Roy, you've lost me now. Told me what?'

'Oh, it'll keep for a bit. Let's get you back and have that hand looked at. Here, use my handkerchief. We got them all, by the way. The Coastguards have apprehended the fishing boat and they're bringing the skipper in. There was a boy waiting in a dinghy in the harbour. Pretty feisty, by all accounts: took three of them to subdue him. We also nabbed the Cortina. It seems it wasn't waiting around to do any return trip.'

Alex settled into the back of an airport security vehicle with a sigh.

'I think our man was set up, Roy. There was no package to pick up at all, and he began to realise it, that's why he ran. I wonder if he's anyone special, not just a courier?'

'We'll have a picture circulated and see if he's known. I doubt he'll volunteer his name and address.'

The lights in the terminal were quite dazzling after the darkness. Alex was half-aware of grins, and thumbs up, and even slaps on the back as he walked up to the Manager's office. His hand was looked at, a deep gash on the side near the wrist which, the airport first aiders informed him, would need a stitch. They then cleaned off the cuts to his face caused by the aircraft debris. He felt in need of a drink but made do with a glass of water.

King told him he'd be taken to a police station where everyone was gathering, and a police doctor would be waiting so that his hand could be dealt with then.

When Alex arrived, he again found that everyone was smiling at him, and congratulating him, and he began to feel embarrassed. The doctor looked at his hand and confirmed it required stitching and proceeded to patch him up and then left to check over the well guarded prisoners.

King handed Alex a small tot of whisky, and poured one for himself.

'Sit down boy, and have this. You're going to need it.' He then looked at the dishevelled young man with a huge grin on his face.

'I'll say this for your crowd, Roy, they all seem to be in high humour,' commented Alex, still trying to see the reason for quite so much elation.

'Nothing like a celebration.' King was still grinning.

Alex looked at him harder. There was something going on here. The door opened and Dougie burst in.

'Boy, am I glad to see you in one piece, Boss. Well, almost,' he amended as he took in Alex's bandaged hand and scruffy appearance. He looked at King. 'Have you told him?'

'Not yet.'

'What's going on? Told me what?'

'You are the proud father of a bouncing baby boy!' announced King.

CHAPTER 18

Alex looked from one grinning face to the other.

'I don't understand.'

'It's right,' said Dougie. 'Catherine called this morning to say something was starting and she was getting to hospital. We had a call just before this thing kicked off tonight to say she's had a boy. We decided not to tell you about anything. You needed all your concentration.'

King spoke up. 'I wondered if that was the right thing to do when I thought you might have got yourself into trouble out there, but it's all turned out alright. Congratulations!'

Alex was still in a daze. 'But she wasn't due yet. Are you sure?'

'Very sure. A Sister Sarah McIntyre rang in the news. They're both OK. Everyone's chuffed to bits for you.'

As the news began to sink in, Alex felt close to tears. 'My poor darling. I wasn't there to help her.'

'Seems as if she's done alright on her own, laddie. Now, back to business. We'll get you to London as soon as we can, but do you want to cast an eye over our catch?'

With great difficulty Alex clawed his mind back to the job in hand. 'Yes, I would like to see what we've got, Roy.'

'OK. I'll organise it. We'll keep them separated and maybe we might get lucky and someone will talk.'

When they were alone, Dougie looked at Alex. 'I'm pleased for you both. Give Catherine a kiss for me when you see her. If you want me to wrap things up here while you get back, I don't mind. You'd better get cleaned up some first, though.'

Alex stood up and looked down at himself. 'Yes, I'd better get to a washroom. Thanks, Dougie. I'll pass your wishes on to Catherine. I'll have some of my own, too!'

He shook his head to try to clear his mind. 'I'll have a first look at what we have here and then we can discuss what needs to be done.'

A while later in the men's washroom after he had smartened himself up as best he could, he looked in the mirror. A father! He still couldn't believe it. He ached to be with his new family, but there was still a job to be done here. He hoped Catherine would understand. He closed his eyes for a moment. 'Thank you, my love. I miss you and love you both, and I'll be with you as soon as I can.'

He then turned and strode out of the room. The sooner he got on with his job the sooner he would be able to leave.

Before the interviewing started, King insisted he rang the hospital. Alex then realised just what the time was, one o'clock in the morning! King told him that they would try to get him on a London plane in the morning, so he should be there by lunchtime.

Alex passed on the information to a Duty Sister, and his love. He was told that Catherine was asleep, but everything was fine. As tired as he was, he couldn't keep the grin off his face as he walked with King to the interview rooms.

*

Catherine looked around the darkened room, and smiled to herself. She had a son! She moved her body, and felt it protest. At her slight gasp, a figure in the chair moved.

'Hello, sweetie. How are you feeling?'

'Oh, Sarah! A bit battered and bruised. What time is it?'

'Just after one o'clock in the morning. I'm supposed to tell them when you wake up.'

'You don't need to stay, Sarah. You need some sleep. You've got to work.'

'I've managed to arrange cover for tomorrow – no, of course, today – so I don't need to worry about that. I'll stay a bit longer, my love. Jerry knows where I am and he sends his best to you both. Guess who rang while you were asleep?'

'Alex? Oh, I wish I could have talked to him.'

'You'll be able to see him in person by lunchtime tomorrow – no, sorry, today. He said he will be catching a morning flight down from Glasgow. He sent you both his love. Now, I'd better tell someone you're awake.'

*

Having been reunited with his top coat, covering up the worst of the damage to his suit, Alex followed Chief Inspector King into the final interview room. He concealed his bandaged hand in his coat pocket.

The other three prisoners had so far said nothing at all, but they displayed varying degrees of emotion. The young boy manning the dinghy looked sullen and resentful, bearing the marks of his attempt to resist arrest. The youngster made an inappropriate comment on being asked if he wished to say anything, but just received a calm stare from King. The other two appeared baffled. One of them was wearing sea boots, and Alex took him for the fishing boat skipper.

The final man, Alex knew, was his fugitive from the airport. He was sitting on the bed, with two uniformed police officers by the door. Alex had passed another half-dozen more in the corridor outside.

He was displaying no emotion at all. He had scratches on one side of his face where he had hit the ground hard when Alex had jumped on him.

King walked to the middle of the room and stood surveying the man. Alex hung back by the door, leaning against the wall, eyes down, studying his shoes.

'Now, then. Let's not waste any time. Do you want to start talking?'

310

Alex became conscious of scrutiny and lifted his head to see the Irishman giving him a considering look. He saw dark eyes travel down to rest on his scuffed shoes. The eyes came back to his again. The man knew that he was his assailant. There was no anger reflected. This one had his emotions well under control. More than ever, Alex was sure that the man was not just an ordinary courier.

King sighed at the silence. 'Alright, my friend, it looks as if it's going to be a long night.'

He turned to Alex and raised an eyebrow, offering him the chance to say or do something. Alex gave what he hoped was an imperceptible shake of his head. For some reason he again looked over at the Irishman and found he was regarding him again, this time with even more interest. It was clear he had noted King's attitude towards Alex, and was trying to work out who he might be. Well, after all, it didn't matter.

Out in the corridor, King turned to Alex. 'I don't think we're going to get much out of the young boy at the moment, apart from bad language. The car driver might be useful. The fishing boat skipper looks as if the sky's fallen in on him. That might produce some results.'

'I think this last one's a pro, Roy. I don't think he's just a courier. He's been sizing me up, and coming to the right conclusions. It would be nice if we could get a name.'

'Photos have already been circulated. We'll see tomorrow if we have any results. Do you want to sit in on anything tonight? You could do with getting your head down for an hour or so. I'll let you know if we turn up anything. In any case, I'll come and take you to the airport.'

'I must admit I'm tempted to let Dougie have a listen to what we have tonight.' His hand was now causing him some discomfort. 'I'll come with you to have a word with him. If he, or you, want me later, give me a call.' He reached into his inside pocket. 'By the way, here's some money for the beer I promised.' He managed a tired grin. 'You can have a double celebration on me.'

Alex thought he wouldn't sleep, but he dropped off in seconds. Although it was for no more than four hours, it took the edge off his tiredness.

The hotel did the best it could during this time with his suit and shoes, and they had been returned to him. He washed and shaved and was getting dressed, surveying the many bruises and scrapes on his body, when the phone rang. For one desperate moment he thought it might be about Catherine, but it was Roy King.

'I hoped you would be up, laddie. I wondered if you wanted to review what we found out last night, which wasn't much. Also, guess what: our Irishman has asked to see you. No one else. Just you. We know who he is, by the way. The intelligence boys will be interested in him, alright. I'll come by now and we can stop off on the way to the airport.'

'I'm not going to miss the plane, Roy. No way!'

'Don't worry, he knows you've a plane to catch. I'll have you on it, my boy. I'll be with you in a minute or two.'

Alex had a quick word with a tired Dougie when he arrived at the station. It seemed that the fishing boat skipper, John Kerry, was being most informative. Dougie said he intended grabbing some sleep and then resuming his talk. They agreed that he should stay in Glasgow for a day or two, and then he could give a full briefing on his return to London.

This would allow Alex two free days with Catherine, which earned Dougie a broad smile of thanks. Alex then followed Roy King to the cell still guarded by two substantial police constables.

The prisoner was named as Liam O'Dowd. He was known to the Northern Irish police, suspected of being involved in activity in the border area and further north, but they had never been lucky in apprehending him – until now.

Alex stepped into the cell. O'Dowd was sitting on the bed with his knees drawn up under his chin. They surveyed each other for a minute or so in silence.

'You wanted to see me?' queried Alex.

O'Dowd regarded him, his dark eyes curious. 'What are you?'

'I'm a police inspector.'

'I know that. You're not ordinary though, are you. Special Branch?'

Alex just shrugged.

'Yes, I bet you are. The one in charge up here outranks you, yet he defers to you.' He stared at Alex for a further moment, and then appeared to make a decision. 'I was set up, wasn't I. Who by?'

'I thought you might be able to tell me that.'

'How were you tipped off?'

'Anonymous letter.'

'Mmm, pity. The skipper might be able to help you some. He seemed quite a decent sort. Doing jobs like this to pay off debts on his boat, he told me.'

Alex made a mental note to tell Dougie, if he hadn't already found out the same thing.

O'Dowd considered him again. 'Were you armed?'

'No. Nor were you, unless you disposed of it somewhere on the airfield.'

'I left it on the boat. I wasn't sure what level of security there might be in the airport. You took a chance, though.'

Alex felt this talk wasn't serving any useful purpose, and turned to go. 'I have to get back to London, but if you want to say anything, ask to speak to my Sergeant Johnson and what you tell him will come straight to me.'

O'Dowd gave a slight smile. 'Oh yes, you've an important date, I gather. Not a good idea – relations, I mean – in my line of work, I've found.' He paused, and his face hardened. 'I could cope with what I'll be getting for things I've done, if that's why I was caught. However, this leaves a sour taste. I don't like being hung out to dry. I'm not going to rest until I find out who's responsible, and then I'll pay them a personal visit. If you find out before I do, you can give them that message.'

There was an ominous finality to the man's statement. Looking at him, Alex saw the coldness in the eyes, and believed every word. He turned and left the room.

*

The persistent throbbing of his hand kept Alex awake on the plane. He'd intended, if he could, to catch some more sleep, but he was too keyed up. All he could think about was rerunning the last few hours, and seeing Catherine.

He found a car waiting at the airport to take him to the hospital. No doubt arranged by King, he thought. He would have liked to have gone home and made himself more presentable, but that would have wasted time.

The nurse on Reception eyed him up and down, her eyes widening; wondering what sort of tramp Catherine had married, he thought. The real reason for her sudden interest didn't occur to him. He was told that the Sister had requested a word with him when he arrived, and he waited, trying to be patient, until she appeared about ten minutes later.

'Good morning Mr… sorry, Inspector Hartman.'

Alex smiled at her. 'Don't worry. I don't mind the "Mr".'

'I'm Sister Barnard. I wasn't on duty when your wife gave birth but the doctor who was will be back tomorrow, and will speak with you then.'

'There's nothing wrong, is there?'

'No, it's all fine, he just wants to explain to you what happened. Your wife's had a rather difficult time, so she'll be uncomfortable for a bit. You'll find them both in the end room on the left. We'll leave you alone for a while.'

Alex followed the directions to the room and pushed open the door. He saw Catherine lying in the bed. She appeared to be sleeping. Her hair had been pulled back from her face and secured, exposing the line of her cheek and neck. How many times, he thought, had he watched her sleeping since he had known her? Every time, it seemed, he felt the urge to place his lips against her throat. He was bending his head towards her when a sound caught his attention. In the cot beside the bed was a small bundle. He moved over and stood looking down – at his son!

'Do you like him Alex?'

He turned his head, and saw the green gaze on him.

'Oh, my love!' He crossed to her and gathered her in his arms. Her small gasp halted him. 'I'm sorry, I didn't mean to hurt you. My darling, you've been so brave.' With gentle hands he laid her back on the pillows.

'Please hold me, Alex. I was so frightened. I needed you so much.'

With great care he slid one arm under her shoulders, murmuring, 'Keep still my love. I'll do all the work.' He lowered his mouth to hers, intending it to be a light kiss but he sensed the remembered fear and anxiety running through her body, and deepened the contact in comfort.

Drawing back from her, he could see now that she was pale and there were dark circles under her eyes.

'Catherine, I'm so proud of you.'

'I had to do it, Alex. There was no one I could contact. I was worried. I thought something had gone wrong. When it was... bad, they played music to me, and I asked them to let me hear the music you like. It made it seem as if you were with me.'

He could feel her body trembling. 'It's alright, my sweet. Always remember, I'm with you, wherever you are.' He stroked her cheek, and she caught sight of his bandaged hand.

'Alex! You're hurt! What have you done?'

'Oh nothing, just a cut which needed a stitch or two. Me being careless.'

She studied his face, and he knew she had also now seen the other marks and taken in his obviously worn appearance. She started to say something, and then stopped. He watched her expression change from concern to one of resignation. She realised he wasn't going to tell her anything, so she wouldn't ask. He kissed her again, by way of a thank-you.

She smiled at him. 'You haven't answered my first question.'

He was looking at her mouth again. 'I've forgotten what that was, my love.'

'Our son, Alex! What do you think of him?'

With a strange reluctance he couldn't understand, he moved off the bed and stood once more looking down into the cot. The small shape was wriggling more now, and as he watched, started to cry.

'He's wondering who the heck I am.'

Just then the door opened and a Staff Nurse appeared.

'Looks as if I came at the right time, dear. Let's get you ready.'

Alex watched as she assisted Catherine to sit upright and then brought over the baby. The small bundle was placed in her arms and she offered a breast enlarged with milk to the infant who, after a moment, stopped crying and began to feed.

The tumult of emotions that flooded through him at this sight unnerved him, and he knew he had to get away by himself. With a quick 'Excuse me', he left the room.

CHAPTER 19

The men's toilet, when he found it, was empty and he stood there, his body shaking as if with a fever. What the hell was wrong with him? Why had he experienced that sudden dreadful anxiety, something akin to… fear, when he had looked at that tender scene? This was his wife and son, for God's sake. He should be brimming over with happiness.

Then, with a growing realisation, he acknowledged that until this moment the fact of having a child, despite it becoming obvious, was still… something in the future. Now it was for real. A wife and child, both depending on him. Did he know how to deal with the responsibilities of being a good father? Had it all come too fast, before he was prepared?

He leant against the wall, the coolness of the tiles soothing the agitation inside him. As he began to calm down he recognised the source of his panic. Catherine, out of necessity, had slipped away from him with her new responsibilities, and from now on it would always be so. She was no longer there just for him – but he still needed her.

It began to dawn on him that Catherine had been all he could think about since she had come into his life, such a short while ago. She had made a huge impact on him. He had delighted in the fact that she was his, and his alone, but now... now he would have to share. Share with this child who had already wreaked such havoc on that beautiful body he loved and desired, and who at this moment was being nourished by her in a way that would still deny him any immediate pleasure.

He straightened up from the wall and paced up and down, trying to think. After a moment or two he knew with certainty how the future must be. Their child had been wanted and created between them, and was a part of them both. As his son grew, he would share his love between his parents, and they with him. Catherine would still be his wife, nothing would change that. When it became possible, she would be his lover again. Yes, this was it, he was sharing her with his son, just as she was sharing her husband, but they still had each other and those special moments between them would happen again.

He began to feel quieter now he had sorted it out in his head. Perhaps he was more tired and muddled than he thought. Had he upset Catherine? He must return to her and show her that they both had all his love, and he would try to be as good a husband and father as it was possible to be.

When he entered the room again she was alone, but still feeding. She looked up as he came towards her. He could see a query in her eyes, but as she recognised his change in attitude she relaxed and smiled at him.

'Feeling better?'

He ran a gentle finger along the side of her breast and on to the cheek of his son. He felt an uplifting surge of sweet emotion. Dear God, he loved them both, and he would do all in his power to look after and protect them.

He smiled at her. 'Perfect, my love. Just perfect.'

*

When Sarah and Jerry arrived during the late afternoon, Alex was on his own. Catherine had just been taken away for a bath. He was sitting in the chair, half-asleep.

'Well, now, how's the proud father!'

Alex knew that he was in for some ribbing from Jerry... but just wait until it was his turn!

With a proud smile, holding his emotions in check, Alex went with Sarah and Jerry to show them his son. He had been into the nursery on several occasions and was beginning to enjoy the feel of the tiny body in his arms. It was getting quite addictive, he thought.

Back in the side room, they waited for Catherine's return.

'He seems a bonny little chap. I hear he gave Catherine a rough time.'

'So I'm told, and she seems pretty uncomfortable. It will all heal up, so they say.'

Sarah had been regarding him with interest but now observed, 'You look as if you've had a rough time as well.'

Alex looked down at his hand. 'Oh, I had an argument with a piece of metal. A couple of stitches, that's all.'

Sarah and Jerry looked at each other. There had been reports on the news bulletins of a security incident at Glasgow airport, and the obvious conclusions were drawn.

'What did Catherine make of it?' Sarah knew the answer. Alex wouldn't tell her anything, and Catherine would know not to ask.

'I'm sure she thinks I'll mend.' He rubbed his hand, 'It's a bit sore at the moment.'

Catherine, rather pale and drawn, came back into the room at that point. The nurse accompanying her saw her seated in a chair, then commented, 'A nice cup of tea is called for after that, I think,' and left the room.

Alex moved over to his wife, lifted her face and placed his mouth over hers. No words needed to be said.

'Well, shall we leave these ladies to congratulate the female species, while we men go off to pat ourselves on the back, or something?' Jerry grinned at Alex.

'Yes, why don't you do that. I'm sure you could both do with a cup of tea. After all, you've been through such a lot!'

Sarah's wry comment brought smiles all round, and Jerry ushered Alex out into the corridor.

'Right,' he stated, his voice firm, 'first thing we do is have that hand looked at.'

*

'I think you'll live! It looks a little angry, but clean. Give it another twenty-four hours and it should have calmed down. Well, Alex, what's it like to be a father?'

Jerry looked up from stirring his tea and was surprised at the serious look he encountered.

'To be honest, it frightened the hell out of me, Jerry. I've never felt emotions like that before. It's now real. We have a child. Something vulnerable that relies on us to look after it... and, you know what, it scares me as to whether I'm going to be any good at it.'

'Well, I don't suppose anyone can be sure of anything like that. Knowing both of you, though, I'd have thought you'll make a damn good go of it. It's not unknown for new fathers to experience various forms of emotion. They can feel out of it a bit at first. The mother is busy looking after the baby, and there's no time left over for the father.'

Alex looked rather sheepish, and glanced up at Jerry. 'Some of my thoughts were rather more... personal than that, Jerry. I watched Catherine feeding him and I went berserk. I almost hated that little scrap for what he had done to Catherine to bring him into this world. I had to leave the room. I went to the Gents and I had a job getting my head around what I was feeling.'

Jerry studied the other man for a moment. Yet again, he was amazed at the level of emotion in what appeared to be a self-confident man. He knew all too well that doctors had to be hard at times in order for them to deal with their profession, and the same must be true in Alex's line of work. It was obvious, though, that he felt certain things deep down, and in his love for Catherine he was at his most vulnerable.

'If I may be blunt, Alex, it's pretty clear to anyone who knows you both that you have a very... how shall we say... intense and intimate relationship. When you consider it, you haven't known each other all that long and the physical side of your feelings is still quite important. The baby has, of necessity, disrupted this and there will be repercussions for a while yet. You have to look long term, Alex. The result of your relations together has been a child. I assume you must have taken this step in joint agreement. When everything is back to normal, you'll wonder what all the fuss was about. Perhaps the baby will be good for you both. It will force you to look outside that close bond the two of you have. I've an idea you've now worked this out for yourself. You seemed quite at home with your son a while ago.'

'Yes, you're right. I came to much the same conclusion. I have to learn to share. Catherine and I love one another, but we both now love our son. Jerry, I want to have her back home, so we can start to be a proper family.'

'She's young and healthy. Give her a few more days, and I'm sure that will happen.'

Alex grinned at him. 'Thanks for the chat, Jerry. I feel happier now you've confirmed some of my thinking.'

'Glad to be of service. I'll send you my professional bill!'

*

Before Alex left for home that evening, he again watched the feeding routine, this time with quiet pleasure, and when their son was wafted away to his nursery place, he and Catherine spoke together.

'We have to give him a name, Alex.'

'I know, my love. We've discussed this before. Are you still thinking the same as you were?'

'Yes, I am. I still like Peter. Do you?'

'I think that would be a very nice name for our son. Peter Hartman. I'll now have to deal with the formalities of registering his birth.'

'It still seems fantastic doesn't it, Alex? I think I'm going to wake up and it's all been a dream.'

'It's your indigestion again!' He paused. 'You knew something when we spoke that night, didn't you.' He saw her eyes drop away from his. 'You weren't going to tell me, were you.' He saw the slight shake of the dark head. 'Oh, my love, no more secrets, eh?'

He touched her mouth with his, and then his heart lurched as he realised what he had just said. That shadow was still there, intertwined with all their happiness.

*

Alex started Monday morning with phone calls. He rang Francis and promised him a full report on the happenings in Scotland as soon as he could. He also told him about his own personal circumstances and after offering his congratulations Francis said he would note the fact that he would be working from home for the next few days.

Alex then contacted Dougie. The poor man sounded shattered and Alex felt a pang of guilt, but Dougie wouldn't hear of Alex making a flying visit back to Scotland.

'I'm almost tied up here now. Should be back either tonight or first thing tomorrow. I'll write up some notes on the plane.'

'OK. Take a day off with your family, and then come round to my house on Wednesday and we'll sift through all your information.'

His next job was the formality of registering Peter, and it was with quiet pride that an hour or so later, looking more presentable, he returned to the hospital and showed an excited Catherine the formal birth certificate.

All the team who had been with Catherine on Saturday were now back on duty again. He met Sister Mason, who said how pleased she was with Catherine's improvement in such a short time. She contacted Andy Newman who, when he arrived, made a favourable impression on Alex with his air of quiet competence.

'I can't thank you, and your team, enough for all the help you gave Catherine. I'm sure she appreciated your skill and attention.'

'No problem. A little out of the usual routine, but we managed. Your wife did very well, all things considered. Remember, though, next time she doesn't give birth that way!'

Alex wanted to query something with him, but felt slight embarrassment about doing so.

'I... er... just wondered, in view of what you had to do... Er... when do you think...?'

Andy Newman grinned at him. He guessed just what this husband

322

was trying to say. 'It might take about six weeks before you have your wife back. Her GP will keep an eye on her, but bring her back to me about then and I'll give her a look as well if you like, and let you know. OK?'

Alex grinned back at him. 'Thanks, I'll do that.'

Catherine was progressing very well and it was hoped that she would be discharged in the next day or two. Alex felt happier. It would be a thrill to bring his new family back home, and start their life together.

However, always at the back of his mind was the situation with Lionel Franklin. He would be seeing Dougie tomorrow morning to hear what he had discovered in Scotland. If there was some tangible evidence, he would have to report back to Francis and Sir John. They were short on factual certainties, this was the trouble. Knowing what was going on was one thing. Proving it was another.

CHAPTER 20

Dougie arrived the next morning with a present from himself and his wife for the new arrival. Alex was quite moved at the thought, and issued an invitation for them both to come and see Peter once Catherine was sorted out at home.

Dougie said he had called into the office before coming out to Fulham, to see what might have arrived in their absence, and was very glad that he had. Seated at the dining room table with a pot of coffee and sandwiches between them, Alex looked at him in enquiry, wondering why his companion seemed rather smug.

They started by reviewing the Scottish interviews.

'The young boy, Fergal, told us nothing, apart from reinforcing the already known opinion of whose side he is on. An angry, but controlled, Liam O'Dowd spoke to me, but added very little. He said it was just unfortunate that he was known by his controllers to be in the vicinity when the pick-up was arranged at the last minute, and they considered that he might as well be used. A decision, in his view, that they may well now regret. Where, or who, the arrangement originated from he wasn't able, or prepared, to say. He just acted on orders given, did the job and left the rest to others. He repeated what he told you, Boss, that when he is in a position to seek information he will do so, and act on it. I'm certain that however long it takes, that man is going to seek retribution.'

He took a long swallow of his coffee, consulted his notes, and a broad grin came on his face.

'The boat owner, John Kerry, was very interesting. Seems he was in some financial difficulties a while ago and ended up in Court, with the possibility of being declared bankrupt. Then at the eleventh hour, as they say, a benefactor came along and stumped up enough collateral to keep the creditors happy. Kerry was supposed to pay back the monies at an easygoing rate, but he soon started to receive phone calls. The unknown caller made it clear that his position regarding payment of debts was known, and he was asked if he was prepared to do a bit more than fishing; which, it was suggested, would be deducted from his outstanding loan. Kerry had a good idea what he was getting into, he's not a complete fool, but if it meant keeping his boat, he was prepared to take the chance. This last job would have gone a long way to paying off his remaining debts, he told me.

'He's devastated. He knows he'll lose everything now. I asked him to contact the solicitor who acted for him, to see where the loan money came from. We heard back just before I left Scotland that it was from a company called Last Finance, some sort of philanthropic organisation funded by donations offering practical emergency financial assistance to deserving cases.' He looked at Alex. 'Keep that name in mind, Boss.'

He rummaged through his notes again. 'Now, the Cortina driver. A young man. No previous form. Unemployed.' He looked up at Alex. 'Guess where he used to work?'

Alex just shook his head.

'He used to be a farmhand on the Ayrshire estate of Sir Gregory Hamilton, that young bastard Duncan Hamilton's father. He was dismissed a year ago for fighting with another employee. I just happened to notice that for someone unemployed for a year he was sporting a nice, expensive wristwatch, which he maintained was years old but it looked pretty new to me. You getting my drift, Boss?'

'Loud and clear, Dougie! Loud and clear!'

'It gets even better! When I went into the office this morning I found Companies House had replied to my query about Franklin, Hamilton or Villiers being company officers. It seems both Hamilton and Villiers are involved in several, but...' – he paused for a moment, consulted his notes, and then grinned at Alex, 'together with an Edwin Thompson they are also trustees in a private company, limited by guarantee. Guess what company, Boss?'

Alex gave a soundless whistle. 'Last Finance?' Somehow he had known that Scotland was going to prove important, and it appeared to be turning out that way.

'Right. Here's how I think they played it with Kerry. They must have contacts in the Court offices keeping an eye open for suitable cases. In this instance, a fishing boat owner in trouble. Bail him out with a loan and he becomes their man. They then have enough potential power over him to do what they want. A useful way of trafficking anything from money to drugs to people. Kerry turns a blind eye, although he knows well enough, but is desperate to keep his boat. We're going to need to know a bit more about these monies, so I've ordered company accounts.'

'I'll bet they're passing the original "donations" through other dummy channels,' put in Alex. 'It can't be as transparent a chain as a trust fund or suchlike to Last Finance to Kerry.'

'Maybe not, but if we can show reasonable doubt about the origins of the money it might be enough to have others dig around a bit more. My bet is Franklin and his chums must have in the past, or still are, using other people in this way.

'I remember one of the staff at The Grosvenor mentioned to me in passing that Franklin uses the pay phone in the lobby an awful lot. Useful for making certain phone calls?'

'It's a good point, Dougie. We'd better work all this up into some sort of cohesive report and put it in front of Francis and the Commissioner. I think we've enough to show that things need to be looked at more closely, with more manpower than just us. To be quite honest, I'll not be sorry to see the back of any involvement.'

'Catherine still has no idea?'

'No. I thought I might say something if we were released from the detail and someone else took it over. I still don't know what her reaction might be if she knew I was investigating her uncle.'

'She can't blame you, Boss. You're following orders.'

'The trouble is, Dougie, that I agreed to do it. In the circumstances I could have said no, and should have done so, but I felt that if I was involved I would know what was going on, for her sake.' He rubbed his hands over his face. 'At least, that's what I tell myself. What if I just wanted to get back at the man in some way?'

'As I see it, you're the law, and he's doing something wrong, and needs to be stopped. End of story!'

'You make it sound nice and simple, Dougie.'

'Well, in any case you need to concentrate on Catherine and the baby now. What do you want me to do?'

'I'll come into the office tomorrow morning and we'll start to knock up our report. If it looks good, I'll try for a meeting with Francis and the Commissioner some time next week. We'll have to practice our two-finger typing, I think.'

*

'I wish you'd keep your voice down Aubrey. Don't get so excited.'

Potter had requested an urgent meeting with Franklin at The Grosvenor, and they had just finished a less than amicable lunch.

'Excited? Of course I'm excited! What else did you expect after Gregory Hamilton's news?'

'I think we'd better go up to my study if you're going to continue in this vein, Aubrey.'

When the two men were settled in Franklin's private quarters, Aubrey Potter turned to his long-time friend.

'Have you lost your head? Do you realise what you're meddling with? I've already forestalled one or two enquiring phone calls as to whether I know anything. For your sake I've denied any involvement, but they're not that daft, and they're angry. Not a good combination. The man picked up was one of their best operatives.'

'Well, if he was that good they were stupid to use him, or he shouldn't have been caught.' Franklin shifted papers around on the desk in front of him. 'I assumed it would be a local police job, a couple of officers, apprehend the messenger at the airport, and that would be it. How was I to know it would amount to a full-scale security operation, and they'd have everywhere covered? We must keep our nerve, Aubrey. Let it all die down. No one can trace anything to us.'

'How can you say that? What about the car driver, with a link to Hamilton? He's furious. He says the rumours are that it wasn't just local police involved, there were people from London. Then there's the skipper. What if someone digs around in his financial affairs?'

Franklin banged his fist down on the desk. 'The driver's been paid enough to keep him quiet. If anyone wants to look harder at Kerry, we can get Gregory's associate Thompson to cover our tracks with the finance matter. Hamilton and Villiers approved the whole idea. So did you!'

'Yes, in principle, against my better judgement; and not done this way. You know, Lionel, I have the strangest feeling that someone is taking a close interest in us, and I don't like it.'

'Why should they, Aubrey?'

'Our man in the Met thinks the Commissioner has some project on the go he's keeping quiet about. He says that detective you have a personal interest in is involved.'

Franklin sat up and fixed Potter with a penetrating stare. 'Hartman? Is that why he was sent to Richmond? What the hell did he hope to find out? At least the girl doesn't know anything, I made sure of that. You said people from London were up in Scotland. Now wouldn't it be a coincidence if it was Hartman? I'd say it was a certainty. I think you're right, Aubrey, the sniffer dogs are out alright. Leave Hartman to me. I'll settle things in that direction once and for all.'

'For Christ's sake, Lionel, don't start stirring anything else up. I think its time you kept a low profile until we find out just what's going on.'

'Don't worry, Aubrey, my plan will have to wait for a little while longer. But the anticipation will make the wait all the sweeter.'

Potter sat back in his chair, a sudden air of deflation about him.

'As I told you, I'm thinking of finishing in a year or two anyway. My bigger ideas haven't met with as much interest as I'd anticipated. Too radical even for these days, and the prospect of change is looking slim. I don't want to raise suspicions by pushing too hard. With any luck I'll be pulled back to help on various committees which might throw up some useful information...' – he glanced up at Franklin -'in a financial sense.' He raised an eyebrow in enquiry.

Franklin just nodded and smiled at him, masking his inner thoughts. On leaving university, once exposed to the real world, he had long ago given up on the ideological changes his group had been introduced to by Professor Helsenberg. In the cold light of day, and practicality, any real political changes were harder to achieve than might have been thought. Aubrey had held on to his dreams a little longer than most, but now he too was becoming disillusioned. Financial gain was far more useful. Franklin had soon found ways to make use of his friend's activities to achieve a higher level of wealth than might have been the case. Far higher indeed than he'd led Aubrey to believe; and from a personal point of view, he needed it to continue.

*

This was the day Alex had been waiting for. It was Thursday afternoon and he had just brought Catherine and Peter home from the hospital.

Their next door neighbour had been very kind and made sure the house was cosy and warm with a roaring fire in the front room as well as the central heating. She told them that a casserole was in the oven for whenever they were ready, and then left them alone to enjoy the experience of their first evening together.

Peter was proving a little fractious; because of the change of surroundings, suggested a nervous Catherine. She was attempting to comfort him when the telephone rang.

It was Luigi, just home from their New Year holiday in Italy, staying with their son.

'Good evening Alex. How is everything? How is Catherine?'

With a huge grin, Alex held out the telephone receiver, and then spoke into it again.

'You heard the noise? She's a little busy at the moment, Luigi, trying to quieten our son.'

He waited for the news to sink in. When it did, there was a riot at the other end. Maria was soon on the phone in floods of tears. Like everyone, they had been counting on the fact that they would be on hand for the birth.

With a confirming nod from Catherine, Alex interrupted the emotional outburst. 'You must both come round tomorrow afternoon and we'll show you our son.'

*

Alex left a little late for the office the next morning. The night had been quite disturbed, but Peter now seemed to have tired himself out and was sound asleep.

When he arrived in the office Dougie was already starting to put down the points he felt they had to make for their report, and they both worked through their information over the next hour or two. Some bits were a little sketchy for their liking, but others showed a definite pattern, now that they were looking for it.

'You know, Dougie, I've been thinking about that letter that started the whole Richmond thing off. If you remember, the envelope had an EC4 postmark. The Court area would have the same. Just suppose that Franklin sent that letter to himself as some sort of smokescreen about the court case...'

'He wouldn't have wanted police crawling all over his house, would he?'

'Maybe he thought it would just be one uniformed officer at the front gates. A miscalculation on his part. He wasn't to know that people are very interested in his affairs. I wonder if the same thing happened in Scotland. He didn't expect the level of policing that caught more than just a minor target.'

'I see your point. It's possible.'

'There's something else. Doesn't it seem strange that when people appear to be superfluous, or in the way, they're not just dropped but something seems to happen to them? There was poor Lucille Prentice.

Just a simple mugging that went wrong, or something more? Did they think she knew too much? Take Scotland. What was the point of whistle-blowing? It's spoilt a useful route for them. If they wanted to finish with it, why not just close it down without all this drama? There could be other things that have happened that we don't know about. I get the impression that someone enjoys wielding a sense of power over people.'

He stood and walked up and down, then turned back to his companion, his face now grave.

'Am I going out on a limb here, or should we have a look at the plane crash that killed Catherine's parents?'

Dougie stared at him. 'Come on, Boss, you're not thinking that it was deliberate?'

'As I said, I could have it wrong, but it might have been a chance to get hold of some extra money, as well as anything going to Catherine on their deaths.'

'But... his own brother?'

'I imagine stranger things than that go on in families.'

'What details do we know about the incident? Has Catherine spoken to you about it?'

'She's done so once. Her father was with the Diplomatic Corps in Cairo and she was at boarding school when the accident happened. They were on their way home to the UK where her father was intending to resign and seek approval as a Conservative candidate for a parliamentary by-election due in a few months.

'She was told they had flown into Rome on a scheduled flight and stayed there for a few days. It seems they then accepted a lift on a private plane to the UK. It came down in the Alps with no survivors.'

With a sudden chill, Alex remembered Catherine's Italian industrialist. Rome! Italy! Could it be that she was supposed to be a payment or thank-you for a job well done? He felt sick. No, not where her own parents had been involved!

He saw Dougie staring at him, a look of dawning comprehension coming over his face.

'Christ, you're not saying he organised it with… that lot? He's playing big if he's getting mixed up with them as well.'

Alex returned his look, his grey eyes solemn.

'I don't think there's any "if" about it, Dougie. I'm almost certain he's playing in that rarefied atmosphere.'

Dougie rubbed his chin. 'How could Franklin be sure about getting his hands on any monies even if he did stage an accident?'

'He might have known of their private affairs and what was in any Will. After all, he could have drawn up the Will and any other documents, or Villiers could.'

'Well, it would take us some while to obtain any report on the incident, but I'll have a go if you like.'

'Yes, see what you can do.'

'Now you've mentioned this, it has me wondering about another bit of information I found out at The Grosvenor. We know that Franklin is a half-owner of the freehold. Well, one night I was chatting to the Manager and it seems that Franklin's former partner sold out his share in something of a hurry about ten years ago, not long after the place was set up. He said he thinks the new co-owner is Italian, but he's never seen him, and only has dealings with an accountant. Might be significant?'

'It's interesting, alright.' Alex looked at his watch. 'We'll give it another hour and then I'll be off home, if you don't mind. I'll think about all this tonight and perhaps we can thrash out some sort of final draft tomorrow.'

He was aware of Dougie still looking at him. Was he right in his thinking, or was he so close to this whole affair that he was reading coincidences into events which weren't even there? If he was right, it made the actions seem almost evil.

CHAPTER 21

Luigi and Maria arrived at Fulham just before Alex. Luigi told them with a laugh that Maria would have been straight round the day before if he hadn't put his foot down. As it was, she had packed a bag and insisted on staying for a week to help out.

As Peter's next feed took the ladies upstairs, Alex spoke in private to Luigi.

'Are you sure you don't mind about Maria staying? I can't deny that it makes me feel happier for Catherine to have someone with experience close at hand. Mary next door has been a brick, but the poor lady knows as much about babies as I do.'

'I don't mind in the least, boy. At this time of year we're never busy. In fact I thought I might do some decorating. Maria will be in seventh heaven.' He smiled over at Alex. 'How does it feel to be a father?'

'I'm still a bit shell-shocked, but already I wouldn't want to be without him. I'll be glad when Catherine's back to full health. It's been pretty rough for her.'

'From my experience its amazing how women bounce back. The next thing they talk about is having another! Maria did, but we weren't lucky. I suppose this is why we both have such a strong attachment to you, Alex. In a way you became another son… and now look what we have: Catherine and Peter. Perhaps we will have the opportunity to help Peter in his life also.'

Alex felt warm pleasure at this remark. He remembered his unconscious reliance on Luigi and Maria being there for him in his youth, even if he hadn't always admitted it at the time. As he had grown older, he knew he could count on Luigi for sound advice if ever he needed it.

'I must say, Luigi, that both Catherine and I look upon you both as adopted parents. Peter will be another grandchild for you.'

Luigi gave him a little smiling salute in thanks.

That evening, under careful tuition, Alex bathed his son. Feeling the warm soapy body under his hands, he had an incredible sense of caring in his actions, and wanted to prolong the event. Catherine, however, was anxious about the cooling water and between them they wrapped Peter in a warm towel and Alex, with gentle care, dried the little body. However, now the sensation of the soothing water had ceased, Peter let them know in no uncertain terms that he was displeased.

Alex held him on his lap, cocooned in the towel, and remonstrated with him. 'Now then, young man, that will be enough of that. This is your father you're dealing with.'

Catherine giggled, leaning against his shoulder. 'I don't think even you can provide him with what he wants now. Come into the bedroom with him.'

She made herself comfortable on the bed, and soon Peter was quiet again. Alex stood for a long while, looking down at the little tableau. He then lay on the bed next to them, once more mulling over the idea that during the last few hours had come to him even stronger. As if sensing his preoccupation, Catherine stirred and looked up at him.

'Is anything wrong?'

'No, my love, I was just thinking.' He turned on his side and gazed into her face. 'Catherine, I can't claim to be a religious person, by that I mean someone who can believe all the Church's teachings, but I

334

do recognise that we should live our lives in a basic Christian way if we can. I've seen plenty of the other side, after all, and it's never the answer. The world out there is a place where pitfalls can occur to even the most wary and you need all the help you can get.

'What do you think about having Peter christened? Right now, I mean, not waiting until he's older? I just wonder if that would give him some extra sort of... protection.' He kissed the tip of her nose, and laughed. 'If you understood any of that you're lucky, because I'm not sure I did.' Then he became serious again. 'Do you know what I mean? I somehow feel a need to do this.'

Catherine stretched up and kissed him on the mouth. 'I do know what you mean, and I think it's a wonderful idea. We'll need godparents. I suppose we're looking at Sarah and Jerry again.'

'Sarah, yes. But I was wondering about Luigi. Then Peter will have youth, and experience.'

'Oh yes, that would be brilliant. You're a clever old thing, aren't you.' She bent her head and gazed at her son still feeding. 'Peter, you have a clever Daddy, did you know.'

Alex bent his head and covered her mouth with his own. After some time he murmured, 'I must be clever if I chose you for my wife.'

He could feel his rising passion, and it wasn't the thing to do, so with an effort he controlled his feelings. In an attempt to take his mind off the problem he added, 'Perhaps I should have a word with Reverend Jones about it.'

With a half-suppressed giggle Catherine observed, 'I'm not sure how much he'll be able to help you with the problem.'

Embarrassed, Alex realised that she had guessed how he felt, and his efforts to get over it. He smiled back and gave her a light kiss.

'I'll go and see if Maria needs any help, as I can't do much for you at the moment!'

He left the room, chuckling at her shocked expression.

*

Dougie and Alex worked on their report over the next few days. Alex was of the opinion that he would try to fix an appointment to see the

Commissioner the next week; after all, he had insisted that this was first and foremost a policing matter. He decided he would outline his views in general and then, depending on how this was received, a joint meeting between himself, Sir John and Francis could be arranged for a discussion on further action.

He scandalised Maria by insisting that he would have to work late on Friday. Catherine just gave him her grave stare, then smiled at him and mollified Maria by stating that Alex must have a good reason.

His actual reason was to once again use the quieter time of day to copy up all the new information to add to his mounting collection. He knew he would have to remove this from the office somehow and store it elsewhere before too long.

*

Peter was growing, so were his lungs, and he was exercising them all the time. Catherine and Maria sat at the dining table finishing their coffee. Peter, for once quiet, lay on Catherine's shoulder. The Health Visitor had just left, after making some suggestions.

'You know, Catherine, I think it is a good idea to introduce Peter to a bottle feed. It might be that he needs the extra nourishment.'

'I can't deny it's making me a little worried, Maria, and I can see the point that as he grows he appears to need more than I can give. Its worth trying. I hope it will make him more contented.'

Right on cue, Peter reminded them of his presence. Once feeding again, Catherine stroked the small cheek.

'You know, Maria, I wondered how Alex would react once a baby was here in real life. I think he panicked at first, but now he seems quite at ease. I've watched him with Peter, and the look on his face is quite moving. I'm sure he loves him.' She stroked the cheek once more. 'As I do.' She planted a soft kiss his forehead.

'I know what you mean. If you'd told me a year ago that Alex would be married with a child, I wouldn't have believed it. Luigi and I are so glad for you both.'

'I couldn't be without either of my men now. I do worry about Alex, though. When he doesn't think I'm around he has a sad look on his face sometimes, but there's no use asking him if anything's wrong. He tells me things when he has to, I know that. I can't think its anything here at home, so it must be work.' She stroked the small cheek again. 'Peter, we must look after your Daddy, you and I, because we love him.'

*

On Saturday morning, Alex set off with his son in the pram and headed for the church. On his way he was stopped on several occasions by interested neighbours keen to glimpse the new arrival. By the time he reached the vestry he felt a warm sense of fellowship with people in the locality, and knew it was his son who had brought this about.

Reverend Jones was working on his sermon but welcomed the intrusion. As he admitted, 'I may be more prepared than most, but it still comes hard at times.'

He admired Peter, now for once fast asleep, and waved Alex to a chair.

'What can I do for you, my boy?'

Alex started to explain the reason for his visit, a little diffident at first, but then with growing conviction. After he had put his views, he waited for the Vicar to respond. He could see that the man was marshalling his thoughts.

'I am glad that you and Catherine wish young Peter to be welcomed into the church. I see no problem with this being done at any age. It makes no difference as I see it. What I would say to you is that for all our best desires and wishes, there is no magic talisman which will prevent any ills befalling even the young and innocent. Having Peter christened will not give him immunity. You are not a fool, and through your job are well aware of what happens in the world. All we can ever hope for is that if a need arises, someone offers help and guidance, and we must believe that this is God-given.'

'I understand that, Reverend. I just need to know that I have done the best for my son.'

'I quite understand that, and I'm happy to oblige. If you are certain you wish to go ahead, I would perhaps like to combine the christening with a normal Sunday service. It makes the community feel part of it all. Would you and Catherine have any objection?'

'I don't suppose so. I hadn't thought that far ahead.'

Reverend Jones consulted his dairy. 'I am going to suggest that we look at about a month from now. Is that satisfactory for you? I'm not sure it would be possible before then.'

'Yes, of course. Er… there was one more thing I would like to ask you. I haven't spoken to Catherine about this. If you agreed, I would like it to be a surprise for her.'

'Well, ask away. I can only say no!'

*

Alex felt his briefing with Sir John had gone quite well. The Commissioner was impressed with the operation in Glasgow and, irrespective of anything to do with the broader enquiry, was pleased with the outcome. He had asked Alex to enlarge on certain points in his enquiries, and then once he had a complete report he would look at the matter again. Just like that, Alex thought. Easy enough to request. He had put forward his point about turning all the information over to a larger dedicated team but Sir John was adamant that he wanted the matter left as it was for the time being.

Walking down the corridor away from Sir John's office he encountered Assistant Commissioner Rankin. To Alex's knowledge the two of them had met on just one previous occasion, and he wasn't sure what he made of the man. He appeared affable and pleasant enough, but Alex had the odd feeling there was something else going on behind this façade.

'Ah, Hartman. I heard you were in with Sir John. Been telling him about your operation in Glasgow? I understand you did some good work. More promotion, eh?'

'I had a lot of help from my partner and the local forces, Sir. Chief Inspector King in particular. We struck lucky.'

'Interesting how the tip-off came about. We have no idea about that?'

'No, sir. Anonymous letter, hand-delivered, person unknown. No prints.'

'Ah well, we can't expect miracles. Good work, Inspector.' He turned to go. 'By the way, I hear you've just become a father. You married Judge Lionel Franklin's niece didn't you?'

'Yes, sir, on both counts.' For some reason Alex went on the defensive, not wanting to be questioned further. To his relief, Rankin just smiled and walked off towards Sir John's office.

The encounter left Alex feeling uneasy but he could discern no reason for this. He shrugged and carried on back to his office to break the news to Dougie that, despite what Rankin had just said, they were being asked to come up with one of those miracles.

CHAPTER 22

On the morning of the christening Catherine came downstairs to find that Peter had been washed, dressed in a clean nappy and Alex was sitting in the kitchen giving him a feed.

'Why didn't you wake me?'

She bent and planted a kiss on her husband's cheek, and then one for her son, who ignored her, more intent on the contents of the bottle.

'It's no problem. I thought I'd let you sleep in. Have your breakfast in peace for once.'

It was then that Catherine saw the parcels on the table: one big, one small. She looked over at Alex.

'What are these?'

'Well, if you open them, you'll find out. One's from me and one's from Peter.'

Catherine sat down and began to open the smaller parcel. Inside was a box she thought she recognised. As soon as she opened it and saw the little velvet bag, she knew! Inside the bag, wrapped in tissue paper, were the emerald earrings to match her ring. They glittered in her hand until her vision was blurred by the gathering tears.

'Oh, Alex, they're beautiful, but you shouldn't have bought them. I'm costing you a fortune.'

He smiled at her. 'As far as Peter and I are concerned, you're worth every penny.'

She came over to him and this time found his lips with her own. 'Thank you my darling. I love you both so very much.'

'Open the other one, then.' Alex hoisted his son on to his shoulder and patted his back, displaying his pride at this new skill, much to Catherine's amusement.

Unwrapping the larger parcel she found more tissue paper. This time it contained what appeared to be a dress. It was pale cream jersey with a soft draped neckline.

'I thought you might like something special to wear on a special day. I'm assured it will fit you. I hope to God it does!'

Catherine held it up against herself. 'It looks as if it will. Oh, Alex, it's beautiful. You've spoilt me.'

'Why not? Now, have your breakfast while this urchin is quiet. What time are we meeting everyone?'

Catherine started to munch on her cereal.

'Luigi and Maria said they would be here at about ten o'clock. Sarah and Jerry said they would come about the same time.'

When Alex had asked Luigi to act as a godfather, Luigi had protested that he was too old. Alex then explained to him that with Sarah as godmother, Peter would have youth, but with Luigi he wouldn't have age, he would have experience. As he said to Luigi, from Sarah he would have love that would allow him to do no wrong in her eyes, but from Luigi he would have a person who wouldn't be quite so accommodating! Luigi saw the logic in this and agreed, a proud smile on his face, which was still there when, later that morning, he and Maria arrived.

Dougie and his wife Janet were joining them at the Church, as were Grace and Arthur. Alex had felt uncomfortable about not discussing with Catherine the inclusion of her uncle, but she hadn't mentioned it, and he was ashamed of his relief at the fact.

Sarah sat on the bed with Peter, now smart in a yellow suit with blue animal motifs, watching while Catherine finished dressing. She was amazed at her friend's rapid recovery and display of confidence with her new baby. All testament, she felt sure, to the security Catherine had found in her marriage.

'I've something to tell you, petal, but it's to be between us at the moment.'

Catherine turned around from the mirror.

Sarah smiled. 'I think I'm pregnant!'

'Oh Sarah, how wonderful! Are you sure?'

'No, I'm not. I haven't had a test, but something's going on. I'll try to see a doctor next week.'

'Does Jerry know? Or even guess?'

Sarah laughed now. 'What do you think? Alex didn't work it out either, did he?'

Catherine stood and hugged her friend. 'I'm so pleased for you. Let me know as soon as you're sure, but I promise I won't say anything until you tell me.'

'I'll take the star of the show downstairs now, shall I, and leave you to finish.'

Catherine picked up her new dress and slid into the soft folds. Its fit was perfect. The casual drapes at the front hid any slight bump she still had. She put on her new earrings and their soft glow was reflected in her eyes. Could she be any happier? she thought. The love of a wonderful husband, and now a beautiful son. She had a lot to be thankful for. It could all have been so different... But she made herself put those thoughts aside. With one final look in the mirror, she picked up her bag and left the room.

Alex stood in the hallway with Peter in his arms. He looked up as Catherine came down the stairs. She was blossoming into a beautiful woman, he thought. Motherhood had lent an extra maturity to her features. The dress looked magnificent and, as far as he was concerned, although he admitted to being biased, fitted her body to perfection. The simple addition of her new earrings was all the extra adornment she needed. Once again he marvelled at the effect the sight of her had on his senses, and he longed more than ever to regain their shared magic. Soon now, please let it be soon!

'You look wonderful, my dear. I'm a very proud man today. A

beautiful wife and a magnificent son. Now, if you're ready, let's join our friends shall we?'

*

The church was crowded as the christening party slipped in at the back, close to the font. After completion of the christening formalities, at Alex's insistence his son was handed to Sarah, much to Catherine's surprise, even more so when Reverend Jones turned his attention to her.

'Catherine, your husband has asked your friends and the congregation here today to join with you both in a blessing of your marriage. If you would care to follow me...?'

Catherine looked in astonishment at her husband, who put his arm round her waist, and drew her down to the front of the church. Alex had even kept the surprise from his friends, who were just as startled as Catherine.

Luigi, now holding his godson, looked at the couple standing in front of the Vicar. The two young people hadn't taken their eyes off each other, and their hands were entwined. He felt moved by their display of total love, and he sent up his own prayer that this would stay with them all their lives.

*

An old Mercedes saloon was parked in the road opposite the church. Harry Fowler had been observing the comings and goings with some amusement. All this fuss over a baby!

Clarke's watchers had been passing on information collected over the last few weeks about the movements of the Hartman family, and he'd been asked to familiarise himself with the vicinity. This Hartman person must be causing Clarke's associates some grief. He was definite now that this was the same person involved with that little prostitute and Fenton's gym. There must be more to it, with the amount of interest being shown, but even if not, he was police – and Fowler liked the chance of having a go at them!

*

On a fine, mild March morning a couple of weeks later, Catherine was attempting to catch up on her course work, which was now way behind. Through the French windows she could see Peter outside, fast asleep in his pram. She had just spent some time on the telephone with an excited Sarah, who confirmed her good news. It would be superb, they said: their children would be able to grow up together. Promising to meet soon, Sarah laughed and suggested that Catherine should bring with her a long list of tips and recommendations.

Trying to refocus her mind, it was with annoyance she heard the front door bell ring. Opening the door she found her uncle standing there.

'Good morning, my dear. I hope I'm not intruding.'

Catherine felt the blood draining from her face, and for a moment, thought she might even faint. She put out a shaking hand to steady herself against the open door. What should she do? She was mindful of her promise to Alex not to be alone with her uncle. She hadn't been aware that her uncle even knew where they lived. He knew about Peter, because Alex had agreed she should to write to him with the news, but on his instructions she hadn't disclosed their address.

However, she felt obliged to show good manners and invited him in, trying to disguise her reluctance. He looked around with apparent great interest as she took him through to the living room, apologising that she needed to keep an eye on Peter in the garden.

'You seem to have a nice house, Catherine.'

Without invitation, he seated himself at the table, but declined her offer of a coffee. 'I am not able to stay long. I have a taxi waiting outside for me.'

He put a parcel on the table. 'I know that things have not always been right between us of late, but I acknowledge that you are now married, with a son, and that this is your choice. I have brought you something which used to belong to your father. I thought it might please you to have it.'

When Catherine unwrapped the parcel she found inside a small, but heavy, bronze statue of a soldier of the Crimean War.

'It has some value, I believe. A house warming present, perhaps?'

Catherine stammered her thanks. Her uncle was being very pleasant. Perhaps he was now regretting some of his past actions. Her generous heart warmed to him.

'Would you care to see Peter? I can fetch him.'

'That would be nice, my dear. I think this statue would look well on your hall table. Perhaps whilst you are outside…?'

'Oh, er… yes. That's fine.'

Her uncle was again sitting at the table when she returned, after a slight delay, while she made sure that Peter was presentable. He was duly admired, but for some reason she sensed that, his duty now performed, her uncle was keen to leave.

With Peter in her arms she followed him to the front door. She saw the statue on the table.

'Thank you for the gift, Uncle. Perhaps we will see you again?'

He turned and smiled at her. 'Perhaps.'

*

Sitting in the taxi Lionel Franklin's face wore an unusual, boyish grin. It had all worked better than maybe he had hoped. What a good thing the child was outside, as this gave him ample time to perform the task as instructed. He removed his gloves and placed the small metal box in his coat pocket. He had seen the handbag on the hall table and found what he wanted with no trouble. Now he could move his plan forward. Everything was in place.

Was there just a moment of regret? No, none.

*

Catherine moved back into the lounge, with Peter still in her arms. What a strange occurrence. Was Uncle Lionel reaching out for contact in some way, now that he was alone? She knew that Alex was wary of her uncle, and at times she felt it was more than that. Why, she didn't know. Something else he hadn't told her. Now, happy in her marriage, she had long ago forgiven her uncle for his views on her future. Perhaps there was a chance for attitudes to change. She sat with Peter in the leather armchair.

'We might be able to be a real family, Peter. You could have a Great Uncle. We'll have to tell your Daddy tonight, but I'm not sure how he'll take it.'

With a small sigh, she stood and placed her son back in his pram, and returned to her work.

Catherine waited until after the evening meal before she told Alex of her visitor. She knew she had to be honest with him.

'How on earth did he know where we lived?'

'I've been thinking about that all day, Alex, and I can't imagine.'

Alex went into the hall and looked at the bronze figure. 'I suppose it's nice for you to have something of your parents. I wonder if it does have any value?'

'I'm not bothered if it doesn't, it was just a nice thought.'

Alex looked at his wife. He knew her well enough by now. She would always think the best of people, until proven otherwise. This gesture had redeemed her uncle in her eyes, but he wasn't so sure. What was the man up to now? His intuition told him that something was wrong... but what? Within a few days his report would be finalised, presented to higher authority, and with any luck, acted upon. What would she think then? He was back to his old dilemma.

During the rest of the evening Alex tried to ignore it, but the problem was worrying him again. He felt Catherine's eyes on him, but didn't know what to say to her. Later, in bed, he watched her sleeping as he had so often. What would he do without her? He felt too restless to sleep and put on his robe and went downstairs. After a moment or two he took a notepad from his desk, sat down at the dining table and began to write.

He folded the letter and slipped it into an envelope and sealed it. The first he knew of her presence was when he smelt her perfume. She was watching him from the doorway, the folds of her long pink gown held around her.

'Alex?'

'It's alright, my love. Go back to bed.'

She came towards him and slipped herself onto his lap. He sighed and folded his arms around her.

346

'What's wrong, Alex? I know something's bothering you. I think it's to do with my uncle, isn't it.'

There it was, he thought, the opening he needed. But he was too afraid to follow it up.

He felt her lips on his neck. 'Alex, we love each other. Whatever difficulties there are, with family, or anything else, they can be overcome. I know certain steps in life have to be taken even if they're painful to others.'

God in Heaven, had she guessed already, and was she telling him it would be alright? His heart leapt with hope.

She was looking up at him. 'Do you remember that awful night when we had that terrible argument? You said you just wanted me to be happy, even if it meant you were not. That's what I mean about love. I want you and I to be happy together, even if we have problems that might hurt. We love each other. We both love Peter.'

She stirred in his arms. 'Come to bed, my love. I need you there with me.' She appeared to hesitate. 'Alex, I'd like you to make love to me. Please.'

He looked down at her with alarm. 'Catherine, I'm not sure. I don't want to hurt you. I know the doctor said everything was fine, but I wanted you to see Newman as well.'

She kissed his mouth, the folds of her silky gown slipping apart. 'There's one way to find out, my darling.' She made a face at him. 'Do I have to beg?'

'There's no way you have to beg for my love, my sweet.' He picked her up in his arms and carried her upstairs.

With great sensitivity, gentleness and care he reignited the old fires, and to the delight of them both they found their feelings overcame any reservations and the result was all they had hoped for. The dawn light was filtering through the bedroom curtains before they slept, wrapped in each other's arms.

CHAPTER 23

Copying more of his file information late on Friday night, Alex was faced with the problem of what to do with it. Was he just paranoid about the whole thing, and no one would come snooping at all? He didn't want to take the chance. The papers needed to be taken out of the office and stored somewhere for safe keeping. His gaze rested on an empty stationery box standing in the corner of the room. This would be ideal.

Excusing himself to Catherine the next day by saying he had some errands to do, he drove to his office. He put all the papers into the box, sealed it with tape, and took it with him when he left the building. He put it in his car, and on the drive home came to the decision that first thing on Monday morning he would place it in the care of Simon Kingsley, to be held to his instructions; also the letter, at the moment hidden in his father's desk.

*

Kingsley, with reluctance, agreed to keep the box. He was unhappy about not knowing the contents, but in the end took Alex's word on the matter. Alex left with him instructions as to what should happen to both the box and the letter if he was ever not in a position to collect them himself.

When Alex had left the office, Kingsley thought about it, and asked his secretary to make a note that both the box and sealed envelope were to be held to his own strict order, together with any files opened by his firm relating to the affairs of Alex and Catherine Hartman. Nothing was to be destroyed without his personal knowledge. He was still having trouble obtaining information about the trust fund, and decided he would have to keep a close eye on matters that concerned them.

*

The next, and with any luck final meeting with Sir John was set for Tuesday morning. Alex was tempted to take Dougie along, but thought better of it. He had managed, so far, to keep up the pretence that his colleague wasn't aware of the whole picture, and it might as well continue. He would make sure, however, that he pointed out how invaluable Dougie's help had been throughout. Dougie always maintained that he wasn't interested in any further promotion, but that didn't mean that Alex could not gain him some rightful appreciation of his services.

On the whole, he was now happy with the report. Some links still seemed tenuous at best, but he felt they were worth mentioning. In contrast, however, their enquiries into various subversive acts over a period of time had shown definite links to earlier court actions. Ripe pickings if you were looking for ways to manipulate vulnerable people. The Scottish exercise had also thrown up coincidences of related association. This morning they had received copies of Last Finance's accounts. They would need to be looked at in more detail, but it appeared that payments had been made on several occasions, even before the one to Kerry.

A particular entry which stood out for Alex was the receipt of a donation made about six months ago from an E. Sullivan. He had the odd feeling that the name meant something to him. He was on the point of leaving for the meeting when he realised where he had heard a similar name. Catherine's mother's maiden name was Sullivan, and her Christian name was Ellen... but it couldn't be the same! Ellen Sullivan had died with her husband some ten years ago!

Was it possible that in some way monies were still being used under that name? It might be, under some sort of fund, but then the money would have come in from another account designation… or were they using forgery? The point would need some further investigation.

Alex gave Sir John a copy of his typed report, with an embarrassed apology for any errors, and then took him through it in detail.

'I admit that some possibilities are just that and nothing more, but they might stand more investigation. Some, as you can see, are far more definite. I consider on balance that there are enough hard facts to be able to make a pretty good case.'

'Yes, I can see that.' Sir John appeared pleased. 'I have a meeting on Wednesday with my senior officers and I intend putting the full report before the meeting. If it's felt, in the light of the investigations, that any action needs to be taken, I wish to discuss it there and then.'

'Sir John, I have to say that although the report indicates further action needs to be taken, we haven't been able to answer the question as to who is part of the set-up and who isn't. By putting this information out into the open it will serve to give advance warning to those involved, and the whole ring could melt away. I think we ought to bring Francis in on the matter again before anything is disclosed, and we should organise another meeting with him.'

It was clear to Alex that Sir John was annoyed at his suggestion, but he had to try to get his point across. He was given a hard stare, but held his own gaze steady. Then, with a shrug of his shoulders, Sir John gave in.

'Alright. Just for the moment, I will give notice to the meeting that certain enquiries have been made and are ongoing. The whole matter will be reported back as soon as possible.'

'I still think, Sir John, that the enquiries should now be taken forward by others.' Alex wanted to try once more to make his views on this point known.

'No, my boy. You and your colleague have done sterling work and I feel you should stay with the matter for the time being.'

Alex felt he was losing an uphill battle, and there was no more he could do.

On the way back to his office Alex again encountered Assistant Commissioner Rankin who, this time, just nodded to him and passed on.

Dougie was on the phone when Alex reached his office.

'Seems as if there's a flap on. Several of the Protection Squad are down with a stomach bug and they're short-handed. We've been requested to assist. The Superintendent wants to see us. Foreign dignatory. Airport to meeting in Whitehall, back to airport.'

'Right, we'd better see him then.'

'How did it go?'

'Oh we got pats on the back alright, but I'm worried about too much information getting out too soon. I'll tell you about it later.'

Over a cup of coffee when they were back in their room Alex outlined Sir John's intentions.

Dougie was annoyed. 'The old fool. He could blow the whole thing!'

'I tend to agree with you. I managed to make him water down his original intention and the meeting will be given nothing more than inferences of the type of enquiries that have been made with possible further action. Even that's enough in my book. If anyone in that room is in on the whole thing they're going to be on the alert and pull the plug.'

'And all our hard work will have been for nothing. Bloody stupid if you ask me.'

Coming to a decision, Alex picked up the phone.

'I'm going to ring Francis and see if he can put a stop to it.'

A strange voice answered, but as Francis had said it was a secure line, Alex left a full message and tried to convey the urgency. He put down the receiver and sighed.

'Well, you can't say that we haven't done our best. I'm going to get off now. I have to draw my firearm as I'm on the first detail at the airport. Catherine will throw a fit if she spots it in the house tonight!'

'Tuck it in your underpants, that's what I've done in the past.' Dougie then looked over at the other man and gave a knowing grin. 'Maybe that's not such a safe place as far as you're concerned!'

Alex stared at him for a moment, and then started to laugh. 'You've got a wicked mind! I'll see you.' He left the room still chuckling.

*

Sir John Fraser felt pleased with himself. His last weeks as Commissioner would be a triumph if this operation could be brought to a conclusion. All the talk of unknown people in the shadows was all very well, but how deep did you dig, and how long would it take? If everyone known was rounded up now, other names might come out, and at the very least the heart of the operation would have been ripped out.

There was a knock on the door and Rankin walked in. Fraser was never certain whether he liked the man. He seemed amiable enough, but there was something unnerving about him; a sense that he always had more than one motive for his actions. However, he had brought off one or two useful operations of late, and Fraser knew that he coveted the post of Commissioner. He was unconvinced, though, that Rankin was the right man.

'Heard you've been seeing that Hartman fellow quite a bit. Saw him here earlier. He's a high flyer alright. Something big on?'

Fraser made a rash decision. He needed to top this man, in policing acumen as well as rank.

'Yes, now you come to mention it, something pretty big indeed. Seems we have certain people wielding unlawful influence to the detriment of the country. Might be terrorism involvement too. Under my instructions, Hartman's been digging around and has collected a lot of evidence. I intend to see it's acted upon.'

Rankin's eyes narrowed. 'Well now! Do we know any names?'

Fraser, now regretting his outburst, decided not to mention any. 'Oh, we have several, don't you worry. I'll be bringing it up at the meeting tomorrow.'

Rankin smiled at him. 'Well, John, you seem to be going out with a bang. I've a nice bottle of port in my room. Suppose we celebrate with a small glass?'

Fraser enjoyed the drink, but Rankin enjoyed it even more,

although he didn't taste a drop. Within a few minutes he excused himself, saying he had to make an important phone call. He made his way back to his office, stopping on the way to speak to Sir John's secretary.

*

Lionel Franklin stood at the pay phone in The Grosvenor. There was no one around. He dialled a number.

'Geoffrey? I heard from Hamilton that the banking matters are in place and you've been provided with paperwork... Good. Now, I need you to get in touch with Clarke, there have been unexpected developments.' He explained on for a few minutes, giving precise details. 'Yes... yes, I said *both* tonight! Remind him that it must be done as instructed, no deviation. This is important.'

He put down the phone, went to the bar and ordered a brandy. He smiled to himself. Aubrey had sanctioned the first part of tonight's events with great reluctance, even more so the second, and if he'd known the exact instructions given he'd have been horrified and vetoed it; but he didn't know, did he!

*

Catherine was surprised to see Alex home. He'd been working late over the last few days, finalising a report of some sort. It was nice to have him home in time to join in Peter's bath time.

The little boy was already growing and Alex cradled him on his lap, pink and sweet-smelling, while Catherine tidied the bathroom. It was then time for his feed. She sat on the bed, propped up with pillows, and Alex lay next to her, as usual just taking in the scene.

After dinner, with Peter contented and asleep, they settled down on the settee in the front room, the red glow of firelight their only illumination.

'I'm going to have to leave earlier tomorrow morning.' Alex nestled his cheek against the soft brown hair.

Catherine looked up at him and smiled. 'Are you suggesting its bedtime by any chance?'

'Depends what's on the television I suppose,' he replied, trying, and failing, to appear nonchalant. 'I thought there was something good on tonight.'

'Oh, there might be, but not on the television.'

He took her hand in his, rubbing his thumb over her soft palm. 'Are you propositioning me by any chance?' His gaze was very direct.

'Would you mind?'

The look between them became more intense.

'I wouldn't mind in the least. I like taking my wife to bed, feeling her body next to mine, knowing that she wants me as much as I want her. May I kiss you, Mrs Hartman?'

As usual, she could feel the excitement building inside her. He brought her hand up to his mouth, kissed the inside of her wrist against her pulse and then lowered it again, and just smiled at her. With frustration, she recognised he was playing the game he did so well, toying with her emotions until she couldn't bear it any longer. He always knew just when she reached that point, and it excited her even more.

'Alex!' Her whisper was more like a moan.

CHAPTER 24

Drawn into the warm circle of his arms, Catherine put her lips against his throat.

'Hush, my sweet. We have all night ahead of us.'

He turned her face up to him, and with his eyes on her mouth, brought his head down to hers, capturing her parting lips.

Oh, how she loved this man. He had brought so many wonderful things into her life, always showing her the greatest care and consideration. When she could, she murmured, 'I love you Alex.'

'I love you too, my darling, and I'm going to spend the rest of the night showing you just how much,' he whispered, and she found herself picked up in his arms. As he carried her upstairs, his mouth continued to plant soft, quick kisses on hers.

Later in the night, Peter woke. Alex heard him crying and looked at Catherine nestled in his arms, still fast asleep. He smiled to himself. He had worn her out! How wonderful it had been, though. He felt more contented now than he had ever done in his life.

On his way home, he had made a decision. Tomorrow he would tell Catherine his secret. Whatever the outcome, he must deal with it. The worry of not knowing her reaction was worse than trying to anticipate the aftermath. Given her recent comments, he hoped that all would be well. Over these last weeks, watching his wife and child together, he couldn't countenance an existence without them.

Unfolding his arms from around her he slipped out of bed. He wouldn't wake her – just yet!

Peter wasn't sure whether he wanted to sleep or feed, and halfway through his bottle Alex decided to try putting him down to sleep again. With a clean nappy he went off like a lamb, and Alex turned off the light and climbed back into bed.

'Is Peter awake?' Catherine murmured, still half-asleep. Alex put his cold hands on her warm body, and chuckled when she gasped. 'You beast, that's unkind. You've woken me up now.'

'That was my intention,' he murmured into her throat. 'Our son has been fed and is fast asleep again. He shouldn't need any attention until the morning. I'm afraid, though, that I'll need some before that.'

He could see Catherine's eyes glittering at him in the faint light coming from the window. He felt her body melt against his. 'Whatever my husband wishes,' he heard her whisper.

Their emotion soared as each tried to convey to the other the depth of their feelings, and they climbed to heights never reached before. She was so beautiful, and he loved her so much, was his last thought before sleep claimed them both, and they lay together in peaceful dreams.

*

Sir John Fraser was regretting his decision to attend the charity meeting that night. He had begun to feel unwell during the afternoon and, he now realised, should have gone straight home. He had also decided to drive himself. Another bad move! The slight dizziness he was experiencing was not the best thing when in charge of a vehicle. However, the traffic out to Bracknell was light, and now he was in the country he would be home in a few minutes. His wife preferred him not to stay in London. He would have a word with his specialist tomorrow. Perhaps this new medication didn't suit him. Shouldn't have had that glass of port with Rankin, either, he thought.

Anxious to be home, he increased his speed a little. He looked in his rear view mirror as the headlights of a car coming up behind caught his attention. It seemed to be coming fast; too fast for these country roads. Wouldn't he love to be in a police vehicle and be able to book this idiot!

Just a mile or so to go now, he thought with relief, increasing his speed further to stay ahead. The lights behind him, however, were beginning to have a strange effect on his eyes. He needed to concentrate now, as there were one or two tight bends coming up, and the land fell away at the side into a line of trees. Why didn't this clown behind him overtake?

Then, as they were coming up to a tight bend, the car began to do just that! The fool, he thought, turning his head as the car started to pass. He felt a slight bump as they touched. What on earth…! The wheel was wrenched out of his hands, and he scrabbled to regain control. His heart was in his mouth as he tried to recall the advice police drivers had given him years before. He began to panic, as his efforts were in vain and the car veered off the road, careering down the embankment and straight towards the trees.

As it hit, and turned over, he felt a sickening pain in his head where it had impacted with the door pillar, and then to his horror he smelt the stench of fuel and saw the first small flames lick up from the bonnet. He could feel himself slipping into unconsciousness, and in desperation, struggled to open the door. Whatever he did, it just wouldn't budge, and through his rising panic he could now hear the noise of the flames. He also thought he heard a scream.

*

The dark-coloured saloon had slowed to a stop and the occupant smiled as, in his rear view mirror, he saw flames begin to light up the night. It had gone well, Fowler thought, considering the short notice and lack of certainty. No further action needed. He drove away at speed, with the smile still lingering.

*

It was about one-thirty when a car turned into Church Road, doused its headlights, and glided to a stop outside a house. A dark figure got out and moved to the front door. The man extracted a brand new key, and with care inserted it in the lock. As it turned he let out his breath, realising that the latch wasn't down. The door moved inward. He'd been warned about a safety chain, but there was nothing. He couldn't believe his luck! It had saved a more risky entry by the French windows at the back of the property, although that would have proved no obstacle to him, and no one would have been any the wiser.

Once in the hall, he located the statue on the small table. As instructed, he picked it up in his gloved hand and made his way up the stairs. He reached the door of the front bedroom and eased it open. Two figures were lying in the bed and he started to cross toward them.

*

Alex was dreaming, but that dream was disturbed. He opened his eyes. Some sixth sense had warned him that something was wrong. He looked over his shoulder and saw a dark figure by the door. A burglar! With an oath he released himself from Catherine's arms, and leapt out of bed. The other man had the advantage. He raised his arm and Alex felt a heavy blow on his left temple. The pain seared through his head. His mind and body went numb, and as darkness crept up on him he heard Catherine cry out his name.

*

Fowler saw that the woman was now awake, and heard her cry out. Noise he did not want! She was struggling to free herself from the bedclothes. He reached the bed and tried to hold the soft body still. This was one part of tonight's operation about which he had felt some strange unease. The man was police, and was fair game. This woman was something different, with her baby sleeping in another room. She was struggling underneath him, and he increased his weight. He could see her eyes looking up at him, and knew when she realised what was to come and lay still. A look of such unutterable sadness

358

came over her face, the green eyes swamped in tears, that for once in his life he was unnerved. But he had to finish it. In the one single act of mercy Harry Fowler had ever shown another person, he hit the woman on the jaw and knocked her out. He reached for the pillow.

When it was over, he checked to see if the prone, naked figure on the floor was still unconscious. There was no sign of movement, and he wasn't surprised. With his gloved hand he retrieved the statue, taking care not to transfer any blood to himself. He placed it in the woman's lifeless right hand and then let it drop to the floor.

Now for the rest of his instructions. He left the bedroom and went downstairs into the back room. He pulled out an envelope from his inside pocket and scattered the printed pages it contained over the table and floor. It was done. He must leave. He went back into the hall and had reached the front door when a sound made him turn. He looked up and saw a pale figure at the bend of the stairs, and the gun pointing at him!

*

Alex came to and tried to move. Something was wrong with his limbs, they felt weak and sluggish, and when he moved the pain in his head crashed into him like a wave. He had to lie back again and recover. But he couldn't stay here, there was an intruder in the house, and he had to protect Catherine and Peter.

Ignoring the searing pain, he struggled to his feet. He was finding it difficult to see and he could feel blood running down his face. He just made out Catherine's figure lying on the bed. She must have fainted. He dare not stop to check on her, his first thought was to tackle the intruder. His gun! Where was it? Then he remembered. He took a while to fumble open the bedside drawer, but with relief felt his hand on the cold metal. With a muffled groan he lurched to the bedroom door. The pain in his head was so intense that the movement almost defeated him, but the fear for his family pushed him on. He stumbled down the first few stairs and stood swaying on the half landing.

Below him in the hall near the front door he could see the outline of a figure. He tried to call out some sort of challenge but he seemed incapable of speech. The dark figure turned and looked up at him. A hand went into a pocket and Alex saw the glint of a gun and the arm lifting toward him. He knew his reflexes were weakened but forced himself to concentrate, aim and fire. He heard the echo… was it his gun, or was it another? Then came the pain in his head and he could feel himself falling headlong, down, and down…

*

Fowler cursed to himself. Nothing had been said about this man being armed! Although he had been under express orders not to use a firearm, out of habit he always carried one. There was no way he was being shot at without some sort of retaliation. Pulling his own gun from his coat pocket, he aimed at the swaying figure on the stairs. At the same time as he pulled the trigger, he felt the wind of a bullet just missing his own head.

He saw the naked form crumple and topple down the rest of the stairs, the head hitting the square newel post at the bottom with a sickening thud. He moved closer to the still figure and examined it in the dim light. He had aimed for the head and from what he could see, with the other damage inflicted, no one was going to discover much. With the woman dead, the man could have committed suicide. That would explain the firearm. He scrabbled around until his searching fingers found an ejected spent casing – hoping it was from his gun. He knew his firearm was of a make used by the police. Anyway, he'd been assured that any forensic formalities would be moved along with haste, so perhaps he could get away with what had happened.

His breathing heavy, he opened the front door and slipped out. All he had to do now was dump the car and make it to his arranged pick-up point. The car hummed into life and cruised away.

Church Road returned to its usual pre-dawn quietness, but an hour or two later a baby started to cry.

CHAPTER 25

The strong spring sunshine poured its brightness and warmth over the churchyard. Variations of colour were everywhere but to Sarah McIntyre the world was just… grey. For her there was no warmth in the sun. She was cold, and knew that the coldness was coming from deep inside her. It had been this way since she had heard the news, and she suspected it would continue.

She had been ready to leave for work when the police officer had arrived. In complete disbelief she had heard him out, and then fainted. On coming to her senses again she had found herself lying in her bed with a worried Jerry holding her hand. It was just a nightmare, she'd told him. Something to do with her pregnancy perhaps… But once again she heard the dreadful words, this time from Jerry himself.

There never seemed to be any tears for most of the time, just a complete empty void. The one thought repeating time and again: her sweet little Catherine – dead! She would never again see those sparkling green eyes smiling at her, or hear her soft voice. They had both been so happy, with motherhood having come to them at the same time. All the plans they had made… like passing on clothes from Peter as he grew out of them. Now it would still happen, but Catherine would no longer be involved. She would not see her own son grow and do all the things children did, for better or worse. She had been so happy about the future and all it held. She would also no longer have her beloved Alex.

Sarah just couldn't work this part out. How could they say all those dreadful things about him? There was no way it could be true! But the authorities were adamant that it was; even Jerry told her it could be possible. Still she refused to accept the conclusions.

Day moved into day and nothing else seemed real; she was drifting. She wasn't bothered whether she ate food or not, and sleep was something she dreaded, as the thoughts crowded in again. Then she became aware that her mother was there. Jerry told her he'd sent out an urgent request for her to return to the UK. She noticed he always had a worried face these days, and at night he would hold her, and talk to her, encouraging her to sleep.

Always, there was little Peter! She wouldn't let anyone else care for him. She had to do it herself. When she held him in her arms she tried to pretend that she was Catherine, imparting to him the love and affection that he would no longer know. This was when she cried, but she always tried to hide it.

She knew she was ill. She could feel it in herself, but somehow was certain that it wouldn't affect her unborn child. She had built a wall inside her, shielding the baby from the rest of herself. She had tried to explain it to her mother and Jerry, but she could see that they didn't understand.

Today had been the funerals. She had fought for the right to organise these as she wished. She weathered a dreadful argument with Jerry, who tried to forbid her being involved, saying that she was taking on too much. She knew he was taking a stand because he was concerned for her, and she understood his obvious worry. However, sensing her implacable resolve, he had given in; and she had never felt more grateful for his continuing love and care for her than at that moment.

She knew what she wanted to happen with the formalities, and afterwards. She conveyed these instructions to the funeral director and also spoke to Reverend Jones of St Luke's about her wishes.

He understood her request and the reason behind it, but was reticent about whether his superiors would agree. She had pushed him on the matter, and at the end everyone acceded to her wishes. Tomorrow her instructions would be carried out; and in a few days she would come back to this graveyard to make sure and say a final goodbye.

*

There was a large turn-out for Catherine's funeral. Lionel Franklin did not attend, pleading ill-health. She was pleased about that. Something deep inside her said that it would be wrong to have him here. She hadn't been able to bring herself to make a final visit to the funeral parlour, although Jerry attended and told her that Catherine looked as beautiful as ever. Seeing the coffin brought into the church, with the one bouquet of cream roses, was almost her undoing. Jerry placed his arm around her waist and supported her throughout the service. Luigi Gandoni stood on her other side, holding himself stiff and erect, his face a mask of sorrow. His wife Maria was beside him, weeping as though her heart would break.

Alex's funeral followed, and she felt vindicated by the number of people who remained in attendance for this.

On leaving the church and standing, for once, alone, she was approached by a man, a total stranger to her.

'Mrs McIntyre? I apologise for intruding at this sad time. My name is Ellison and I'm a former… colleague of Alex Hartman. We knew each other in our youth and I felt I wanted to attend for old times' sake.' He then made a somewhat cryptic remark that she didn't understand. 'I am of the opinion that the authorities have made a grave mistake in this whole matter, but…' – he gave a shrug – 'once again, my condolences.'

As he walked away she noticed several thick-set men surrounding him. Who could he be? Without her being aware, Alex's colleague Sergeant Johnson had come to stand at her side.

'I hope he didn't upset you, Mrs McIntyre?'

'No, he was very polite.' She told him what the man had said.

Looking, with narrowed eyes, after the departing limousine she heard him mutter, 'Someone else thinking straight, for a change.'

Then he left her, still wondering what it all meant.

She watched the last people departing and saw Jerry and her mother coming towards her. It was time to go home – to see Peter.

*

Lionel Franklin glanced up from the papers he was perusing, to look at the clock on the desk in front of him. The funerals should be over by now. It would have looked better if he'd gone to Catherine's, but as the day approached he'd become conscious of an uncomfortable feeling about attending, and pleading illness was a good way out. So far he felt he had managed to portray the appropriate attitude that others would consider necessary during the legal formalities, but to attend the funeral itself might have been, even to his own conscience, less than tasteful. He doubted Sarah McIntyre would mind. He never had the impression she thought much of him; he likewise of her.

When he was told about the two deaths, at first he was incandescent with rage that his plan had been thwarted. But then he realised that the ramifications might prove to be even more beneficial. It had therefore come as a shock when he found out that there were Wills, and the McIntyres had been made guardians of Peter.

This would, of necessity, lead to disclosure of information re the trust fund, but it would be an easy matter to massage the figures somewhat. Above all, he had to keep some sort of control, and this meant having to maintain a level of civil contact. He decided that he would appear generous in offering financial assistance, and when the boy was ready for schooling he would assist there also. It was imperative that the McIntyres be kept as amenable as possible in order to avoid any awkward financial questions, and to keep Hartman's solicitor quiet. With subtle pressure he would attempt to steer the boy into an ideal career, but for the time being, with any luck, their matters could still proceed as before.

*

In the quiet of the evening, Sarah sat with Peter in her arms and told him all about the events of the day.

'So many people have shown they cared for your parents, Peter. You were so lucky to have their love, even for a short while. But Jerry and I, and everyone else, love you and will always do so. You might not have your real parents as you grow up, but you have so many people who will care for you, that you'll not be on your own. In a short while, you'll have a little playmate too!'

Tears streaming down her face, she stroked his soft cheek. 'Oh, my dear Peter, we'll try so hard to make up to you for your loss. Aim to be good in all you do, and Catherine and Alex will be proud of you. I know it won't be easy, but I'm sure you'll grow into a fine boy.'

Holding the small body close to her, hearing his even breathing in the silence of the room, she became conscious of a growing certainty which softened the harsh edges of grief still inside her.

'Peter, some day the truth of what has happened will be discovered. I know it. I'll always believe it, and I'll hold on to that belief no matter how long it takes.'

PART THREE

CHAPTER 1

With the sun shining out of a cloudless blue sky, Peter Hartman let his gaze travel over the dazzling white slope in front of him. There were fewer skiers on the top part of this run at Canada's prestigious Lake Louise resort. None but the more confident attempted the challenge, and most started lower down the treacherous slope. As an expert skier, he himself had no problem with the awkward terrain.

Then he spotted her. The bright red ski jacket stood out well against the snow. She was moving fast and he would have to ski at full speed to catch up with her. Could he put his plan into action? Without giving himself any more time to debate the matter, he launched himself down the slope. He was soon overhauling her, but skiing well within his capability. Watching her fluent, assured turns, he realised that she also skied to a high standard. As he came nearer, he washed off some of his speed. He didn't want to cause a real accident, after all!

Closing in level with the flying figure, he called out a warning and passed her, near enough to bump her shoulder, sending her off line. He braked to a stop at the side of the run and rolled into the soft snow, losing a ski. He picked himself up and looked round. The girl was a few yards away from him. She too had ended up in the soft snow and was just attempting to sit up. Discarding his goggles and remaining ski, he struggled up the slope towards her.

'I'm so sorry. Are you alright? I'm afraid I lost an edge further up and couldn't stop in time.'

He caught hold of her arm, and steadied her for a moment as she regained her footing. The girl shook off his hand, and busied herself retrieving her skis and poles. She then turned and looked at him.

'You know that it's dangerous to be in areas like this if you're not a good skier? We could have been hurt!'

Now he was closer, he was able to confirm his first impression when he had seen her in the hotel, that she was a pretty girl. Snow flecked her honey gold hair, and her clear skin was a pale pink from her exertions. Her eyes were the colour of caramel, several shades darker than her hair, but their expression at the moment was as frosty as the landscape around them.

'I must apologise again.' He contrived to adopt a chastened look. 'If we skied down the rest of the way together, perhaps I could buy you a drink in the café.'

She was still looking at him, but the expression in the brown eyes had now changed. He found out why a few seconds later.

'After an experience like this, I wouldn't be sure of my safety; either skiing, or anything else.'

To his consternation he realised that she had misinterpreted his actions. Too embarrassed to explain, he watched her straightening herself and preparing to launch off again down the slope. In a moment she would be gone, and it would all have been for nothing.

Then, to his astonishment, the girl paused and turned to study him again. 'Rather than attempting such a dangerous way of introducing yourself, perhaps you could take a safer course and buy me a drink in the hotel bar tonight.'

With a slight smile she skied away, leaving him standing there, mortified. All the planning and effort on his part, and it was so obvious to her. What on earth had made him think up the whole crazy idea anyway? Bored with his own company, he'd wanted someone of his own age to talk to but, as usual, didn't feel able to just walk over and talk to her.

Could he, now? After all, she had invited him to do so. Feeling happier, he retrieved his skis and carried on down the run. There was still time to get back up to the top again and try a final fast descent.

Changing for dinner in his hotel room that night, Peter began to feel nervous again. For goodness' sake, why was he being such an idiot? Here he was, twenty-four years of age, and his experience with the opposite sex was lamentable. Rob would put it stronger than that, he thought! If he'd been here with him, as planned, he would have achieved several conquests by now. He knew that wasn't his own style, though. He always shied away from the idea of commitment, and found even casual acquaintance difficult. There had been a couple of girls at college, but he'd felt no particular need to extend their relationship into anything serious.

Yet, he acknowledged his loneliness. Although, during his life, there had been people around who cared for him, there was still... something missing. He knew what it was, of course, but tried never to dwell on it.

He looked in the mirror. Aunt Sarah said that he had his father's eyes and his mother's hair colour. He knew this was true. No one guessed that he kept a photograph of his parents in his wallet. It was taken on their wedding day, and he looked at it often. He had wondered whether to separate the two figures and keep them apart, reflecting what had happened, but felt a strange reluctance to do so. Perhaps he was influenced by Aunt Sarah's vehement denial of any idea of a rift between his parents, despite others accepting the irrefutable facts.

Once again, he acknowledged that the events of the past had coloured his own view of relationships. As with his parents, how could you guarantee anything was permanent, however much it might seem so... just to have it fall apart? Better not to get involved in the first place, wasn't it? He shook his head in anger. He went through this over and over, so many times, and never reconciled it within himself.

He'd been on his own too much over these last few days, and he made up his mind. Yes, he would see the girl tonight.

Christa Benjamin decided to take extra care with her appearance. The fresh air and exercise had brought the glow back to her skin after months of being in an office. She brushed her long hair until it shone, curling over her shoulders. Stepping into her dark green dress, she then sat down at the dressing table to fix her gold earrings. Her brown eyes softened as she smiled, thinking about the events on the ski slope this afternoon.

She and her father had arrived three days ago and it wasn't long before her naturally warm nature was disturbed at seeing the young man always alone in the restaurant, and she had commented on this to her father. After a moment of study, he suggested that she asked him to join them. It was odd... in normal circumstances she would have done just that, but for once she felt a strange reluctance. There was an air of solitude about him which troubled her.

She smiled again at his contrived introduction, which had surprised her in more ways than one! You would have to be a fool trying to negotiate the higher parts of that slope if you couldn't ski well, and she somehow judged that he was not a fool. In fact, to have achieved that mock crash, without either of them being hurt, was the mark of an experienced skier. This was borne out by the fact that she had seen him take the cable car up to the summit again and watched most of his subsequent descent, executed to perfection.

She hoped he would accept her invitation tonight.

She was sitting with her father in the restaurant when the young man walked in. Holding her breath, she waited to see what would happen. He made his way towards his table, paused, and then came towards them. She started breathing again.

How nice he looked in his navy suit, his dark brown hair curling on the collar of his jacket... and from nowhere she had the urge to know what it would feel like under her fingers. She was startled by her thoughts. What on earth was she thinking about? She'd just met the man, and not in a conventional way at that.

He walked up to their table and, with a slight smile in his grey eyes, spoke to her in a rather formal fashion.

'Good evening. I hope you've had no ill effects from your tumble this afternoon?'

'Er, no. I'm fine, thank you, Mr…?'

'Sorry, I should have introduced myself. My name is Peter Hartman.' He held out his hand to her.

'I'm Christa Benjamin, and this is my father.'

Rising to his feet, her father shook the younger man's proffered hand. 'I'm Frank Benjamin. Glad to meet you, Peter. I hear you had a bruising meeting with my daughter. I know the feeling. I have them all the time!' Despite his words, there was a fondness in the smile he gave her.

'It was my mistake, sir, and once again I offer my apologies.'

Christa listened, almost entranced. There was an old-world charm about this young man with his speech and manners, nothing like the rough and tumble she had become used to in others of her age.

Her father also must have been impressed. 'If you're dining alone, Peter, why don't you share our table? Save the waiters a bit of trouble. Oh, and the name's Frank.'

'Thank you, er… Frank. I would like that, if Christa would have no objection.'

His immediate use of her Christian name pleased her, and she smiled at him and shook her head.

Over dinner she learnt that he was staying for ten days, with only three further days remaining. The sudden sense of disappointment she felt was so great that she lost track of the conversation flowing between the two men. Whether or not her father was astute enough to notice her slight change of mood, she didn't know, but he spoke to the younger man with a laugh.

'As I'm finding that my old legs can't keep up with the youngsters any more, if you have the time, I would deem it a favour if you could keep Christa company whilst you're still here. I'd like to feel I've derived some benefit from my holiday.'

Christa looked across at her father. He hadn't shown any signs of flagging when he'd been skiing with her before. He caught her look and stared back at her with no apparent expression, but she sensed that he was asking for her approval.

She found Peter Hartman looking at her with a strange, sombre look in his grey eyes, but the tone of his voice was warm enough when he answered, 'I'd be delighted to help out, if you wish.'

Christa sensed that the remark was being directed at her, and not her father. 'Thank you. That would be very kind. My father does suffer so.'

She watched with inner mirth as her father choked on his wine, just recovering by the time they ordered their meal.

CHAPTER 2

Over coffee, she sat in discomfort as her father began his well-practiced inquisition of the younger man.

'By your accent, I assume you're British. Are you working in Canada? I say that, because it seems a long way to come on your own for just a holiday.'

'In fact, strange as it may seem, I am in this country on holiday. It's an unexpected but marvellous present from a great uncle, for doing well in my law studies. I should have been here with a friend but he broke his leg just before we left.' A smile began to play around his mouth. 'He fell off a horse.'

'Oh, bad luck. Some of them can be awkward creatures.'

'No animal could be as bad as Rob's senior officer.' Seeing their puzzled looks, he explained, 'My friend is a junior officer in the Household Cavalry. Falling off your horse is not an option, I gather.'

His smile broadened as he recounted to them Rob's pained expression when they brought him home from the hospital, not all as a result of his injury. 'His sister hasn't stopped laughing yet.' He paused for a moment. 'I thought about cancelling the holiday, but in the end decided to come on my own.'

Christa was watching with interest as Peter's face became lighter and more animated. He should smile more often, she thought. He was quite handsome. Since she had first seen him, she knew there was something about him that had attracted her – but she wasn't quite sure at the moment just what it was.

'A pity your plans were spoilt somewhat, but I hope you've enjoyed seeing something of the country?'

'I have indeed. I've been very impressed.'

Frank Benjamin went on with his cross-examination. 'You say you've just taken law exams?'

'Yes. Now I have my degree, I'm due to join a barrister's chambers in London when I get back. My great uncle seems pleased, and perhaps that's why he's been generous with the holiday. He's a retired Judge. He's been an enormous help to me all through my studies, and I owe him a lot.'

'You say that your career move has pleased your great uncle. What about you or your parents?' Christa couldn't help but make the comment.

Their companion seemed to draw in on himself, remaining silent for several moments. Christa looked at her father, who shrugged, and was about to speak when the young man seemed to rouse himself.

'My parents died… in an accident… when I was a few weeks old. I was brought up by their good friends, a doctor and his wife. Aunt Sarah and Uncle Jerry have been brilliant, and their two children, Robert, who should have been here with me, and Amy, have been like a brother and sister. I also have a wonderful godfather. So, between them all, I've been well taken care of.

'However, to answer your question, if I'm honest, I went into law because I found it easy. My great uncle has been generous in his financial assistance with my schooling, and began to teach me law even as a young boy. I suppose I just absorbed it without being conscious of the fact. When I started studying at university, he acted as a private legal tutor, which was a terrific benefit. I found I was way ahead of everyone else, so after all the help and support he's given me, I owe it to Great Uncle Lionel to do as well as I can.'

Christa felt dreadful for being instrumental in having brought up his sad past, and her heart warmed to him. Perhaps this explained some of the strange solitary quality about him, and why she felt herself drawn to him.

'I know it won't help to say we're sorry, but we are. What happened to your parents is not an ideal start in life, is it.'

'No, but I can't change anything. I must make my own life, and as I said, I've had all the care and help from everyone that I needed. At least I'll have no trouble remembering 2000 as the year when I started gainful employment!'

Music could be heard playing in the background and Christa, making a sudden decision, looked at Peter in query.

'Do you dance?'

'Oh Lord, I'm not very good.'

Laughing at him, Christa took hold of his arm and half-dragged him out of his seat.

'Well, you can get in some practice now. See you, Dad.'

Frank Benjamin rose to his feet. 'I feel an old man's game of bridge coming on. Have fun, you two.'

*

Peter found he enjoyed the next few days. The weather was good, and he and Christa were able to ski each day, and it was nice to have company at mealtimes. With interest, he watched the easy relationship between Christa and her father. The generation gap was non-existent as they sparred off each other. He found himself laughing more than he could remember.

It was obvious that Christa was well educated, and when he had enquired about her father's occupation she replied, 'He builds boats'. She herself had just started work in journalism after leaving college, and again the close relationship with her father became apparent as she mentioned that he had left her to choose her own career path.

With his own experience, Peter was reluctant to make any query about her mother, but one day while they were having a warming drink after one of their skiing sessions, she volunteered the information.

'Mum and Dad divorced several years ago. They went through a bad patch while I was away at school. Dad says it was his fault. He was concentrating on his business so much that they drifted apart. Just one of those things that happen, he said. They've remained on good terms, and I see my mother from time to time. She's married again and seems to be happy enough. I was given the choice of who I wanted to live with, and I chose my Dad. I sensed he had taken the whole thing hard. I'm glad I made that choice. We get on so well, and I love him to bits.'

Peter thought about what she had told him and became envious of the good relationship she had with her father. Would he have had the same with his?

On his last day, as they stopped to rest out on the slope, Peter stood looking at the view.

'This is a very beautiful country.' Without knowing why, he found himself adding, 'Do you know, I might have a grandfather living in Canada.'

Christa came and caught his arm. 'Oh, Peter. How wonderful! Do you know where he lives?'

He turned to her. 'No. He emigrated when my father was in the Army. All I know is that his name is Michael and he came out here in his late thirties, in about 1958, after resigning from the police force in London. According to my godfather, he corresponded with him for a few years when he was living in Halifax, but then lost touch. I suppose I could attempt to trace him if I wanted, but I'm not sure about making contact after such a length of time. My father never did, so I'm told. It's perhaps better left as it is.'

He returned his gaze to the view and, watching him, Christa began to form a plan.

*

Both Christa and her father insisted on seeing him off at the airport. Frank Benjamin shook his hand.

'Make sure, if you're ever this way again, that you look us up. Have a good journey, Peter.'

Then, in a tactful move, he left to retrieve the car.

Peter looked at Christa. Her long hair was held back off her face, exposing her smooth skin and showing off her tan. He would miss her. She was like quicksilver, in both mind and movements. He felt energised in her company. He noted that for once the brown eyes regarding him were serious. It was impossible for him to read her thoughts, but he sensed she was coming to some sort of decision.

'As Dad said, keep in touch won't you? You have all my details.' She paused. 'Peter, I know this will sound a bit contrived, but I was considering coming to England to work on a British newspaper. If I did, could we meet?'

As he thought over her statement, Peter was at first taken aback, but then as the idea grew in his mind he decided that, yes, he would look forward to it.

'Of course, Christa. Let me know.'

'Alright, I will.' Her smile became mischievous. 'You'd better go now or you'll miss your plane.'

'Oh! Yes... right... I'd better.' He felt foolish, not knowing what to do or say.

Before he realised it, she had reached up and kissed him on the cheek and then disappeared into the crowd. He stood there for a moment looking after her and then, with a quiet smile, turned toward the boarding gate.

CHAPTER 3

Sarah and Amy were waiting at the barrier. Peter's plane was late in, and for the third time in as many minutes Amy began fretting about her date that evening.

'Oh, do come on Peter, please.' She tucked errant strands of red-dyed hair back behind her ear and pulled the multicoloured scarf tighter around her neck.

'It's not Peter's fault, Amy. Now calm down, he'll be here any moment.'

Sarah looked at her daughter's startling and vivid appearance. She loved her independent spirit but felt unnerved at being with her in public when she was in one of her 'arty' dress moods. The Art College had a lot to answer for, she decided.

She hoped Peter's holiday had gone well. It was a shame he'd been forced to go on his own. He was too much on his own already. Rob, in typical fashion, just had to do something idiotic at the wrong time!

Peter would be even more in debt to Lionel Franklin now, was her unhappy thought. Right from the beginning of caring for him she had been apprehensive about any involvement with the man. But then he had offered to assist with school fees, enabling Peter to have a far better education than might have been the case. As Jerry had said, for Peter's sake they had to accept. All she wanted was for him to be happy in whatever he was doing.

It became obvious that Peter was a bright boy and he had done well. Sarah considered that Lionel Franklin had been too hard on him by encouraging him to do extra, over and above his school work, but it had paid off with grades that gave him an easy university entrance. Then there was the choice between reading law or something else, and again his great uncle won by encouraging him to read law under an old friend at Cambridge. Once more, how much opposition could she have mounted? It would have looked as if she was not doing her best for Peter. She knew his Uncle Luigi felt the same; indeed, she sensed he disliked any involvement with Lionel Franklin at all. However, it seemed that through the law Peter had found a common bond with his great uncle, displaying affection for him and singing his praises on a regular basis.

As they stood waiting, try as she might to ignore it, she felt the familiar apprehension building in her. Whenever Peter was away for even a short while, the first moment of seeing him again was like having three people there instead of just one. His physical appearance and mannerisms were a vivid reminder of the people she still could not believe she would never see again. It had been so difficult over all these years, and the pain of hearing that dreadful, unimagined news was still as fresh inside her.

'Are you OK, Mum?'

Amy's enquiry brought her back to reality, and the arm around her shoulders was comforting.

'Come on, Mum. Don't go there again. You know it makes Dad upset. Buck up. Peter will be here any moment.'

Sarah had made the deliberate decision of asking Amy to come to the airport with her, and she knew very well that her daughter understood the reason. They all knew how she felt, although she tried hard to hide it. When Rob and Amy were considered old enough, they were told the full situation regarding Peter's parents; and, bless them, they had been even more supportive of their special brother.

'Here he comes, at last!' Amy jumped up and down and waved her arms, never considering that it was impossible she could be missed in the crowd.

Sarah saw Peter wave back and come towards them. He was a nice-looking boy, she thought. Not quite the film star good looks of his father, but still attractive enough in his own way. However, there was that air of vulnerability about him, much like Catherine. It always concerned her; although it might bring out the mothering instinct in some females… but, she sighed, not yet it seemed. He had a tan. It's done him good to be out in the fresh air, she thought.

Peter came straight to her, enveloping her in a hug, and kissing each cheek. His body felt lean and hard and he seemed more relaxed than before he went away. His holiday must have been worthwhile.

'Hi, Aunt Sarah. Thanks for coming to meet me.'

He then turned to Amy, and Sarah hid a smile as he winced. 'I did see you, you know. I think it was when the plane was still at ten thousand feet!'

Amy was unmoved and just made a face at him. She grabbed his arm. 'Come on, Peter, I can't hang around here all night. I've got a date.'

'Poor boy,' Peter murmured, with a grin at Sarah.

Amy turned back to him with a saccharine sweet smile. 'I was going to say it's nice to have you back, but I'm not sure now.' And she marched off towards the car park.

Sarah put her arm through Peter's as they walked. It was always so nice to have the children together, with their amicable bickering. She knew very well that, when pushed, they were always protective of each other, and Jerry and herself.

*

The car eased off the road into the parking area at the front of the large four-storey semi-detached Victorian villa.

'Dad's not back yet,' Amy commented to her mother.

'So I see, but he shouldn't be long now. I hope I've left him enough room to park.'

It was a running family joke that Sarah wasn't the world's best driver, and time and again Jerry had to move her car in order for him to fit his own into the rather limited space.

He was now a Consultant Paediatrician at St Thomas's and was often away either at conferences or on courses. The house was convenient for the hospital and also big enough for their extended family. Peter had been given the basement as his own self-contained living area, and had his own key so he could come and go as he liked.

Sarah loved the house. It was always full of bustle and laughter; and some tantrums now and again. It was a home in the true sense of the word, and the big extended kitchen at the rear was the hub. All major discussions took place around the big wooden table, and even when guests came they seemed to gravitate from the best rooms into the warmth of the kitchen.

Sarah had always encouraged the children to assist in the running of the house, and now that she herself was back at work full-time, it came in handy. Despite appearing a scatterbrain, Amy was, in fact, quite organised and methodical, and Sarah was very glad of her practical help.

She had worked part-time at first when the children were young, but once they were all away at college, decided to go full-time. She was now at last working in the Rheumatology Department at St Thomas's, and was studying hard.

Moving her books to one side of the table, she motioned to Peter. 'Dump your bag there. We'll sort it out in a minute and put the washer on later. I'll see how the meal's doing first.'

'Don't worry, Aunt, I'll sort it out. There's not much anyway. I did some in the hotel. Is Rob upstairs?'

Busy at the oven, Sarah turned to him. 'I would imagine so. He can't go far at the moment, can he!' With a chuckle she turned back to her casserole.

'I'll just nip up and say hello. I'll tell him the meal's on the go, shall I?'

'Fine. His father should be home at any time, and he can show him his cast.'

A little perplexed at her remark, Peter left the room.

CHAPTER 4

As nice as it had been to be away, Peter acknowledged that he was glad to be home, with the people he was fond of and familiar sights and smells. Hotels were alright, but pretty soulless. He went up to the top floor, knocked on the door marked 'Do Not Enter', and walked in.

Rob was lying on his bed playing a video game, his plastered leg propped up on a pillow. Tall, blond and blue-eyed, he never had any problems attracting the opposite sex, all the more so when in uniform; but Peter knew that underneath all that machismo was a kind and caring person. Although a year younger than himself, Rob was a good listener for his problems and came up with sound advice. At times, however, he could be a little impatient with Peter's hesitancy and caution.

'Hey, the wanderer returns! Have a good time, old son?'

Peter sat down on the bed. 'Yes, great. The skiing was good. Nice country.'

'What about the après-ski, eh? Anything tasty?'

'Not that I saw. I did meet a Canadian couple – father and daughter – in the hotel. I had about three days left when they came, but we joined up for meals and we skied a bit.'

'So? What was the daughter like?'

'Quite pleasant. She seemed pretty bright. She's a trainee journalist. Her father builds boats. She skis well.'

'And...?'

Peter looked up. 'And what?'

'Peter, for God's sake, what are you like! Are you going to keep in touch, you idiot?'

'Well, I have her phone number and she has mine. Now I think about it, I'd better send a text to say I've arrived.'

As he busied himself for a minute or two, Rob lay back on the bed and watched with amusement. When Peter had finished his task, he went on, 'Did you get on with her alright, if you know what I mean?'

'I enjoyed being with her, but nothing happened, if that's what you're referring to.'

'Not that you'd have done it anyway, I suspect, knowing you. But we've got to start somewhere, I suppose. Make sure you keep in touch. You know what they say, "absence makes the heart grow fonder", my old son.'

Peter thought about this for a minute. He already missed her sparkling conversation. Perhaps he could ring and speak to her.

'She did say that she might be coming over here to work on a British newspaper.'

'Well, there you are then!' Rob leant forward and clapped him on the back. 'You've cracked it there, and without the help of yours truly.'

They grinned at each other. Peter then remembered he ought to have asked about the leg.

'How have you been getting on?' pointing to the well-decorated cast. 'I see Amy's been busy prettying it up.'

'Oh, I'm managing, but I'll be darned glad to get it off. The boys have been busy as well.' He pointed with a sly look to one particular portion of the cast. Peter leant over for a closer look, and then whistled.

'I'll say they have. It's almost pornographic, Rob.'

'I don't know about "almost", I think it already is,' Rob chuckled, and then sobered. 'Mum turned quite pink when she saw it and says that if Dad sees it, he'll put a coat of whitewash over it, and the rest of me!'

They both heard voices and a door slam down below.

'Oh boy,' Rob sighed, 'here we go, sounds like one in, one out. If Dad's back, it won't be long before I'm hauled over the coals about it. I wonder if Amy has any correction fluid?'

'Speaking of Amy, what's with the fire engine red hair? Who's she going out with who can put up with her like that?'

'I think she sees herself as a rebellious art student. Don't worry, if she came across someone she liked who put their foot down, she'd be all Miss Prim and Proper in no time at all. It'll come, mark my words. What's your girl like?'

'She's not "my girl", for goodness' sake.' Peter shot him an exasperated look. 'She's a natural honey blonde with brown eyes, if you must know.'

Rob studied him with a serious look for a moment. 'Did you tell them about… well, you know.'

'Your aversion to horses?'

'No, you fool. You know what I mean.'

Peter knew just what he meant. 'We talked a bit about my career choice and there was a reference to my parents. I just said the usual: that they'd been in an accident.' He looked at Rob and his grey eyes were now bleak.

'It's not the right sort of small talk at dinner to mention that your father was suspected of accepting bribes in his profession, and added to that, killing his wife after a violent row, and then taking his own life!' The anguish came through in his voice.

Rob eyed him, his face reflecting his unhappiness. 'Sorry, I was an idiot to mention it. It's obvious you don't want to bring it up. There's no reason for anyone to know, is there? Keep cool about it, Peter. This is your life, to do as you want, without any throwback to anything else. Focus on where you're going now, not back to the past. Nothing can change that.'

Peter gave him a fond smile. 'Yes, oh wise one!'

Looking a little more relieved, Rob began to shuffle himself off the bed.

'Dinnertime soon, I shouldn't wonder. We'd better get downstairs.'

386

*

Jerry sidestepped out of the way of what he took to be his daughter tearing out of the front door with a quick, 'Hi, Dad. Bye.'

Shaking his head, he dropped his bags in the hall and went in search of his wife. Sarah turned with a smile as he entered the kitchen, and he crossed over and wrapped his arms around her waist and gave her a peck on the cheek.

'How's my girl, eh?'

'Much better for having you back home. Good trip?'

'The conference was a bit boring. One or two of the speakers knew less about the subject than I did. I had a good run home, though, which was a blessing. Was that apparition that passed me in the hall our one and only daughter? I'm glad it was dark. She's going to give us a bad name with the neighbours.'

Sarah laughed at him. 'You should be so lucky. She came with me to the airport like that.'

'Ah, so Peter's back then. Did he have a good time?'

'As far as you can tell with him. He's a close one. You have to dig deep to find anything out. He's up with Rob at the moment.'

Jerry looked hard at his wife. He knew as well as the rest of the family what effect Peter sometimes had on her, but she appeared to be quite calm.

'I'd better change before dinner. Do you mind if I make a quick couple of phone calls? I'll be ten minutes, I promise.'

Sarah's look at her husband was disbelieving. 'Oh yes, and the rest. I'll give you twenty, and that's all. Give the boys a shout, will you, Jerry.'

'Sure thing.' Jerry went out into the hall and retrieved his briefcase. When he reached his landing he called up the top flight of stairs, 'Dinner, boys. Help in the kitchen needed, please.'

He went into the main bedroom, and a couple of minutes later as he made his first call he smiled to himself, hearing Rob's laborious clump down the stairs.

Dinner was the usual warm family gathering. Everyone pitched in and helped. Jerry pressed Peter for a description of his holiday and it appeared that he had enjoyed himself. When Peter made a brief mention of his contact with Frank Benjamin and his daughter, Sarah and Jerry exchanged a look.

'You say that this girl might come over to the UK?' Jerry enquired.

'It's possible, I'm not sure.' Peter replied.

'Well, if she does, don't forget, as they showed hospitality to you, you must bring her along to us and make her feel welcome over here.'

'Thanks, I will. If it happens.'

Jerry looked at his wife, who nodded. It was time to mention the idea they had both talked about while Peter was away.

'Pete, lad,' Jerry began, 'on Monday you're about to start the next step of your life with a proper career, and...' – he smiled – 'as you can now be classed as an intrepid lone traveller, we wondered how you would feel about dropping the "Aunt" and "Uncle" bit. It's your choice. We don't mind either way.' He eyed his son, moving his cast on the supporting stool next to him. 'After all, we've been called other things from time to time.'

'Oh, I'm over all that now, Dad. I'm all grown up,' was Rob's immediate reply.

'I'll believe that when I see it!' Chuckling, Jerry turned back to Peter. 'What do you think?'

Peter was thinking. When told as a small boy about his parents, he remembered adoption being discussed. Something inside him hadn't wanted that. He had real parents, even though they weren't with him. The 'Aunt' and 'Uncle' thing became the norm. Over the years, he'd become so intertwined with this household there didn't seem any difference anyway, apart from the surname. He realised that he was now being offered an adult option to his status. It was typical of the caring attitude towards him that this had even been considered.

'Yes, I think I'd like that, if you're sure about it,' he said.

'OK, consider it done then.'

While Peter had been thinking, Jerry had been eyeing his son's leg on the stool next to him.

'You've a pretty good art collection there, Rob.' He looked a little closer, and raised an eyebrow. 'Not very correct from an anatomical point of view, or even possible, come to that! Might be an idea to cover it over in public. We don't want you scaring any little old ladies, do we.'

Rob grinned at Peter and sighed with relief. 'Thanks, Dad. The boys went a bit mad, I think. I'll make sure it doesn't offend.'

'Good. Well, I think maybe you two could deal with the washing up while my wife and I have some time to ourselves in the front room.'

As Sarah and he left, Rob gave a loud whistle. 'Good old Dad. You know he's mad, but he doesn't make a meal of it. Treats you like an adult. That was a nice suggestion they made to you, Peter.'

Peter stood and began to clear the table. 'I've always thought they were terrific people. They've done their best for me. Has it ever bothered you and Amy, about me being here?'

Rob looked at him in genuine surprise. 'Lord no, it's been so natural I haven't given it much thought. I don't think Amy has either. She's never mentioned it to me. We think of you as a proper brother, and that's it. It's nice having you around.'

Such displays of care and support, Peter realised, continued to warm the lonelier areas inside him.

CHAPTER 5

Without, for once, the involvement of his great uncle, Peter had obtained a position as a pupil with an old and well-respected barristers chambers. Although this had not been a conscious independent decision, he was pleased about making the choice for himself. At his interviews he had been impressed by the atmosphere of genuine friendliness in the chambers.

Despite this, however, it was with some trepidation that he presented himself on the Monday morning. The Chief Clerk, John Moore, introduced him to a blur of names and faces and then took him through to a room overlooking a courtyard garden. Jonathan Raven was a man in his forties, but already with a shock of iron grey hair. He was a senior barrister and son of the present head of chambers. He was to steer Peter through his first months. They had met once and Peter had taken an instant liking to him.

'Well now, welcome, Peter. All ready for the fray?'

'I think so, sir.'

'Right, well we'll start by you not calling me "sir" all the time. In front of clients it's Mr Raven, but otherwise try Jonathan. OK?'

'Thanks… Jonathan.'

'Right. Well then, pull up a chair. I imagine you'll feel a little out of your depth at first, but if I think you can manage it, I'll put some work your way. We have a busy time coming up just now. One or two big cases. I suggest you read through some of the case notes and Court documents I'm dealing with at the moment just to familiarise yourself with the contents and how things have panned out. I'm not in Court until tomorrow and I think John Moore will take you along so you that can see things in operation. Sound OK?'

'Oh yes, I'm looking forward to it. I seem to have been studying for so long, and now I'm almost at the end of it, it's nice to be doing some proper work.'

Jonathan Raven considered him for a moment or two.

'Judge Lionel Franklin is a relative of yours, and he's been your mentor, I believe?'

There was something in his tone of voice that alerted Peter.

'He's my great uncle. My mother's uncle. He was of tremendous help by giving me extra coaching when I was at school, which helped my grades. He wanted me to study at Cambridge under an old associate of his, Professor Davenport.'

'Mmm... my father has spoken of Franklin. He's had several sparring matches with him in Court, I understand. Tended to come up with points relating to some outrageous old cases which made him unpopular with many a counsel.'

'But isn't a full disclosure of any legal issues of paramount importance?'

'Indeed, but where do you draw the line of obscurity? The law is the law, of course, but things have to move forward and change with the times; even law, to a certain extent. Any information has its part, but there is also common sense, fairness and justice; which is, after all, what we are supposed to be upholding.'

Peter went on the defensive, his voice taking on an unconsciously belligerent tone. 'Are you suggesting that my great uncle wasn't doing that?'

Jonathan Raven gave him a stern look through narrowed eyes. 'Well, perhaps we can have a theoretical conversation on the point some other time, Peter, but for now we'd better get on with some work.'

Peter picked up on the slight censure in the other man's voice and calmed himself down. 'Yes, of course. What would you like me to do?'

*

Peter found himself so engrossed by all he was seeing and learning, that he realised he had forgotten to contact his great uncle since his return. On the Friday evening he mentioned to Sarah that he would like to make arrangements to see him at his Club the next day. Peter had learnt to drive and, when needed, Sarah gave up her car to him.

'Of course, you can have the car. I'm not on duty until Monday, and I don't need to go out.'

She appeared to be about to say something else, but then thought better of it. Again, he recognised the disapproving attitude both Sarah and Uncle Luigi always took whenever his great uncle was mentioned. For a long while now, Peter had been given the clear impression that they were unhappy about any association with him. Nothing explicit was said as to why they held this stance; and if he was honest, he resented their feelings.

'You're never happy about me seeing Great Uncle Lionel, are you?'

He noticed Sarah didn't turn to face him, but continued preparing the evening meal. 'You must do as you wish, Peter, but I can't deny the fact that I don't like the man.'

'I can't see why. After all, as well as his professional guidance, he's been generous with his financial assistance over the years, and we owe him a lot. Besides, I feel a fondness for him. He is my one true blood relative, although a little removed, but proper family all the same.'

Sarah then turned to look at him and he saw the sheen of tears in her blue eyes. Realising far too late how his words must have sounded, he moved over and put his arms around her. He was annoyed with himself for making such a careless remark, and held her close.

'I'm sorry, Sarah. I'd never hurt you for the world. You know how much I love you and Jerry, and the "terrible two", and I can never repay you for what you've done for me.' He gave a sigh. 'I just can't deny the family association. I hope you can see that.'

Sarah sniffed and looked up at him. 'Yes, I know. It's just—'

'Look, perhaps we should agree to keep off the whole subject, eh? If I need the car I'll just ask for it and not tell you where I'm going. Is that OK?'

She gave him a watery smile, nodded and turned back to her task.

*

Lionel Franklin now lived on the top floor of the Grosvenor Club. He was in his middle seventies, and although still sharp enough in his mental faculties was less able with his mobility.

So, he mused to himself, Peter was back, and coming to see him. He had done well enough in all his exams. Brian Davenport said he was quite bright, and thought he would succeed in his career, although remarking that attempts to instil various views in him had met with a certain amount of resistance. Some throwback to that damn father of his! Franklin felt the anger rising in him again at missing out on the pleasure of seeing Hartman brought down to his knees. However, he had been able to maintain a certain amount of control over the boy and, despite the feeling of animosity from Sarah McIntyre, had pressed home his advantage and steered him towards the ideal career goal.

It was a nuisance that Peter had found his own place in chambers. There were other firms more suited to him than Ravens. Old Anthony Raven had been a thorn in his side at times in the past, trying to outsmart him.

It seemed the boy still had the odd spark of independent spirit, and was nowhere near compliant enough yet, but he had time to do a bit more work on him. Over the years the McIntyres, and that Italian godfather, must have had an influence on him. He would have to increase the pressure, he decided. Test him now and again. Keep him unsettled. Make him more reliant.

The telephone rang to announce Peter's arrival, and a few moments later he breezed into the room. Franklin noticed the tan and had the uncomfortable feeling that Peter was looking more and more like his father. The sharpness of his initial greeting betrayed his frustration.

'Took your time in contacting me, didn't you?'

He noticed Peter looked a bit sheepish.

'Yes, I know. I'm sorry, Great Uncle Lionel, things have been a bit busy since I came back.'

Franklin relented. Now was not the time to alienate him. He knew well enough that from a young age Peter had formed an emotional bond with him as a true relative. This was something he had fostered for his own benefit.

He gave a slight smile. 'Good holiday?'

'Brilliant, thank you,' said Peter, settling himself into a chair, his relief obvious. 'It was very generous of you to treat me. Shame that Rob couldn't make it. Jerry McIntyre said that he would repay you for the other unused ticket.'

'Tell him not to bother. Nice country, I believe. Never been there myself. How are you adapting to the job?'

'I'm enjoying it. So far, I've just been reading case notes and going to observe at Court a couple of times. I'm under Jonathan Raven.'

'Mmm... I know his father, Anthony, from the old days. Thought he knew a thing or two, but I made a point of coming out on top.'

'Jonathan said that his father had been in Court with you.'

Franklin sat up. 'What else did he say?'

Peter appeared taken aback by the abruptness of the question. 'Well, just that sometimes you were able to produce some old law information that might have influenced the proceedings. He seemed to take a dim view of how relevant this was.'

'Law information is there for anyone, if you look hard enough. It's knowing where to look. Your mother used to do my research. Damn good at it, too.'

The boy looked shocked, and Franklin regretted his comment. If Peter ever tried to ask a question about the past, he was always swift to change the topic of conversation. He could see Peter forming an inevitable question.

'Sarah said my mother was studying for a history degree via a correspondence course. Didn't she want to go to college?'

Franklin would not let himself be drawn into any further

discussion on the matter. 'I had certain plans for her, and she had others. Now, let's get back to what you've been learning. By the way, what happened to the respectful title "Aunt"?'

'Oh, the McIntyres have suggested that I now call them by their Christian names. They consider I'm adult enough.'

'I see. Perhaps you should do the same with me.'

This would seem like a nice gesture, he thought to himself with a smile. He had to make sure that at this critical stage Peter was still content with his influence, which could be used to advantage in the future.

CHAPTER 6

Christa Benjamin twisted the pencil round in her fingers, thinking hard.

'A penny for them, girlie.'

She looked over at the man sitting opposite her. Dick Hudson was a veteran reporter, now working out his time with the *Chronicle Herald*, and had been detailed to steer her through the minefield of features writing. In his day he'd been one of the best, working for the Canadian national daily the *Globe and Mail*, and had many front-page stories to his name. She got on well with him, although many didn't. He was short-tempered and taciturn, but she stood her ground, and she felt he respected that.

'Perhaps I shouldn't tell you,' she laughed. 'I'm afraid I wasn't thinking about work.'

'You won't work well if you've something on your mind. Is there a problem?'

Christa regarded the older man for a moment. Although she always valued her father's advice, there was no harm in running problems by others. Dick was an experienced man, after all.

'There's a... friend, in England, who lost touch with a relative when he emigrated here in the late 1950s. He was speaking about him a little while ago and I had the idea that I might try to see if I could find this person. It's my own decision, and it might be impossible.'

Hudson walked over to the coffee machine, returning with cups for each of them. He sat on the corner of her desk.

'You could always make enquiries. You needn't take it any further by contacting anyone. What information do you have to go on?'

'The man's name is Michael Hartman. He emigrated in about 1958, aged late thirties. He used to work for the British police. Initial correspondence had him living in Halifax, but after a year or two that contact was lost.'

'So we have to assume that he moved away, or didn't wish to correspond any longer, or even died.'

'That's about it. He would be in his seventies now.'

Hudson regarded her for a long moment. 'I think you should go ahead. It will be a good exercise for you in researching information, so I think we'll class it as work. Don't spend all your time on it, though, fit it in with your other assignments.'

Now that her search was semi-official, Christa became engrossed with her task. She decided that for the moment she would work on the premise that Michael Hartman was still alive, and establish whether he had ever left Halifax. This meant a check through the City Directories, the archival records for which were held by Library and Archives in Ottawa and would require a personal search. She decided to contact a college friend who worked in the city, to ask whether he would be prepared to do some research for her. After writing with her request she heard nothing from him for a week, but one evening, at last, the call came.

'Hi Larry. I wondered when I was going to hear from you!'

She smiled at the reply she received to this remark.

'I see, she's that pretty is she? Look, if you ever get the time, do you think you can help me out?'

After she had made her request, it was obvious that a hard bargain was being set at the other end.

'OK, OK... consider the deal done! Let me know when you're on leave, and I'll ask Dad to take you out again on the racing catamaran.'

Luigi Gandoni was the first to arrive at the restaurant, and waited for Peter to join him. He was looking forward to seeing the boy again. In his view he was growing up into a nice young man.

As always, though, his pleasant thoughts were tinged with that same old sadness; not just for the loss of Alex and Catherine, but also for the loss of his wife. Maria had passed away some five years ago after fighting a long battle with cancer; brought on, he was sure, by the anguish and shock of those terrible events. He had sold the business and thought about moving to Italy to live with his son, but felt an obligation to be close to Peter and help to watch over him.

It had been hard, very hard, and even today there was anger in his heart at the waste. All those innocent hopes and dreams, shattered in one tragic night, with the ripples moving out to touch other people. He knew that Sarah McIntyre had suffered, and like him, was still suffering. He had seen her raw emotion at the funerals and there was a strange empathy between them at their many meetings since, as if they both shared secret thoughts.

He had sensed her frustration, like his own, during the inquests. According to the authorities, there was no proof to implicate anyone else in what was perceived to have occurred; but he was sure, and he felt it was the same for Sarah, that the truth of what happened that night had not come out. It was inconceivable that Alex would have acted in the manner alleged, leaving Peter to fend for himself. But despite a body of evidence put forward as to the loving nature of the marriage, in the face of the known facts, the verdict was given.

Alex would always have this slur against his name, and at times the knowledge weighed heavy on Luigi's heart. He always impressed on Peter how much his parents had loved him, and even when he was old enough to be told the full story of that night, Luigi tried to instill in him that perhaps one moment's madness could not wipe out all the care and love shown to him before.

After the funerals, he took it upon himself to contact the solicitor who had acted for Alex and imparted to him his concerns, although they seemed, even to his ears, quite weak and judgmental. The short answer he received was that unless any new concrete evidence surrounding the events could be obtained, it would be difficult to mount any challenge. Further, as financial support was voluntarily offered by Lionel Franklin, it would be construed that he had the best of intentions regarding Peter Hartman's welfare.

As far as Alex's work colleague Sergeant Johnson was concerned, Luigi had been angry and disappointed that, for some reason, the man refused to have any contact with him. In fact, he was so angry that he thought about confronting Franklin himself, but good sense stopped him from making what he later considered would have been a mistake.

As Lionel Franklin became involved in Peter's education, he felt grave misgivings. His concerns about the man still lingered, and sat like a cloud over Peter's head. Over the years, he tried to temper Peter's enthusiasm for Franklin's ideas on his future, with the advice that he must make his own choices and also take the views of others around him. However, he often noticed Peter's resistance to his comments, and refrained from taking matters too far in case it endangered any dialogue between them at all.

For the boy's sake, he had to remain alert and keep an eye on the situation.

Peter arrived in a rush, apologising for being late. 'It's a little busy at the moment in chambers.'

'Are you enjoying it? That's the main thing, Peter.'

'I am, now I'm doing things for real. Study is all very well, but dealing with something that you know is affecting someone at this moment, is quite exciting. Jonathan Raven is a good teacher. I've learnt a lot from him already.'

'Are you still happy that you chose law? At times I've felt that you had very little choice.'

Peter looked at him, with eyes so like Alex's.

'Don't start that again, Uncle Luigi. You're as bad as Sarah. I've told you, Lionel didn't make the decision for me. I made it myself. You seem to forget that he's gone out of his way to give me a lot of help over the years.'

'That doesn't mean that you have to do what he says. He doesn't own you. He should have done what he did out of family love, not expect you to follow a path he has set out for you.'

'You make Lionel sound as if he's been manipulating me! I've been happy with all I've done, and what's more, I found my job without any help from him.'

Luigi just shrugged and threw his hands up in defeat.

'What's this "Lionel" business?'

Peter had looked a little uncomfortable under his comments, but now appeared to relax again. 'Sarah and Jerry suggested that I should drop the "Aunt" and "Uncle" bit. I mentioned it to Lionel and he said I could do the same with him.'

Luigi bit back a retort that the old schemer had done so to try to keep in with the boy, and gave the young man a rueful smile. 'I suppose I'd better follow suit, then, don't you think? Now, let's order.'

Over the meal they discussed the holiday, and Luigi was interested to note Peter's attitude when he spoke about the girl he had met.

Luigi commented, 'It would be nice if she did come over to work here. At least she would have someone she knew. It's good to have a friend to talk things through with, even more so when you're away from home.'

Peter gave him a fond smile, which warmed the old man's heart. 'Thank you, Luigi, for not going on about a girlfriend, like everyone else, with all the winks and nods. I dread to think what might have happened if Rob had been over there with me. Why do people always have to have this love baggage with everything? Why can't you have a girl as just a good friend?'

'There's no reason whatsoever, Peter. Nothing better than a good friend of any gender. All I would say to you is not to close your heart to emotion. I understand very well what's in the back of your mind, but don't let it cloud your judgement in any of your own relationships.'

Peter looked down at his coffee cup, his face tense. 'What's the use of love between a man and a woman if it can all go so wrong?'

Luigi laid his hand on the young man's arm. 'I had the privilege of knowing both your parents. I saw their love for each other, and for you. As I've told you, the truth of what happened that night is known to two people, and they are unable to tell us. There might be other factors of which we are unaware. These could make a difference. Remember that.

'Sarah, Jerry and I have tried to guide you through your formative years, and for my part I think you have become a very nice young man. Now you must steer your own course, even if you make mistakes along the way. Keep an open mind and don't be swayed by anyone in particular. Always remember that we are still here to give our thoughts and guidance if you require them at any time.'

Peter smiled at him again. 'Thanks, Luigi. I'll remember that.'

CHAPTER 7

Christa looked up as Dick Hudson came and stood in front of her desk.

'So, a dead end?'

'It seems so. Larry looked through Might's Halifax and Dartmouth City Directories for 1960 and 1961. Michael Hartman was listed in 1960 but not 1961, so he must have moved. I've checked, and there's no record of death. So he's alive somewhere.'

Hudson perched on her desk, rubbing his chin, a thoughtful look on his face. 'You said he was ex British police?'

'Yes, that's right. Have you had a thought?'

'Well, it's a wild guess. Won't get you very far, but I was just thinking… a fit young man, firearms training… would he have gone north, offered his services to one of the organised hunting outfits?'

'He would have been retired from that long ago, Dick. Even if I contacted some of the big groups, I doubt their employment records would go back that far. He might have kept independent, or not even done it at all. I'm going to have to give this a lot more thought.'

'Ah well, life's never that easy.'

*

Peter stifled a yawn. He was feeling tired. Perhaps it was time to call it a day. He looked at his watch, it was seven p.m. He'd stayed late at chambers, working on a piece for Jonathan tomorrow, but his mind was beginning to close down. Perhaps he should go home.

The door opened and Anthony Raven stepped into the room.

'I thought someone was still about. Working late?'

Peter had stood up as he entered, but the older man waved him down and perched on the edge of his desk. With piercing blue eyes, and iron-grey hair like his son, Peter could well see how his manner would both intimidate and influence in Court. This reinforced Peter's secret misgivings about his chosen profession. Did he have the necessary qualities to be a successful barrister? As far as he could see, you needed to be something of a showman and storyteller, and he knew his own failings of confidence. Perhaps you acquired the necessary attributes needed over a period of time.

'Yes, sir, I'm working on a piece for Jonathan tomorrow.'

'House rules, Peter. Remember? No "sir".'

Peter knew very well the informal way Ravens preferred to run their chambers, but after two meetings he still felt diffident about calling this imposing man by his Christian name.

'You're related to that scoundrel Lionel Franklin, aren't you?'

Peter bristled at the description. Biting back a retort, he shuffled the papers on his desk to distract himself.

'Yes… Anthony. He's my great uncle.'

'He used to cause me some grief, I can tell you. On occasions it seemed to me that he made a point of hunting out the most obscure legal points he could find when giving his judgments, which in my view had marginal relevance to the case in point. It must have meant a lot of diligent work in those days before computerisation, for whoever did his research.'

'It was my mother.'

Anthony Raven glanced down at him.

'Yes. I'm sorry about all that. Not very pleasant for you. I remember the incident. In fact I was surprised how little coverage it received in the press. Bent copper, crime of passion, etcetera. There was also, at the same time, a car accident which killed the then Met Police Commissioner. I'd have thought the press would have snapped up stories like that and made more of them, but it all faded away. Often wondered if someone wanted the lid screwed down tight for some reason. There was a funny mood about in the country at the time.'

He shook his grey head. Peter sat still, just watching him, not wanting his mind to explore what he had just heard.

'You know, I was surprised Lionel Franklin was happy for you to join us.'

Peter adjusted to Raven's sudden change of tack.

'He didn't have anything to do with my selection. I made my own evaluation.'

'Well, all I can say is that I run the best firm I can, and I want the best people in it. You were head and shoulders ahead of any of the other applicants, and I was prepared to take you on despite that connection. I don't have to remind you, of course, not to mention anything you see here to him in any way, or impart any of his views into your own work. It's easy to do. If I found it happening, I would be very displeased.'

Peter looked at the older man, his gaze steady. 'Everyone is telling me to live my own life, and that's what I intend to do.'

Anthony Raven stood and walked to the door.

'Good, good. Best way. Listen to advice, but work it out for yourself. Jonathan tells me you're doing very well. Keep it up. Don't work too late. Goodnight.'

Peter looked at the closing door, his mind revolving like a carousel. He needed to talk about it all with someone, and the first person he thought of was Christa.

*

Frank Benjamin knew his daughter was leading up to something and was not surprised when she came and cuddled down next to him on the old baggy sofa in the den. It was always her way of discussing things with him.

'Dad, you know I mentioned some while ago about maybe going to work in England? Would you mind if I did? Always assuming I got the chance.'

'My dear girl, you're twenty-two years of age. You can do anything you want without asking me.'

She squeezed his arm. 'I know that, Dad, but I still like to run things by you. I value your advice.'

Frank's fondness for his daughter grew on hearing such words. Since her mother left they had become very close, and he always treasured the time he was able to spend with her.

'I'm glad to hear that, baby. I've tried to do the best for you. I like the young woman you've grown into, and you make me very proud. If you wish to go to England I can't stop you. I know I'll miss you, but you must do what you feel is right. Can I ask one thing?'

His daughter looked up at him with misty eyes. 'Of course you can.'

'This move to England. Is it for your career, or for that young man?'

He watched Christa plucking at her jersey. A sure sign that she was thinking hard.

'I would like to work abroad. Dick Hudson says it would be good experience for me. I can't deny, though, that I would like to be nearer Peter. I don't know how to explain it, Dad, but I feel he needs me... or someone. He seems so down at times, unsure. I think it all stems from his being orphaned. By the way, he still has no idea of your financial circumstances, so don't worry that he's enticing me over there for any underhand benefit. I'll keep it as quiet as I can.'

'You're right, Christa. It's always been a worry to me. First and foremost, I want you to be happy with anyone you choose. The financial considerations must be second place. I like Peter. He's polite and well mannered. He's without doubt a bright young man, and I feel he'll move on well in his career. I agree with you that he has a strange air about him at times. If you feel that a friendship with you could help him, then by all means go, with my blessing. Don't forget about your old Dad, though, will you?'

He placed a kiss on her forehead, and she smiled up at him.

'You're the best Dad ever.'

*

405

'Let me get this straight. What are you trying to tell me, Larry?'

The phone had rung just as Christa was leaving for work.

'What? Are you sure?… Well, yes, I know. I appreciate that, but it's not that common a name. So you say Toronto?… Yes, I'll look it up myself. You're brilliant. If it turns out to be the one, I'll ask Dad to lay on something special… Yeah, bye.'

She flopped down onto the settee and stared into space for a few moments, before racing out to her car with a wide grin on her face.

*

'So you're telling me he came upon the name, just like that?'

'Yes, I know, without even looking for it! After I asked him to do my initial research he thought the whole idea might be a neat line in some extra cash for him, so he advertised his services. One night he was doing some work for a client and tried out some leads for them on Canada411 phone directories. He was looking through for the information he needed and came across the name Michael Hartman. When he told me, I followed it up, and sure enough there's a current listing for a Michael Hartman in the Toronto directory. This is the address quoted.'

Hudson looked again at the paper in his hand. 'That's a spot of luck. The chances of that happening are… But we still don't know if it's the same person.'

'I know, Dick, but I've had this idea. It might take a while, but it could give me an opportunity to find out. I've been giving some thought to an article it might be interesting to run, and it could fit this situation. Now, you know that over the years people have been emigrating to this country. I wondered, now that we've started a new millennium, if there was a story in picking out particular examples and finding out what their lives have been like over here, and if they think it was worthwhile. That sort of thing.'

Dick rubbed his chin. 'You'll be spoilt for choice, that's for sure.'

'I wondered if we could do the angle of choosing immigrants from particular time periods and finding out if this made any difference to how the country gave them initial help.'

Dick leant forward on the desk. 'Mmm… that sounds interesting. Did this country work out for them or not, kind of angle, depending when they came here. How are you going to tie that in with your Hartman person? We can't go national on this; unless, of course, it takes off, then there might be a chance.'

'I know, Dick, but if the idea is accepted in principle, and it did go national, I might then include the query as to whether previous employment was useful in finding jobs over here. If your thought about linking policing with hunting through firearms experience is feasible, it might just strike a chord. If all else fails and he doesn't respond to the article, I might have to try a more personal and direct approach.'

Hudson gave her a quizzical look. 'OK. Let's run this by the boss and see what gives, eh?'

The boss liked it, but with the proviso of just using their local circulation at first, and then, if it went well, interesting the nationals. So, given the go-ahead, Dick left Christa to start work. He was already impressed by her writing skills, and it now looked as though she had a quick mind for ideas as well, reinforcing his belief that she should be given as much experience as possible. Between them they worked out a preliminary article, asking for members of the public to volunteer any information.

As predicted, they received floods of replies. It was agreed that out of the participants chosen, some would be asked to write in their experiences, and others would be interviewed in person by Christa and two other journalists. This took several weeks and Christa was beginning to feel that it had been a good idea from the paper's point of view, and for her career; but for her own personal goal, not so good. She had to move things along somehow.

With the help of Dick Hudson they both put pressure on their Editor to agree to go national and, worn down by their perseverance, he agreed to their idea of canvassing the big cities, starting with Dick Hudson's suggestion of Toronto. He queried the choice of city, but Hudson, with an innocent glance at Christa, just shrugged and remarked that they might as well start somewhere. As her Editor spoke to his opposite number, Christa held her breath in case just local journalists would be preferred, but Hudson had pushed for Christa to be involved, as the originator of the whole successful feature, and this was agreed.

As replies started to come in from Toronto residents, each day Christa would look through the growing list of names passed through by her city colleagues. Then, with a shriek of excitement, which startled the whole newsroom, she saw the name she'd been waiting for. She requested the Toronto office to send through a copy of the letter, and with sanction from Toronto she rang the number. After asking some questions from a curious-sounding Michael Hartman, and finding the right answers, she was sure he was the person she was seeking. He agreed to be interviewed and, still not quite believing her luck, Christa arranged to meet him in Toronto for the interview.

CHAPTER 8

Three weeks later, after spending a morning with two other Toronto contributors to the article, Christa sat in a taxi as it drove through the East York district of the city, feeling nervous and sick. The buildings in this area were, in the main, mature, post-World War I single dwellings or small apartment blocks, and it was in front of one of these that the taxi stopped.

Michael Hartman lived in a ground-floor apartment. As Christa pressed the bell on the front door, she could hear her heart pounding. After a moment or two the door opened and a man in his mid-seventies stood there, surveying her.

She noticed that, for all his years, he seemed fit and erect. His grey hair was a little longer than normal for a man of his age, but his eyes were what arrested her. They were the same as Peter's! Grey eyes that looked as if they were used to seeing into the distance, and even in old age were bright and clear. She also had the notion that there was still a sharp mind behind them.

'I'm Christa Benjamin, Mr Hartman. I believe we have an appointment.'

'I believe we have,' he replied, and stood aside to let her enter.

He motioned her through into the living room and watched while she sorted out her recorder.

'I understand that you would like my views on my emigration to Canada.'

Christa smiled at him. 'Yes, Mr Hartman. As I informed you, my local paper, and now the nationals, are running articles on immigrants over the years. Perhaps we could first start with your reasons for leaving England.'

'Let's just say I fancied a new start.'

Christa concentrated on her notebook. 'Did you leave family?'

There was a pause and Christa was forced to look up. The grey eyes were studying her.

'I don't see the necessity of going there, young lady. It's nothing to do with my life here.'

Alright, she thought, we'll close that avenue for the time being. She didn't want to antagonise him.

'Very well. Tell me what jobs were open to you when you arrived.'

'I found some odd casual jobs to start with. As I mentioned in my reply to the article, after a while it was suggested to me that, as I was familiar with firearms, it made sense to offer my services to the hunting fraternity. I was fit and healthy. Once I had my various licences in place I picked up jobs with summer hunting parties before I joined an organised outfit. I enjoyed the open air life and it's kept me fit. When it came to retirement I stayed up in Manitoba, but after a while decided I'd seen enough of open country, and a month or two ago thought I'd try an urban lifestyle. My private funding seems to have given me a reasonable enough set-up here. All in all, I can say that I am pleased with the experiences this country has given me, which is why I felt I wanted to reply to your article and voice my appreciation.'

She just had to ask, 'Did you marry here, Mr Hartman?'

'No, Miss Benjamin, I did not.' The reply was emphatic.

For the next hour, Christa worked through her list of questions. She'd been right about the sharp mind. For all his age, this man appeared to be well informed about the modern world. She found herself agreeing with a lot of what he said about her country and the world in general. He offered her some refreshment when she suggested they took a break from recording, and found herself enjoying his company. However, she knew that before she left she would have to come back to her main query. She was putting on her coat and collecting her belongings, waiting for her taxi back to the airport, when she plucked up the courage.

'Would you like to return to England, and maybe see any of your relations, Mr Hartman?'

'Do I have any?'

The bold question caught her off-guard, and for a moment she could think of nothing to say. She managed to stammer, 'Unless you search for them you won't know, will you?'

His grey eyes were assessing her, and... was it her guilty conscience, or did she imagine they were looking right into her mind?

He then shrugged and said, 'The same applies to them, doesn't it. You found me; so, I presume, could they.'

Christa caught her breath, and managed a weak smile. 'Well, you never know, Mr Hartman. Thank you for your time. It's been very enjoyable. I'll send you a copy of the article before it goes to print so that you can confirm you are happy with it.'

He showed her to the door. 'Thank you for the very interesting talk, Miss Benjamin.'

She walked out to the taxi, her mind replaying his final words.

During the flight home, Christa began to check her notes on the various interviews of the day, but found she always returned to Michael Hartman. Thinking back over his comments, she had the distinct impression that he had guessed her article wasn't the real reason for visiting him. It had been, at times, as if they were both having two conversations, neither of them quite telling the whole truth. The remark he had made about any family wanting to trace him being able to do so, might be construed in two ways, but she was sure that it wasn't just her imagination making her certain he was suspicious.

Now she had to face the dilemma of whether to take the real reason for her investigations any further. She needed to judge whether news like this would be in Peter's best interests, and in order to do so she had to get to know him better. More than ever, she must concentrate on a move to England. With the obvious success of her immigration idea, this might be the right time to push for assistance with her goal. She would have to speak with Dick Hudson again.

*

Sarah sighed with pleasure. Jerry had woken her as the dawn light filtered in through the curtains, and they had just made love. She was lying in his arms, warm and content, waiting for another busy day to unfold.

'I'm so very lucky.'

Jerry rubbed his bristled chin against her shoulder, and murmured an automatic, 'Yes, my darling', still half-asleep.

Sarah laughed and snuggled closer against him. 'I'm very lucky that I married you, I mean.'

Jerry turned his head and kissed her hair. 'Well, of course, I could have told you that. As far as I'm concerned that day I proposed to you in the hospital canteen was the best day's work I've ever done.'

Sarah reached up and kissed his mouth. 'I'm so glad you did. I think I love you even more now than I did then.' She stroked his shoulder. 'Jerry?'

'Mmm?'

'Do we need to get up just yet?'

'Oh, I'm sure there's plenty of time. Did you have anything planned?' He turned over and pinned her beneath him. 'Or perhaps I can suggest something, my love.'

He covered her mouth with his, and slid his hand down her body.

Sitting at the kitchen table enjoying their breakfast an hour or two later, they exchanged an amused glance as Amy, grabbing a slice of toast, raced off to college.

'One of these days this house will be quiet and still, when the children all leave. If that day ever comes.' Jerry grimaced. 'I think they like it here too much, that's the trouble; plus its cheaper!'

Sarah started to clear the table.

'We'll always have each other, and if we get more time like this morning, that will be…'

She felt Jerry come behind her and his arms slid round her waist.

'I know, my dear. As you said earlier, we've had luck. We have jobs and a house we love, and two marvellous children. On the whole,' he amended with a chuckle. 'At least they're individuals with minds of their own.'

He sighed and planted a soft kiss on her bright curls. 'Time for me to retreat to my study, I'm afraid. I've notes to read through for this afternoon.'

He retrieved his briefcase from the hall and started sorting through some papers. Sarah finished loading the dishwasher and then turned to him.

'I still worry about Peter. He's very like Catherine in character. A bit too diffident at times. He needs more confidence. I often think he's searching for something.'

Jerry looked at his wife, came over to her and wrapped her in his arms again.

'My love, we've done the very best we could.' He lifted her face and looked into her blue eyes. 'Peter is twenty four years old. He has to look after himself now. I'm sure Alex and Catherine would be proud of how he's turned out. You've been marvellous since the beginning. I was in despair all those years ago. I saw what the whole thing was doing to you. You were ill, and at one point I thought I was going to lose my wife, or my unborn child. I couldn't seem to reach you, all I could do was watch and hope. As Peter grew and Rob came along, you came back to us again, but I know it still affects you. I just thank God we've worked our way through it. Perhaps now we can have more time for ourselves, like this morning.'

Sarah gave him a quick kiss. 'I'm sorry I worried you. I was locked into a dark place and it took me some while to escape.' She looked up at him with a shy smile. 'I liked this morning, too.' Snuggling back into his arms, she went on, 'I'm glad this girl Peter met is coming over to England. I'm sure he didn't ask her to come, but I think it would be good for him if it worked out. I've noticed, though, that he's seemed very tense and nervous these last two months since she said she was coming. I think that's why he's asked me to go with him to the airport today to meet her. Jerry, what do we do if they want to stay together in Peter's rooms?'

'We stick to the rules Sarah,' Jerry sounded adamant, and released her. 'Same for Peter as it is for Rob and Amy. No goings-on under our roof. I'm enlightened on some things, but not as far as that.'

He picked up his briefcase and made to leave the room, but turned back and, giving her a smiling wink, commented, 'A cup of coffee in an hour might be welcomed… to your advantage. We are the exception, of course!'

Even after all these years, Sarah felt herself turn pink.

CHAPTER 9

Peter couldn't stand still. The nervous tension inside him was growing, as it had since Christa's news. For so long the idea of her coming to England had been something in the future, but now she would arrive at any moment. Over many months they had shared numerous telephone conversations and he always found himself looking forward to hearing her voice. However, seeing her again in person, what would happen if it wasn't the same? There would be nothing he could do. And then he saw her, the bright head and that same smile, and he realised it felt good.

*

Sarah watched as Peter paced up and down behind the line of people waiting to greet new arrivals, the knot of anxiety building inside her. She had never seen him quite so agitated. Was he regretting becoming involved with this girl? If so it was a little late to do anything about it. Then she knew he had spotted her. He stopped pacing and half-raised his arm in greeting. Sarah stood back and took a good look. The young woman was honey blonde and about her own height, dressed in a smart green trouser suit, but it was the spontaneous smile when she first saw Peter, and his answering grin, which made the greatest impression on Sarah. She sighed with relief. It was going to be alright.

Noticing that Peter had only given the girl a smiling hug, she decided to give her a kiss on the cheek.

'Welcome to England, Christa. I'm so pleased to see you.'

'Thank you, Mrs McIntyre. It's nice to be here.'

The girl must have worked out who she was, thought Sarah. She detected a slight accent in her speech, but had the immediate impression that she was well educated and well mannered.

'Well now, come along. I'm going to suggest that you come to ours at first and catch your breath, and then Peter can take you to your accommodation later. Is that OK?'

Christa looked at Peter, who nodded.

'Right, let's go then.'

The kitchen table was again the meeting place for the house. Over mugs of tea and sandwiches, Christa was introduced to Jerry, just on his way out for his afternoon clinic, and Amy, on afternoon home study leave from college, who came down from her room-cum-studio to meet the guest. Rob, by now back on his two feet, was on duty away somewhere, so introductions there would have to wait.

Sarah was amused to see that Amy, who had toned down her hair colour, was studying the real honey shades of the other girl. Even so, she noticed that Christa's eyes had widened when they were first introduced. They were of the same age, and maybe Christa would make a good role model. Sarah's own first impression was confirmed as the talk flowed around the table. She liked the open friendliness and confidence the girl displayed, seeming at ease with near strangers, but in particular she noticed her caring, considerate attitude to Peter, making sure that he was included in the conversation. Peter, she saw, was just looking and listening to her, but she sensed that he was back to his normal self.

'I gather you've been lucky enough to take over a flat from a friend, Christa?'

'Er, yes. That's right, Mrs McIntyre.'

Sarah noticed the slight hesitation in the girl's reply, but let it go. It was none of her business after all.

Christa gave Peter an apologetic glance. 'I don't wish to appear rude, but I'm afraid perhaps I ought to get settled in. It looks as though I'm going to hit the ground running. I'm starting work tomorrow. As I've been given this chance to exchange places with an English journalist for a year, I'll have to give it my best shot for a while. Also, my previous Editor wants me to do a monthly article for them on how I find England, so I'm going to be a busy person!'

Peter rose to his feet. 'Yes, that's fine. No problem. I'll find the car keys.'

As he left the table, Sarah came to a decision, and voiced her thoughts. 'Christa, you know you're always welcome to drop in at any time, but I wondered, if you were free, would you like to come for a typical British Sunday roast this weekend?'

Christa looked over at Peter, who nodded, looking pleased, and then she turned with a bright smile. 'Thank you, Mrs McIntyre. I'd like that a lot.'

As they left, Jerry came up behind his wife and gave her a light smack on her behind, whispering in her ear, 'Matchmaker!'

*

It became the normal pattern for Peter to collect Christa on a Sunday morning. They would work together in Peter's room, then come upstairs for lunch and spend the afternoon with the rest of the household, before Peter took her home. Christa insisted on joining in with the household chores and soon became as much of a fixture in the routine life of the house as the other young people. Sarah was delighted as she observed the quiet growth in confidence that Peter was displaying.

*

Lionel Franklin too had observed the change, and on one visit suggested that Peter might like to bring his friend along to be introduced.

Peter appeared delighted at the invitation when he brought the matter up with Christa. She, herself, was intrigued by the idea, having heard Peter speak about his great uncle so often. It seemed that a

417

Sunday afternoon was a convenient time, and on the particular day chosen, Christa was at the McIntyre's for lunch as usual. She detected an air of unease about Sarah McIntyre. Until now, she had always appeared to be a bubbly sort of person, but today she seemed more subdued, and Christa intercepted one or two glances between her and her husband. Peter seemed oblivious to any undercurrents, however, and so Christa tried to put it out of her mind.

Her first impression of Lionel Franklin was not favourable. She felt a strange force about him which she couldn't explain. She also knew without any doubt that he didn't like her. It was instant, almost pre-formed, without any knowledge of her or her character. Peter seemed not to notice, and treated the old man like a venerated elder. The difference, she thought, between Lionel Franklin and Michael Hartman, both about the same age, was huge. She knew which she preferred.

After polite introductions and conversation over a pot of tea, Christa sensed that Judge Franklin was biding his time, and before long he steered the conversation her way.

'So, Miss Benjamin, you appear to have made a courageous leap in your fledgling career to come to the UK. A little soon, it might be said?'

Christa picked up on the faint censure in his tone, but looked straight back into the cold pale blue eyes.

'Some might think so, but I hope to gain an enormous amount of experience. Absorbing other cultures can benefit me in my creative ideas and I felt it was better to do this now rather than become too immersed in just my own country's affairs.'

She saw Franklin's eyes narrow, but she couldn't gauge what he was thinking. Quite useful in Court, she thought.

'So, you are interested in the political side of your country?'

'As much as anyone, I suppose. What any government decides to do will have an effect on everyone at some point. If you keep abreast of what might happen you can be more prepared in planning your life. It pays to have an idea of what's going on.'

'Yes, like if they're putting up the price of beer!'

Despite Peter's jovial comment, Christa noticed that Franklin didn't take his gaze from her or even acknowledge the remark.

'Is that why you wished to enter journalism, so that you could find out things, poking and prying into affairs that are no one's concern?'

Christa had the distinct impression that this man was trying to needle her into an unwise comment, but she held back the immediate retort she might have made.

'No doubt, Judge, some investigative journalists have gone too far in their pursuit of a story. But I'm sure, given your profession, you will acknowledge that journalism has uncovered things which needed to be brought out into the open.'

'Indeed. If you say so. It also sells newspapers, of course!'

He gave her a slight smile and then seemed to lose interest. His next question came out of the blue.

'Peter tells me your father is a boat builder. By using the term "boat" I assume he doesn't build supertankers! Is there still a call for craftsmanship in this modern era?'

Christa glanced over at Peter. She had no intention of discussing her father's business affairs, but she had to give a credible answer. After a slight hesitation she answered, 'No, he doesn't build supertankers, but he seems to manage. He's given me the benefit of a good education, which is why I want to succeed in my chosen career, for his sake.'

'Commendable, I'm sure.'

The remark was patronising, and deliberate. She gave the man a hard stare. She might have made a comment, but in deference to Peter she remained silent. The fact that Franklin was aware of her displeasure became evident in the smile that for a moment touched his mouth.

She was thankful when Peter began to describe a recent visit to Court as an observer of general routine, and pressed his great uncle for more information. It gave her time to restore her equilibrium. For some reason this man wanted to get under her skin, and trip her up in some way; and she thought she knew why. He wanted her to make a comment which would upset Peter, and spoil their friendship. She was seen as some sort of rival!

She knew that when Peter and his great uncle were alone, she would be spoken of by Franklin in disparaging terms. She was an interloper who he did not want around. But why? She was glad when it was time to leave and return to the McIntyres' home.

CHAPTER 10

Jerry offered to take Peter to the local pub for a drink in the evening, leaving Sarah and Christa sitting at the kitchen table chatting. It was no surprise to Christa when she was asked how the afternoon had gone. She decided to be truthful.

'All I can say, Mrs McIntyre, is that I was glad to come away. Lionel Franklin is not my idea of a nice person. He didn't like me at all, and that was before I had even entered the room! Peter, however, seems to treat him with great fondness and respect.'

She saw Mrs McIntyre sigh, and then her whole body slumped. 'I hate the man.'

Christa stared at Mrs McIntyre, not knowing quite what to say. It had sounded such a heartfelt statement.

'Christa, how much has Peter told you about his parents?'

'I understand they died in an accident when he was a baby. Is that something to do with Lionel Franklin?'

She could see the other woman trying to come to a decision.

'Christa, are you fond of Peter? I mean, very fond?'

She found herself replying without hesitation. 'Yes, Mrs McIntyre, I am. I'm not so sure about Peter, though. He sees me as a friend, I'm sure, but anything more... I just don't know. I think he finds it hard to deal with relationships.'

'I'm going to tell you some things, even things Peter doesn't know. Although it all happened a long time ago, it's still painful, but I will do my best.'

'Oh please, Mrs McIntyre, I don't want to know any personal details that I shouldn't.'

'It's alright, my dear. I feel you ought to know.'

Christa watched as she rose from her seat and went to a shelf containing cookery books, bringing one back to the table. Leafing through the pages, she drew out a photograph. Looking at it for a moment, she gave a fond smile and then handed it to Christa.

'This is a photograph Jerry took of Peter's parents on their wedding day. I keep it there, so that I can take it out and look at it when… I need to. No one else knows about it.'

Christa looked at the couple in the photograph. What a striking pair they made. The young woman was beautiful, with amazing green eyes. The man so handsome, and… oh, eyes like Peter's. With parents like that he would have been lucky either way, she thought.

Mrs McIntyre had not spoken again, and Christa wondered if she had changed her mind about what she wanted to say, but then she began to speak. Christa sat spellbound as the tale unfolded of the schoolgirl friendship, the involvement with Alex, the story of the engagement ring, the marriage and house, and Peter's arrival. Christa formed an impression of a deep bond between Catherine and her handsome husband. How wonderful it would have been for Peter to have known loving parents like this.

Her companion now appeared to be in the grip of a powerful emotion, making it difficult for her to proceed with the story. Christa laid a hand on the other woman's arm.

'I can see how upsetting this is for you. Let's not talk about it any more.'

'But I must. You need to know what is thought to have happened that dreadful night.'

What she then went on to reveal left Christa appalled. She found it hard to take in all the details, and with continuing horror listened to

422

Mrs McIntyre's description of the following events and the subsequent decisions of the appropriate authorities.

'Christa, I will never believe what they said is true. I feel in my heart that Lionel Franklin knows more than he has divulged, and all these years he has had an influence on Peter... almost like a puppeteer. I think that's what he does. He tries to control people. He tried to do that to Catherine, until Alex came on the scene and took her away. I think she paid for that with her life, and Alex became expendable too. Christa, they were so much in love, with so many dreams for the future, but in the end they had little more than a year together. My heart still breaks for them.'

She put her head down on the table and sobbed, her anguish very evident.

Christa sat there for some moments in a state of shock. She could find no words to express her emotions. Peter had been carrying this around with him for all these years! Her heart overflowed for him, and she felt her own tears pricking behind her eyes. Mrs McIntyre was still crying, and in an effort to comfort her, she reached out and put an arm round her shoulders.

'Please don't cry, Mrs McIntyre.'

She had to do something for this poor distraught woman. She went into the front lounge and brought back a small glass of brandy from the drinks cupboard.

'Here, please drink this, it might make you feel better.'

'Thank you, my dear.' A tear-streaked face tried to smile at her. 'I'm sorry for all this. Even after all these years it seems to affect me now as much as it did then. I was carrying Robert at the time and I became quite ill. Jerry even brought my mother back from abroad to look after me. It wasn't an easy time. We had been made guardians of Peter and we had to think of him also. We coped – just about.'

Despite herself, Christa had to ask the question. 'Why do you think Lionel Franklin knows something about these events, Mrs McIntyre?'

'I don't know anything, I just have this feeling! And I think Peter's godfather Luigi feels the same. He and his wife treated Alex like a son, and they also loved Catherine and Peter. When Lionel Franklin asked to be involved with Peter in his education, I sensed in Luigi the same wary reserve about that influence, as I felt myself. We have never spoken about it together, but I know it's there.

'Jerry says I'm just being oversensitive. He has reminded me about Alex's sometimes volatile temper, and also told me to read my medical textbooks about the problems some males can have when a new baby is introduced into a family. He says that however loving a relationship the two of them had, it's always possible that for a split second something went wrong, although he hates to think that. I've thought about it, and accepted that there's a case for this, but my inner being tells me that it wasn't a factor here. It didn't happen that way. I know there is nothing now that can be done, but it hurts to think that Alex has been accused of something I'm sure he did not do.'

She sighed and sipped at the brandy. 'I spoke with Reverend Jones at St Luke's before the funerals and asked for, and in the end received, permission for Alex and Catherine's ashes to be interred together in the churchyard. He knew both of them, and also witnessed the closeness between them. He, and other members of his church, although shocked at what had happened, took the view that forgiveness was the key, and in another world the couple would again share that same bond. We had the ashes buried in a corner of the graveyard, in urns side by side, together, with just a simple plaque. I remembered the words Alex said to Catherine at the end of their wedding ceremony when he placed the rings on her finger. "Together always", he said. I put their wedding rings and Catherine's engagement ring in a watertight container and placed it with the urns, so they would always be together. No one knows that apart from me – and now you.' She sighed. 'I've done the best I can for them. I hope they would have approved.'

She looked so sad, just sitting there with her memories. Christa gave her a hug and held her close.

'You're a good girl, Christa. I knew that the moment I saw you. I do so hope Peter can see it too.' She took a deep breath and straightened her shoulders. 'Please, my dear, don't keep calling me "Mrs McIntyre", call me "Sarah". Now, if you don't mind, I think I'll go upstairs and have a lie down. I've a bit of a headache.' She gave an apologetic smile. 'Jerry hates to see me upset about all of this.'

Christa sat by herself at the big table, trying to take in all she had been told, waiting for Peter and Jerry to return and thinking of the man in Canada who knew nothing.

*

'You know there will have been tears when we get back?'

Jerry looked over at Peter. The young man bent his head and studied his glass.

'Yes, I know. I've begun to think that it might be better for all of you if I start life on my own somewhere, without my presence around all the time – a reminder.'

'You must do what you think is best for you. I hope we've helped you in the past, and we intend to continue to do so. I can't deny that I worry about the effect the whole matter is still having on Sarah. I get the impression, though, that if you were away from us she might worry even more. Peter, she was so very fond of your mother – and of your father – and for her, nothing will replace them. The loyalty she has for them cannot accept the facts of what happened, and until she does, the situation for her will remain unresolved. I, too, find what happened hard to believe, but the facts are there.'

'What would you like me to do, Jerry?'

The resigned weariness in Peter's voice caused Jerry some discomfort. He was being unfair to the boy, placing blame on his shoulders for something of which he was innocent. He thought back to the day in the hospital just after Peter had been born, when Alex had disclosed to him the momentary resentment he had felt against his own child. The boy had already been through enough. Now wasn't the time to heap onto him the worries Jerry had about his wife. They had to stand by him for the whole journey.

'Let it rest for now, Peter. With Christa being so involved with our family, questions were bound to be asked. I'm sure it will all settle down again. Just concentrate on your work, that's more than enough for you at the moment.'

*

Frank Benjamin was not, as normal, enjoying the regular conversation with his daughter.

'I never realised how bad the situation was, Dad, or I'd never have asked questions. I feel so awful now. You could see when they came back that Jerry was worried about Sarah, and Peter looked so down.'

Frank Benjamin heard the distress in his daughter's voice. She had just recounted to him the whole dreadful story.

'It's not your fault, Christa. They accepted you into their home and told you family history, as bad as it was. No one forced them to say a thing. They could have glossed it over. You could take it as a compliment that you were told the truth. As I see it, you now have a chance to help. Peter needs support. He's received this from the McIntyres and others since he was a baby, but now he needs the confidence from outsiders who know the story but are more interested in him than anything else that has happened in his past. I know your warm heart has always gone out to him, and now we know why you feel this way, but he must be treated as normal, not like a rare specimen. You're both young people; enjoy yourselves together as any others would do.'

'Do you think I should make contact with Michael Hartman, Dad? Ought he to know about all this? I've been worrying about it all night.'

He knew from the past that caution had to be instilled into his sometimes impulsive daughter.

'I'm not sure, Christa. It seems he hasn't done much over all these years to make contact in any way. It's never an easy thing, though, attempting to build bridges. Did you say that you were told Peter's Italian godfather had kept in touch with Hartman at the beginning?'

'Yes, Dad, but I gather even he lost contact.'

'Why don't you try to meet with this man, perhaps in private, and tell him what you've found out, and see what he suggests?'

He heard Christa sigh with relief. 'I knew I could always count on you for some answers. That's a brilliant idea. I'm going to do that. I'll see if I can get in touch with him somehow. Thanks, Dad.'

He was relieved to hear the bounce back in her voice.

'I might be able to come over in a week or so. Would I be intruding?'

'Oh, that would be marvellous. I do miss you. Please come if you can.'

'Alright, I'll see what I can do. Take care of yourself, and don't worry. You have a job to think about, after all. Give Peter my regards.'

CHAPTER 11

After a mini council of war between them regarding the latest upset, Rob could see that Amy was worried by the continuing effect on their mother. He had himself noticed that she had lost some of her usual sparkle.

'What do you imagine Peter will do, Amy? We mustn't allow him to leave and find somewhere on his own. Mum will be sure to worry about him more.'

'I'll say. We all know she has a down on that Franklin creep, and she'll be afraid Peter will mix with him more than ever. Christa is worried that she's stirred it all up again. You know, I think she likes Peter.'

Rob stirred himself from his habitual prone position on his bed. 'We must talk to him and persuade him to stay. Is he downstairs?'

'I think so.'

'OK. Come on, Sis. Time to call out the cavalry.'

He led the way downstairs.

Peter was trying to concentrate on his work, but it was difficult. His mind kept returning to the look of shock in Christa's eyes when he and Jerry had returned from the pub the other night. She hadn't spoken about anything, but he guessed that she had been made aware of the whole story. Would she now consider him someone with a strange past and choose to keep a wide berth? Should he even not make any further contact with her? That would be a pity, he acknowledged to himself. He had come to look forward to seeing her, and enjoyed her company. Perhaps it was best, as Jerry had said, to let things settle down again and see what happened.

He heard footsteps on the stairs and knew he was about to have company.

'Hi, old son!' Rob's head appeared round the door. 'Are we intruding on your thought waves?'

Peter grinned back at him. 'I don't seem to have any at the moment, so come on in.'

Rob sank his tall frame onto Peter's bed, ignoring the exasperated look from his sister who had followed him into the room.

She looked around. 'I still think you could do with some pictures in here, Peter. Shall I sort something out for you?'

'Ah… thanks all the same Amy, but I'm fine with it as it is.' He was sure that the vivid images she would prefer were not conducive to study.

'What he wants is that sketch of me looking handsome in my state uniform you've got tucked away in your portfolio! Something classy like that.'

If it was possible for Rob to look more comfortable than he appeared to be, sprawled on the bed, it would have been difficult. However, he opened a lazy eye and fixed it on Peter.

'What's all this rot we hear about you leaving the nest? What've we done to make you want to do that? If you go, then guess who has to do more helping around the house! You're dropping us right in it, you know. Correct, Amy?' He cocked an eye at his sister.

'That's right. Besides, I'll miss seeing Christa. She's just great.'

Peter looked from one to the other. Being so close in age, they had all grown up together, and he had a great fondness for them both. He knew the reason for their joint visit, and felt an even greater warmth towards them for their obvious caring attitude.

'You both know why it crossed my mind. I can't keep on upsetting your mother. There has to be some sort of closure.'

429

Amy put her arm across his shoulders. 'The closure is that we're all in it together, for good or bad, supporting each other. That's the good that will come out of it. Like a phoenix from the ashes.'

Rob groaned.

'For goodness' sake, Amy, you'll have us manning the barricades in a minute. But I do tend to agree with you. As a family we've all learnt that you should give help and support if needed. We just wanted to remind you of that...' – he stood up, a look of anticipation on his face – 'and to suggest that now you're in gainful employment, you buy us a drink at the pub.'

Peter burst out laughing. 'I knew there had to be an ulterior motive. Come on, you two, before you break out the violins and make me cry.'

He switched off his computer, grabbed a jacket and led the way out of the room, missing the wink Rob gave to his sister. Mission accomplished.

*

Christa found it easier than expected to make contact with Luigi Gandoni. He turned up for lunch as a guest of the McIntyres the very next Sunday. She liked his obvious warm, smiling attitude, but she judged that there was a shrewd mind behind his air of benevolence. It was clear that he had a great fondness for Peter.

After lunch the two of them were excused the clearing up and found themselves alone in the front room.

'I'm pleased that you have been able to join Peter in England. He has spoken to me of you.' The warm dark eyes studied her. 'He needs a friend. Sometimes families are too close to the emotion in troubled times.'

It was obvious what he was trying to tell her.

Christa looked back at him, her brown eyes steady. 'I like Peter a lot, and I admire him for the way he's dealt with all his troubles. It can't have been easy.'

'We have all tried to help, but as we all know, in those quiet moments at night unbidden thoughts can intrude.'

Christa saw the pain mirrored deep in the dark eyes, and on impulse put out her hand to him, which he took and squeezed.

'Mr Gandoni, I wanted to have a talk with you, but somewhere private so we're not overheard. Would you meet me, perhaps at my flat?'

She could see the question on his face, but then he smiled. 'How can I resist an invitation like that? Yes, I will meet you, young lady, and in view of our clandestine arrangement may I suggest you call me "Luigi".'

Christa answered his grin with one of her own. She scribbled her address and telephone number on a scrap of paper and handed it to him. 'Give me a call and we'll fix something up. Perhaps next week?'

Luigi pocketed the paper just as the rest of the family joined them with coffee.

Christa enjoyed the afternoon, knowing that she would at last tell someone in this family the truth.

*

Lionel Franklin was bored. Peter had been going on about how work was organised at Ravens, and also the girl, for some time now, as if he was interested in any of it. He had noticed of late that the boy was more articulate than he used to be. In the past he would listen, rather than talk so much himself. It must be these new influences. He had to do something about both before it was too late.

'Well, Peter, you seem to have plenty going on in your life at the moment. I would, however, caution you about too much involvement with this Benjamin girl. She seems to have chased after you with a lame excuse of wanting to work over here. I didn't wish to say so to you, but I did find her a bit evasive in answering some of my questions. What do you know about her?'

He could see the slight confusion in the young man's face, and pressed home the advantage.

'Is she by any chance aware of your financial circumstances? Your inheritance from your mother? You can't be too careful, Peter.'

'She knows nothing about that.' A pause followed. 'From me anyway.'

431

Franklin could see the boy thinking. This was good!

'Have the McIntyres told her, do you suppose? Peter, I hate to say this, but you are unused to the sometimes unscrupulous ways people have of engineering certain circumstances. This girl might well have come to this country to follow her career, but now she is here she might be seeking other potential possibilities. Do you understand what I'm saying?'

'I can't think Christa is that kind of a person, Lionel.'

His tone of voice was adamant; but was there just a trace of doubt? Better to let the idea lie for a while. Now implanted, it might grow.

Franklin shrugged and waved a nonchalant hand. 'Well, of course, you must know best, Peter. But I do still urge caution. Your career must be your first thought; there will be plenty of time for, er, dalliances, once you are well set up.' He patted the boy's knee. 'Now, if you want to trot down and see Chef, we can have a nice meal together. Take your time. Choose something you fancy, and I'll have my usual.'

When Peter had left the room, Franklin rose with difficulty, and walked over to his desk. He took out two sheets of paper and crossed back to where Peter had left his briefcase, opened it, and studied the contents for some time. He then slipped the sheets of paper into one of the files and replaced the items in the briefcase, before settling back in his chair.

When Peter returned, Franklin decided to complete the second part of his strategy.

'So you're liking the Ravens set-up, Peter?'

'Oh, yes. They all seem a nice crowd to work with. We have to work hard, but they're fair in other ways. I do sometimes wonder how good I would be in Court. I enjoy the researching side, but I can't say I'm so comfortable with having to be an orator. Jonathan Raven is a class act. I watched him have a witness in a complete muddle the other day.'

'Barristers are just showmen, Peter. The Judge rules the Court. Sometimes play-acting covers a lack of knowledge, either of law itself, or of the case in particular. Take a tip from me: know your law, that's the basis. Dig around in archives, and you'll be surprised what you find to help you. Use it to make or nullify legal arguments. Become used to looking for it. Train yourself. I know I wasn't popular with some of my decisions, but they couldn't be argued with. Some barristers are more amenable than others. I always thought Ravens took a too rigid stance. Show them what you're capable of in independent thought, Peter, although they might not appreciate what you have to offer. If they don't, we can find someone else who will. Another point is to take notice of the people involved in the courtroom and their personal circumstances. You never know when that knowledge could be useful to you.'

That was enough for today, he thought to himself. Now let's see how things work out. With any luck, when this new-found confidence had been stripped away he would be able to regain his full control again.

*

Peter lay in bed, staring up at the ceiling. His disturbed thoughts were keeping him awake. For the first time he found himself questioning some of the advice Lionel had given him. When he thought about it, he realised that in the past he had accepted what his great uncle said without much argument.

Now he found that he didn't altogether agree with Lionel's ideas of barristers, and of Judges ruling in Court in the sense he felt Lionel had meant. There had been the inference that all the other participants were bit players, there to make up the numbers at most, and could be treated as irrelevant. But over the years, numerous clever barristers had been successful and, more important still, correct to challenge on points of law. Lionel was advocating that the Judge's word was law and all others were subservient, without any discussion. No, he considered, there was a dangerous flaw there.

When he thought about it, this was something like the topic he and Jonathan had begun discussing a while ago. He would be interested in bringing up the point with Jonathan again. Also, what was it Lionel meant about noticing the sort of people who were in the Court, and that they might be useful in the future? He had no idea why that should be important.

However, the thing that disturbed him most was what Lionel

had said about Christa. He knew he'd not mentioned his impending financial windfall to her, and knowing the McIntyres so well he was sure that they also had mentioned nothing to her. On what basis, then, could Lionel make the assumption that Christa had befriended him for her own financial gain? Peter thought back over his conversations with her since they had met, and could remember no questioning by her, casual or otherwise, of his financial situation. She seemed to just enjoy his company.

Now he was taking the time to examine his feelings, Peter realised that he always looked forward to seeing her, and thought about her often when they were not together. Was this how it all began: a feeling of contentment in being with someone? Did his parents feel the same way about each other at first, as he did about Christa? He would never be able to ask them; and once again his thoughts returned to what had happened between them.

Unsettled now, he turned over on to his side and looked out of the window at the night sky. Why did he always come back to this problem, which he never managed to resolve? Statistics showed that only a low percentage of marriages ended in violence, as opposed to living in relative harmony for years. He had to believe that it could be so for him; but there was always that lingering doubt. He knew he wasn't cut out for one night stands. He'd found that out when he first ventured into the adult world of college. He'd come to realise that he was the kind of person who would need the reassurance of long-term commitment; but being sure enough to give that commitment was difficult. Although it wasn't satisfactory for him to move from one brief affair to another, how could you be certain that the one you chose would turn out to be the right one? He gave a sigh. His association with Christa might not lead anywhere long term, but the one certainty was that he needed her as part of his life at the moment, and he was very glad they had met.

Rolling on to his back, he came to a sudden decision. He would just let things move forward at their own pace. They got along well, and he for one would try to keep it that way. He closed his eyes and at last settled to sleep.

CHAPTER 12

Luigi checked the address on his piece of paper. Yes, the taxi had deposited him at the right place. He looked around. An affluent district, not the sort of area you might assume a young working journalist might inhabit, but you never could tell these days. The girl seemed nice enough. It was obvious that she and Peter were getting on well together, and the McIntyres liked her. He rang the intercom bell, and when he heard the girl's voice, announced himself.

She was waiting for him on the first-floor landing with a welcoming smile.

'I'm so glad you could come, Luigi. This way.'

She led him into the flat, which lived up to its promise from outside. She offered him a glass of wine and then came and sat down opposite him.

'Dinner in a few minutes, if that's alright?'

'That's fine, my dear. This is a nice flat. I believe you have taken it over from a friend who is in Canada?'

He saw her head go down, and began to worry.

'Luigi, this flat belongs to my father. He uses it when he comes over to the UK and Europe on business, which he does quite often. I haven't told Peter or the McIntyres this.'

'I see. Peter told me that he builds boats.'

The girl laughed. 'Oh, he does that, alright. He owns one of the biggest shipyards in Canada and builds ships of most sizes, and for all purposes. Dad and I are in the habit of not making too much of the situation with strangers who don't need to know. He has this morbid fear of a string of suitors chasing me, in the hope that they can cash in. Back in Canada it doesn't always work as Dad is better known, but elsewhere it pays off. That's why I said what I did about borrowing this from a friend.'

'I can see the logic behind that, and also the fears of your father. He must worry about it.'

'Oh, he does. Many a young man has been warned off by a glare from him if he thinks they're unsuitable.'

'What does he think about Peter?'

He watched the girl twisting the stem of her wine glass round and round.

'He likes him. He was impressed with his manner when we met in the hotel. The poor boy was given the third degree during the time we had together, but Dad has it down to such a fine art by now that the targeted specimens don't even know they're being dissected. Peter came out OK. Dad is well aware that I've come over to the UK as much for Peter as for the job experience. He's a brilliant Dad, he lets me have plenty of rope to make my own decisions, but he's always there in the background keeping an eye on things.'

'That sounds the perfect arrangement. Peter is a good boy. Despite everything, I think on the whole he's turned out alright.' He smiled at her. 'On the other hand, I could just be biased.'

Christa stood up. 'I like him a lot, Luigi, but perhaps I'm biased as well.' She smiled back at him, her brown eyes warm. 'Time for our dinner now, I think.'

During the meal, Luigi confirmed his opinion: the more he knew of this girl, the more he liked her. As they settled down with coffee, and in Luigi's case a much appreciated brandy, it was obvious to him that Christa wanted to say something but was unsure how to start. Perhaps a little help was necessary.

'I think you wanted to talk to me about something?'

'Yes, I did. I'm not sure how you're going to take this. I don't want you to think the wrong thing about me.'

'Well, try me, and we'll see where we go from there.'

He watched as she took a deep breath.

'I understand that you knew Peter's grandfather, Michael. Also that he had emigrated to Canada and you were in touch with him at first, but then contact was lost?'

The words had come out in an embarrassed rush, and Luigi now had the strangest feeling that he knew what she was going to say.

'Yes, all you have said is correct.'

'When Peter was in the hotel with us both, Dad and I remarked that there was an air of loneliness about him. We understood it a bit more when he told us about his parents. Later, Peter mentioned to me his grandfather's emigration. It stuck in my mind that there was the chance of a family somewhere for him, if he just knew where.'

There was a defiant air about her now. 'I know what you're going to say. If Peter wanted to trace any family, he could have attempted it himself, but he chose not to do so.'

The sudden defiance left her and he sensed that she needed his approval.

'I thought I would help, and see if I could trace his grandfather. Through an article I did for my paper, I managed to make contact with him.'

Luigi had somehow known this was coming, but he was still unprepared for his reaction to her disclosure. As she continued, he listened, with hope starting to build inside him.

'We spoke on the telephone. I asked one or two questions, and the dates seemed to fit. I asked if I could visit and interview him for this article. He seemed interested, and we fixed an appointment. Luigi, as soon as I saw him I knew it was the right person. He has Peter's eyes!'

Luigi didn't need to be told this. He could remember remarking on the same thing to Michael when Alex was a toddler. He had, of course, noticed the same coincidence with Peter.

'He told me what he had done over the years, which was linked

437

to the hunting fraternity, but he wouldn't be drawn on why he had emigrated or if there was still family in England. I formed the impression that he suspected there was something else behind my questions.'

Luigi grinned to himself. It seemed as though Michael was still as sharp as he had always been.

'Did he look well?'

'Yes, indeed, very agile and bright.'

'Well, Christa, so far no harm's been done. We're still at the status quo. Are you now suggesting that you somehow bring Peter and his grandfather together?'

'That's why I wanted to speak to you about it. I'm not sure what to do for the best. I don't want to upset people's lives, but it seems such a shame that after all that's happened, they don't know about each other. Perhaps it's just wishful thinking on my part, and it's better left as it is.'

She now looked rather dejected, and Luigi leant forward and patted her arm.

'Don't worry about it, Christa. I know that you did this out of the best of motives, for Peter. I'm pleased that you care enough about him to have even attempted it. I agree with you that it's a difficult choice. I continued to write to Michael after he left, telling him the news about Alex and his progress in the Army. After a while there was no reply to my letters and I didn't know the reason. In the end, I too stopped writing. Alex never mentioned his father to me and never asked for any information so that he could try to re-establish contact.'

He pondered for a moment or two. 'I wonder if the best thing to do would be for me to write to him at the address you now have, asking if he would be interested in communicating again? Neither of us are getting any younger, after all! I won't mention how I found an address; just wait for any comment he might make. If I hear from him at all. I won't tell him anything else until I see what happens.'

'Oh, Luigi, that would be perfect. Would you do that?'

Luigi looked at the pretty young face turned to him, her desire for his help plain to see. It mattered to her! He didn't dare hope for too much, but perhaps out of all these years of pain, something good might now come.

'I can but try, my dear. And try I will.'

*

Peter was so engrossed that he wasn't aware of the Clerk of the Chambers coming into his room.

'Sorry to disturb you, Peter, but Jonathan wants to have a quick look at your Chambers file.'

'Oh sure, John.' He fished the file out of his briefcase. 'I haven't finished working on it yet, though.'

He returned to his deliberations and it was perhaps an hour later when a rather serious-looking John Moore came back into his room.

'Anthony would like to see you, if you please, Peter.'

Peter looked up, perplexed. 'Anthony? Not Jonathan?'

Moore looked a little discomforted and made to leave the room.

'I'd cut along there now, if I was you.'

Still mystified, Peter walked along to Anthony Raven's office and knocked on the door. He was bidden to enter and found not only Anthony but also Jonathan waiting for him. He thought they both looked rather stern.

'Come and sit down, Peter.'

Anthony indicated a vacant chair and when Peter was seated he picked up a file.

'This Chambers file you've been working on. Do you know the content of the papers? By that I mean, do you know what papers are in the file?'

Peter looked from one to the other. What was going on?

'Well, there's the usual correspondence with the Solicitor, the Court papers so far, and certain pieces of photographic evidence.'

'Do you know anything about this?'

Anthony passed two sheets of paper over to him. They were typewritten and appeared to be a list of legal references, some of them pretty old by the look of the dates. It didn't mean anything to him. He looked up at the two men.

'I don't know. I have a feeling that I didn't see it in the file when I first went through it, but perhaps it must have been.'

'It's not something you have compiled yourself, then?' It was Jonathan's turn to question him.

Peter looked again at the papers in his hand. 'No. I don't remember seeing this before.'

Anthony resumed his questioning. 'At any time when you have visited Lionel Franklin, has your briefcase been with you, and have you ever discussed its contents?'

Peter looked from one to the other in amazement. 'I might have had my briefcase with me, but of course I haven't discussed anything! It wouldn't have entered my head to do so. What are you trying to say?'

The other two men looked at each other, and Anthony spoke again. 'Peter, the content of this list seems to indicate that you also are interested in using ancient legal information to inform your thinking. I believe we have discussed this with you before. Either at your own behest, or that of your great uncle, time has been spent in compiling this information.'

'I refute that! I've never seen the list before.' Peter's denial was adamant. What was going on? What were they trying to say?

'If that is the case, Peter, we might have to assume that this list is the work of Lionel Franklin and it was placed by him in the file. Which presupposes that he had free access to the confidential files in your possession.'

Peter now didn't know what to say. He'd not seen the damned list before, but he couldn't reject Anthony's last statement.

'I've no idea.'

'Peter, my son and I have discussed this matter. In short, despite one or two misgivings to begin with, we offered you the post with our firm because you were a worthy applicant, but also acknowledged your association with Lionel Franklin and our views on certain aspects of his conduct. However, we were prepared to give you the benefit of the doubt. You have already proved to us that you have a good legal mind, but this matter has shown that there is still a misplaced trust in your association with Franklin which goes against the principles of how we wish to run our firm.'

Without stopping to consider his position, Peter interrupted. 'He said you might not like independent thinking.'

Anthony Raven glanced at his son, and then sighed. 'My boy, I fear you have just incriminated yourself by appearing to have discussed aspects of our firm with Judge Franklin. If you remain with us, how much else might be disclosed? I am afraid, therefore, that I must tell you that this firm no longer has a place for you.'

Peter looked at each man in turn, his mind a whirl. What was happening? Had all that effort and hard work over the years been for nothing? In silence, he rose to his feet and left the room.

Back at his desk he stared, unseeing, at the papers still in his hand. Had Lionel compiled them and somehow put them in that file? If so, how? And why?

The door opened and Jonathan Raven walked in. He stood there regarding him for a moment.

'I'm sorry about this, Peter. If it's any consolation to you, I think you've been manipulated into this position. At the moment, I can't think why.' He came and sat down opposite the younger man. 'You have a good brain, Peter, but in all honesty I have my doubts that you would succeed as a barrister. I'm not sure this is where your talents lie. If you are truthful, I think you have reached the same conclusion.'

Peter gave a deep sigh and leant back in his chair. 'I think you're right.'

'Peter, I know your feelings toward my father and I will not be very amicable at the moment, but we want to help you if we can. I have a friend who is a senior partner in a corporate law firm. He's mentioned to me that he's looking for an assistant. This might be more the right vehicle for your talents. Why don't you go to see him about the vacancy? If you like, I'll ring him tonight and see if I can fix up a meeting. I won't mention anything that has happened today. Perhaps we can expand on the unsuitability for barrister excuse. What do you say?'

Peter wasn't sure. He wasn't sure of anything at the moment. But it was something, wasn't it?

He nodded. 'Thank you, Jonathan. I'll get my things together, shall I?'

'You do that. I'll text you when I've set something up. Peter, just one last word of advice. Make your own way in life. Perhaps you would be better to remove yourself from the sphere of influence surrounding Lionel Franklin. I think it would be in your best interests.'

CHAPTER 13

Without conscious thought, Peter found himself taking a taxi to Christa's flat, hoping she'd be there. It just seemed the right place to be. His mind was reeling. He'd been sacked – and for what?

When Christa answered the door, she seemed so pleased to see him that it went some way to steadying his churning thoughts.

'I'm sorry just to drop in on you like this.'

'Don't be silly, you're welcome any time. Is something wrong, Peter? You look a bit upset.' She took in the carrier bag of oddments he was carrying besides his briefcase. 'Are you moving?'

Peter followed her into the lounge, and flopped down on to the settee.

'You could say that. I've just been given the sack.'

'What!'

He could see that Christa was now as shocked as he had been.

'What do you mean, Peter? They can't have done that!'

His grin held no mirth, it was more a grimace.

'Oh, believe me, they have.'

'But what's wrong? What's happened?'

He sat forward, resting his arms on his knees, and stared at the carpet. Feeling his way, he began to tell her of his interview with the

Ravens. When he had finished, Christa came and sat beside him. Glancing up at her he could see that an unaccustomed hard look had come over her face.

'Peter, to be less than polite, your marvellous great uncle has stitched you up!'

Taken aback at her words, mirroring those of Jonathan Raven, he stood and paced up and down for a moment, thinking hard.

'It seems too unbelievable. The implication seems to be that I've been sharing with him some of the confidential documents in my possession, and accepting his guidance on the conduct of those matters.' He turned to face her. 'Christa, I've done nothing of the sort, and I've told the Ravens this. I know they have a less than favourable attitude towards Lionel. Jonathan came to see me before I left, and pretty much suggested that I stay away from him in future.

'Christa, he's my one blood relative, and that's important to me, and I thought it was the same for him too! Why else would he give me both educational and financial help over all these years? Because of that, I've tried to do well for his sake, as well as my own. If in some way this whole matter was engineered, as the Ravens suggest, I can't understand what he would gain by getting me the sack. I'm appalled to think he would do such a thing.'

He ran his hands through his hair, and slumped back on the settee. Christa put her arm across his shoulders.

'Peter, listen to me. I think your great uncle likes to manipulate people for his own purposes. I'm certain all this trouble has been staged for a reason. Like you, I can't suggest at the moment why, but I do think I'm right. Will you tell me something, Peter? Has he said anything to you about me?'

Peter now felt uncomfortable. 'Oh, it doesn't matter, Christa.'

'Yes, it does matter, Peter. I think it matters a great deal. Please tell me.'

He looked into her clear brown eyes, honest and straightforward. He didn't want to upset her; he realised at that moment just how much he valued her presence in his life. But he couldn't lie to her.

'Christa, when I'm twenty-five I'll inherit an amount of money

444

from my parents, my mother, to be exact. It was money she would have had herself if she had lived. I'm not sure how much is involved, and to be honest I don't care. I doubt it's a fortune. Lionel said you had been a bit evasive on answering some of his questions. He suggested to me that you might have become aware of my windfall and were interested in me for that reason.'

To his complete astonishment, Christa became convulsed with laughter. At what, he couldn't imagine.

'Oh, that's priceless, Peter. It shows how much he knows.' She became more serious. 'Look around you, Peter, at this flat, where it is in London, at its contents. Haven't you been curious as to what sort of friend I might have who has lent this to me?'

Peter looked around with a vague air of disinterest. 'I can't say it's bothered me.'

'I haven't told you the complete truth, Peter, but you'll see why when I explain. You know I said that my father builds boats?'

Peter nodded, still mystified.

'He owns one of the biggest shipyards in Canada. He builds boats of most sizes and descriptions, for anyone worldwide. This flat is where he stays when he comes to Europe for business, which he does often. I keep my family circumstances as quiet as I can, for obvious reasons. I want people to like me for who I am, not what I might have. So, you see, far from me being after your money, now you're unemployed, the reverse could be true!

'Dad was impressed by you when we met in the hotel. I think he felt the same as me, that if you liked me, even if you knew the truth about my financial status, it wouldn't make any difference.' She put her head on one side and stared at him. 'Do you like me, Peter?'

As the initial shock of her revelation began to pass, he too saw the funny side of the situation – well, almost. He curled his arms around her and leant his head on her hair, a smile starting to form on his face.

'I think you can say that I do like you, Miss Benjamin. By the way, you couldn't by any chance lend me a fiver?'

They both started laughing. For Peter it was a release, washing away all the disbelief and hurt of earlier in the evening. When they had sobered somewhat, Christa offered to make him something to eat.

Over the meal, Peter told her about Jonathan Raven's offer of assistance.

'You know, Peter, in my view, this is a much better career choice for you. It's still the law, but without all the public performance. Getting to know your character, I don't think deep down you're suited to that Court sort of thing. Your great uncle should have seen that for himself.'

'I need to have a talk with Lionel to see if I can get to the bottom of things. If this is some sort of deliberate ploy, God knows what it could be for. It's as if he was trying to get me away from the Ravens. But why? I wonder what Sarah and Luigi will say when they know. They've never been that keen on him, and this will make it worse.' He gave a deep sigh. 'You know, now the first shock has passed, I'm not looking forward to dredging it all up again. I just want to move on, start again.'

He looked at his watch. It was getting late. He'd better call a taxi and get home. He checked his phone and much to his amazement, true to his word, there was a message from Jonathan Raven. A meeting had been fixed with his friend for lunchtime on Monday, and he gave the contact details required. Peter sighed with relief.

'I'd better be getting along, Christa. Thanks for everything.'

She stopped in the act of closing the curtains and turned towards him, her brown eyes dark and serious. She was a very attractive girl, he thought, watching the muted lighting reflected in her long gold hair. He had the ridiculous urge to stroke it and feel its softness. He was glad he had come to see her. There was nowhere else he'd wanted to be tonight.

'You don't have to go, Peter.'

The implication was there in her quiet words. Her voice was steady, with no discernible emotion. He now had the choice. Refuse her implied offer and risk offending her, spoiling their friendship after all the quiet support she had given him, or accept the gesture and move their association to a different level. He didn't hesitate in his decision. Remembering his thoughts of a moment ago, he needed to see her brown eyes soft with pleasure, and know he was the one she

446

wanted. Walking over to where she stood, he tipped up her chin and planted a soft kiss on her pink lips.

'Thank you, Christa. I'd like to stay very much.'

*

Christa sat at the kitchen table in her bathrobe, it was six-thirty and Peter had just left. She smiled to herself. He had been a gentle and considerate lover. At first she had sensed the diffidence in him, nothing like the other two occasions when she had allowed a man to get close to her. It had been refreshing to be treated as something delicate and precious, and her feelings of warmth and caring toward him had increased.

He had wakened her again in the dawn and had been more assured and confident in his love-making. She was aware that their relationship so far had been based on mutual companionship; now there was a subtle shift. What would happen between them, she was not sure. They were at a crossroads. The important thing was that he had sought her out last night when he was in trouble. Seeing his distress, she had been tempted to tell him of Sarah's worries about his great uncle, and also her news from Canada, but she dare not encroach on his affairs too far, and had remained silent. For the time being, support and comfort was her role, and after last night she thought he realised it too. It was impossible to tell how much more their relationship would change, but of one thing she was certain, she wanted to continue being part of his life. Perhaps with her support Peter could wean himself away from the influence of that wretched man, with a future, perhaps, for them both.

She would have a lot to tell her father tonight in their regular telephone call (although perhaps not everything…). But more than that, she was looking forward to seeing Peter again on Sunday.

*

'You need to get him on board pretty fast now, Lionel.'

Villiers took another appreciative sip of his wine. The Club kept a very good cellar.

447

'I'm aware of that, Geoffrey.'

'I'm just hanging on at the firm part-time so I can keep an eye on our affairs and facilitate the winding up of the trust. We'll have to make provision for dealing with the money. He might make a fuss when he understands our involvement. Have you thought how you're going to sell the idea to him?'

'Not at the moment. We've enough time for all that. I'm hoping my little ploy has worked as far as the Ravens are concerned. I'll hear from him soon. No doubt he's still in a state of shock.' Franklin pushed away his now empty dinner plate. 'I'll have to do something about the girl, though. The sooner she's off the scene the better.'

'For God's sake be careful, Lionel. You're turning this into another personal crusade. Look what happened last time!'

'Don't fuss, Geoffrey. Clarke's man messed up the Fulham business, but it turned out quite well in the end. Anyway, that's one thing which is all in the past.'

Tossing back the rest of his drink, he pulled some papers towards him, and after a pause cleared his throat.

'We'd better give some thought as to how we deal with Bonetti's latest "donation". I understand a bigger return is required.'

Looking up, Villiers caught his quick glance, and noted that for once Franklin's pale blue eyes lacked their usual power.

*

Dougie Johnson shifted his glass of beer around on the scuffed table. It was one of those days; the days when his feelings of guilt came bubbling to the surface. He had come to know them well over the last twenty-odd years. His wife knew them too, and over time had resorted to banishing him from the house until he pulled himself together again.

Even after all this time, it was always the same. He should have done more. He knew this, but it was difficult to face up to the fact. Then again, in the circumstances as they had unfolded, what could he have done? That was always his excuse.

He felt the emotions rising in him and his palms began to sweat. Once more, the old memories crowded in.

CHAPTER 14

On that dreadful morning so many years ago, the building had already been agog with the news of the fatal car accident involving the Commissioner. Arriving at the office, he found that he was on his own. It was unexpected, as Alex's part in the scheduled protection duty should have been over a while ago. He wasn't aware of any appointment out of the office. Perhaps Alex had been asked to investigate something to do with the Commissioner's accident. There might even have been a problem with Peter or Catherine.

He was contemplating making a phone call when the door opened and Superintendent Charles appeared, grim-faced.

'Sergeant, I think you ought to get over to Fulham. Hartman didn't turn up for his scheduled duty this morning, and I'm hearing rumours of a multiple fatality.'

He wanted to query the instruction, but something in the manner of the older man made him grab a coat and head for his car.

Turning into Church Road he spotted a police car outside the house. Parking behind it, he encountered a young police constable stationed at the front door. He showed him his card as authority.

'Let me in, Constable.'

'I'm afraid I can't do that, Sergeant. I've been instructed to let no one into the premises.'

Faced, however, with the implacable stare of a superior, the young man gave in and opened the front door.

Dougie was shocked to see a massive bloodstain near the foot of the stairs.

'What's happened here, Constable?'

The constable relayed how he was first on the scene and found the two bodies and the gun. He said at that point he had called for full back-up. Within a few minutes, there had been the usual flurry of people in and out.

As they went upstairs into the front bedroom Dougie was half-listening to the young man relaying the scene he had discovered. His imagination pictured the young woman lying on the bed with a pillow over her face, one arm outflung, holding a bloodied ornament. He could see blood on the carpet.

'What about the child?' He had dreaded hearing the answer.

'The baby was unharmed. The neighbour who raised the alarm took him in.'

That was one blessing. Poor little bugger: both parents dead.

The constable then took Dougie back downstairs and indicated where various papers, including bank statements, had been found strewn around the back room. A Superintendent in plain clothes had arrived at the same time as the forensics people. The man was unknown to the constable, but he understood he had been sent by Assistant Commissioner Rankin. With some embarrassment he related how he had overheard the senior officers discussing the contents of the statements, saying these indicated regular cash and some cheque payments into an account but no withdrawals. Certain handwritten notations of names were recognised by one officer, who took the view that Hartman might have been 'on the take' and, on this being discovered, there must have been some sort of violent domestic argument during which he suffocated his wife and then shot himself.

The bodies had been quickly removed and, as far as he was aware, the Superintendent had taken the papers away with him when he left.

Dougie was overwhelmed by his feelings as the bare details sank in. It sounded crazy! The last person on earth he would have thought possible of taking bribes was Alex Hartman, and it was unthinkable that he could have hurt Catherine in any way. Yes, Alex had a temper, but he was able to control it when he had to, even in circumstances with the provocation of emotional involvement.

'If this was discovered only this morning, I'm surprised forensics aren't still here.'

'They've been and gone.'

'Gone? Already?' He was unable to hide his amazement.

'Said it was pretty clear-cut.'

Dougie refrained from making a retort about some people not being able to see the nose on their face.

The young man said he had formed the impression that due to the sensitive nature of the persons involved, the whole matter was to be wrapped up as soon as possible and no more than a rudimentary examination of the property was undertaken.

'How did you get into the property when you arrived, Constable?'

'The next-door neighbour had a front door key. She sensed something was wrong, but was afraid to use it.'

'Is there any sign of forced entry elsewhere in the property?'

'No, Sergeant. I'm sure it was investigated.'

Dougie double-checked for himself, but there wasn't even a slight scratch anywhere.

'Have neighbours been interviewed to see if they heard anything?'

'I couldn't say, Sergeant. I know the next-door neighbour told me she had heard nothing until the baby started crying for a long while. She admitted her hearing isn't as good as it used to be, and she's a heavy sleeper.'

'Even so, it must have been a rather quiet violent argument, wouldn't you say?' Dougie was unable to resist the remark. 'Where have the bodies and evidence been taken?'

The constable informed him, and without another word, Dougie left. He didn't want to take the next steps, but knew he had no alternative.

The mortuary technician was less than keen on him viewing the bodies without any sort of paperwork, but Dougie persisted. He felt sick at what he saw. There appeared to be no damage anywhere on Alex's body, but even he had a job to recognise that handsome head. There was cranial damage on both sides of the skull; some, it could be presumed, from an initial blow and the rest resulting from a probable connection with the banister newel post. On close examination it was just possible to discern what he took to be the partial outline of a bullet hole on the left-hand side of the forehead. His immediate thought was that it was at a strange angle. Knowing Alex was right-handed, he would have expected to see damage in the right temple. Perhaps the head injuries already sustained had caused some problem and miscalculation.

He stood there for a moment, remembering some of the events in the past months that he had shared with this man. He then said a silent goodbye.

The worst thing was Catherine. She looked as if she was sleeping, and would wake at any moment and fix him with those wonderful green eyes. There wasn't a mark on her, apart from a small bruise on the left side of her chin. As he felt the tears welling up inside him, without conscious thought he bent and kissed her cold, pale cheek.

He sat in his car for a long time, wishing he could dispel the vivid pictures in his mind. That poor little girl, so full of excitement at the future – and now this! What must her last thoughts have been? His mind didn't want to even begin to compute that. He made himself concentrate on the facts.

Out of all this, one thing stood out. He could not believe that Catherine had been able to wield an implement capable of injuring Alex to any great extent. She just wasn't strong enough. And she would have been very lucky indeed to have been able to surprise Alex. He would have taken any weapon from her with ease. Then there was the amount of time it would take to suffocate a struggling girl. Plenty of time for Alex, however angry, to realise what he was doing. Knowing the people involved, he just couldn't picture the scene.

He knew his next job was to track down the whereabouts of the items taken from the property. Again, he met initial reluctance from the forensic department when he asked to see them, but at his insistence permission was granted. He was told that from records it had been established that the gun was the firearm issued to Alex the previous day. He was informed that it had been fired once. One spent casing had been found. He examined the bronze statue with interest. Although small, it was quite heavy. Again, he could not imagine Catherine wielding this with sufficient force to injure Alex to the extent of his apparent injuries. After further pressing, he was told that the papers found at the house had been taken away by a senior police officer.

Dougie reported back all he had discovered to a shocked Superintendent Charles. In something of a daze, he then went back to his office and sat at his desk, staring at the other empty chair, wondering what on earth he should do next.

After an hour, and two cups of coffee, neither of which he tasted, he found himself no further forward with his dilemma. With Sir John and Alex gone, who was now in charge of the investigation? Who could he trust? He had no way of knowing how to contact Francis. Perhaps he himself would be contacted as soon as the news leaked out. The newspapers would have a field day with this one!

Then his door had opened and a man entered, followed by two uniformed constables, none of them known to him.

The man announced, in a cool voice, 'I'm Superintendent Fox. I've been brought in on this matter. Assistant Commissioner Rankin has given instructions that he will take full charge of your investigation and all your papers are to be removed into his keeping. Here's a signed letter of authority. You are to be reassigned back to other duties.'

There was nothing Dougie could do. It was a direct order from a superior. He watched as the filing cabinets were emptied and their files carried away. The Superintendent remained behind and fixed Dougie with a hard stare.

'I understand you've been to Fulham and other places.'

So, his movements had been reported, thought Dougie.

'Yes, I have. Alex Hartman was my colleague, and I knew his wife. I wanted to know what had happened.'

'What happened is that a bent copper killed his wife and then killed himself. End of story. There won't be a fuss about it. Gets the Force a bad name, this sort of thing. There'll be no need for you to do any more investigating, it might not go down too well. You have your pension to think about.'

With a slight smile, he left. There was no doubt about the meaning of his remarks. Don't poke around, or your career could be on the line.

Should he have a word with Superintendent Charles? He'd always felt he was a reasonable man. What if Charles had been warned as well?

Then another thought had come into his mind, one that worried him. The Commissioner had been about to report to others on their findings. Now the Commissioner was... dead. Had that been an unfortunate accident? Then Alex: dead. Could it be that someone was trying to stop any further investigation by removing those persons involved? If it was, where did that leave him? Or his family, for that matter. He remembered Alex's thoughts on the deaths of Catherine's parents; and now Catherine herself was dead. Had Alex been right to worry, after all?

He was still of the same mind when, on attending the inquests, he found himself disagreeing with the rudimentary submissions from pathology and ballistics, and the Coroner's eventual final decision.

The whole thing preyed on his mind over the following weeks, to such an extent it culminated in him asking to be removed from Special Branch and returned to ordinary CID work. Keep your head down, and work out the rest of your time for your pension. That was best.

It was no surprise when Luigi Gandoni attempted to contact him. He was sure to ask him to push for more investigation, but without any new evidence he knew this was pointless. As for the other matter... how could he explain? Perhaps he should just keep quiet.

His worries deepened when he was informed about the box awaiting his collection. A glance inside was all he needed to realise that they were copies of all their reports and file notes. Had Alex foreseen something like this happening and made sure that the information was safe? But what could he now do with it all? No one named Francis, nor anyone else, had yet made any contact with him. It then dawned on him that if it became known that there were copies of all their documentation in existence, and in his possession, this again could bring danger to him or his family. He put the box in his loft and tried to forget about it.

That was when the guilt had started.

CHAPTER 15

The noise in the public house began to intrude on Dougie's thoughts. It had been a regular of his for a number of years on these particular days, taking him back to the area where he had been brought up and people knew him and the start of his career. He laughed to himself. A psychiatrist would no doubt say he was trying to return to his youth, to a time before the guilt had started to invade his waking thoughts.

He had noticed a man sitting at the bar looking his way a few times. Although he knew several people from the old days who still lived in the vicinity and frequented the pub, this person he did not recognise.

As if making up his mind, the man turned from the bar and came his way.

'Its Dougie Johnson, isn't it?'

Dougie still didn't recognise him.

'Yes, that's me. Sorry, should I know you?'

With a grin the man slipped into a seat next to him.

'A good few years ago I'd have been glad you didn't… if you're still in the same profession that is. The name's Ron Henshaw. You're the law, or you were, and I was… well, I wasn't.'

Dougie gave him a straight look. 'Well I'm still the law. But not for much longer,' he amended. 'Almost time to quit now.'

'Are you living back this way? I've seen you drinking in here several times on your own.' Henshaw gave a short laugh. 'Wondered if you were looking for someone.'

'No, I don't live around here. I just come to… keep in touch with the past.'

'I'm all the way retired now. Used to work for Jack Ellison. He packed it in a long time ago now, of course. Let that little so and so Johnny Carter have the run in the eighties. Now, there's one person I wouldn't work for. Had the chance, but he could play rough, or he had people do it for him. Knew one or two of them. Paid well, but I wasn't prepared to get into deep water for him. He was supposed to have some influential friends. Liked the ladies too, and they did alright out of it, as long as they put up with what he wanted! No, I was better off with Jack Ellison, he always knew just how far to go. You know, its funny, but I formed the impression that he had a certain respect for the law. Even went to the funeral of a copper killed in some domestic argument back in the late seventies. I went along as one of his minders. Yeah, funny that!'

Henshaw didn't notice the reaction his words had on his companion.

'Well, it's been nice to have a chat. Brought back some memories. Perhaps I'll come across you here again.'

Dougie managed a faint smile and a nod, his mind too full with the memories conjured up by what he had just heard. Would it ever go away? No, not until he had the courage to do something about it. He thought again about Henshaw. Was that why he kept coming here, hoping he would meet someone who knew about those days, from the other side? He banged his glass down on the table, slopping some of the beer over his hand. By Christ, he'd do it! He'd meet Henshaw again and find out all he knew and maybe, just maybe, there might still be something he could do.

*

Peter lay on his bed, looking at the ceiling, music playing in the background. His father's music. He had attended his interview earlier in the day, and to his amazement, and relief, was offered the vacant position straight away. Jonathan Raven's friend appeared to be impressed with his qualifications, and made light of his change in career direction, commenting, with a cheerful grin, that he would never have suited Court work either. Peter liked the outline of the job he would be expected to do, and met one or two of his new colleagues, who seemed keen that he should start as soon as possible. As he was free, he offered to come in the next day.

The first thing he did was to send a text to Christa, letting her know his good news. All he received in reply was a smiley face. It was typical of her sense of humour.

He heard a car arriving and knew Sarah was home. He wanted to ask her if he could borrow the car. He now had to confront Lionel. He had been trying to work out what to say to him about the Ravens episode. There were questions to be asked, but should he make any accusations? After all, Lionel was no longer a young man. In the end, he decided to just wait and see the reaction to his news, and take his cue from there. He was now so keen to start the new job that it no longer even seemed to matter.

He was, however, relieved that he had something good to tell Sarah. Both she and Jerry had taken the sudden change in his situation pretty well. He climbed the stairs up to the kitchen. Sarah looked up from unpacking her shopping, and gave him a smile.

'Oh good, you're around. I'd kill for a cup of tea!'

'Perhaps we ought to make it stronger than that. I've a new job.'

He watched the look of relief cross her face, and she came and gave him a hug.

'I'm so pleased for you Peter. I'm sure this will all work out for the best now. A new millennium, and a brand new start.'

'Let's hope so, I'm quite looking forward to it. I'll get the kettle on, shall I? Oh, by the way, Sarah, could I borrow the car tonight?'

'Are you going to celebrate with Christa?'

He paused in the act of filling the kettle. 'Well, no. I've already sent her a text. I was going somewhere else.'

There was a sudden silence in the room. He turned around

and Sarah was standing looking at him, her face now pale and anxious.

'I had a feeling you didn't tell us everything about this matter. Franklin's behind it all isn't he. Is he telling you what to do again?' Her voice sounded sharp and accusing.

Peter had made a conscious decision to be economical with the truth about Ravens, and he might have guessed that Sarah, in particular, would have picked up on this. However, he didn't want another fight, so he just smiled at her.

'Jonathan Raven put forward my name for this job, Sarah, and I must have measured up. Out of courtesy I need to inform Lionel about the changes, and like you, I hope he'll think it's for the best.'

As he turned back to his task, he could see from the worried look in her eyes and the nervous way she had of playing with her hair that she remained unconvinced, and that his words had failed to reassure her.

*

Once Lionel Franklin recovered from his initial annoyance at the unexpected turn of events, and exasperation that the boy was shooting about like a loose cannon, he reflected on the situation and saw an advantage in what he had just been told. After all, there were other barristers who had, and would, dance to his tune; ones with experience, as well. If Peter was now to move in the moneyed world of corporate dealings, there might be even more opportunities presenting themselves.

'I must say, this is something of a shock, Peter. I did warn you about the Ravens. They seem to have a particular way they like to run things.' He studied the young man. 'So they just thought that, after all, you were unsuitable?'

He noted Peter had said nothing about any difficulties with the papers being found in one of his files. Perhaps he had come across them himself and just destroyed them… but he knew the boy was too intelligent not to recognise them for what they were. Curious, though: he had at least expected some questioning. Perhaps the Ravens had decided not to bring the matter out into the open, and dismissed him through the back door without creating a fuss.

'There was a discussion, Lionel, with the outcome I've told you. Now I just want to concentrate on this new start.'

So, it appeared that he was still in the boy's good books, thought Franklin. And he needed to keep it that way. Perhaps Peter was just trying to humour him by not making a scene of any kind; another example of his emotional attachment.

'Well, one thing about moving into the corporate field is that you can make some useful investment contacts. With the money you have coming your way, you could do very well for yourself. Remember that, Peter. Over the years, Hamilton, Villiers and I have all made useful contacts. I'll be interested in how you get on.'

Heading home, Peter wondered why he had decided not to confront Lionel. Was he just a coward? The bottom line was that he still couldn't bring himself to think that there had been anything deliberate in Lionel's actions, however mystifying. He had seemed calm enough when told the news, and about the eventual outcome. In fact, he'd appeared pleased that he was going into this other branch of the law. As Lionel had said, he might make some useful contacts, for himself as well as his new employers. He couldn't wait to begin.

*

Dougie saw his quarry coming into the pub, and beckoned him over. Not weakening in his decision to start his enquiries, he had now tried on two occasions to meet up with Henshaw. Third time lucky!

'Well, Dougie, we seem to be congregating here again. Just been speaking outside to another old face.'

Dougie kept his expression blank. 'An old colleague?'

'Funny you should say that. He used to be on Clarke's payroll, but changed horses to Ellison about the time, like I mentioned to you, when that copper was killed. I can remember he always got off the subject pretty smartish. Still, it's never wise to discuss certain things, if you get my drift.'

Dougie prodded some more. 'He must know quite a bit about Clarke's affairs.'

'Oh, I dare say. But as I said, you learn not to talk about them. If Clarke got to hear about it, you'd get a visit one night, like he did to that other poor sod a few years ago. It must have been nice for you lot to get him banged up for something.'

Dougie remembered his own satisfaction on hearing that Clarke had been caught and charged with grievous bodily harm, and sent to do a stretch at Her Majesty's pleasure. He looked at his companion.

'Like I said, I'm finishing soon. Just going through some old files and tying up loose ends. You said before that, on the whole, Clarke didn't do his own dirty work, he had others do it for him?'

'Oh sure, same as Ellison. You don't have a dog and bark yourself. I admit I've leant on a number of people in my time, but like I said, Ellison would allow it to go so far, and that was it. Clarke was a different ball game. I'm pretty sure Monty didn't get into the heavy stuff for Clarke, but I bet he has a few ideas who did.' He gave Dougie a shrewd look. 'You want me to introduce you to him, don't you?'

Dougie returned his look. 'He might be able to fill in one or two blanks. Like I said, tidying up old files.'

Henshaw finished his beer. 'I might have a word with him. Can't promise anything, though.'

Dougie tried not to show his sudden excitement.

'No, of course not. I'll make it worth his while. Shall we say same time next week? I'll stand the drinks.'

In the intervening week Dougie made a point of seeking out a retired colleague who had been involved with the Lucille Prentice case. He confirmed the suspicions noted on the file, that Clarke had been behind it, but there was no proof. His very convenient alibi for the time period involved was cast iron, and nothing had emerged to incriminate anyone else. Various men she had known, besides Clarke, had all been interviewed and discounted for one reason or another. Dougie also took the opportunity of speaking to him about the circumstances of the Fenton death. Although not involved, his former colleague took the view that it was just an accidental fire causing an unfortunate death. Why the deceased had not made his escape from the premises while he still could was perhaps a little odd. He then put forward the idea that Fenton might have tried to put the fire out and left his escape too late, or for some reason had passed out having by some chance started the fire himself. When the building collapsed there would have been very little evidence left for anyone to find. The authorities had, after all, passed it off in this way.

Good reasoning, Dougie thought, but viewing it all from his standpoint he was certain that a real professional had been involved. Someone so good at his craft that, as yet, he was invisible to the law.

*

Henshaw was sitting alone at a corner table when, as arranged, Dougie entered the pub. He bought his beer and crossed over to him.

'Evening. On your own, I see.'

'I had a word, as promised. Monty's not too keen.'

'Did you tell him it would be worth something to him?'

'Oh yeah, but that won't go far if you find yourself in a dark alley with your legs smashed up.'

Dougie felt he had to push the matter. 'I'm not asking him to walk into a police station. I'm sure we can find a way of not being observed.'

Henshaw studied him for a moment or two.

'This is important, isn't it. Not just clearing old cases.'

'It's a bit of both. Now, this is my idea…'

CHAPTER 16

For a Saturday night there was quite a good crowd, Dougie thought, looking at the people milling around. Greyhound racing wasn't as popular as it used to be, and some areas of the Walthamstow track were showing it, although the large neon stadium sign still advertised it as a going concern. He leant against the fence close to the starting traps, pulling his yellow scarf up round his ears in the brisk wind. They were parading the dogs for Race Two. He had put a bet on number four as a whim, because of the name, 'Catherine's Folly'.

He felt someone wedge in against him, and moved over to give the person more room.

'You'll never get anything back on number four, it's too long in the tooth. Number one's the bet here.'

Dougie didn't turn his head.

'Monty?'

'Yeah. I saw you with your yellow scarf in the betting area. I've been keeping an eye on you for a bit. Making sure you're alone.'

The loud speakers announced the start of Race Two. The traps sprang open and the dogs were running. True enough, number one was the winner, with number four coming in a good last. Dougie tore his betting slip into pieces and let them drift to the ground. His companion clapped him on the back and took his arm.

'Come on, let's get my winnings and I'll treat you to a tea.'

They stood together drinking their tea, out of earshot of people in the queue still waiting to be served. For the first time, Dougie regarded the man standing beside him. He was a year or two younger than himself, medium height and build. In other words, ordinary; wouldn't stand out in a crowd. There was, however a certain air about him which, to anyone in the know, warned you not to take him for granted.

'Ron said you wanted to talk about the old days.'

'Yeah. Trying to tie up some loose ends.'

'Such as what? Something specific?'

'Clarke. The sort of things he used to get up to, round about the late seventies.'

'Looking back, I think he'd consider those were his best days. At the time, a lot of his fame came from the police suspecting him of being involved in things but never having enough to pin on him. He did alright when Ellison backed right off, but Johnny's star is beginning to wane a bit now. He's getting past it, younger people coming in. Mark you, I'm not sure even that would quieten him down: he's still a maniac. Lost a lot of credibility, though, when he did that stretch.'

'You moved on, I believe.'

'I was putting two and two together and didn't want to be caught up in it. Took a risk and changed horses. Made me look over my shoulder for a bit, I can tell you. Pretty pointless, I wouldn't have known much about it if Clarke had given the order.'

Dougie finished the rest of his tea and threw the paper cup into the waste bin beside him. Perhaps a bit of pressure was in order.

'Who would he have given the word to?'

'That's what this is all about, is it?'

Monty disposed of his cup and walked off. Dougie kept pace with him.

'I've come to the conclusion that Clarke had a professional – I mean, a real professional – working for him. Someone who's managed to keep himself out of the spotlight.'

They were leaning back on the rail again, the loudspeakers drowning out their conversation.

'You're not wrong. I had an idea, just an idea, about someone but it was safer not to ask too many questions.'

Dougie decided now was the time.

'I'm interested in a particular night when the top man in the Met was in a fatal accident, and also a policeman and his wife were wasted in Fulham.'

There was silence for a while.

'I somehow had the feeling you were coming to that. That was the time I decided to quit. Too heavy for me, and I was too close in for comfort.'

'What do you know of it?'

'I was asked last minute, urgent, to provide a fast car and have it parked with keys left in it outside a hotel at a particular time. We had a stolen vehicle suitable, tucked away in a lock-up. I was then instructed to be around to pick up a certain person outside the Fulham football ground in the small hours of the next morning. I read the newspapers the next day and came to a few conclusions.'

'Who was the person you picked up?'

Monty turned and looked at Dougie, and in the dim light his face looked strained.

'Even after all this time, you're asking a lot, you know. If I'm right, he still gives me the shivers.'

'I'll make it worth your while.'

Dougie moved his scarf aside and reached into the inside pocket of his jacket. He partially revealed a bundle of bank notes and made sure Monty had a good look.

There was silence between them again.

'He used to work for Clarke in one of his betting shops. Worked irregular hours, often disappearing for a day or two, and nothing was ever said. I saw him once or twice at Clarke's house. Never got into casual conversation with him. He was pretty closed off. He's the one I picked up from Fulham that night.'

'I need a name, Monty.'

'Sorry, I'm not going that far. When I left I ought to have been taken care of with what I knew, but it must have been considered I could keep my mouth shut. That's still the case. I'll help you so far, because the copper's wife should have been left alone, in my book. The person you're after is about ten years younger than me. Used to drive a clapped-out Merc. I know he was married, but I don't know anything more. Now that's all!'

Dougie moved closer and passed him the notes.

'Thanks, Monty.'

He turned away and merged in with the crowds, watching the final race of the evening.

*

Franklin was again thinking about the girl. He had come to the conclusion that Peter would not react as hoped to the suggestion that she was motivated by greed. At their meeting he had sensed the strength of will in her, and it was obvious that this was being communicated to Peter. She had to be encouraged to go back to Canada; as soon as possible. It was just a few months before Peter's twenty-fifth birthday and the boy was nowhere near satisfactory material yet. Yes, he needed her out of the running. Now.

*

Christa had worked late on a particular story which for days she could never seem to quite complete to her satisfaction. Tonight, however, she had felt inspiration and had stayed on to finish the article before her ideas left her again.

Walking the couple of streets from the Tube to her flat, she welcomed the fresh air clearing the stuffiness from her head. Taking her keys from her bag, she heard steps behind her, and then felt a push in her back. As she stumbled, hands grabbed her bag. She clung on as hard as she could, and screamed. A light came on in a porch further up the road and someone called out.

'Help me!' Christa shouted with the remaining breath left in her. 'Get the police! I'm being attacked!'

Other lights came on, but by now Christa was on her knees and in the end had to give up the unequal struggle and release her grip on the bag. The dark figure ran off back down the road. Christa was trying to get her breath when a woman's voice spoke to her.

'Are you alright, my dear? The police are on their way. Can you stand up?'

With assistance, Christa made it to her feet. She was taken inside a nearby house to await the police. When they arrived she found there was little information she could give them. They took details of her assailant, as much as she knew, and also her bag and its contents. She had to think about this. Why could you never remember what you carried around with you on a daily basis? Asked about a phone, she remembered that this was in the side pocket of her coat. That was something, at least.

She declined the need for any medical treatment or a lift home, but now, looking out into the darkness, even the distance of a couple of streets seemed daunting. She wanted Peter. With shaking fingers she rang his number.

CHAPTER 17

Peter was enjoying Luigi's description of a telephone call received that afternoon from his granddaughter. They were just finishing a meal together, a last-minute arrangement in order to bring Luigi up to date on his change of career.

Luigi was making him laugh, trying to mimic the young girl's chatter, when Peter's phone rang. On answering it, his laughter faded.

'God!… Damn the handbag, are you alright, Christa?'

He saw Luigi watching him, now concerned.

'OK, Christa. I'm coming for you. What's the address?' He listened for a moment. 'I'll get a taxi and be right round. You're sure you're not hurt?… I'm on my way.'

He closed the call and looked at Luigi.

'Christa's been mugged on her way home. Someone's taken her handbag. I need a taxi.'

'I'll come with you.'

*

Peter was not satisfied until Christa was tucked up in bed after a warm bath and a hot drink. She seemed quite controlled, but shock was a funny thing. By the time he and Luigi had reached her she had made a phone call to arrange for her cards to be cancelled. There was nothing else of real importance in the bag, she told him; it was more of a nuisance. What a blessing she had kept her phone elsewhere.

Once Luigi had seen Christa was unharmed, he took his leave.

Peter rang the McIntyres and spoke to Jerry, telling him what had happened and that he would spend the night with Christa. Jerry offered to come round and check her over, but Peter decided that was not necessary.

'Everyone has been so kind.' Christa was sipping her drink, propped up on her pillows.

Peter sat on the side of the bed and took her hand. He felt immense relief that she seemed unaffected by her ordeal, and also a quiet pleasure from the knowledge that he was the first person she thought to ring when she was in trouble. The more he saw of her, it was now registering, the more she meant to him.

'You're easy to be kind to,' he smiled, kissing the tip of her nose. Then he said the words he knew he must, dreading her response. 'Christa, if you decided you wanted to go back home to Canada, I'd quite understand.'

She reached up and stroked his cheek. 'Don't be silly, I've no intention of going.'

He opened his mouth to make his point again, but she placed a finger against his lips and shook her head. Relenting, and trying to hide his relief, he smiled at her, sliding his hand down the warm skin of her back.

'Now you've rested a bit, how do you feel?'

She looked at him, her brown eyes soft and warm. 'I'd feel much better if you came to bed.'

He took the unfinished drink from her, and folded her in his arms, his mouth covering hers. 'Let's see if that's true, shall we,' he murmured.

*

'I don't know what you expect me to do. I'm not taking that sort of message to him.'

Villiers had been surprised, and not a little annoyed, at the sudden arrival of Johnny Clarke. It was fortunate that his wife was not at home tonight.

Clarke was pacing up and down the large sitting room, leaving dirty footprints on the Indian rug in front of the fireplace. Then he stopped and gestured around at the elegant furnishings.

'Looks like you've done very well for yourself over the years. I'm the one asked to do all the nasty jobs, and in my view, I've been paid a pittance in comparison. Franklin sits there on high just issuing instructions, like last night. Just do this, just do that.'

'You get paid for it.'

'Yes, but not as much as others make out of it, I bet.' Clarke threw another look around the well-appointed room. 'He didn't do much to help when I got banged up, did he. I'm sure he could have oiled some wheels if he'd wanted, but he didn't. Well, he'd better not forget that I know quite a bit about him, things certain people would be very interested in.'

Villiers began to worry. If Clarke was serious in his threat and he brought Franklin down, he would fall as well.

'Alright, I'll speak with him. Don't go and do anything stupid, for God's sake.'

Unasked, Clarke helped himself to a whisky from the cut-glass decanter on the sideboard.

'That's up to you then, isn't it.'

With an insolent smile, he gave a mock salute and walked out. Villiers watched him leave and then sat down in the plush armchair, trying to control the sudden shaking in his legs.

*

Dougie was getting nowhere. This was the third and last of the betting shops owned by Clarke, and it was almost closing time. He was using the story of looking up a friend of a friend to pass on a message about a death. His main problem was that most of the current staff were too young to remember more than a few years back. He used the scant information Monty had imparted to him, but with not even a name to go on the task was looking impossible.

One older-looking man tapped his forehead.

'There's something I remember, when I did a Saturday job here as a lad, about one chap who was always in and out at odd times. The others used to grumble a bit about it. I think the story was that he was in poor health.'

'Can you remember a name? It's important.'

Dougie was hoping against hope. He was running out of ideas.

'I know it was a common sort of Christian name. I just can't remember it though. Sorry.'

With a sigh, and a mumbled 'Thanks', Dougie turned for the door, all but colliding with an elderly man who was hovering in the doorway. As he left the premises, the man watched him go.

What to do now, that was the question. It was two days since his enquiries had come to a full stop, and Dougie was back at his old haunt. Maybe he would see Ron Henshaw again, ask him to put some more pressure on Monty to give him a name. Failing that, he might have to speak with his superiors to see if there was a case for getting Clarke in for a chat, but he rather doubted that anyone would give his enquiry serious consideration.

Deep in thought, he failed to notice the man he had collided with in the betting shop sitting in a far corner. The man rose, went to the bar, and asked to use the telephone. After finishing his short call he had a word with the landlord, and without another look left the pub.

It was time to go home. Two pints was Dougie's limit these days. Feeling rather despondent he shrugged into his coat, and drained the last dregs from his glass. He became conscious of a man in the long black robes of a priest talking to the landlord; they were both looking his way. Did they think he was in need of saving! He watched as the priest moved over to him through the tables.

'Excuse me, are you Sergeant Johnson?'

'Yes, that's right, Father.'

'May I sit down for a moment?'

Dougie wondered what all this was about, but pointed to an empty chair.

'Be my guest.'

'Sergeant, I have a man over at my church who has asked to speak with you. He says he has to pass on some important information, and it has to be right now. The poor man has terminal cancer, with not much longer to go.'

'This isn't my patch, Father. He needs to speak with someone local.'

'He says you've been seen in here over a long period of time. People know who you are. He says it must be you, no one else.'

Dougie was intrigued. 'Who is this man?'

'His name is Harry.'

It meant nothing to Dougie. With a resigned sigh he stood and motioned for the priest to lead the way.

'Right. Come on then, Father, let's see this Harry of yours.'

They crossed the road and entered the church. The priest led him to a pew at the back, tucked in a corner. A man sat there huddled in a thick coat, but on their approached he looked up. As far as Dougie could remember he had never seen this person before, but then the man's own mother might have had trouble recognising him. His face was thin and shrunken, the skin drawn tight, with a yellowish sheen. His eyes were dark and sunken into his skull. Not much longer to go, alright.

'I'm Sergeant Johnson. You wanted to see me?'

'Someone from the old days thinks maybe you're asking after me. He knows you're the law.' The voice was low-pitched and harsh. 'The bastard thought he could make a bob or two by threatening to inform on me. Years ago I'd have rewarded him in a way he would have regretted, the f—' He looked up at the priest and gave a sigh. 'Then I got to thinking about it, and perhaps it's as it should be, just in time. I need to tell you something, before it's too late.'

Dougie sat down on the pew next to the man. The priest made to move away, but the man reached out a thin hand and stopped him.

'No, Father, I'd like you to stay if you will.'

'By all means, my son.' The priest joined Dougie on the pew, the other side of the man.

'I suppose during all these years I wondered if anyone would come for me. This thing's been gnawing away at my insides, much like the cancer, and I can't get it out of my mind.'

Dougie recognised that sort of feeling. Then something registered in his mind – 'Ordinary Christian name, nothing fancy' – and he began to concentrate harder.

'What do you want to tell me?'

The man began, as if giving a formal statement, with his full name and address. 'My name's Harry Fowler. I live at 32 Statham Road, Plaistow.' After a pause, he went on, 'I killed a young girl many years ago now, and I still can't get it out of my mind.'

Dougie felt the hairs standing up all over his body. Could it be…!

CHAPTER 18

Fowler seemed to gather himself and then he began his story.

'I worked as an enforcer for Johnny Clarke back in the seventies and eighties. You're still the law, and the word is you used to be in Special Branch. This job I'm going to tell you about was something to do with another Special Branch officer.'

Dougie was sure now, and a feeling, cold as ice, began to form inside him. His hands started to tremble.

'Clarke had instructions from someone for a job. He called me in. I was good at my work, and if I was given a free hand I would craft it just like any other professional, but this job had to be done one way. I was given strict instructions – no deviation. That's where the amateur goes wrong. Things can always happen you don't allow for, just like it did here. Anyway, I was to await further instructions on when the job had to be dealt with. As it turned out, it was at short notice.

'I was given something else to do that night as well, a rush job. A car accident that was to look genuine, with a definite fatality. Unknown to the victim he'd been given a small amount of slow-acting sedative, to dull his responses. The vehicle caught fire after the crash. Even better as far as I was concerned.

'I then had to get back into town to put this other operation into effect. I'd been given a key to enter a particular property, and papers to leave about the premises. I was supposed to surprise the occupants, disable a male police officer with a heavy ornament which I was told where to find, and while he was unconscious, kill his wife. It went well at first. I got in with no problem, and upstairs without being heard. The man became aware of me but I was able to use the ornament and he went down. Should have been out of it for hours. The woman woke up and, I thought, was about to scream. I didn't want any sound. I grabbed the pillow as instructed, and...'

Fowler stopped and bent his head. The priest put an arm round his shoulders. Dougie by this time had a far different urge, and half-rose out of his seat. He then remembered where they were, and tried to subdue his feelings.

'I saw her face looking up at me. She was young and beautiful with large green eyes. She can't have failed to know what was coming. In the end, she made no sound, and didn't even struggle. But the sadness in those eyes... I can't forget.'

Hearing these words Dougie had difficulty in restraining himself. His hands were balled into fists, which he ached to use.

Fowler glanced at the priest before he continued.

'I had my orders, but somehow I knew I couldn't do it to her while she was conscious. I hit her and knocked her out, then I did it. I'd been told to put the ornament in her hand to make sure her prints were on it. I was to go downstairs and leave the papers I'd been given, and then get out. I was under strict instructions not to touch the baby.'

He looked over at the priest again, who patted his shoulder.

'I'd just dealt with the papers and was going back to the front door when I looked up and the copper was coming down the stairs with a gun in his hand. How he was even on his feet, I've no idea; he must have been in one hell of a state. I'd been warned, no firearms, but I never go anywhere without one. The copper fired at me but missed. He must have had a job to even see straight. I wasn't going to let him get in another shot that might be lucky, so I fired back. He fell down the stairs and hit his head one hell of a crack on the banister. I had to get away, so I just let myself out again.'

475

'You evil bastard!' Dougie's voice was a low snarl. 'That officer was my friend and colleague, and one of the best. But we're fair game to the likes of you. The little girl, though, she'd done you no harm. She was a young mother with her baby sleeping in the next room.'

He stood and picked the other man up by his coat and shook him. 'I'll see you rot in Hell for this.'

The priest intervened. 'Gentlemen, please, remember where you are!'

Dougie released Fowler back onto the pew and ground out, 'A church is no place for the likes of him. He deserves the worst anyone can throw at him.'

Fowler's smile had little mirth. 'That might happen to me yet, but perhaps my judgment has already begun. I know it's near the end now, and maybe I can make some sort of amends by telling what I know.'

Dougie tried to calm himself and think.

'You said that Clarke was instructed by someone else to do this job. Do you know who?'

'No. I gather Clarke had done work for him before and gave me the impression that he was someone high up with a bit of influence. Whoever it was had got a key to the property, and most of the papers appeared to be bank statements. I read in the newspaper report that this copper was supposed to be accepting bribes, which I assume were shown up in the statements. He was a bit stupid to pay things into a bank, if you ask me. Was he bent?'

'No, he wasn't.'

'So it was a frame-up, then, and the bank statements were crooked. That's what I mean: someone with influence.'

Dougie slumped back in the pew. Yes, someone with a lawyer and a banker as friends. God! So Alex had been right! Franklin wasn't above destroying his own flesh and blood for whatever his devious mind was dreaming up. What was the point here, though? It was obvious the plan was for Alex to be framed for his wife's murder and disgraced in his profession. What did that leave for Franklin? The child? That was it! Of course, Franklin needed the child: it meant he could keep the money under his control. Catherine had failed him, so it was the turn of her child. Plus he would have revenge on Alex, who would languish in prison for a murder he didn't commit, also knowing that his child was being influenced by the instigator. Alex would have gone out of his mind!

'What other jobs have you done? Have you ever worked for Jack Ellison?'

'Not Ellison. He never had any use for my, er... talents. He packed everything up in London years ago. He's found more lucrative pastures abroad, so I'm told.'

'What do you know about a Joe Fenton?'

Fowler gave him a shrewd look. 'Yes, that was one of mine. Clarke was sore at Ellison for side-stepping a fixer Clarke had planned for him. He thought he was tipped off by Fenton, influenced by that copper.'

'How about a young prostitute, Lucille Prentice?'

'Well, you're going back a bit now, aren't you? Yes, I can remember that. She was a favourite of Clarke's but he thought she'd split on him. I was following her on his orders. Saw her with that same copper. She was a junkie, anyway.'

The man was getting cocky again now he'd unburdened himself, thought Dougie. He took out his phone, and called for a car.

'I'm going to put you under formal arrest for the murder of Catherine Hartman.' He stared at Fowler as he read him his rights. 'We'll do it all by the book, although my personal inclination is to do it another way.' The cold, hard look that went along with his words could not have been misinterpreted. 'Fowler, if it's the last thing I do, I'll see you pay for everything you've done.'

'I don't think I have that long, Sergeant,' was Fowler's reply.

Dougie could feel no sympathy for him. 'Until the car comes I'll leave you with your priest. Maybe he'll convince you of mercy, but at the moment I can't find any in my heart for you.'

Dougie accompanied Fowler as he was taken into custody. His obvious state of health caused some concern and, as Dougie feared, a doctor was called, who advised that Fowler be admitted to hospital.

This, he knew, would mean that the process of taking a formal statement would be delayed, and in his view, time was critical.

*

The telephone rang the next morning at five-fifteen and Dougie struggled awake to answer it. He listened to the voice at the other end, said nothing, and replaced the receiver. For some long moments he sat on the edge of the bed with his head in his hands, then with a deep sigh stood up and left the bedroom.

He went downstairs into the lounge and poured himself a large whisky. He drew back the curtains and stood looking out at the lightening sky, running through in his head the words he had just heard.

So Fowler had had less time than he himself imagined. During the night, under police guard, and with his wife at his bedside, Fowler had escaped man-made justice once and for all.

Dougie took a long swallow of his whisky. He was full of remorse; not for Fowler, but for all those he had once more let down. He cursed himself for being a coward and not tackling the matter sooner. He turned and threw his glass and the remaining contents into the fireplace.

His wife appeared in the doorway, looking at him in concern. 'Dougie, for the love of God, tell me what's wrong.'

Until this morning Dougie realised he had never appreciated how much support Janet had given him over the years. For over two hours she sat in silence, listening to him explain all that had occurred. When he finished, she suggested that he showered while she made breakfast. Working on autopilot, he obeyed her without conscious thought, and it was not until he reappeared, bathed and dressed, and had somehow eaten his meal, that she sat beside him and spoke.

'Dougie, you are a good and honourable man. I'm sure you don't need me to tell you what you now have to do. The truth must be told to everyone, in particular Peter Hartman, whatever it costs.'

He smiled at her and stroked her hand. 'That's just what I'm going to do, my dear. I'm not going to stop now. I'd already made up my mind on that.'

On his way into the office he started to make plans. He had to speak with his superiors about Fowler's verbal confession and what, in legal terms, could be done. The priest had been a witness, but would he be bound by the rules of the confessional? It had, after all, been more of an open talk. He would have to seek guidance on this. Clarke would need to be interviewed as to his part in the matter. Could he be persuaded to reveal his source?

But it left the matter of the Franklin investigation unresolved. This was still his main worry. What he would give to bounce Lionel Franklin around in a padded cell for a bit! He would have all his answers then.

He must speak to Peter Hartman and the McIntyres. If anything about Fowler started to leak out in the press, they would be unprepared. He also knew he must tell them the complete truth about everything. He acknowledged to himself that he would welcome some independent guidance on his actions.

*

Sarah felt the happiest she had been in a long time. It was the perfect Sunday. Her husband and both children at home for lunch, also Peter and Christa, and even Luigi Gandoni had popped in. It was a boisterous meal with everyone in good spirits.

Going about her preparations, she had observed Luigi and Christa talking together. The two of them seemed to get on well. Christa was such a nice girl, none the worse for her recent bad encounter, thank goodness. She had noticed a subtle change in Peter's attitude to her of late. The warm looks between them were very noticeable, and Sarah had even seen them holding hands. Since Peter's problem at the legal chambers and the start of his new job, he had grown in stature. He was more assured and confident, and a ready smile often lit up his face as never before. Please God, she said to herself, after all this time, let him know some happiness.

The front door bell rang as they were having coffee, and Amy left to answer it. She came back a moment or two later and whispered something to her father, who left the room. Strange, thought Sarah, if it was a call-out someone would have rung.

It was some time before Jerry came back into the kitchen, and when he did she could see from his face that it was something serious. He had a man with him who seemed familiar. Not placing him at first, she then remembered. It was Sergeant Johnson, Alex's former colleague; but, of course, now much older. Her light mood of the day vanished and with sudden insight she dreaded what was to come next.

CHAPTER 19

Sarah tried to keep herself calm, but it was difficult, seeing the anxiety registered on Jerry's face as he looked at her.

'Sarah, you remember Sergeant Johnson? He has asked to speak with us about an important matter.' His glance moved over to Peter. 'This affects you, Peter. I gather that some of what he has to say may not prove easy listening.' He looked around the room. 'If anyone feels it's not their concern and wishes to leave us for a while, that's fine.'

There was a moment's silence and then Rob stood and moved over to Peter, placing a hand on his shoulder. For once he radiated the mature, assured young man he was underneath all his good-natured fooling around.

'We've been with Peter all these years and I, for one, don't intend to stop now.' He looked around the room, defying anyone to contradict him. No one did and no one moved.

Jerry glanced again at his wife, and smiled at her. 'You told me a while ago you thought we were lucky with our family. You were right.'

He turned to their visitor. 'Well, Sergeant, you'd better take a seat. We appear to be ready to hear what you have to say.'

Sarah watched as their visitor gazed around the room, seeming to study each person. He stiffened when his eyes lighted on Luigi

Gandoni, and gave a slight shake of his head. He took a few moments longer in his perusal of Peter. He appeared to be weighing him up. Then his eyes came back to Sarah.

'I should be telling you just part of the information I have, but I believe that you need, and deserve, to know it all; even my own failings of errors and inaction. As to this, all I can offer you is my sincere apology and hope that you will be able to forgive me.'

Sarah smiled at him. 'I'm sure when you tell us your news we'll understand.' Turning to her daughter she said, 'I think we'd better have the coffee replenished, Amy, if you will.'

Turning back to Sergeant Johnson, Sarah thought he looked tired and defeated and on impulse moved to sit next to him, putting her arm across his shoulders. When everyone was again settled, with Peter sitting opposite, she squeezed his arm. 'Now, please tell us.'

'I've spoken with someone who admits to killing Alex and Catherine Hartman.'

The gasps of shock following this announcement rippled around the room. Sarah could feel tears pricking behind her eyes. She dared not look at Peter.

'Thank God! I just knew it had to be like that. Go on, Sergeant Johnson, please.'

He gave her a sad smile. 'Call me "Dougie". Catherine did. I now have to tell you, however, that the actual perpetrator will never be prosecuted. The person involved died from cancer the day after he confessed.'

Jerry broke the subsequent silence in the room.

'Suppose you start from the beginning.'

Sarah found herself half-listening while Dougie explained his meeting with this… this person. All these years, she had been so sure that the truth had not come out, but that it would one day. Even so, of late, she had been finding it hard to hold on to that faith. Now…!

She looked over at Peter. His face was set and still, his eyes riveted on Dougie Johnson. She longed to reach over to him, but dared not. When she returned her full attention to the man next to her, Dougie was still speaking, recounting the actual details of that awful night as this man Fowler had described them, his audience reacting in their own individual way, from stony-faced acceptance to shock and tears.

'The matter is now with my superiors for further action. I am hoping that the priest will verify my own statement. I am taking the view that it was an open discussion and not a proper confessional. The next thing would be to obtain a hearing where the initial inquest result could be amended.'

Peter spoke for the first time, his voice quiet. 'So my father's name will be cleared of murder?'

'That is what I will push for. I suggest you seek some expert legal advice, someone with experience.'

'I'm now a qualified lawyer. I'll sort that out.' Peter sounded firm and decisive, and his grey eyes looked focused and determined. 'This Johnny Clarke will need to be interviewed.'

'He will be, but he'll deny everything, of course. You know what he'll say in his defence: "Just the ramblings of a dying man with a grudge". He'll have his lawyers as well.'

Luigi spoke into the following silence. 'It's a pity that all this couldn't have been discovered years ago; perhaps with a bit more police work, Sergeant Johnson?' His voice had a distinct edge to it.

Dougie looked over at him. 'I understand your continuing dislike of me, Mr Gandoni, but if you hear me out you might then realise the position I found myself in. However, I repeat that it doesn't absolve me of all blame.'

Luigi gave a sigh. 'From what you've just told us, I gather this assassin confirms that the bribery accusation was faked.'

'I'm going to suggest that the old files are trawled to see if we can pick up those bank statements and other papers. I'm also going to ask if we can investigate which police officers might have been involved with the matter back then. After this length of time, some may already have left the force. I'll keep on it, though.

'To confirm Mr Gandoni's comments of a moment ago… Like him, at the time I thought the whole affair should have been better investigated. In my view the conclusions were based on obvious available evidence, and there were definite inconsistencies, in particular with relevance to the pathology.'

He looked around the room again, and returned his gaze to Peter.

'You need to know that at the time I was – how shall we say? – "discouraged" from making any more investigations myself without jeopardising my career and pension. This was made very clear to me. I was given the distinct impression that my superiors wanted everything concluded with as much speed as possible, and I'm ashamed to say that I went along with it. In all honesty, there wasn't much more I could do. However, I'm still hopeful that we'll turn up something, even after all this time.'

With an apologetic glance at Peter, Christa made an observation. 'This Fowler person mentioned that his boss received instructions from another to carry out these acts. Do we have any idea who that might be, and why?'

Sarah looked over at Luigi, and found him studying her with the same question in his eyes. Oh no… if her worst fears were realised, how on earth would Peter cope with news like that?

Dougie Johnson was silent for a few moments, fiddling with his coffee cup.

'I'm still undecided as to whether I should mention anything else to you which may, or may not, shed some light on the young lady's comment. My reluctance is due to the fact that there might be an element of danger involved to persons who become aware of the information.'

He looked round at them again, taking in their reactions to his statement.

'I know it sounds melodramatic, and I might be overstating the case after all these years, but I still have nightmares about it. This whole matter has wider implications than just something to do with your family.'

Rob, sitting on the other side of Dougie, touched his arm. 'If, as I think, you mean something to do with national security, then as a member of the armed forces I feel I should be made aware of the facts. I can then judge whether I need to take any further action.'

'Very laudable, young man, but we're not dealing with *Boy's Own* stuff here.' Dougie's voice was hard and stern. 'People have already died in order to suppress facts, and my inaction on the matter was prompted by the fear that either I or my family would go the same way.'

'Dougie,' Peter was staring at the other man, his voice calm and controlled. 'are you saying that my parents were murdered because of some national security problem?'

'In a roundabout way, yes.'

Again, the reaction in the room to this statement was electric.

Luigi spoke again. 'Sergeant Johnson, I myself am prepared to take the chance of hearing your other information, because I feel it is still relevant today and can, even now, affect people in this room. If the others here choose to do the same, then I think we should hear you out and then decide what is best to do.'

Dougie looked over at Peter again. 'I think it needs to be left to you, young man, to say whether you are prepared to hear more.'

Sarah watched as Peter closed his eyes for a moment. She saw Christa's hand slip into his. Then, squaring his shoulders, he opened his eyes again and stared straight ahead, looking at no one in particular.

'If what you have to say still affects my parents, I wish to know everything. And I mean everything.'

Dougie studied him for a moment longer, then nodded. He paused to collect his thoughts and then began by relating the initial contact with Judge Franklin, plus the intervention of Sir John Fraser and Francis.

Sarah could see the shock registering on Peter's face, but he was holding himself together.

'I'm afraid to say, Peter, that Judge Franklin didn't impress either Alex or I in his dealings with us, but in particular his attitude to your mother.

'When it became obvious that feelings were growing between Alex and Catherine, I am sure this didn't go unnoticed. When I later joined Alex in the wider investigations he was asked to pursue, I found out that he'd been warned to keep me in the dark about the real reason for our investigations; but knowing that good police work depends on sharing thoughts and views, Alex decided to tell me everything, although no one else knew that. Perhaps because no one thought I knew everything, that has kept me out of harm's way.'

He looked around the room and then back to Peter, who motioned for him to continue.

'We began to collect evidence which, on the face of it, appeared to suggest that Judge Franklin and others were using monies from various sources, some of which belonged in the Franklin family, to facilitate the instigation of activities designed to destabilise this country, through various means. I'm afraid there was even involvement with the Irish.

'Considering Alex and I were just a two-man team, without the use of today's computer technology, I think we managed to put together quite a good case. Alex presented it to Sir John, who was going to bring up the findings at a policy meeting, but he never had the chance.'

Dougie stopped and looked around his audience. 'That meeting was to be held the day after he was killed in a road accident. The same night that Alex and Catherine were killed.'

The atmosphere in the room was now one of silent shock, each person busy with their own reaction to what they had just heard.

Into this silence Peter spoke, his voice just a whisper. 'Someone else either knew or guessed what was about to be revealed, and wanted to stop it?'

Dougie nodded. 'This was always the trouble. Who was in the know? I gathered from Alex that this Mr Francis believed the whole set-up might even be stemming from someone in the Civil Service or government. I am certain that nothing of our investigation was known to others from a perusal of our files. We made sure that our papers were kept secure, by various means. Did Sir John let something slip? Fowler indicated that there were emergency last-minute instructions to deal with the road traffic incident and also to put the pre-planned operation at Fulham into effect that very night. My feeling is that someone in the Force at the time became aware that certain evidence had been obtained, and it needed to be covered up.

'My own warning not to meddle came from a Superintendent who I had not seen before, who claimed to be acting on orders from the then Assistant Commissioner. It was he who had given instructions for all our files to be taken away. There was nothing I could do to stop it. As far as I could see, there was no reason for them to be removed, unless someone was worried about what information they contained. It did cross my mind that maybe Mr Francis had instructed the removal, but somehow I just don't think so.'

'Well, you were right when you said that all this could sound melodramatic!' Jerry spoke for the first time. 'It's almost hard to believe. One thing surprises me, though. What's happened to this Mr Francis? You say you were never contacted. Why, as you say, didn't he arrange to take over your files?'

'I agree, and it's puzzled me. I didn't know how to contact him. I can't even be sure that Francis was his real name. I never heard from anyone.'

'Did something happen to him too?' Rob queried.

'I've no way of knowing. Perhaps he decided it was better to lie low. I myself requested a transfer out of Special Branch and back into the CID.' He paused for a moment, then sighed. 'I am now coming to the difficult part about my own actions, and once again I must offer my further sincere regrets.'

CHAPTER 20

At this point Sarah signalled Amy for more coffee. She looked around the room. Peter seemed to be lost in thought, staring down at his hands. Luigi, Jerry and Rob were still and silent. Glancing at Christa, she detected the sheen of tears on her face, much like her own. Dougie Johnson looked even more tired, but smiled at her when she touched his arm.

With the room quiet again, he cleared his throat and continued with the story.

'A week or two after the funerals, I was contacted by solicitors acting for Alex and Catherine. They told me that Alex had left a box in their safekeeping addressed to me, for if anything happened to him. I opened it and found…' he hesitated and looked around the room, 'copies of our files. Alex must have been copying all our evidence as he went along. He had also made sure before Sir John's meeting was supposed to be held that the copies were safe, and out of our office. No one had any idea of their existence, not even me. Alex insisted on carbon copies of anything we typed up and I thought he might be passing these on to this Mr Francis, but I was wrong. It appears he was also making handwritten notes of our other evidence.

'My problem was, what could I do with all this? I would have turned it over to Francis if he'd contacted me, but he didn't. Who else could I go to? The very person I chose might well have been part of the set-up, and even if they weren't, I was putting my neck out in advertising the fact that I held certain evidence and knew more than people thought. I admit I was afraid, pure and simple. I put the box in my attic, and left it there. I've felt a weight of guilt ever since.'

His voice began to break. 'I let Alex down. I let that little girl's murderer live out his life, and she had once trusted me. I can't undo all those wasted years, but I have now made up my mind to investigate further. I have contacted you in case anything happens to me, as I need someone else to know the truth; but not someone in the force. Again I say to you, this knowledge could bring with it danger. That's my dilemma, but I can't cope with it myself any more.' He leant back in his chair and closed his eyes, the lines of worry etched on his face.

As silence descended again, Sarah was sure that every person in the room felt the same way she did: as if they were in some sort of dreadful nightmare.

She was so lost in thought that it took a moment or two for her to register that Peter had risen to his feet. With a pale, set face and eyes bleak and hard as stone, he looked down at the man opposite him.

'Dougie, I'm prepared to help you. Come and see me as soon as you can with all your evidence and we'll go through it together, and I promise you I'll be with you every step of the way.' He looked around the room. 'I think I'll go downstairs now, if you will excuse me.'

Everyone watched as he walked out, closing the door behind him. No one spoke, but a moment or two later Christa left her seat and followed him.

Worrying whether she was doing the right thing, Christa went down the stairs to Peter's rooms. She could hear music playing. As she entered, she saw him standing at the window looking up into the evening sky. She hovered in the doorway, uncertain of his reaction. Would he rather be alone? He had made no acknowledgement of her presence.

'Am I intruding?'

Not turning from the window, Peter held out an arm to her.

She crossed the room and he folded her close. It was obvious that he must be reeling from all he had just heard, and every fibre of her being wanted to offer him any solace he needed. As they stood together, Christa became aware of the haunting melody playing in the background, the notes seeming to swirl around and fill the whole room with their sound.

'This is beautiful music, Peter.'

He sighed. 'It's from Rachmaninov's Second Symphony. According to Sarah, my father always loved his music. I inherited his vinyl collection, as well as his wristwatch and writing desk. I found I liked the music too, so I now have it on disc, and it's a kind of connection with him.'

Christa realised that, for the moment, Peter needed to speak about inconsequential things, while his mind dealt with the shattering revelations. Both silent again as they continued listening to the music, Christa's heart ached for him. What he had just been told must have shocked him to the core, and torn apart the supposed truths by which he had lived for so long. But he would still never know his parents.

As the notes died away, Peter looked down at her and spoke, the expression on his face confirming the anguish she could hear in his voice.

'Dear God, I've been such a fool, Christa. My father would be ashamed of me. How could I have been so blind? Over all these years, Lionel has let me believe all those lies, when he knew the truth all the time, because he instigated it. I can see now how I've been manipulated by him, steered into making choices without question just because I thought of him as family. Why didn't I query things more? Make my own decisions earlier than I have?'

He took his arm from around her and slumped down on his bed.

'I could never understand why Lionel wasn't keen on me working for the Ravens. I thought he would be pleased: they're a top, well-respected chambers. You see, Christa, it's him wanting to be in control again, making the choices. But why? To what end? Is it the money? Perhaps there's more for me to learn about this... mess. All I do know is that I now have a chance to do something to rectify matters, and I'm going to do it, no matter what happens. I owe it to my parents.' His voice started to break. 'Oh dear God, why did all this have to happen!'

Seeing the pain on his face, Christa moved over to sit beside him. Once more he folded her close and buried his face in her hair. She could feel as his body gave way to the tears, the outward sign of the rawness of his internal emotions. Her heart joined in with his sadness.

As she held Peter close, Christa could see how it had happened. The young, vulnerable boy befriended by his supposed true relative who appeared helpful and caring, but who, over the years, was drip-feeding the young mind with his own ideas. He must have tried to do the same with Catherine. Sarah had been right. The man was a kind of puppeteer, but like Peter she could not understand what he intended to gain by this influence.

When Peter seemed quieter, she spoke. 'I'll do everything I can to help you, Peter. We all will, I'm sure.'

For a moment longer he hugged her closer in silent thanks, then let her go, and disappeared into the bathroom. On his return she could see that he had himself under control, and was now brisk and efficient.

'I'm going to suggest to Dougie that we collect all the evidence he has and speak to my solicitor, Simon Kingsley, and also the Ravens about it. I trust them, and they'll be able to judge if the evidence is strong enough to bring it out into the open. I think we must take that chance.'

'I'm sure something can be done, Peter.'

To her ear his remarks seemed bright and animated, but she sensed underneath that he was still frustrated at the years of misguided infatuation.

She squeezed his arm. 'Would you like to run me home?'

He planted a quick kiss on her forehead. Smiling down at her, he murmured, 'Thank you. I would like that.'

*

Later that night, something woke Christa. Her head was on Peter's outstretched arm and she was curled into his side. She looked up at him and saw that he was awake, staring at the ceiling.

'What's the matter, Peter?'

'I'm sorry, did I wake you?'

'It's alright. Can't you sleep?'

He turned to face her, and, in an absentminded gesture, stroked her arm. 'I keep thinking about all I've heard. You know, one thing upsets me more than anything. Did my father know that my mother was dead before he got himself out onto the stairs? If he did, what was he feeling? Why didn't he stay with her?'

Christa looked into the pain-filled grey eyes, and wanted to cry. 'He wouldn't have known that it was all planned, and I suppose he thought it was more important to apprehend what he believed was an intruder and safeguard you, and his home.'

'If, as he thought, it was a burglar, he would have just taken stuff, not lives. It wasn't worth it.'

Christa took his hand from her arm and kissed his fingers. 'Perhaps if he knew about your mother he wanted to catch the person who had done it. Loving her as he did, he would have been beside himself. Then again, Peter, he might not have known anything. He could have been spared that, and then would never know. I prefer to think it was like that.'

Peter turned on to his back, staring once more at the ceiling. He sighed. 'Perhaps. I hope it was that way too. Maybe he didn't know, but I'll never be sure about that, and so many other things. Do you understand, Christa, just how much I would like to have the chance to talk to them now, as an adult? To know them as real people? They're like shadows... almost there, but just out of reach.'

Christa could hear the desperation in his voice.

'Then all the time I've been pandering to that... that bastard of a man, who created all this unhappiness! Messing around with other people's lives for some ideal of his own. And I thought he was so marvellous. It makes me look an idiot – which I am! I wish I'd taken more notice of the comments Sarah and Luigi made over the years about him. I thought they were just envious of the time he spent with me, and in a way I resented their attitude.'

'Without knowing all this other information, Peter, would you have listened to them or believed them? They must have been nervous about speaking out too much. It could have alienated them in your eyes and reduced their contact with you, pushing you more towards Franklin. I think he had all this weighed up from when you were a baby. He had practiced it all once before on your mother, don't forget. I think anyone in your position would have done the same. Why should you question his supposed helpfulness?

'What worries me is what he would do if he ever found out you knew about him. If Sergeant Johnson is right, awful things happen to people who cross him.' She clutched his arm. 'I'm frightened, Peter.'

He turned her head up to him and stroked her cheek.

'Don't worry, Christa. It's up to me to make sure we don't alert him before we find more answers. Now we've been given the chance, we must finish this thing once and for all.'

He bent his head and kissed her. 'Thank you for being here for me. It means more than I can say.' His smile was gentle as he stroked her cheek. 'Now, although I can think of other nicer things to do, we'd better try to get some sleep.'

Christa lay for some time listening to Peter's even breathing. She had realised from the beginning that his attitude to relationships was coloured by what he had been led to believe about his parents. He had been afraid of commitment which in the end might turn out to be in vain. Perhaps, with what he now knew to be the truth, he could start to see things in a different light. She was sure Peter felt something for her, but how deep did it go? One thing she was certain of: he needed her now more than ever, and she would support him in any way she could.

CHAPTER 21

Sarah sat in the hospital canteen enjoying a last cup of tea before returning to her afternoon clinic. She was reflecting on the last few days, from the momentous news brought to them by Dougie, to the events still happening.

When Peter and Christa had left the room that afternoon, Luigi told Dougie what Alex had revealed to him about Lionel Franklin and Catherine's young life.

'Alex has told me some of what you say, Mr Gandoni, and it seems obvious that some of the monies being used by Franklin was Catherine's inheritance – now Peter's.' With what seemed like reluctance, he went on, 'Alex also had thoughts about Franklin's possible involvement with the death of Catherine's parents. He had the feeling that it, too, was no accident. We were going to try to investigate.'

This information shook everyone. To think of someone planning Catherine's death was bad enough, but to contemplate that this sort of thing had happened before was something else.

When it seemed that Peter would not be returning, Dougie made to leave.

'I'm sorry to have brought you all such distressing news, but thank you for listening to me.' He looked at Sarah. 'I'll bring my papers along one evening during the week, maybe Wednesday. Anything different, and I'll ring you.'

Luigi stood and shook hands with him. 'I apologise for my previous attitude towards you. I think, for Peter's sake, that there needs to be another person involved to give him moral support, and I would like to join you and Peter if you have no objection.'

Dougie smiled at him. 'Thank you, Mr Gandoni. I would be pleased to have you with us.'

*

On the Monday morning, Sarah noticed that her car was missing. She assumed Peter had taken Christa home as usual, and not returned. It was her rest day and she did not intend to go out, but it was unlike Peter to keep the vehicle without a word. Before long, however, she heard the sound of car tyres crunching on the driveway. She expected him to go straight to his rooms and was surprised when he came into the kitchen. He would know that she could not fail to realise where he had been for the night, but even if he anticipated any comment from her, she decided she would make none.

She expected him to be subdued and shattered by the revelations of the day before, but she noted with amazement that there was none of this. He was looking confident and assured, as if he had thrown off a cloak hiding the real person. With this new attitude, the glint in his grey eyes and the hint of stubble on his face, Sarah thought he looked lean and dangerous, awakening fond reminders of his father.

'Sorry I took the car without asking, Sarah. I drove Christa home last night, and didn't want to come and tell you before we left, not with everyone still there. I'll get changed and then I'm off to work. Did Dougie make any arrangements with you?'

'He and Luigi will come here on Wednesday evening, if that's OK with you.'

'Yes, fine. I want to get on with it. I'll contact Simon Kingsley today and fix an appointment to see him on Friday, if he can make it.'

He had turned to leave, but then came back and wrapped his arms around her.

'I'm glad I belong to this family.' He kissed her on the cheek and left.

Sarah was certain that whatever happened in the end, some good had already come from these last few weeks.

*

Luigi had been toying with the idea of mentioning his news from Canada, but after a discussion with Christa it was decided to wait. Michael Hartman had replied to his letter, saying that he too had been thinking of trying to re-establish contact. He apologised to his old friend for the break. He had considered that when he knew Alex was doing well there was no reason to seek news, and anyway delivery of mail was pretty haphazard where he intended going. Luigi in his letter said that he had been assisted by a friend in Canada in finding his address. Michael's sole comment on this was to mention a visit from a journalist for an article, and that he had wondered whether there was another reason behind the contact. Luigi smiled at this. He would be amazed if he knew the truth. At least it proved that his friend was still as sharp-witted as ever.

Michael was shocked to hear of Maria's death, but was glad that Luigi was gaining comfort from his son and grandchildren. He said that he himself had never remarried, and then made the heart-stopping remark that Alex could be a grandfather himself by now. Luigi wanted to write back and tell him the whole story, but on reflection thought that perhaps now was not the time.

*

Dougie arrived as arranged on the Wednesday evening. Luigi was already with Peter and, like Sarah, was amazed at the change in him. Had he at last cast off the shadow of Lionel Franklin, to emerge as his true self, rather like his mother had done? He judged that Peter would need all this new confidence in the weeks to come.

The box of papers was soon sorted out, and the three men sat down to sift through the information they contained. Dougie explained the line of reasoning that he and Alex had developed in looking for information, and Luigi could see that Peter was impressed by the astuteness of Alex's thought processes. He began to appreciate the amount of work the two men must have done to amass all this evidence.

'One of the key moments,' Dougie told them, 'was when Alex realised that the troubled company he became aware of might well fit the pattern we were looking for.'

'You see, Luigi,' Peter explained to him, 'how certain events could only have happened with inside influence?'

They then studied the subsequent information obtained on that case and several other similar instances of firms in trouble. In one, the link was made to a man who had been in Court, and his hearing had been presided over by Judge Franklin.

Peter made particular note of this. 'Franklin was always giving me advice to take notice of people in Court. Now I know what he meant: establish a connection with people known to be in trouble, and prey on their misfortune by using that knowledge to your advantage. No doubt that's why he was so keen for me to pursue that particular branch of the law. It would give a continuing supply of people who could be used – like me. But no longer!' The last few words were uttered in a firm voice, full of resolve.

Luigi patted Peter's hand. He had noticed the change to his normal form of address for Franklin, betraying his innermost feelings, and hoped that he would be able to remain calm and focused.

Dougie went on to explain their other various lines of enquiry. 'The Ardrossan episode was pivotal. The events there were conclusive, and the best bet yet for tying everyone in, including the Irish connection. The company information we found as to Kelly's benefactors was also crucial.'

'I'm going to see Simon Kingsley on Friday,' Peter informed them, 'and I'm taking all this stuff with me. I want his take on the legal side of the whole thing. I'm going to suggest that we bring in the Ravens for guidance on the bigger picture.'

'I think this is something that needs to be dealt with as fast as possible, Peter,' cautioned Dougie. 'If Clarke is called in to be interviewed about the murders, any others involved on the fringes are going to hear about it and start reacting to cover their tracks. We want to keep the element of surprise. Also, I'm still concerned about who might still be involved within the force itself. If word gets about that we're bringing people in for questioning, they'll be on the alert.'

'I take your point, Dougie. I'll impress that on Simon. Christa has offered to have a look at back copies of newspapers to see if fresh eyes can pick up anything else. She's a great girl.'

For the first time that evening the other two noticed a smile lighten the serious young face. Luigi regretted having to make his next statement, and spoil that small moment of pleasure.

'I have been thinking that you will have to keep to your usual pattern of visiting Franklin, although I'm sure at the moment it's the last thing you want to do. He, of all people, mustn't be alerted.'

Peter looked from Luigi to Dougie. 'I know. I've thought about that too. I'm not sure how I can carry it off at the moment, but I'll have to try.'

Dougie nodded in agreement. 'That's another reason for moving all this on as fast as we can. He's canny, he picks things up. You'll have to be on your guard, Peter.'

Luigi considered that Dougie's warning was not overstating the situation.

'Have you any idea when Clarke might be interviewed, Dougie?' questioned Peter.

'It's not in my hands, I'm afraid. As far as my superiors are concerned we're just opening up an old case, and there might not be so much urgency attributed to it, however much we might want the opposite.'

'It will buy us a bit more time to see what we have and where we can take it in a legal sense, I suppose.'

Dougie reached for his coat and prepared to leave. 'I'll keep in touch. I must say I feel a lot better now something's being done. I feel more like a detective again.' With an embarrassed smile, he left.

Peter and Luigi looked at each other.

'All this was a heavy weight on his mind, Peter.'

'It's enough to make you think you're going crazy – wondering who you can trust. Jerry was right: at times it all sounds unbelievable, until you remember some of the cold, hard facts.'

Luigi accepted the offer of another coffee and they sat together at the table. He sensed Peter had something on his mind.

'Tell me about my parents, Luigi,' Peter said. 'Tell me all you know about them; as people, I mean. I know the big story, but I don't know the… little things, the feelings.'

They sat together for several hours and Luigi's emotions began to overwhelm him as he recalled the young couple and their interaction with each other. He sensed that Peter needed, now more than ever, to know them as real people; and this was borne out by his comment just as Luigi was preparing to leave.

'I so wish I'd known them both, Luigi. Now this has happened, I don't regard Lionel Franklin as family any more, so I've no one else.' He forestalled Luigi's immediate denial. 'Yes, I know I have another special family that cares for me, and I'll always be grateful for that… but do you understand, Luigi if I say that it's not quite the same?'

Luigi almost blurted out his news, but that would not help just yet. At the moment, Peter's emotions were too ravaged to accept further revelations; and as yet, Michael was an unknown quantity. No, for the moment Luigi considered he would keep his own counsel.

'I understand, Peter, but at the moment you have to be stronger than you have ever been. If we are to get justice for all those involved, you of all people must keep calm and reasoned. Alex has given you the tools with which to carry on his fight, and he would want you to do all in your power to avenge his beloved Catherine and the robbing of their lives with you. Do you understand?'

'I understand Luigi, and I'll make him proud of me.'

Luigi patted the young man on the back. 'I'm sure you will, Peter.'

*

With a rather thoughtful frown, Lionel Franklin put down the phone and started to make some notes. He had just been informed that Clarke's former expert had died, and there was a rumour he had been arrested by the police the previous day. Clarke's man had never been implicated in any activities over the years, so what were police interested in? Had he decided to give away some information just before his death?

Although patchy, Franklin had managed to keep some sort of useful presence available to him in the Met over the years. The effort to promote Rankin to the top spot had not worked out to their advantage, but he had cultivated other outlets, and now it was time to call in some of those favours. He had to know what the police were interested in, and whether any incriminating details had been passed on.

He would make some phone calls from the lobby tonight.

CHAPTER 22

Peter's meeting with Simon Kingsley was long and difficult. He realised that to a dispassionate outsider much of his story would appear melodramatic, but Kingsley's immediate reaction was still disappointing. However, Peter was determined, and continued to press his point until Kingsley agreed to take the papers home with him for the weekend and read through them. He promised Peter some sort of answer on Monday.

'To be honest with you, Peter, I did have some misgivings about your parent's affairs in relation to your mother's inheritance, the terms of the Wills that were made, and then being asked to retain your father's possessions for safe-keeping. So much so, in fact, that I put a stop on any of the firm's papers dealing with your parents from being destroyed without my express permission. Whether or not that will prove to have been a good course of action will depend on what I determine we can do with any of your new evidence. After this length of time though, Peter, things will be difficult. You appreciate that, of course.'

'Yes, I know Simon, but something must be done. I can't let it all wither away to nothing after so much work and heartache.'

'If we can clear your father's name, that will be a major result. Anything else... well, we'll have to see, Peter.'

Feeling a little despondent, Peter headed for Christa's apartment. He needed her cheerful common sense to lift his spirits.

After listening to his news, her immediate reaction was not the one he had been expecting. 'I suppose his attitude isn't surprising. If you have a legal mind you can't go leaping about with excitement at every tall tale someone brings you, without looking at all the facts. You of all people should know that.'

'Yes, of course I know that.'

Realising, too late, the sharpness of his tone, he knew he was taking out his frustration on her when she had, after all, spoken the truth. He sighed and ran his hands through his hair. 'I'm sorry. I suppose I'm just too involved. I'll have to wait until Monday. It's going to be a long weekend.'

He noticed her studying him, her bright head on one side.

'What's the matter?'

'Is Rob home at the moment?'

Surprised by her question, Peter racked his brains. 'I think Sarah said this was his weekend at home. Why?'

'I'm going to suggest that tomorrow we make up a foursome. You, me, Rob and any girl he fancies – or Amy if she's free – do some shopping in town and then have a meal or go to a show. I think we could all do with cheering up. What do you think?'

Peter was by no means stupid. He knew why she was making the suggestion, and he felt a warm sense of pleasure inside him at her caring attitude.

'I think it's a splendid idea. I'll get off home now and see what I can arrange.'

*

Monday came sooner than Peter had anticipated. Sitting at his desk he thought over the last two days. The whole weekend had been a resounding success, and he found it difficult to remember when he'd enjoyed himself more. He was still smiling at some of Rob's antics when the phone on his desk rang.

It was Simon Kingsley. Peter's stomach churned as he waited to hear his verdict.

'I've read your papers and I think we ought to do as you suggested and arrange with your barrister contacts for a full discussion.'

Peter breathed a sigh of relief. He could sense from Simon's business-like tone that he was considering some sort of action.

'I'll get in touch with Jonathan or Anthony Raven right away.'

'Let me know when you've done that, and I'll get these papers to them. They will need to read through them, as I have done, before they can give us any useful indication of their thoughts.'

'I don't want them lost by any sloppy courier service, Simon.'

'No, I'm aware of that, Peter. I'll go round in person.'

'That's fine. I'll get onto it right now.'

Peter put the phone down and looked out of his window for a moment. Was something going to come from this at last? Calming his thoughts, he picked up the phone again.

He was lucky, and was put straight through to Jonathan Raven. He outlined in broad terms the reason for his call, and asked if they would be prepared to help him.

'Subject to a perusal of your papers, we'll see if there's anything we can do, Peter. Have them delivered, and we'll set up an initial meeting for, say, Wednesday afternoon, so that we can have a discussion as to what might, or might not, be possible.'

'Would it be a useful idea,' Peter suggested, 'if all interested parties could be present? I might see if, as well as Simon Kingsley, perhaps Dougie Johnson and maybe Luigi Gandoni could also attend? It would give everyone a chance to make their own comments.'

Jonathan Raven agreed. 'I'll leave you to arrange that, Peter, if you will.'

Now, thought Peter, that left him with the ticklish problem of trying to arrange time off work for himself.

*

The six men in the Ravens' conference room were enjoying a welcome break for coffee. It had been a good meeting so far, thought Peter. Both Jonathan and Anthony Raven had read through his father's paperwork, and Peter had the impression that they were treating the matter in a serious fashion.

Dougie's informal statements detailing the initial enquiries at Fulham, and his meeting with Fowler in the church, had also been perused. Jonathan Raven had questioned him further about his views on the investigation of the murders.

'I gather from Simon's notes, and your own statement, that you were unhappy with the way matters were conducted at the time, Sergeant Johnson.'

'Yes, indeed. I felt that everything was rushed, and certain of the conclusions drawn were, in my view, suspect. As we all know, bloodstains and fingerprints can be arranged if needs be; and according to Fowler's instructions, they were. My comments regarding the non-evaluation of Catherine's physical abilities, and Alex's apparent self-inflicted wound, in my view still stand. At the time, the supposed facts of what happened were assumed on the basis of the obvious evidence found, and as we are now aware, the whole incident was staged. My opinion continues to be that the evidence was laid out on a plate in such a way that it was accepted, and, of more importance, encouraged to be accepted, by all concerned without any further enquiry.'

Jonathan Raven queried, 'You are, therefore, suggesting that pressure was brought to bear on all parties concerned to have the matter disposed of as soon as possible, with the least investigation possible?'

'That is my view. As I have admitted, I was encouraged to join in with this idea, and to my eternal shame, I went along with it.'

'From what you've said, your reasoning on this was quite understandable at the time.'

Anthony Raven joined in the conversation then. 'You say that the instructions to remove your files came from the Acting Commissioner – Rankin, wasn't it? – carried out by a Superintendent who was unfamiliar to you? If my memory serves me correctly, the young Constable told you that a Superintendant had arrived at the Fulham property to take charge of the investigation there, and perhaps commandeered the bank statement evidence. If this person was perhaps one and the same, could we assume that his orders stemmed from Rankin? Perhaps we need to take a closer look at

Rankin himself, with particular relevance to the terms of your other investigation.'

Peter watched Dougie stare at the other man for a moment.

'Are you suggesting that Rankin was in on the whole thing, under orders, and used his position to short-circuit the investigation?'

Anthony Raven just shrugged his shoulders, and said nothing further.

'Holy...' Dougie stopped his comment just in time. 'This seems to get worse and worse.'

Just before the coffee break was called, the discussion touched on the box of papers. Kingsley still seemed sceptical, as if the whole idea was far-fetched, but again Peter had the feeling that the Ravens were more inclined to accept the possibilities.

Peter was looking down into his coffee cup, thinking about what had been discussed so far, when Luigi came over and sat next to him.

'Christa told me last night that Lionel Franklin has asked you to visit him.'

'Yes, he has. It had to happen some time. I'll have to put my playacting face on, although I'm not sure I have one.'

'Take some guidance from our two learned gentlemen about that. I have the feeling they are past masters at it. I've watched them so far and they don't give much away.'

Anthony Raven then called everyone back to the table.

'Both Jonathan and myself feel that strenuous effort must be made to overturn the inquest results in view of the new evidence, and we will liaise with Simon here and Sergeant Johnson with a view to achieving that. We feel it would be useful if enquiries could be ongoing to find these supposed forged bank statements, but also a review should be made, if possible, of Alex Hartman's finances in general so that the bribery allegations can be addressed.

'Sergeant Johnson, a question for you, please. If, as appears, the bullet wound to Alex Hartman's head was the shot from the murderer, but Hartman fired his own gun, where do you suppose that bullet went?'

Dougie thought for a moment, picturing the scene in his mind.

'From the trajectory, I would assume that it went into the wall near to the front door of the property. If it buried itself in the plaster it could even still be there now. Someone might have redecorated during the years, not taking any notice of a small hole.'

'Mmm. It just makes you wonder how easy it might be to make that discovery. One more string to our bow... Not that I'm suggesting anything, of course, you understand.' The innocent smile accompanying the words was explanation enough.

'It would indeed, Mr Raven,' said Dougie with an answering smile.

'Turning to your other matter, this Mr Francis intrigues me. Who is, or was, he and why did he drop out of sight? Alex Hartman told you no more about him than you have already been able to tell us, Sgt Johnson?'

'No. Nothing. Not even a physical description or where the office was that Alex visited. To put out a search for the name of "Francis" in the Civil Service employment records of the time would, I suggest, be a problem; and we can't be sure that Francis was his real name anyway. My view is that he was as frightened as I was, or that he was suspected and ended up as the others did. I just don't know where to go on that one.'

Luigi spoke into the following silence. 'Excuse me for interrupting, but I wondered if anyone working at the time for Sir John Fraser, like his secretary, might know if he ever contacted anyone by that name, or had any other clue?'

'Indeed, Mr Gandoni. A good point. It's possible that the secretary might well have retired by now, Sergeant Johnson?'

'I'll make some enquiries on that.' Dougie made a note.

Jonathan Raven addressed Peter. 'Lionel Franklin was very keen on you being tutored by an old friend at Cambridge, I understand, Peter.'

'Yes, a Professor Donaldson. They had studied together.'

'What was Donaldson like as a tutor?'

Peter was rather nonplussed at that question, and for a moment wondered how to answer it.

'I found him a bit brusque. He had some pretty dogmatic opinions about things; in fact, most things. As a group we had several heated arguments, not always about interpretation of the law, but politics as well. He appeared ultra left wing by persuasion, I would have said. I wasn't that interested. I was studying law, not politics. Why do you ask?'

'I just wondered who Franklin and Donaldson might themselves have been tutored by at college, and whether any of their fellow students, or the like, ever found their way into the Civil Service or government. This Francis person, as I understand it, mentioned to Alex Hartman that he thought the whole scheme might have emanated from someone close to political circles. He overheard part of a telephone conversation, I gather, but didn't let on who was involved.'

'That's as I understood it from Alex; and you've got a point there.' Dougie made another note and then looked over at Peter. 'I don't suppose that, from any talks with Franklin, you have any idea?'

'No, he hasn't said much about his own time at college.' Peter cleared his throat. 'I've been asked to go and see him. I'll have to, of course, although I'm not looking forward to it. I suppose I could try asking him a few discreet questions.'

'I think you might have to, Peter.'

Jonathan Raven smiled at him. 'If you want any advice on how to deal with it, just pretend you're someone else. Make believe you're in one of those Hitchcock-type court dramas and you're playing the lead role. I've no doubt your father had to have his poker face on during some of his investigations.'

Anthony Raven spoke then, also glancing at Peter. 'I think we have to discuss the question of funding. It seems to be the suggestion that monies due to your mother, and now you, Peter, have been misappropriated. It is also quite possible that other funds have gone the same way. I see Hartman had thoughts that monies from Catherine's mother might also be involved, still under her own name. If so, we must assume that when her estate was finalised not all funds were disclosed; and we might be looking at other serious irregularities. I admit that I always considered Lionel Franklin had

507

some eccentric ways about him, but I would never have believed this level of corruption.'

He turned to Simon Kingsley. 'You intimated that you had found it difficult to get information from the trustees of Catherine Hartman's fund. Who are the trustees?'

'They were Franklin, Geoffrey Villiers and Sir Gregory Hamilton. Hamilton died some time ago and I put myself forward as a new trustee but found that one had already been appointed, at Hamilton's request before he died. His son Duncan is the third trustee.'

'That little...'

CHAPTER 23

It was obvious that Dougie had managed to stop himself from uttering a profanity.

Anthony Raven looked over at him. 'You know of him, Sergeant Johnson?'

Peter sensed there was something behind this exchange. 'If you have anything to tell us, Dougie, go ahead.'

With an uncomfortable glance at Peter, Dougie outlined the episode with Duncan Hamilton at Richmond, and Alex's subsequent interview with Franklin about the matter. Peter listened with disbelief and began to wonder how much more there was for him to learn, and it wasn't long in coming.

'I have some knowledge of Alex in this respect.' Luigi's voice was quiet, and all eyes turned to him. 'Alex told me of an interview he had with Judge Franklin when they disclosed their marriage. I gather Franklin made some inappropriate remarks about Catherine, of a... sexual nature, and taunted Alex with suggestions that he had married her for her money. I'll be the first to admit that Alex had a temper, as well as pride in his integrity, and he was always vulnerable where Catherine was concerned. I think it was a deliberate act to goad him, and Alex ended up signing a letter of disclaimer regarding any benefit from the monies.'

Simon Kingsley looked at Luigi. 'I didn't see any draft of this, or a signed copy.'

'I understand Franklin produced a letter he had already prepared, and Alex signed it there and then, in anger.'

'Of all the stupid…! No wonder he was adamant that his Will was to be drawn up in a certain way. Why didn't he tell me then?'

Dougie smacked his forehead with his hand. 'I've just thought of something! Supposing, with Franklin's involvement with Clarke, as well as hitmen available to him, he also had forgers of various kinds. Now, think of this: if Alex signed a paper which was retained by Franklin it's just possible that his original signature was then forged, which might explain the other bank account.' He looked around the room for confirmation of his idea.

Jonathan Raven was the first to speak. 'It's an interesting theory, Sergeant.'

He then looked down at his watch. 'I think, for a first meeting, that we have achieved quite a lot. We know where we need to look for further evidence. In light of Sergeant Johnson's warning, I think it would be as well if we all remembered that there could be much more to all this than we know at the moment, and we should take care in our investigations.'

He looked around the room, and received nods from all present.

'It would be much simpler if Lionel Franklin could be encouraged to tell us what he knows. It might even have to come to that. I'm still unclear as to his basic motives. However, for now I suggest we dig around some more and perhaps have another meeting next week, and I'll liaise with you all on that.'

As everyone started to leave the room, Luigi came and placed his arm around Peter's shoulder. 'I'm sorry you're hearing all this sort of thing, my boy. It won't help when you see Franklin, will it.'

Peter sighed. 'No. I think I'll take Jonathan's point about pretending to be someone else. However, what I've heard tonight has made me even more resolved, and I must deal with it.'

Luigi saw the determination in the grey eyes, and gave him a pat on the back. 'Good boy. All I would counsel is not to underestimate

Franklin. I warned Alex about him, and if I'd been aware of his actual investigation I'd have been even more troubled. He's clever, and you will need to be on your guard.'

*

As the evening of Peter's visit to Franklin arrived, he still had no idea how he could keep himself from blurting out his knowledge of the man's actions. However, he knew that somehow he must hold everything back and try to behave in his normal way. He had given some thought to the questions he would try to ask. It was obvious that he would have to lie, and he hoped he could do so well enough to convince Franklin.

When he arrived at the Club, Franklin appeared to be in good spirits, a little more so than Peter had ever seen him. Stamping down on the immediate desire to confront this man with his knowledge about the past, he accepted a glass of whisky and concentrated hard on what he had to do. He tried to turn the conversation round to college days, speaking about his own memories of the evenings with Donaldson and others.

'Oh yes, I remember many a fascinating evening myself. Those were interesting times, when you had serious discussions with like minds.' Franklin was sitting back in his chair staring into the fire, appearing relaxed, with a refilled whisky glass. 'One of the Dons during my time, Helsenburgh, was quite a hothead. He was a good speaker: used to impress us. Richard was in our group, then, until he began to change his views.' He went silent.

Peter tried to keep the thread of the conversation going. 'I've kept in touch with one or two of my class. Do you still see any of the people you were at college with? Did you all go on to do well in careers?'

'Well, you know Brian Donaldson, of course. He wanted to stay on in academia. He didn't fancy the rough and tumble of the outside world. Aubrey Potter went into the Civil Service, like Richard. I'm in touch with him still. He's retired now, although he's called back from time to time to assist with committees and the like.'

He seemed to come out of his mood of reminiscence. 'How's the job going?'

The change of topic threw Peter's concentration, and he had to work hard to keep the game going.

'I'm enjoying it. I'm getting to know plenty of people in the corporate world, both here and abroad. I already have lines of communication to some very influential people. It could do me some good in the future, in a personal way, if you know what I mean.' Untrue, of course, but it sounded good, he thought.

'Oh yes, Peter, I do indeed know what you mean. Cultivate them. Find out what they're like on a personal level. If you can get to know what makes someone tick, any weaknesses, you can work out ways it might benefit you.'

'This is the same sort of thing you used to tell me to watch out for in Court? Keep an eye on the people involved?'

'Yes. I did just that, and it's proved very useful. In your new situation I think you could find this working for you… if you wanted it to.'

Peter found himself being watched by pale blue eyes, and with what he now knew about this man, wondered what was going on behind that gaze. Was Franklin suspicious of his questioning, or was it his own imagination? He made himself keep his face relaxed, and sipped at his whisky. He had never liked the stuff, but hoped it created the right sort of atmosphere.

'Do you still see that girl?'

Again, the sudden change of topic.

'Not as much. She's involved with her own crowd now. There'll be someone else.'

'Choose well, Peter. Remember, this can bring you more influence. The old adage of marrying for money or position still has its place in modern times. You're a nice enough looking boy, well brought up, you shouldn't have much trouble. Another reason to use your contacts.'

'Yes, you could well be right Lionel. As usual.' A quick smile over his whisky glass accompanied this remark.

Steady, he chided himself. He was starting to play-act too much.

Perhaps it was the whisky. His grip on the glass tightened. He must be careful not to overdo it. The truth was that he was beginning to feel strained and tired, trying to keep up the act when all he wanted to do was let all his true feelings pour out. It was perhaps time for him to go.

'Well, I think I'd better be on my way now. Thanks for the chat, Lionel. See you again soon eh?'

*

Lionel Franklin stared into the heart of the fire, thinking hard. Was it his imagination or had the boy been overeager in his company tonight? It was unusual for him to drink whisky too. Perhaps he was becoming influenced by some of his new contacts! Then there was the out-of-character questioning. Just innocent interest, or was there something more behind it? Also, surprising news about the girl: he had seemed keen, and Peter had never struck him as the sort of person who would flit from one woman to another. As she was still around, it appeared she had not reacted as hoped to her mugging episode. Pity! He would have to watch that situation.

He thought again about the police and Clarke's man. Yes, he must find out more about that. With slow steps he made his way down to the lobby phone.

*

Peter found Sarah waiting for him when he arrived back home.

'Sorry to have let myself into your sanctuary, but I thought you might be feeling peckish. You can come up to the kitchen and I'll fix you something if you like.'

'That's OK, Sarah, but I'll get to bed, I think. I'm a bit tired. I've also had a glass of whisky which hasn't helped.'

He sensed that Sarah was anxious about his reaction to tonight's meeting and wanted to talk, but first he needed to calm himself and sort out in his mind everything he had heard. He could still feel the tension in him. As he watched Sarah fiddling with her hair, he had the curious impression there was something else on her mind.

'I'll leave you to it, then.'

She turned to go and then appeared to make a decision. She pulled out an envelope from her skirt pocket and handed it to him.

'As well as the box Alex left with Simon Kingsley, there was a letter addressed to me. In it, Alex asked me to give you this envelope when I thought the moment was right. I don't know if this is the right moment, and I don't know what's in the letter, but I think it's about time for you to have it. Goodnight, Peter.'

Left on his own, Peter looked at the envelope. He recognised his father's handwriting. It was addressed 'To my dear Peter'. Sitting down on his bed he opened the envelope and drew out the contents. It appeared to be two pages of a hand written letter. What else was he now about to learn? He cleared his mind and began to read.

My dear son,

You will never know how much pleasure just using that phrase gives me. If you are reading this letter then you will know that I have not been able to be with you in your life so far. This does not mean that I do not love you; in fact, quite the opposite. It is for the love of you, and your mother, that I have taken the decision to remove myself from your lives.

I do not know whether your mother will inform you about the circumstances for my leaving you; that is entirely a matter for her. But I wanted you to know as much as I can tell you of my reasons.

I love your mother with all my heart, and always will. She has brought more happiness into my life than I had ever known before we met. I looked forward to living the rest of our lives together and enjoying shared experiences with you. Unfortunately she became aware of certain actions I was forced to take in the course of my work which caused her much unhappiness and distress; a fear I always had, but one that I hoped we could overcome. This has not proved possible, and as I have no wish to cause any further pain to her I felt it was better to leave and let her live in peace. My decision was not taken lightly. It caused me great sorrow to

know that I would no longer be part of her life, and to enjoy
seeing you grow.

Your mother loves you very much and I ask you to take care
of her, as I always tried to do. I know that she will bring you up
with the right attitude in life, and for my part I would urge you
to try to be the best you can in anything you undertake. Sarah
McIntyre and Luigi Gandoni will also give you good counsel if
you require guidance.

Please do not think too badly of my decision. It was meant
for the best. Where ever I am I will be thinking of you both, and
you will forever have all my love.

I wish you luck and happiness in your life.
Your loving father, always,
Alex

Peter read the letter again and again, with tears running down his cheeks. As he refolded the pages and put them back in the envelope he wondered at the agonising his father must have gone through worrying all the time whether his investigations might drive him away from his family.

Sitting there alone, he whispered into the quiet of the room. 'I'm sure it would never have happened, Father, but you weren't to know that. I didn't get the chance to take care of either of you, but I hope you're proud of me, and I'll try to be worthy of you. I'm sure you're both together again, and I will do all in my power to right all the wrongs against you. I love you both.'

With even stronger resolve in his heart, he made ready for bed.

CHAPTER 24

Dougie Johnson was informed that Johnny Clarke was going to be brought in for questioning within days. He would have liked to be involved, but on reflection, thought it better to keep out of it. The less direct contact the better.

He had tracked down Sir John Fraser's secretary who, though nearing retirement age, still worked part-time for the force. Using a round-about reason for his enquiry he asked her what she recalled of the time leading up to the Commissioner's death. After some thought, she remembered Alex Hartman's visits to see Sir John. She always enjoyed seeing him, she said, as he was such a nice-looking, polite man. She also remembered Assistant Commissioner Rankin calling to see Sir John that particular evening. She had the feeling that there was some sort of celebration as she remembered seeing a bottle of some description. She also remembered Rankin, as he left, asking her if Sir John had any engagements for that evening as he thought he looked a little tired. She had told him of Sir John's charity engagement.

She promised Dougie that she would give some thought as to any names of contacts Sir John might have made round about this time. He impressed upon her the confidentiality of his enquiry and, with a smile, she assured him of her understanding.

He was still working on tracing the young constable at the Fulham property and also the unknown Superintendent Fox. He had contacted the now retired Superintendent Charles who confirmed that no approach was made through him for permission to remove their investigation files, and that although he had not been involved, it would have been normal for him to have passed on instructions to Dougie for organising the removal rather than a stranger. He promised to give some thought as to other Superintendents known to him on the force at that time. Dougie was sure he suspected something about these enquiries, but he had made no comment.

He had turned his mind to Anthony Raven's idea of finding the bullet from Alex's gun. With no real plan he had driven out to the Fulham property, trying to work out some vague idea of how to gain entry. He was trying to avoid, if he could, the necessity for obtaining a proper search warrant, as the fewer people who knew about these investigations, the better. He was surprised to see a For Sale board outside the house. On enquiry he found that the property had just been sold and renovation works were being undertaken. This might be the right time to try to get inside. He would contact Peter Hartman, and see if they could use some pretext or other.

He wondered how the boy had fared with his visit to Franklin. It was uncanny, he mused, just how much there was about Peter that conjured up his parents. How did Franklin deal with it? Was there any remorse? He doubted it.

*

Sarah had passed on a message to Peter when he arrived home from work that Dougie was calling round at any moment, and in fact he arrived a few minutes afterwards.

As the three sat down at the kitchen table with a pot of tea, Dougie was trying to convince a sceptical Peter that they would be able to gain access to the property by saying that they were local amateur crime writers keen to view the scene of a past incident. Peter was not too sure at all. It sounded pretty thin as far as an excuse went.

'Why don't you just flash them your card or something? After all, they're just workmen, they're not going to live there, and even if they were I'm sure neighbours would at some time talk about past events.'

'I'd prefer them not to think the police were snooping around. They might be more inclined to mention it to someone.'

Peter shrugged. 'We can try your way, I suppose. It sounds a bit illegal to me.'

Dougie grinned at him. 'It probably is, but I'm beyond all that now.'

He turned to Sarah. 'Do you know what happened to Alex's paperwork in the house when it was cleared?'

'Yes, it's all up in the attic. I keep thinking I ought to look through it sometime, but I never do.' She looked at Peter. 'Perhaps that's something we should tackle.'

'Would there be anything amongst it relating to Alex's finances, do you know?' continued Dougie.

Sarah smiled at him. 'Oh, I'm sure there is. Catherine was meticulous in keeping a note of all their housekeeping details. It used to amuse Alex. He said it would be easier for him to get money out of Fort Knox than his own bank account. I know that he once had some shares in a small company that did very well, which is how he bought the Porsche and rented a good-quality flat. I believe he said that the remainder bought Catherine's engagement ring. When he sold the Porsche to a friend of his, he had cash to buy the other car and also Catherine's earrings. He told me this when he asked me to keep the jewellery so that she wouldn't find it until Peter's christening.' She looked over at Peter with misty eyes. 'He was so proud, that day, of his beautiful wife and son.'

After reading his father's letter, Peter could well believe that to be true.

'I agree with Dougie, it might be a good idea if everything was sorted through and we could piece together some sort of picture of my father's finances and how he funded things. It might shed some light on this bank statement thing.'

'I think Amy's the best person to help in something like this, Peter. Shall I ask her to take a look?'

'That would be fine, Sarah.'

He turned to Dougie. 'Well, come on then, let's go and try our Sherlock Holmes disguises. Do we want a camera or anything?'

*

Dougie had already established that work at the Fulham property was being carried out during the evenings, and sure enough, as they turned into Church Road, there was a builder's van outside the property.

Peter had been back to the vicinity twice in his adult life: first with Sarah, who had shown him the grave in St Luke's churchyard; and then he had come back himself, for some strange reason, just before he took his final law exams. On each occasion he had felt a strange mixture of familiarity and connection, together with a tremendous sense of loss. He stood for a moment, looking at the house. This was the property which had meant so much to his parents. If things had been different, it could have been his home for many years while he grew up, and he could have had brothers or sisters and played with them in the garden. Now it was just a building, and someone else's at that.

The front door stood open and banging could be heard at the rear. Dougie called out, and after a moment a man appeared, covered in brick dust.

'I know this is going to sound strange to you, but my friend and I are local amateur crime writers. We understand that many years ago an incident happened in this house, and we were hoping to have a look around in this hallway area and do some reconstruction of the events, role play, measuring, that sort of thing. Do you have a problem with that?'

The workman looked at the two of them for a moment, a perplexed look on his face, then shrugged his shoulders. 'No problem of mine, there's nothing you can nick, anyway, is there.' He indicated the bare walls and stairs. He ambled back to the rear of the property.

Dougie winked at Peter and beckoned him inside.

'Go up to the bend in the stairs, Peter and hold your arm out

519

straight as if you were aiming a gun. I'll stand here near the front door where Fowler said he was.'

Peter did as he was told, although not liking the idea. He was here where it had all happened, and he could sense the ghosts. Standing on the stairs, pretending with an imaginary gun, was far too close to reality.

'Right. Now, Peter, take a rough look along your arm. What part of the wall are you aiming at?'

After a moment of concentration Peter fixed on an area at the intersection of the internal and external walls about three feet up from the skirting board, and guided Dougie to the spot.

'Right, Peter, let's have a look. It's been wallpapered a couple of times by the look of it.' He scraped and prodded around the area for a good five minutes, widening his search all the time. Then he turned to Peter with a smile. 'See what I see?'

Peter crouched down and looked at the spot on the wall indicated by Dougie. There was a small depression in the bare plaster, and running his fingers over it he could feel there was something at the centre.

'See if you can ease it out with this, Peter.'

Dougie handed over a penknife and as he bent to the wall, cautioned him, 'Work to get the plaster away, and try not to touch the metal. We need all the evidence we can get, still intact.'

After a few moments of careful prodding around, with a grunt of satisfaction Peter eased out a small piece of metal. He handed it to Dougie.

'Bingo! You see what I mean, Peter? It's been here all the time. If the whole event had been explored a bit more at the time, it would have been discovered then. We'll have this checked out, but I'm sure we've found what we're looking for. We'd better do some measuring and take some photographs.'

After another twenty minutes they had all they needed. Dougie called out to the workman that they were just leaving, and received a shout in reply.

As they left, Peter turned back to look at the house. For so many years it had kept its secret safe, just waiting for him to come back and find it. He shook his head in anger. He was just being fanciful now, but he said a small, silent 'thank-you' anyway.

Dougie dropped him back home. Another meeting with the Ravens had been fixed for Friday evening, and he said he hoped to have some further information to report then.

Peter asked to borrow Sarah's car. He needed to see Christa.

*

As Peter arrived, Christa had just finished one of her regular telephone calls with her father. She had made a point of not telling him of her mugging, knowing full well that he would have demanded she return home. She was missing him, however. Now, much to her disappointment, he had told her that his anticipated visit to the UK would have to be postponed. For once, she found it hard to be her usual positive self.

She listened while Peter told her about his father's letter.

'The poor man must have been so worried. It's nice for you to have such a personal memento of him, though. I'd like to read it some day, if you'd let me.'

'Of course I will.'

Peter then went on to tell her of his visit to Franklin, and his worries about how his questioning might have been received. He finished by telling her of tonight's developments at the house.

She gave a heavy sigh. 'There seems to be so much evidence to find, Peter. We're amassing bits and pieces, but is it getting us anywhere?'

They were sitting together on the settee and Peter regarded her, his grey eyes now rather sombre. She guessed he had sensed her mood, and she found herself drawn into his arms with her head against his shoulder. He placed a soft kiss on her forehead.

'I know, Christa. But everything we do find is a step in the right direction. What Dougie and I have discovered tonight is a major step, and above all else I want my father's name to be cleared. This other business might have to be handed over to professional agencies to unravel.' He put his chin down onto her hair. 'You can see what my

521

father thought he was up against in gathering evidence with his small resources.'

He was quiet for a moment.

'I don't suppose you've had time to search for anything?'

It had not been a productive search so far with the limited time available to her, but she offered one report which had caught her eye.

'One thing I came across was that late in 1975 the Parliamentary offices of the Labour Party were broken into and drawers were rifled through. MI5 became involved. There was no follow-up report. It might be something – or nothing.'

'Mmm. It's difficult to say, I agree. Still, we'll add it to the pile. I want to find out a bit more about this Aubrey Potter who Franklin mentioned. If he went into the Civil Service he might tie in with this Francis person.'

Christa twisted around in his arms and looked up at him. 'Peter, how concerned are you about Franklin's reaction to your questions? I agree with Luigi. I don't trust him an inch.'

'He didn't appear to be curious. I tried to be as casual as I could. I found it more difficult than I thought to be there with him, Christa. For so many years I've believed the story as told, and now everything's been stood on its head. Watching him sitting there, I kept thinking about the things I had heard, and wondered how he could be so calm, talking with me over a glass of whisky, but knowing the truth all the time.'

'The crime writer on my Canadian paper said that some criminals justify their actions to themselves and don't have a conscience. It was never their fault they were doing what they did; someone else did an act against them which started it all off. They were the victims. He also said they enjoyed the power of manipulating people. It was a game they played; because they could.'

'I'll bet he's not far off. I wonder what Franklin's tipping point was? I'm beginning to think that Jonathan Raven's right: we need Franklin to tell us himself.'

'He would never admit to anything.'

'You never know. He might have such a high opinion of himself that he would feel flattered he was being considered as a master criminal.'

Christa took hold of Peter's hand. 'Please be careful. I don't like the man. I'm afraid.'

Without warning, Peter stood up. She watched in puzzlement as he turned on the radio and found some dance music. With a slight smile he came back towards her. As all those weeks ago at the hotel, in his navy blue suit and wavy dark brown hair curling on his collar, she thought what an attractive man he was. He gathered her into his arms, and began to dance in time to the soft, slow rhythm.

As his mouth covered hers she heard him whisper, 'Don't worry, sweet Christa, there's nothing to be afraid of.'

*

In a car parked in the street below, a man lit his third cigarette, looked at his watch and made another note. 'Subject visited girl again. Still there at 10.30.'

CHAPTER 25

Luigi finished his telephone conversation. It had been on his mind for days before he came to a final decision. Michael Hartman should know what was happening. Luigi was worried for Peter. He was fearful of Franklin and his sinister power, and if Peter, without being aware of it, alerted him to any investigation, Luigi was certain he would not hesitate to act.

Michael Hartman had missed out on Alex's life. He should not miss out on another. Although Luigi would have preferred to speak to Michael face to face, or even written of the past events in a letter, something had to be done now; therefore his telephone call had to be made.

His friend listened to Luigi's story in total silence. For one moment after Luigi had finished speaking, as the silence continued, Luigi wondered if Michael had broken the call. Then he heard a long, heavy sigh.

'Why did I have the feeling that something had happened? All that time ago, I thought it better to leave Alex to his own resources rather than taint his life with my wrongdoings. I sensed he had enough inner strength to make something of himself, given half a chance, and it sounds as though he did. I'm glad he found a good wife. If I'd done so, things might have been different.

'What matters now is Peter. You are right, Luigi, my old friend, we must do what we can to help the boy. I have no doubt that your feelings about this Franklin person are not unfounded. He can still cause another tragedy to happen. I must come over. I'll have to raise the cash this end—'

'Michael,' interrupted Luigi, 'I've more than enough to live on in comfort. We'll sort out the cost between us. Just come. Let me know when you can get over. Make it soon, my friend.'

*

The Ravens' chambers were quiet, and almost eerie, at this time of night. Simon Kingsley, because of other commitments, was absent from the meeting. Peter had just reported on the financial information uncovered by Amy in working through his parents' papers. He passed over her handwritten statement which, as he said, showed everything in order and accounted for in some detail, and no obvious financial problems with their lifestyle. Nothing indicated the existence of another bank account or other monies.

He then went on to recount his visit to Franklin.

'I'm certain I've seen books written by someone called Helsenburgh. Heavy political doctrines, far left wing, if I remember.' Anthony Raven rubbed his chin. 'I'll look into it. As you say, Peter, we'd better investigate this Aubrey Potter. I might make some innocent enquiries at my Club tonight.'

He looked at the younger man. 'Do you think you got away with it?'

'I'm not sure. Lying isn't my best talent. He didn't appear to react. He seemed more keen on drinking; more than I've seen him do before.'

Anthony turned his gaze on Dougie. 'Well, Sergeant, anything to report your end?'

Dougie filled them in on his interviews with Sir John's secretary and Superintendent Charles, and promised to report back as soon as any further information came to hand.

Peter looked over at Dougie. 'Just a thought, but Rankin looks a good bet as the chosen candidate of Franklin's group for the vacant Met Commissioner's post. How did it work out in the end?'

'He was in charge on a temporary basis, but the permanent job was offered elsewhere. I'm told he went abroad, and I imagine we'll have to try to track him down. By the way, Clarke's being brought in for questioning. This will stir things up a bit. Might make people nervous.'

'All the more reason for us to keep on top of the matter,' Jonathan Raven commented.

Dougie looked around the room. 'I've had a thought. It must have been going back to the house the other night that jogged my memory of something Alex mentioned to me. I should have twigged it before. I remember him saying that Franklin had made a surprise visit to the Fulham property when Catherine was alone. She told him that her uncle appeared to wish for some sort of reconciliation. He brought a belated house-warming present with him; some sort of ornament, I believe. Young Peter was admired, and then he left.

'Alex was a little unsettled about all this because their address hadn't been disclosed to Franklin, and he mistrusted his motives. Catherine, as usual, was prepared to give him the benefit of the doubt. I'm just wondering if Alex's misgivings were quite correct. What was the ornament? The bronze figurine, by any chance? If you remember, Fowler was told just where to find his weapon. Also, Fowler said he'd been given a new key to let himself into the house. Maybe an imprint of the original was taken, and a copy made. Could Franklin have managed to do this on his visit? It's possible, if he was told how, and had the time.'

'Isn't this giving Franklin a more active role in events than normal?' queried Luigi.

'Indeed, but perhaps he thought this way he could cover himself in the light of any future events, which he knew very well would happen. He would appear as a genuine visitor trying to re-establish family relations. The good guy. I think he played this sort of game before with the death threat letter that brought Alex and I into the matter in the first place. We suspected there never was a threat, and he might have written the damn thing himself. He was trying to throw a smoke screen over his court case actions.

'Don't forget, his plan at Fulham didn't intend for Alex to be killed. He wanted Alex in prison for murder, and anticipated that he would then have almost total control of Peter, as an upstanding, respected family member. No doubt he allowed for the fact that Alex would protest his innocence, but what proof was there to back it up, with the evidence stacked against him, and Rankin in a position to block any further investigation? Francis, and whoever was in charge of him, might not have wanted or been able to show their hand. What Franklin didn't bargain for were the Wills. I bet that must have thrown him into a panic.'

Luigi spoke up. 'Both Sarah and I were unhappy about any involvement with Franklin as far as Peter was concerned, but we also had to do the best for him, and felt bound to accept Franklin's offer of financial and educational assistance.' He looked over at Peter, genuine regret etched on his face. 'I'm sorry, my boy.'

Peter gave him a fond look. 'Don't worry about it, Luigi. You were all doing your best for me at the time.'

He looked around the room. 'You know, I've been thinking, if Franklin still wants to keep control of any monies coming to me, something has to happen soon. I think you were right Jonathan when you indicated that I had been manoeuvred into losing my position in these chambers. He doesn't appear to like me making independent decisions. He hoped that I would fall back on his assistance again to find another position, and seemed surprised that once more I had done so by myself. The other night I went to great pains to try to convince him that through this new job I was making useful contacts for myself. He became quite upbeat about that, and encouraged me. Perhaps he now sees me as an avenue to other financial influences for him.'

'I think you're right, Peter. We might need to cultivate that idea in him. He might just trip himself up,' confirmed Jonathan Raven. 'Anything else, Sergeant?'

Dougie glanced over at Peter with a grin. 'We've found the missing bullet.'

'What?' Astonished glances shot around the room.

Dougie went on to explain the visit to Fulham and its result. 'The downside is that I was hauled over the coals for not doing it by the book. They're not sure what the Courts are going to make of it. The bullet's been tested and appears, as far as can be seen, to be the same standard calibre as would have been issued to Alex for his weapon that last evening. We have the written records still, but not the firearm itself to make further tests; and, of course, just one spent casing was ever found. We could always surmise that Fowler picked one up before he left, as damage limitation when things went wrong, hoping it would look like suicide.'

Anthony Raven was making notes. 'Alright, leave that with us. We'll see what the legal ramifications are of that discovery.'

For what it was worth, Peter offered the information Christa had managed to find from back copies of the newspapers.

'OK.' Anthony Raven sounded brisk. 'We've moved things on a bit. I'll contact you all for another meeting in a few days when we might have some further news. Sergeant, when is Clarke being brought in?'

'Tomorrow, I gather, Mr Raven.'

'Right, keep your ear to the ground. As you say, this might stir things up a bit. I'm off to my Club now to see if I can put out a few feelers there.'

*

In a parked car another note was made. 'Subject attended Ravens' barristers chambers with two others. Spent two hours and left with one other male. Others watching.'

*

Anthony Raven settled into the deep leather chair with his favourite whisky, scanning a newspaper. He had made one or two what he hoped were innocent enquiries about Aubrey Potter and found that he had been a senior civil servant at the Home Office. He had been retired now for some years but was still called upon from time to time to assist on various committees. Raven decided he would attempt to make further enquiries about the subject of those committees.

'Too engrossed in your paper for a chat, Anthony?'

Raven looked up to see an old former colleague, Derek Watson, regarding him with a smile. Watson, he had heard, was now attached to the Civil Service in some vague way.

'Course not, Derek. Sit yourself down.'

They made small talk for a moment or two, and when this began to peter out, Raven was not surprised to see Watson regarding him over his glass. It was obvious that he had something on his mind.

'I understand you've been asking about Aubrey Potter.'

'Yes, that's right. Someone else was asking me about him. I said I'd make enquiries.'

'Of course.' Watson appeared to consider for a moment. 'Don't suppose you're free for lunch tomorrow, by any chance?'

Anthony Raven regarded him with a thoughtful look.

'I think I could be, Derek.'

'Good. I'll book the private dining room here for tomorrow at, say, twelve-thirty.' He stood up to leave. 'I'll see you then. Oh, by the way, let's just keep it between ourselves for the moment.'

Raven watched Watson walk away and thought even deeper.

*

Peter, in company with Luigi, had decided to take a stroll on the Embankment. He felt frustrated following tonight's meeting. Progress was being made, but Christa was right, it was all so slow!

'At this rate we could be months amassing any evidence. I'm beginning to think Jonathan was right when he said that we needed Franklin to talk.'

'What about his associates, Peter? The lawyer, Villiers, and that Hamilton fellow?'

'I think once we corner Franklin they will talk, but I'm betting that until then they will keep quiet. I still wonder what's driving Franklin. Past influences like this Helsenburgh person, some sort of ideological perfect society, or is it something more personal? The other night he made a comment about his brother Richard changing his views. Did Franklin think that he and his brother were of like minds, and then, as Richard diverged from the chosen path, did he feel let down in some way?'

He stopped walking and Luigi, surprised, turned back to face him. Peter was warming to his sudden idea.

'Luigi, just imagine that Richard did diverge from a supposed chosen path and this annoyed Franklin. Was my father right? Did he cause something to happen to his brother and sister-in-law as some sort of revenge? Likewise, my mother. Did she disappoint him in not following the path he envisaged for her, so he planned another "accident"?'

Luigi came close and placed his hands on the young man's shoulders, and looked up at him, his face serious.

'Peter, if what you say is true, then you yourself could be in danger. Franklin has already steered your education and career in a particular way, but by your own admission, you have diverged from that. Please, boy, be careful. If anything should happen to you… too.' His voice broke.

Peter was overwhelmed by the emotion he could feel in this man who had been his staunch supporter for so long. He remembered Sarah's comment that Maria Gandoni's death might be attributed to the stress and grief of what happened to his parents, who were more like family. Luigi had already been hurt in so many ways by what happened, but he was still prepared to offer his support.

Peter forced himself to laugh, and clapped him on the shoulder. 'I've no intention of going anywhere just yet.'

*

Just as anticipated! Dougie was that morning informed of the outcome of Clarke's interview. Total denials and no comments. A waste of time; but it had to be tried. It was now a case of what would happen next. Would Clarke contact Franklin? It would have been good to have a warrant to tap the line, but then he remembered the payphone booth in the lobby at the Club: a far safer channel of communication.

CHAPTER 26

Derek Watson folded his napkin and laid it on the table.

'Well, I must say, Anthony, they do an excellent meal here.'

Anthony Raven looked over at his lunch companion. 'I've never had a problem with it Derek. Since Monica passed away I've eaten here quite a bit. Can't expect Jonathan and Susan to keep feeding me.'

'Jonathan's doing well, Anthony. You must be pleased that the firm will keep going if you decide to give up.'

'Oh, I've no complaints, but I hope to put in a few more years yet!'

'Am I right in thinking that you have a Peter Hartman working for you?'

Well, thought Raven, at last we get down to business. 'He did for a bit, but we made a mutual decision that he wasn't cut out for a barrister, and he's left to work for a firm in the city.'

'I see.'

Raven remained silent. He was giving no more away just yet. He still needed to know what this was all about.

'Peter Hartman's father found himself in a bit of hot water several years ago, didn't he?'

'I think both his parents died when he was a baby.'

Raven grinned to himself, still not prepared to be drawn any further.

'Hartman is some sort of relation to Judge Lionel Franklin, isn't he?'

'A bit removed. Something like a great uncle.'

'You had dealings with Franklin in Court once or twice, didn't you?'

'Oh, he livened up proceedings on occasions.'

Raven regarded Watson with a calm stare. Come on, Derek, he thought, say what you've come for.

'I understand there are some rumours about Franklin. Have you heard anything?'

'Rumours about what?' Raven again smiled to himself. Still over to you, Derek.

'Things like inappropriate use of his position.'

'Well, Derek, if there's any evidence it will have to be submitted to the correct body and investigated further.' The voice of innocence, he thought.

'Aubrey Potter was an old college chum of Franklin's, I believe. Why do you want to know about him, Anthony?'

'I told you. I'm making enquiries on behalf of another. Derek, as far as I'm aware I know of nothing on the statute books which prevents me from making general enquiries about another person. Is there something about Potter that I should know – or, maybe, shouldn't know?' Time to start asking some questions myself, Derek, old son.

Watson shook his head and grinned at him. 'You're still a wily old fox, Anthony. If I'm ever up in Court you'll be the first person I'll call to represent me.'

'Any time, Derek, but don't expect preferential rates! Shall we now cut out all this nonsense and speak in plain English?'

Watson passed over the brandy decanter, but Raven declined.

'We've had suspicions about Potter for some while.'

'You say "we". Who are "we" Derek? No murky corners. Everything up front, my lad.'

Raven found himself being studied for a moment and then

Watson put down his brandy glass and, sounding casual, said, 'Oh, I think some of the security people are keeping an eye on him.'

'Security? As in…?'

Watson hesitated again, glanced at him, and said, 'MI5.'

Anthony Raven gave his companion a straight look. 'Been up to no good, then, has he?'

'He's been a concern for some while now. Possible involvement in misusing his position. Then he retired, but of late he's been helping on one or two committees which have interested us again.'

'And how do you know all this, Derek? Or shouldn't I ask?'

'Better not to, but shall we say… I have connections.' He leant closer to Raven. 'Anthony, there have been certain political questions about him since he first came into the Civil Service.'

'Rather a long time to play out your line without catching anything, isn't it?' Raven's remark was dry.

'I agree, but things have been hard to pick up on and prove. We thought in the seventies that he was active enough to nail down. Someone came close to achieving this, but we never quite made it, and due to certain… circumstances, we missed out on a lot of evidence. Now he looks as if he may be active again and we want to try to nab him this time.

'We know that he still associates with Franklin. One of their Cambridge tutors back in the thirties was known to be of a particular political affiliation, and there might be some ongoing connection, but again, no strong evidence to back it up. Anthony, how close is Peter Hartman to Franklin? Is that who you are finding out information for? And if so, why?'

'Mmm, several questions there, Derek. You know I cannot betray client confidentiality.'

'I could quote all manner of security of the realm nonsense to you, Anthony, and make it awkward for you not to tell me, but I've known you for long enough to hope that this won't be necessary.'

'Not even matchsticks under the finger nails in a dark dungeon!'

Watson sat back in his chair and gave him a steady look. 'Well, Anthony, if that's your bag, I'm sure we can arrange it.'

Anthony Raven was thinking hard behind the jocular remarks. Was Derek Watson one of the dark shadows fishing to see how much collateral damage had been done by the resurrection of the Hartman murders? Or was he, on balance of probabilities, connected, as he had said, to British security?

Raven kept up his air of innocent enquiry. 'You mentioned that someone had the matter in hand some years ago, but nothing happened, and now you're scrabbling for evidence?'

Watson looked at him. 'Alright, Anthony, I can see you're not going to tell me anything unless I come clean.' He took another sip of his whisky and then set down the glass.

'You remember all the various political shenanigans in the seventies? Well, we decided to have certain people placed in the Civil Service, seeing what they could pick up. We had one report suggesting that Potter was passing on information to do with government contracts, and that this was being used by others as a form of destabilisation. Lionel Franklin's name also came up. He had been tracked back, through sources I'm not going to tell you about, to maybe assisting the Irish in moving monies and other services, using contacts through his legal and banking connections.

'At the same time, Peter Hartman's father was getting a name for himself in the Met and was brought in to see what he could pick up about Franklin's activities. Our man felt he was onto several good leads, and then Hartman hit the jackpot in nabbing an Irish operator at Glasgow airport, acting on an anonymous tip-off. Through other channels, we'd been hearing rumours that the Irish were becoming restive with someone over on this side, and were none too pleased when their man was caught. He wasn't just a nondescript courier, but one of their top people, who we'd been after for some while. To this day I still can't understand why they didn't exact their own revenge. Anyway, it appears Potter's been offering them information again. I'm not going to tell you how we know that either!'

He looked hard at Raven. 'As you said earlier, you are aware of the deaths of Alex and Catherine Hartman. Also connected, in all probability, was the death of the then Met Police Commissioner.'

Receiving no discernible reaction from Anthony Raven, he continued, 'Hartman must have reported in full to Sir John Fraser, who, against advice to the contrary, wanted to take action before referring everything to our man. I'm sorry to say that failure on our part to act on a warning from Hartman of trouble, and then reluctance in showing our hand by claiming his written evidence, led to others getting there before us. Someone in the Met at the time of the three deaths had enough clout to close down any investigation pretty fast. Far quicker than we had anticipated.

'With the suicide in custody of one person apprehended in the Glasgow operation, and outright denials from another on the source of his instructions, we couldn't be sure what evidence Hartman might have committed to his file about the matter and, indeed, our own involvement, so we told our man to pull out and lie low. We found ourselves on the back foot, losing out on vital information and giving the other side an advantage. They appeared to cool things off for a while, trying to gauge just how much was known and whether any action would be taken.

'Now, we've heard that the police are working on a supposed confession to the Hartman and Fraser deaths by a former operator for a thug called Johnny Clarke, who's also known to Franklin. We're aware that Peter Hartman and others have been in consultation with you, and now you're asking about Potter. We want to know what's happening, Anthony.'

Raven had to make a decision: trust Watson, or not. From what he had just said, the Francis question had now been explained, and it was obvious that they were all being watched. He took a deep breath.

'Alright, Derek. You've been frank with me and I'll take a chance on doing the same with you. Alex Hartman was warned about not trusting anyone as it wasn't clear who was on what side. I've now found myself with the same dilemma. However, I'm going to stick my neck out and run with you, and I hope to God I'm doing the right thing.'

Over the next hour he explained to Watson all he knew. When the existence of the copied files was disclosed, Watson became excited.

'Bloody good show of Hartman's. Shame we didn't just wade in and contact his colleague, but we thought he'd been kept a bit in the dark about things, as Hartman had been instructed. When we'd decided to act in response to Hartman's message that there was trouble brewing, it was too late, and with the Fraser and Hartman deaths we concluded that no one would start removing files in a hurry. From what you've said, it's obvious that Rankin was given instructions to get them away as soon as possible. If we'd known Hartman's colleague knew the lot... Mmm... bad move by us. It was a big, big error, and we missed a trick there.'

He leant closer to Raven. 'Anthony, I must meet Peter Hartman and Sergeant Johnson to discuss things. We all need to be singing from the same hymn book this time.' He grinned. 'I must say, I'm impressed with the detective work so far.'

'Oh, there are still a few brains left outside the rarefied world of espionage, Derek,' was Anthony Raven's mild response.

*

Lionel Franklin tapped his pen on the blotter in front of him in annoyance. He had just been brought up to date on Clarke's interview with the police and the content of their questioning. It appeared that Clarke's man had given a certain amount away, if not all, about his activities; and although Clarke had dodged any pitfalls of complicity so far, Franklin was sure that the police would dig deeper. Were they just reacting to information proffered in a dubious deathbed confession, or did they have any other hard evidence to work on? His current source indicated that the CID was reviewing the Hartman murders, and one of Hartman's former colleagues was also involved.

Franklin had little concern about Clarke being implicated in any of this. If he failed to keep his subordinates quiet, that was his problem. However, he was banking on Clarke not revealing anything more sensitive. When Villiers had come to him in a panic with Clarke's ultimatum for further money, a deal had been struck which appeared to defuse the situation. After all, Clarke must be aware that Franklin also knew a lot about other things he had been involved in, and could see to it that these were also leaked to the police. The reality was that they both had a lot to gain in not disclosing each other's activities. This time he would get Clarke a good lawyer and use any other influence he still had to mitigate any sentence, if it came to that. No, Clarke would not be a problem as he saw it.

The main worry was the bigger picture. It was fortunate that they had been able to take Hartman's files out of circulation. Franklin was amazed and shocked at how much information had been accumulated, most of it accurate. Aubrey's advice to curtail the majority of their activities for a while had been sound. Over time they had detected no further investigation and Hartman's colleague had dropped back into the ordinary policing world; that is, until now! It was annoying that just as Potter had something for sale, this whole matter had flared up.

Franklin had also begun to have concerns about Peter Hartman's involvement. It was fortunate that Clarke had been instructed to arrange for the boy to be followed. Of late he had been observed with various people, including the Ravens, and now it all seemed too much of a coincidence. Was that why he had asked those apparently innocent questions about old college acquaintances? The boy had also lied about the girl. Despite what he had said, he was still seeing a lot of her.

He must talk to Peter again, probe him a bit more, and find out what was going on.

On a personal note, he also had to think about his imminent telephone call with Bonetti. It was imperative that he found an end to that situation – somehow.

CHAPTER 27

Peter was impressed by Derek Watson. He could sense that Dougie, like himself, was amazed at the disclosures this man had just made to them. He agreed with Anthony Raven's assessment that Watson was on their side. When he and Dougie had arrived at the Ravens' chambers earlier in the evening, they were told that he had spent several hours going through the papers. It was a proud moment for Peter when Watson complimented his father on his professional expertise in amassing the evidence. Peter made sure that Dougie was also given credit, and could tell that it was a relief to the other man that at last his responsibility for the matter could be relinquished to another agency.

'When Potter and chums realised these papers covered the extent of the investigations about their activities, it's no wonder they went quiet. When it appeared that no follow-up was happening, they still, for the most part, kept it pretty well buttoned down. Potter's retirement must also have curtailed matters a good deal. They can have no idea that we still have Hartman's evidence intact, and I think now we must try to strike as fast as possible.'

Watson looked around the room. 'For your information, gentlemen, over the years, in attempting to engineer certain political changes, Potter has been utilising or selling information gleaned from his various sources in Whitehall, with particular relevance to government contracts. As Alex Hartman discovered, in the wrong hands, such information could be used to the detriment of the country as a whole.

'What contacts Potter didn't already have to assist him, Franklin and his associates provided through misuse of their professions. Suitable vulnerable candidates were blackmailed, or outright monetary payments were offered to individuals to perform certain tasks. At the moment Potter is involved on a committee discussing restructuring of security at air and sea ports, and some of that information, as you can guess, might be useful to others. Our information suggests that someone has been in touch with persons – shall we say – over the water, and I think you can guess the reason why.

'All parties are being monitored at the moment, but it seems possible that information will be offered either to them, if they're interested, or I'm sure another... outlet will be found. We have everything covered and we're ready to jump on Potter.

'As with all these things, hard evidence is necessary, but that takes a lot of manpower and effort. It would be nice if someone was to talk, but that would be very lucky.'

Watson looked over at Peter, his gaze sharp and intent. 'I was interested in your comments about your last discussion with Franklin. You made an observation that you thought he was drinking more.'

Peter shrugged his shoulders. 'I formed that impression. I could be wrong, of course.'

'I just wonder if Franklin might be anxious at the prospect of being involved with that organisation again. I'm still surprised that, when we nabbed O'Dowd, there were no reprisals. I can't imagine that they didn't do a bit of backtracking and work it out for themselves.' He kept his gaze fixed on Peter. 'Are you seeing him again, by any chance?'

Peter cleared his throat. 'Well, he did contact me today, asking if I can see him tomorrow night. He wants a meeting of the trustees of my fund and a general talk about finance.'

'Hmm.' Watson rubbed his chin. 'I'm thinking of suggesting something, but I'll let you know.'

Peter was a little alarmed. He looked over at Dougie, who just raised one eyebrow and smiled.

*

'What do you suppose he was getting at, Dougie?'

Peter put their beers down on the table. The two of them had decided to have a drink before they parted.

Dougie looked around the bar to check who was in earshot.

'I'm wondering if they're going to suggest you have a go at "F" to see what you can find out.'

Peter's eyes widened. 'He'll never say anything.'

'You said yourself, with this drinking thing, maybe he is a worried man. If he's pushed a little bit, he might say too much. They might want you to do the pushing. If you made him think that you were beginning to guess what he might have been up to, and were intrigued enough to play their game with them, he might be flattered and say more than he should.'

'Strewth, Dougie, isn't this getting a bit much? I'm not sure he believes what I'm saying to him now, let alone trying him with anything else. Anyway, it would be my word against his.'

'We could have you wired up, so we can record what he's saying. I've got a hunch it's what Watson is thinking of. When they pick up their catch, I've an idea that they would like to confront him with certain facts to see if he's prepared to say what he knows. It's been done before: drop into the interview a few pieces of knowledge that must have come from others in the know, and you have your suspect wondering who else you've caught and how much they've said. Makes them nervous.'

Peter shook his head, polishing off his beer. 'Well, I'm hoping that you're wrong on this, Dougie. In any case, for the moment I'm not going to think about it. I'm off to see Christa now, and will try to forget all about it for a while. Try to be normal.'

Dougie watched the young man leave the bar. I'm not sure we'll ever be that again, he thought. Too much had happened to too many people.

*

'Do you think he'll come, Luigi?' Christa was excited.

'I think he will, my dear. It was obvious that Michael was quite shocked at the news, but there was an instant decision that he ought to help Peter. I could tell he felt the family connection. I'll let you know as soon as I hear when he's coming. How is Peter?'

'I think he's coping. He doesn't say much. I haven't seen him for several days now. I don't want to chase him if he's busy. I do so wish everything could be sorted out now. I still worry about what Franklin might get up to.'

The door bell rang.

'Oh, this might be Peter now. If it is, do you want a word with him, Luigi?'

She went to the door and waved Peter inside. 'Luigi's on the phone, Peter.'

She handed the phone to him as they settled down on the settee. She snuggled into his side. It was always so good to see him. He looked tired, she thought, and in a reflex action she reached up and placed her mouth on his. Surprised grey eyes smiled down at her, and she felt that familiar warmth curling inside.

'Hi... I'm fine, Luigi, a bit busy that's all. Things are moving along, and it's taking up a fair amount of my time... Yes, I'm hoping it may be. We've got an outside agency involved now which is a help... I'll do that, Luigi... Goodnight.'

Christa sat up and looked at him. 'Do you mean that this might all be over soon?'

His grey eyes sobered, and she sensed the worry returning in him.

'I don't know, Christa. I have a feeling that it's going to get worse.'

'Worse! Oh Peter, how? They can't ask you to do more than you're doing! I worry so for you. You're not a policeman; let them do their own work. Can't Dougie take over?'

She found herself pulled back into his arms and he kissed her hair.

'It's not as simple as that, but there's no need for you to worry. Not that I'm complaining, mind you!'

She heard the smile back in his voice. All she wanted was to be here with this man she was certain now she loved with all her heart. She felt herself being picked up and heard his soft words, 'Let's forego the music for once, shall we?' She wasn't going to argue with that.

*

In the chill darkness of the street outside a further entry was logged.

*

'For God's sake, Dougie, is all this necessary?'

Peter was standing in an empty office, fretting, as a technician wired him up with a microphone.

'It's simple, Peter. With this set-up we can listen in to everything that's being said where you are, and we can record it. There will be a van parked nearby, listening in. I'll be there too. It's safer to do it this way because I want some instant back-up for you. With that little so-and-so Duncan Hamilton there, if something did go wrong I don't want him going berserk at you with no one around.

'Now, all you need to do is make Franklin aware that you have an idea of what's been going on with their financial capers, and say you want in. Get him to open up about it. Tell you as much as he can. Also, get Potter mentioned by name, if possible. Just see how it goes. The more information we can obtain, the better.'

The technician had finished and was speaking through the microphone to his colleagues in the van outside, making sure the circuit worked. He gave the thumbs-up to Dougie, and departed.

'What if he doesn't believe me and won't talk?'

'Well, there's nothing we can do about that. We'll have to haul him in with the others and do it the hard way. This is worth trying, though.'

Peter wasn't so sure. It was one thing to lie through his teeth in the first place, but to be trussed up like an electrical chicken whilst doing it was another! However, it seemed there was nothing for it but to try.

His thoughts turned to his father. If he'd been in this situation he was positive he would have done the same. He owed it to all those whose lives, each in their individual ways, had been touched by Franklin's scheming. His grey eyes became determined, and his attractive face hardened.

'OK. It's eight-thirty now. Let's get this thing rolling, Dougie, before I change my mind.'

*

One of these days he would enjoy a glass of whisky, Peter thought to himself – but not at the moment. He was sitting here with these three men, pretending, and hoping that, shrewd as they must be, no one would notice. He reminded himself again of his instructions. Dougie had warned him that he should take a relaxed approach to anything that might be brought up about his parents. Maybe letting on that he knew investigations were taking place, but to appear unconcerned about it. Peter took another sip of whisky and, for what seemed the millionth time in the last hour, cautioned himself that this play-acting was for real.

He looked around the room. He had not met Villiers for years. He could remember not taking to him then, and this impression was confirmed within the first few minutes of meeting him again tonight.

Duncan Hamilton was new to him. Dougie's vivid description of the treatment his mother had received at this man's hands made it almost impossible to maintain a civil attitude towards him; but he had to try.

'As I said, I thought it was time we all met together, and with Duncan in town I thought now was a good opportunity. Come next year, I'm sure we'll be seeing much more of each other as we sort out this young man's affairs.'

Tonight, Lionel Franklin was all good-natured bonhomie – and whisky, thought Peter. It was definite: the man was drinking more.

'Yes, it was a nice thought, Lionel. I'm now realising that it's easier doing business with someone you know on a social basis.' Lie number one!

'I understand you work in the City now.' Villiers waved his whisky glass at him, not sounding in the least interested.

'Yes, I'm enjoying it.' Peter gave him an embarrassed conspiratorial wink. 'And I'm beginning to see definite possibilities of advancing my personal financial situation, even more so next year. I know where deals can be made, and I think it could be quite lucrative, if you see what I mean.'

Villiers narrowed his eyes as he regarded him. 'Oh, I know what you mean alright, Peter. Perhaps my contacts and yours should get together – for the mutual good of all. Eh?'

Peter considered this a good cue, and launched into his prepared story. 'Yes indeed. Talking of that, Lionel, I wanted to have a word with you about the discussion we had the other night. An opportunity has come my way and I'd like to run with it. I had intended speaking with you sooner or later, but seeing you tonight has given me a chance to mention it.'

He studied Franklin for a moment. He looked genial and open, but by now Peter had learned to be wary of him.

'What did you want to talk about, Peter?'

'As you told me, I know that you, Villiers here and Hamilton's father were involved in certain financial deals together. I have the feeling that my mother's trust money has been part of it. For some time my solicitor has had a hard time obtaining anything concrete about the fund details. I would imagine that this is because you couldn't afford to have too close a scrutiny. Am I on the right track?'

Franklin moved in his chair, and he heard Villiers give a false-sounding cough.

'You could be correct, but I think you'll find a tidy profit has been made for you.'

'What sort of investments have been made, Lionel?'

'Ah, well, "investments" might not be the correct description, Peter.' Franklin's smile was thin. 'Money can be made to do what you want it to do, in many ways.' He paused for a moment.

'It seems there might be some point in… joining forces, shall we say. I've been wondering for some while whether you might be persuaded to join our little enterprise. Over the years I've done all I can to help you on the right path. I must admit, it is gratifying to see that you appear to have taken on board some of the ideas I have tried to teach you.'

Peter decided he must press now.

'I'm curious as to whether your "investments" might be of the same kind as my recent offer. You see, Lionel, I have the chance of obtaining some intellectual information about a company that could be very useful to its competitors. The rewards are quite staggering. Villiers has just mentioned his contacts. With my increase in funding, I might be interested in meeting some of them.'

Franklin leant forward. 'For your information Peter, through our professional contacts, Villiers, Gregory Hamilton, his banking associates and myself have, like you, also obtained various pieces of marketable material through which we were able to manipulate certain circumstances to our personal benefit. Hamilton was able to, ah… encourage various bank employees to assist us. Villiers used his legal prowess, availing himself of an expert or two who were not averse to – shall we say – creating various documents on occasion.'

Peter ploughed on. 'You mentioned marketable material just now. What sort of material, and where did it come from?'

'As you yourself have just illustrated, there are always people, in business, and even in government circles, who are prepared to trade what they know. The trick is to sell it on to the highest bidder, or make financial gains in other ways.'

With his throat almost closing up, Peter knew it was now time for him to move the conversation to the point where he could voice his most important question.

CHAPTER 28

'Are you saying that you knew someone who dealt in classified material? I must say, Lionel, I'm quite impressed by all I've heard so far. I had no idea this was going on. I should have spoken to you sooner!'

He could see the flattery was working. Franklin appeared eager and keen.

'Well, thank you, Peter. I must admit we've done pretty well over the years. You realise, of course, we have had to be careful about these things. Doesn't do to be careless with the talk.'

'Of course not, Lionel. I quite understand. What sort of contacts do you have? Civil Service, that sort of thing?'

'One very good source, over quite a number of years until his retirement. He was, in fact, the lynchpin of the whole enterprise.'

Peter took a breath and pressed again. 'You were speaking to me a while ago about old college friends. You mentioned to me then about one friend in particular who was in the Civil Service. Now, what was his name…?'

Peter saw Franklin looking at him, long and hard. Would he bite? Out of the corner of his eye he saw Villiers shaking his head. Franklin appeared to ignore him.

'Now, now Peter. Remember, never reveal your sources. But you are on the right lines.'

So, he had not achieved a name, but Peter felt the quiet excitement growing in him. What was happening in the van outside, he could only imagine.

'Was the basic motive financial gain, or something more ideological than that?'

'Ideology might have been the reason at first, maybe. It does no harm to keep politicians on their toes. They're just the mouthpieces, after all. It's the civil servants, the backbone of Whitehall, and the judiciary who keep things turning around. A little prod here, a little poke there, might create a climate for political change, but in reality this is difficult to achieve. Financial reward is more certain. If certain circumstances can be engineered in some way to manipulate a situation, and this is known in advance, financial actions can be taken of a profitable nature, if you understand me; the Stock Market and the like. We have availed ourselves of many occasions which have proved very lucrative over the years.'

'Interesting. You must have covered your tracks from the authorities pretty well.'

'It's become a little more difficult with new legislation, but we manage. We did have a scare some time ago but we… took care of that.'

Peter knew what he meant, and had to exert all his control to keep his expression bland. He returned his gaze to his whisky glass, but did not miss the look between the two older men.

'Well, all this sounds very interesting, Lionel.'

Franklin smiled at him, 'I always took you for an intelligent young man. Thought you'd soon pick up the clever way of doing things. We must talk about the possibilities of your offer in detail some other time. Your new avenues of contact could be very useful.' With abruptness he changed the subject. 'How's the love life? Is that Canadian girl still on the scene?'

Peter drained the rest of his whisky. He had read in a book somewhere that if you are being interrogated you should keep as close to the truth in your answers as possible.

'Oh, she's about still. I find she can be quite... entertaining. Until I latch on to someone else.'

He smiled around the room, inferring that they were all men of the world. It made him feel sick, but it had to be done.

'She was mugged a little while ago. It was quite rewarding to play the concerned, comforting lover.'

'Good, is she?'

Peter turned and stared at Duncan Hamilton. The man must be in his forties, he thought, and looked as if he enjoyed the privileged life his father's inheritance had given him. There was a particular look in his eyes now, and Peter could well believe Dougie's story.

'I've no complaints.'

'Mmm. Might be worth meeting her?'

Over my dead body thought Peter, but he just smiled in reply. 'We'll have to see.'

'Come now, Duncan,' Franklin admonished Hamilton with a smile. 'Young Peter here might not be in your same line of, er... entertainment.'

Peter's rising distaste for this sort of talk grew as he recalled the feel of Christa's hair against his skin, and its smell, clean and fresh. The idea of her involved with this man was sickening. He had an urge to blurt out his true thoughts, but a sudden alarm went off inside him. Was this how his father had been goaded all those years ago? If so, that was bait he must not rise to. Would there be more?

As if on cue, Franklin changed the subject yet again. 'Oh, by the way, Peter, I hate to bring this up but I'm hearing rumours of some villain or other saying he had something to do with the events surrounding your parents.'

'Yes, that's right, Lionel. Someone seems to have made a supposed confession and then died a few hours later. The police have told me they are making some enquiries, but it's all such a long time ago now, the matter's pretty irrelevant to me. I've other things on my mind now.'

That was almost the truth; but not in the way these men thought he meant! He glanced at his watch. He knew he couldn't keep this up for much longer.

'I think I'll have to go, Lionel, if you don't mind. I still have to prepare for a meeting tomorrow. I squeezed you in tonight at short notice.'

'Yes, of course, my boy. Nice of you to come for a little chat. You get off now and we'll see you again soon, eh?'

*

Villiers returned to his seat after refilling his glass.

'What possessed you to go so far tonight, Lionel? You told him too much! You said you're still not sure of him.'

'It's a calculated risk, Geoffrey. Oh, I'm aware he's meeting the Ravens and Hartman's previous colleague, but what do they know? We destroyed all the evidence years ago. His attitude tonight indicates that he might just be amenable to joining us. It sounds as if the lure of money is beginning to sway him. Think how convenient it would be to take our venture on into the future, with his new contacts, and the possibility of more financial profits.

'At times, however, I do still sense a lack of conviction in him, which is why I didn't answer all his questions. Questions which have come at a quite coincidental time, it seems to me.'

'Get Clarke to rough him up, warn him to keep his mouth shut.' Duncan Hamilton's voice held a distinct relish.

'Oh no, Duncan, I have a much better idea.'

*

Outside the Grosvenor Club, two sets of watchers made further notes.

*

As the same technician divested Peter of all his equipment, Dougie clapped him on the shoulder and grinned at him.

'Brilliant job. So near to getting the cherry on the cake, eh? What we have learnt will be useful to Watson and his people. I'll get off round to him now. You'd better head for home, you look dead beat.'

Peter paid off the taxi and let himself into his quiet flat. There was no way he could face taking Sarah's car and driving to Christa tonight.

He felt unable to even cope with a phone call to her. He was drained of all emotion, and very tired.

He was also hungry, he realised. Sarah would have something she had baked tucked away, he was sure. He went up the stairs and saw a light in the kitchen. He knew Sarah and Jerry were out tonight at a function, and Amy was with friends, so who was in the house apart from him? He found Rob sitting at the kitchen table, munching a sandwich and reading a newspaper. He looked up as Peter entered.

'Hi, old son. Had an evening free, so I thought I'd pop round, but found the place like the *Mary Celeste*.' He looked closer. 'Are you OK? You look a bit frazzled?'

Peter slumped down in a chair opposite him. 'I've been given the third degree by Franklin and chums. I've been in spy mode. It's a bit wearing.' He looked around, then eyed Rob's sandwich. 'I'm starving.'

'Say no more, salvation is at hand! Chef McIntyre to the rescue. Here, have this to be going on with.' He passed over his other untouched sandwich. 'I'll make some more. Mum's also bound to have some fruit cake here somewhere. I'll make some coffee too, OK?'

Peter began to relax. It all seemed so normal again, sitting here in the familiar kitchen with this loveable lunatic, now sporting Sarah's frilly apron, creating culinary havoc. Why couldn't life be as uncomplicated as this all the time? He sighed.

A plate of doorstep sandwiches with a questionable selection of fillings was thrust in front of him, together with what seemed like half a large fruit cake. Sarah was going to go crazy when she found out!

'Coffee coming up.' And with a flourish Chef McIntyre relinquished his role for the evening.

Peter knew he was being observed as he chewed away, but felt disinclined to make conversation.

'It's for a good cause, you know.'

The quiet comment when it came was not what he had expected. He looked up at Rob, and saw his serious face and concerned eyes.

'I know you're going through it a bit at the moment, but if it means we can get these SOBs, your Dad would be proud of you. I know Mum and Dad are impressed by how you're handling this.'

Peter pushed his now empty plate away. 'I know how my father felt, Rob. They started to talk about Christa tonight and I had to join in and make some… comments. I hated it, but there was nothing I could do. All good local colour.'

Rob banged his fist on the table. 'That's as big a reason to get these monsters as I've heard. What I'd give to get three or four of the lads and pay them a visit. Just hang in there, Pete. Remember, if you need me for a chat, just whistle.'

'Yes, I know, Rob. Thanks.'

Peter took out his phone which showed one missed message from Christa. He sent a one-line text saying that he was OK and he would be in touch.

'I'd better get off to bed. Are you going or staying?'

'I was going, but I'd better clear up here first, I think.' Rob grimaced, looking around the untidy mess of the kitchen. 'Or else I'll be on latrine duty for a month!'

Despite himself Peter began to laugh. He turned back at the door. 'Thanks Rob, you're a brick.'

They both knew what was meant, and Peter received a wink in return.

As the door closed, Rob stood still for a moment, his face serious again. Then, with a shake of his head, he started cleaning up.

CHAPTER 29

Out of the blue, two days later, Peter took a call at work from Dougie.

'It's about to happen! Watson's with two of the bosses at the moment, who he knows are clean. He's briefing them on the situation and organising manpower for some raids. To avoid any warning being passed on he's insisting nothing is to be known by the people taking part as to their targets, until the last minute.

'At ten o'clock tomorrow night, his own team will go and arrest "Mr P". "F" will be picked up at the same time. Other teams will be waiting to go for the other two. Steps are in place to make it impossible for them to have any means of contacting each other. We'll also pick up one or two others who appear to be on the fringes, and we've been told to grab "JC" again.

'There'll be days of interviewing to unravel this lot. I understand you'll be asked to give a statement as well, Peter.'

'What can I tell them they don't already know, Dougie?'

'It's just for the record, lad. Keeping things neat and tidy. We're getting somewhere at last, Peter. Feels good, doesn't it?'

Peter was not so sure. He had settled into a kind of lethargy over the last day or two, but still felt something had been left undone.

In his room that night, he realised what it was. He was still a coward, for all his James Bond antics. He had never confronted Lionel Franklin about his parents and the lies told to him. He wanted to see the man's face as he revealed that he knew everything. He was sure his father would have done so, given the chance. Once Franklin was in custody, he might never be given the opportunity to talk to him in private again.

He made up his mind. He would see Franklin just before the police were due to pick him up. There was no way he would disclose what was about to happen, but he decided not to tell anyone his plan in case they tried to stop him; even arrest him! No, he would keep quiet – this was personal.

*

Franklin gazed into his empty glass with a troubled look on his face. His conversation with Bonetti had been disappointing, to say the least. Not quite a flat refusal to his proposition, but near enough. In his previous dealings with the man, he knew him to be hard and unemotional, but today he had sensed something else behind the few curt phrases, something worrying and more ominous. His suggestion to sell the half-share of the Grosvenor Club, he was told, would of course be discussed, but the likelihood of it being accepted was slight. If the answer was a rejection, he would have to reconsider matters. He would put Villiers on notice anyway, just in case it was agreed.

Also, Aubrey Potter was being a nuisance. Instead of offering his latest information out to the highest bidder, Aubrey had been in touch with those wretched Irish people again, despite his objection. This time they indicated only mild interest, and Aubrey was disappointed at the figure offered. For his part, he found himself relieved, not relishing the prospect of being involved with them again. In the past he had felt in total control, but now, after that Glasgow episode, he was a little unsure.

Aubrey, like a fool, had continued to press them and this time they wanted a face-to-face talk to negotiate. Not their normal method in the past, but of course new people were in charge now. Without his knowledge, Aubrey had agreed to a meeting, with Franklin as the go-between. A representative was due to come to the Club at nine-forty-five tonight. Franklin's face became closed and hard. He would make it tough for them. They thought they held all the cards; but he had the information!

The other problem was the Hartman thing. Villiers had told him Clarke had reported that the police were sniffing around for information and were not going to be put off. In the circumstances, Villiers insisted that they had to be sure of Peter Hartman. He needed to be warned about divulging details of their new-found relationship. Clarke passed on information that he had been with that girl again the other night. Randy little... just like his father! He should be giving all his attention to more important things.

At that point, he made his decision. For once, he dismissed the idea of going down to the lobby to make his call, and picked up the receiver on his desk.

*

Peter had taken the chance that his great uncle would not have a visitor at the Club tonight. The desk clerk told him he appeared to be on an outside call in his suite, and Peter decided to go straight up. He had to watch the time. It was almost nine-thirty already.

He knocked on the door and went in. Franklin was sitting at his desk, just replacing the receiver. Peter thought he seemed startled to see him, and not a little annoyed. Good! He sat himself down in one of the deep leather chairs in front of the desk.

'What do you call this, young man, barging in without my permission? I haven't time to speak to you now. I'm expecting a... business colleague at any moment. I'll have to arrange to see you another time.'

'What I have to discuss won't take long. After our talk the other night I've decided I need answers to some questions. About things that took place a long time ago.'

He was subjected to a frosty glare. 'You said you weren't interested in the past.'

'I meant what I said, but on further thought it might be interesting to hear your view as to what happened.'

Franklin relaxed back into his chair. 'I take it you're referring to your father. I know you've been talking to a former colleague of his.' Peter could not help his start of surprise, and saw a look of amusement come over the other man's face. 'Oh yes, Peter, you've been watched. I know about your visits to the Ravens too. Perhaps *you* need to do some explaining. I remain a little unconvinced by your recent protestations of interest in our... group. Maybe you need to consider that it would be wise to keep us amenable.'

His blue eyes were now flat and lifeless, devoid of any expression, and for a moment Peter felt a shiver of fear run down his back.

Franklin continued speaking. 'As I believe you tried to find out the other night, Aubrey Potter was the original architect of our... little plans. All those years ago, he thought someone was poking around, asking questions. Then through a contact we were informed of a special enquiry headed up by your father. Rather a coincidence, as he'd been involved a few weeks before in a security matter to do with my household. We became a little suspicious about this. At the same time, one of our other contacts in a manufacturing firm informed us of enquiries being made, also by your father, relating to a little problem that had occurred a year or two before. We knew then that there was definite interest in our affairs, and we had to take steps. Aubrey curtailed his activities, and I waited for the right moment to put plans into action which I had been... considering... for a while.'

Peter had by now collected himself again and found his voice. 'And just what were these plans?'

A hard, malevolent look came over Franklin's face. He leant forward and spoke with such venom that Peter jerked back in his chair, startled.

'Your father thought he was so clever, but he was a fool, allowing himself to become blinded with pious indignation about insinuations regarding him and your mother. He swallowed the bait whole. He didn't realise that a paper he signed, in a fit of temper, gave me not just the means for ruination of his career, but also the way in which

I could bring matters to their inevitable conclusion. The death of his wife.'

Peter sat immobile, pinned down by that mesmerising stare and those dreadful words.

'I planned it all, every step, and Clarke's man should have carried it out to perfection. I wanted your father broken. His career ruined, and languishing in prison for a crime he knew he hadn't committed. The wife he professed to care for so much, now dead, and also knowing that I was in control of you, his precious son. I wanted to see him on his knees.

'He'd spoilt all my plans for Catherine, coming into our house with his good looks and charm, taking her away from the path I'd planned for her. I'd groomed her to make a good marriage, for either money or influence; something that could have been useful to us. Instead he filled her head with stupid romantic notions, and she failed me. She failed me, do you hear!' His voice had risen, his lips curling back revealing his teeth in something like a snarl. 'She had to pay. Just like her mother.'

Peter listened in horror at the pure hatred coming through the words. Then Franklin was mumbling, half to himself.

'Ellen was *my* girl. She came over to Cambridge to be with me, then Richard took her, and she turned her back on me. She influenced him in his career, away from the ideas we had discussed in our group with Helsenburg. They both failed me. I couldn't let it go unpunished, could I?'

Peter's mind was racing. So that was the tipping point he had discussed with Christa. The loss of Catherine's mother to Richard, his own brother. It was pure evil, disposing of people because they failed to follow a plan set down for them by another.

He could feel the raw emotion boiling up in him now. He jumped to his feet, leaning forward over the desk, staring down into the cold blue eyes.

'How dare you believe your ideas are so right, and have to be obeyed! People are entitled to make their own way in the world, with their own plans, not ones imposed by others. You were free to go on attempting to achieve your own particular goals if you wished. Your actions were pure vengeance. You took away the innocent dreams of the future for my parents and robbed me of my chance of knowing them. In doing so, and letting me believe all those lies about them for so many years, my own view of relationships became damaged, and you just stood by, knowing the truth all the time.'

He felt desperate to leave, to be out in the fresh air, away from all these warped and twisted ideas. He looked at his watch. It was nearly nine-forty-five. Potter would be picked up at any moment; and all the rest, including this sick and evil man sitting in front of him. He stood up straight and stared at Franklin, his grey eyes steady.

'As you appear to have guessed, I have also been playing a game. But one, I think, with better ideals. I have the evidence to bring you and your partners to justice. For my part, what you have done to our family is unforgivable, and I intend to make you pay for every life you have ruined by your actions.'

'Evidence! All you have is talk and supposition, nothing more. Who will they believe anyway: a Judge, an upholder of the law, or the son of a crooked police officer and a murderer!'

With his emotions at bursting point Peter opened his mouth to denounce the man he had once thought of as important in his life, letting him know that his father's evidence still existed, and just what was about to happen. However, he was interrupted when Franklin slammed his fist down onto the desk.

'You're the same as all the others, it seems! Every one of you, dismissing all my years of planning.' His voice was harsh and raw. 'Well, perhaps after tonight you might reflect on what will turn out to be an ineffectual course of action. You remember the Canadian girl, the one you profess not to like so much, but whom you seem to spend the night with so often? It wouldn't do to have someone like her, a journalist, poking around in our affairs, and I could sense she didn't like me. She could do the same sort of damage as others in the past, and I couldn't allow that. Maybe, tonight, once again a big city will prove to be a dangerous place for young females.'

He glanced up at Peter again, and there was no warmth in his smile. 'You see, no proof again, only talk. Perhaps you need to learn a lesson, after which you might reconsider and do the smart thing by joining in and benefiting from our activities. Everyone has to pay, somehow, sometime...' His voice dropped away. 'Just like me.'

Then he roused himself again, but the words were just a hiss. 'Yes, Peter, payment is now due!'

As Franklin's words sank in, Peter's mind went into freefall. Fear was in his heart – and in his voice. 'What are you talking about?'

Franklin sat back in his chair, now calm and controlled, smiling up at him.

Although he had uttered the question, Peter already knew the answer. He could feel his body turning to ice, and his limbs began to tremble. Oh dear God, no. It was like a replay of some terrible nightmare. Once more this man intended to cause harm to someone dear to him. First his mother, and now...

Pain lanced through him at the thought of what might happen because of his own stupid, misguided, selfish actions. What did justice and honour mean when he had brought danger to the one thing in his life he had come to care for, to love?

'You're crazy!' he shouted. 'If you've hurt Christa I'll...!'

Franklin looked back at him, his face still quite calm and composed. Peter turned and raced out of the room, scrabbling for his phone. He dared not wait for the lift, but hurtled down the stairs and through the lobby, almost bowling over a man standing near the front desk. As he raced out into the fresh air, he heard Dougie answer.

CHAPTER 30

Liam O'Dowd stood on the opposite side of the street from the Grosvenor Club, under the shadowy overhang of a tree. He kept still, just watching and listening. The parked cars in the road were dark and quiet. He had seen no discernible movement for some while now. The odd car and taxi had passed and continued on down the road, likewise a couple of pedestrians.

The wind had picked up since he had been standing there, and it was now cold and dark. He looked up. It was strange how, since being in prison, he took more notice of the sky and its moods and changes. There was plenty of cloud cover over the moon tonight. One of the first winter storms was supposed to be coming in from the west, but before it hit he would be long gone.

Quarter to ten. Time to move. He crossed the road and walked up to the entrance of the Club. He passed into the foyer, pulling down the brim of his hat.

'Mr Greville to see Judge Franklin. I'm expected.' He kept as much accent out of his voice as possible.

The desk clerk nodded and picked up a phone.

'Sir, Mr Greville is here for his appointment... Yes, yes I will, sir.'

At that moment a young man ran through the foyer, alarm etched on his face. O'Dowd had to sidestep out of his way. Their eyes met for a second. Grey eyes, so like someone else.

The clerk, replacing the receiver, looked after the departing figure and then nodded to O'Dowd.

'You may go up, Mr Greville. First floor, the last door on the right.'

O'Dowd moved over to the lift. Was he right? Could that have been Peter Hartman? The coincidence was too great for him to be anyone other than Alex Hartman's son. Visiting Judge Franklin. What did this mean? Was he on an innocent family visit with no knowledge of how Franklin had impacted upon his parents lives? Or had he been drawn into the web in some way? Franklin could have tutored the boy over the years. He felt a twinge of something like sadness for Alex Hartman if that was the case.

The lift stopped and he exited into a corridor. He made immediate note of the flight of stairs leading back down the way he had come. Another exit, if he needed it. There was a window at the end of the corridor, but when he looked out it was a sheer drop from the first floor. Not a good idea! He turned to the appropriate door, knocked, and a voice bade him enter.

Judge Franklin was sitting behind his desk. He did not rise to greet him. O'Dowd smiled to himself. Playing mind games, eh?

'Good evening, Judge.'

He took a chair opposite the desk, although he had not been invited to sit down.

'If you'd care to get down to business I haven't got all night.' Franklin's tone was clipped and formal, and without warmth.

Well, you're a cool one and no mistake, thought O'Dowd. Fair enough… for the moment.

'Oh, I'm sure I'll take up very little of your time. I believe there's some information on offer,' he began.

'That is correct, but not for the price which has been stated.'

'This is the sum I am instructed to offer.'

'Then, as it is not deemed acceptable, I feel our discussion is at an end. Rather a waste of time all round.'

'Not quite, Judge.'

O'Dowd stood, and in a casual move perched himself on the corner of the desk. He saw Franklin staring at him, a little nervous now. 'There was one small matter I thought we might have a little chat about.' He paused. 'Does Glasgow airport mean anything to you?'

He saw Franklin's eyes narrow and a slight paleness to his face. Yes, you remember alright!

'I have no idea what you're talking about. It would be a good idea if you left, or I'll call a member of the staff and have you escorted out.'

O'Dowd rose, but did not move to the door. Instead, he walked to the side of the desk, bent to the skirting board, and pulled out the telephone wire. Franklin watched him, and his expression was now one of serious alarm.

'We don't want you making any telephone calls now, do we?'

O'Dowd sounded quite affable as he came back to his perch on the desk, swinging one leg, to all intents and purposes relaxed and untroubled.

'Now, returning to Glasgow. It may interest you to know that I was the operative picked up that night.' He watched with interest as the blood drained from the face staring at him. 'Even if I hadn't spent a lot of my time back tracking that anonymous letter to yourself, I think your reaction would have given me the answer.'

With a casual gesture he picked up the letter opener from the desk blotter with his gloved hand, and studied it. He saw the Judge's eyes following his every move.

'I had a hard time convincing my friends not to come and see you a long time ago, but asked them to wait until I was in a position to do so myself. You know, Judge, they were not very pleased about the events of that night. Needless to say, I was even more unhappy.' His voice and look hardened.

'I've spent a considerable number of uncomfortable years because of your actions, and I think there should be some recompense. For others, also. Take the fishing boat skipper. I dare say you are uninterested in the fact that he committed suicide, believing he'd lost everything. Recompense also for Alex Hartman and his wife.'

He watched as Franklin's face appeared to crumple in on itself.

561

'Oh yes, I read all about it in the newspapers, and I've had a lot of time to think and work things out. It's strange, you know, how professionals in any walk of life always appreciate the professionalism of another. Alex Hartman struck me as an honest policeman, doing his job rather well. He found things out about you, didn't he, Judge? And so he had to be silenced. I didn't buy all that rubbish about a violent domestic argument. It was set up wasn't it, but why you had to kill the girl, your own niece, is beyond me. Didn't you care about their young child? That night in Glasgow I saw Hartman's reaction to the idea of going back to London to see his new baby. You took that away from them both, and blighted the child's life. Why? Did you want your claws in him as well, or was that the whole idea. He's been here tonight hasn't he.'

He saw the nervous twitch in the hands.

'I trust, for Alex Hartman's sake, you haven't perverted the boy into your line of work. Let's hope he has as much integrity as his father. Taking bribes, indeed! You can tell which people play it straight, and Alex Hartman was one of those.'

Franklin attempted to stand. With insolent ease, O'Dowd pushed him back down. He looked at his watch. Five minutes to ten; he had told his driver ten o'clock. Without any discernible haste he leant closer, putting one arm across Franklin's shoulder to hold him against the back of the chair, and struck twice with the letter opener. Franklin's eyes widened and a slight gasp came from him.

'I'm good at my job, Judge. Already you're past saving. You'll last a bit longer, though, as you bleed away inside. Time for an honest talk with your conscience, eh? Get some things off your chest, maybe.'

O'Dowd stood and placed the letter opener in the Judge's hands in his lap.

'Might look like suicide, perhaps. Sins too weighty!'

With a casual smile and a tip of his hat brim, he left the room.

He saw the lift coming up and decided to take the stairs. He slowed as he neared the foyer. He sensed that something was wrong. There were several people milling around and he knew it was trouble.

He saw a door on his left and slipped through it, finding himself in a corridor leading to the kitchen area. He spotted a fire escape door and walked to it, and let himself out. As his eyes adjusted to the dark he could see that he was in a small yard off the street used for rubbish bins. A quick look, and in a few moments he had melted away into the night.

*

Christa was annoyed with herself. Luigi had just called to say he was popping round in a few minutes. She knew how he liked his milky coffee, and there was almost no milk left in the fridge. There was nothing for it but to go round to the deli; she would just make it before they shut at nine-thirty.

Fifteen minutes later she was on her way back home, trudging head down into the wind. This would be her first winter in England and she wondered how it would compare to Canada. The night was dark and cool and the wind whipped the dried leaves into eddies about her feet as she walked. Their rustling sound was ominous, as if there were other feet walking with her. She resisted the urge to turn and look behind. Glancing up, she could see the light above her doorway and knew she would soon be home again.

The arm that reached around her shoulders was unexpected. It was strong and hard, and she was swiftly pinned against the metal railings. A gloved hand closed over her mouth and she could make no sound. She tried to struggle, but to no avail, her assailant was too strong. She saw the metal blade glint in the pale light and her heart failed her. Dear God, no! Oh Peter, help me, please!

CHAPTER 31

Franklin could not believe what had just happened, and yet he felt the pain in his chest and stomach, and saw the blood on his hands. He had to get help. He tried to stand, the letter opener falling to the floor as he did so. There was a noise outside in the corridor and his door burst open.

'Police! Keep still!'

His mouth twisted into a smile. He sank back in his chair and closed his eyes. He somehow doubted they were here to save him. So, who had talked? Someone abroad, or... closer to home? There was, after all, a growing list. It was bound to happen one day, but not yet... it was too soon. He still had people and situations to influence and direct, but... Why could he no longer remember what it was he had to do? He felt tired... and it was becoming too much of an effort to think.

*

Christa was paralysed with fear as she felt the cold metal against her throat. The scream was inside her head, but she knew that no sound would come out.

Then she heard a grunt of expelled air and the grip on her body relaxed. Her assailant's weight was hauled away from her and there were sounds of a scuffle. She clung to the railings, her mind trying to grasp what was happening. She heard shouts and the sound of running feet.

Knowing she had to get away somehow, she attempted to move, but her legs would not respond. A gentle hand grasped her arm and a voice she thought she recognised spoke to her.

'Don't worry, little girl. You're safe now.'

She turned and looked up... into the face of Michael Hartman.

*

Christa registered that she was lying on her settee... then she remembered! She tried to struggle up as the horror returned, but she was wrapped in a blanket. Luigi's face came into view, concerned at first, and then smiling.

'Keep still for the moment, my dear. You've had a nasty shock, but you're fine.'

'There was someone outside, Luigi! He had a knife!' She felt the fear returning again.

'You're quite safe. He's in custody. It was fortunate that Michael and I came along when we did.'

'Michael? Yes, that's right, Luigi. Michael Hartman! I saw him Luigi, didn't I?'

Luigi grinned at her. 'Yes, you saw him.'

He pointed over to the other side of the room where two men were in conversation with his friend.

'I was bringing him round to see you, as you had said Peter was going to be tied up tonight. I thought we could discuss a first meeting. We were walking from the Tube, and as we turned the corner into your road, Michael raced away from me and the next thing I knew he was grappling with someone. Then there were shouts and other people came running.

Michael had seen the man approach you from behind and he must have sensed what was about to happen. He had the man on the floor before the others reached you. Apparently there was a surveillance team parked in a car up the road, but they might have been too far away...'

He tailed off, and Christa saw the concern darken his eyes.

She struggled up and took his hand. 'Peter? Does he know what's happened? Luigi, I must talk to him.'

'Yes, he knows, Christa. He's been told that you're safe and that I'm with you. He wants to be with you himself, but he's tied up with Sergeant Johnson somewhere. He says I'm to stay with you and bring you round to Sarah's tomorrow. He was very insistent when I spoke with him, about sending you his love.'

Christa watched as Michael Hartman walked across the room towards her.

'How are you feeling, Miss Benjamin?'

Looking at him, the grey eyes, lined at the corners, but so like the ones she thought she might never see again, Christa was once more overcome.

Seeing her obvious distress, Michael Hartman sat beside her and put his arm round her shoulders.

'Don't even think about it, my dear. Nothing happened. There appear to have been others looking after you. I just got there first.'

Christa turned her head onto his chest. 'You saved my life. How can I ever thank you.'

She felt a slight chuckle run through him.

'Well, you've proved to me tonight that there's still life in this old body. But more important still, from what Luigi has been telling me, you can make sure that you take good care of my grandson.'

Christa turned her face up to his, a smile breaking through her tears.

'Oh, you can be sure of that!'

*

Having arrived home well after dawn, and snatching a few hours sleep, Peter had just finished dressing when Christa came into his room. Seeing her standing there, he thought she looked the most beautiful thing he had ever seen, her rich gold hair loose on her shoulders and her brown eyes shimmering with unshed tears.

In one stride he crossed to her and folded her in his arms, burying his head in her hair.

'Oh, my dear, it's so good to hold you. Are you sure you're alright?'

'I am now… here with you.'

He had to listen hard to catch the words between her sobs. He knew he had to be honest with her.

'Christa, it was my fault that you were put in danger. I'd been trying to convince Franklin that I was keen to be a part of his little scheme. Because of that, he deemed you unsuitable, and decided to do something about it. I went to visit him last night to confront him over my parents, but when he told me what might happen to you, I was beside myself. There was nothing I could do. I didn't know then that people were watching you.'

He drew back and looked deep into her brown eyes. 'Christa, I could have caused you harm by my actions, and I would never have forgiven myself. What could I have said to your father?'

He felt her soft hand on his cheek.

'You did what you felt you had to do, Peter. You couldn't know that dreadful person was planning to hurt me. I'm proud of you for doing what you have for your parents… And, Peter… I have something to tell you.'

She made him sit beside her on his bed, and he listened, the shock registering on his face, as she told him her news.

'You mean… he's here? And he was the one who…?'

He could not believe the sheer coincidence of events. That his own grandfather should be the one to save the life of this precious girl sitting beside him was… inconceivable.

She was looking at him now, her brown eyes dark with worry.

'Are you angry with me for prying into your affairs?'

He pulled her close. 'Angry? Of course I'm not angry! I think it's wonderful that you did it.'

He looked at her, then, apprehension flooding through him. 'He knows what happened?'

He saw the sadness in her eyes.

'Yes, Luigi told him. He said he had a feeling that something was wrong. I think he has regrets for not trying to make contact years ago. But you, of all people, can appreciate that sometimes a step like that is not easy to make. Peter, don't be too harsh on him. After all, he has lost a son. He's an old man now, but you both have a chance of time together. Will you come and meet him?'

Peter searched his feelings. Did he want to do this? Now? All the recent events and disclosures were still raw inside him. However, perhaps now was the best time, before he thought about it too much.

'Yes, Christa, I'll come and meet him.'

He kissed her and held her close for a moment, taking strength from her care and support, and with sudden insight, the certainty of her love.

*

In the privacy of their front room Sarah and Jerry were introduced to Michael Hartman. Sarah noted the family likeness, and despite herself could not find any animosity towards this man who had left Alex to his own devices so long ago. She felt an overwhelming sadness that he had not been a part of Alex and Catherine's life. It was such a shame, but perhaps now things could be different.

Christa had been gone some time, and Sarah began to feel nervous. Might Peter refuse to see his grandfather? Was this the right time to introduce them? Peter had been through so much.

She need not have worried. When Peter and Christa came into the kitchen she could see how much more relaxed he looked. Christa took him through to the front room and came back a moment later with Luigi. They were both smiling. Perhaps it would be alright!

*

Peter gazed at his grandfather. The old man was studying him, with grey eyes, so like his own, filled at the moment with conflicting emotions of pleasure and… yes… regret.

This was the man who had walked out on his father, but perhaps at the time he had done it for the best of reasons. Nothing could be altered now, and Peter acknowledged that he was indebted to him for saving Christa's life. What would his father have done, meeting in these same circumstances? From his own experiences of the last few weeks, he now understood how difficult it was to keep professional and personal feelings separated. He, too, had known that agonising pain of potential loss because of the actions of others, until the moment he was informed that Christa was safe.

He decided he must not allow any more years to slip by with recriminations about the past. He had to look to the future, and this man standing so erect before him now had hope, as well as regret, in his eyes. Peter took a step forward and embraced him.

CHAPTER 32

Looking down into the lined face, Peter saw the anxiety still registered there.

'My boy, I'm so sorry.'

He heard the note of despair in the voice, and sighed.

'There's nothing to be sorry for. Life just… happens. Perhaps these things are meant to be. You being in the right place to help Christa for instance. Something for which I will always be grateful.'

'Thank you, Peter. I was wrong to leave Alex, I know that now, but I thought I was doing the best for him. I wasn't sure I was a good influence. I knew there was strength in him and I thought he could do better on his own, if he was forced to. I realise I should have tried to make contact again somehow, and because of that we've all missed out on so much. It might even have made a difference to what happened… Luigi tells me that Alex loved your mother very much and was so proud of you.'

Peter nodded. 'After what I've found out over the past few weeks, I can now believe that. I have a letter he wrote to me. It made me understand things much more and I could tell from it the powerful feelings he had for Mother and I. I'd like you to read it, sometime. Over these last few weeks I've tried to keep that in mind and do what I had to do.

'I've learnt a lot of hard truths, some quite shocking, but I've done my best to help right the wrongs that were done by unscrupulous people. I've tried to discharge my responsibilities in the way I think Father would have done himself.'

Michael Hartman patted his shoulder. 'If Luigi is to be believed, I think Alex would be very proud of his son, as I am of my grandson.'

Hearing these words, Peter realised that the strange sense of loneliness which had been with him all his life so far, had now disappeared. His heart was lighter. Despite having been surrounded by people who had loved him, and the recent delight Christa had brought to him, it was now, with the obvious love of his grandfather, that he knew he would no longer be alone. To make it perfect, his father and mother should have been here to share this day, but he knew he must now dwell on the positives and take his life on into the future.

'We have so much to talk about, just you and I. But for now, shall we join the others?' He led the way out of the room.

*

Over lunch Peter told them all of his last talk with Lionel Franklin.

'So they believe it was suicide, then?' Jerry commented.

'That might be the official version. Dougie has a theory of his own. Franklin had an appointment that night with a representative from people who might have been interested in some information for sale. The desk clerk at the Club verifies that just after I left, and before the police arrived, Franklin had another visitor. I remember bumping into a man in the foyer as I ran out. I told Dougie that he gave me quite a stare as we passed. Dougie just grinned and said that if it was the man he thought it was, I would have given him quite a shock. He wouldn't be drawn any further, but he gave me the impression that he was somehow satisfied with the outcome. The police are still trying to trace this person.

'After my call to Dougie I raced out to get my car to drive to Christa, but I was stopped by two of the police waiting to see Franklin. Dougie had managed to warn them I was around. When the ambulance was called and they informed me that Franklin was dead, I just couldn't believe it. For a moment I thought they might even arrest me, until the desk clerk confirmed that after I had left he had spoken to a normal-sounding Franklin. I was told I'd been all sorts of a fool for going to see him on such a night, and I suppose I was, but I just had to do it.'

He looked at his grandfather. 'I had to confront him. At least he knew how I felt about him.'

'Have all the others been apprehended, Peter?' There was a nervous edge to Christa's voice.

Peter reached over and squeezed her hand. 'Yes, they've apprehended all the main players. Duncan Hamilton was picked up in Scotland, and the other agency have Potter and two others they seemed to know about.'

He gave her a steady look. 'It was Clarke himself who attacked you, so he was caught red-handed. He's been spilling the beans about everything. He's corroborated Dougie's understanding of what happened that dreadful night at Fulham. Fowler had reported it all back to him. It appears Clarke's people had been tailing me for the last few weeks, which explains why Franklin knew some of my movements. Watson's people have also been watching me, not knowing which side of the fence I was on. That's why they were outside Christa's flat.'

Ever the practical person, Jerry commented, 'It's going to take some while to sort all this out I should imagine, court cases and the like.'

'Yes indeed. As I understand it, Rankin is being tracked down and will be interviewed about his role. Villiers confirmed that Rankin had provided them with inside information on the force, and was instrumental in assisting the setting up of the accident to Sir John Fraser, and afterwards suppressing the various investigations. There will be quite a number of doors which will receive a sharp knock in the not too distant future, to tie everything up. It also transpires that the pathologist who did the post mortem on my parents had been under their influence for years. I gather they had blackmail evidence on him of some sort, useful in case Clarke's escapades ever needed some covering up, as in the situation with my parents.

'You're right though, Jerry, there will be a mammoth legal paper trail to unravel. Someone will have to revisit Ellen and Richard Franklin's deaths, and their financial affairs to see if monies were misappropriated from their estate. If so, they suspect this was done with the assistance of Gregory Hamilton, his banking connections, and Villiers.

'Of course, all this has a knock-on effect for me too. I imagine Simon Kingsley will have a devil of a job sorting it all out. The Revenue will also be involved. It could all take ages. But that's no bother as far as I'm concerned.

'Villiers is falling over himself to tell everything he knows. As a lawyer he'll be aware that it's in his best interests. It seems that for years they've been paying lip service to Potter's political ideas, their main concern being financial gain for themselves, far more than Potter ever realised. With their inside knowledge of government contracts and company problems they've done very well on the Stock Market, and in other dubious financial schemes, even up to the present day. Franklin's plan all along was to have me on board in the right career to be useful to them. However, I had to be made aware what might happen if I disclosed anything.'

His face registered his remembered pain. 'I never thought anything like...'

He looked over at his grandfather. 'I'm positive the outcome would have been so very different, but for you. As I said before, whatever regret you feel about letting down my father, you have more than made up for by your actions last night.'

Peter watched a quiet smile appear on Michael's weathered face.

'Thank you, my boy. Glad to be of service.'

Looking around the table at the people who were so dear to him, Peter wondered whether to mention his last piece of news.

'There is one final fact, something that Villiers appeared quite smug about. It appears that, all along, Franklin himself was being blackmailed by the Italians he paid to stage the plane accident. He's been pressured into laundering monies for them, and other such favours. Villiers had the impression that these were the only people

Franklin ever worried about, and dare not annoy. Try as he might, he was never able to get them off his back. So, it seems, over all these years, because of his first act of revenge, he too became a victim.'

He gave a small sigh. 'Perhaps, some sort of justice.'

*

Snow was in the air and a strong wind blew through the churchyard. Michael Hartman had just left the graveside and returned to the waiting taxi. He, Peter and Christa were flying to Canada. On hearing what had almost happened to his daughter, Frank Benjamin had demanded Christa return home, but she had resisted, pleading with him to let her stay and support Peter. Matters were now well in hand, and so she had decided to agree to her father's request. He had sent his private jet with the wish that, if possible, Peter accompanied her together with his grandfather.

Now Peter stood by the small grave, holding Christa against him, out of the wind. Over these last weeks the difficult process of unravelling his affairs had begun, but there was still a long way to go. It would be good, however, to get away from it all for a while.

He looked from the simple square plaque to the bright head on his shoulder. He now knew why his father needed the woman he loved to be in his life, no matter what. Even though he had put Christa in danger, he would not have been able to see things through without her constant support, which she had given without asking anything in return. His heart was full with the emotion he felt for her. Turning up her chin, he searched her soft brown eyes. He hesitated for a moment, but then spoke to her in a voice that was quiet, but firm.

'Christa, my parents have been unable to share in most of my life, but I would like them to witness this moment. I love you with all my heart, and want you for my wife, if you will have me.'

He saw her brown eyes widen, and her soft mouth open in shock. As he bent his head to kiss her lips, he heard the soft murmur, 'Yes please.'

After several moments he raised his head and, from his coat pocket, pulled out a small bag.

'This is for you, Christa. I'll buy you a ring as soon as I can, but in the meantime I want you to have these.'

He watched her unwrap the bag with shaking fingers and take out the velvet cloth containing the emerald earrings. She looked up at him, consternation in her eyes.

'Peter, you want me to have these? They are so beautiful.'

'Just like you, my dearest girl. They are yours now, with my love.'

He kissed her again. She then turned in his arms and looked down at the grave.

'Peter, I can't bear to think that we're all going away, leaving them here on their own.'

'Don't worry, my love. They're together, and have been for all these years, thanks to Sarah. It's how they always wanted to be. We'll be back to see them often, to tell them our news. Now, come along, we've a taxi waiting, and a plane to catch.'

With a last look over his shoulder, he took her hand and they walked together out of the churchyard.

The wind blew through the trees, scattering the last of the leaves, but a fitful ray of winter sunshine fell on the small stone, and it glowed with warmth.

EPILOGUE

Peter and Christa married and set up home in Canada. They went on to have two children, a boy and a girl, doted on by a grandfather and a great-grandfather. Christa became a best-selling author, her first novel based on the events in England. Frank Benjamin took Peter into his firm, and on Frank's retirement he became Chief Executive Officer. Luigi Gandoni went to live in Italy with his son, but kept in close touch with them all.

When all legal and financial matters were concluded, Peter obtained his inheritance. He decided that the money should be used to set up a specialist children's clinic to be run by Sarah and Jerry McIntyre, called the Hartman Centre. An allowance was also given to St Luke's, Fulham, for the upkeep of the churchyard, and for a bunch of cream roses to be laid on the small stone in the corner every March, the inscription on the card always the same: 'Generations of love, together always'.